W9-BYQ-808

NIGHTMARE IN SAVANNAH

LAURA CHACÓN
FOUNDER

MARK LONDON
CEO AND CHIEF CREATIVE OFFICER

GIOVANNA T. OROZCO
VP OF OPERATIONS

CHRIS FERNANDEZ
PUBLISHER

CHRIS SANCHEZ
EDITOR-IN-CHIEF

CECILIA MEDINA
CHIEF FINANCIAL OFFICER

MANUEL CASTELLANOS
DIRECTOR OF SALES & RETAILER
RELATIONS

ALLISON POND
MARKETING DIRECTOR

MIGUEL ANGEL ZAPATA
DESIGN DIRECTOR

BRIAN HAWKINS
ASSISTANT EDITOR

DIANA BERMÚDEZ
GRAPHIC DESIGNER

DAVID REYES
GRAPHIC DESIGNER

ADRIANA T. OROZCO
INTERACTIVE MEDIA DESIGNER

NICOLÁS ZEA ARIAS
AUDIOVISUAL PRODUCTION

FRANK SILVA
EXECUTIVE ASSISTANT

STEPHANIE HIDALGO
EXECUTIVE ASSISTANT

FOR MAD CAVE COMICS, INC.
Nightmare in Savannah™ Published by Mad Cave Studios, Inc. 8838 SW 129th St. Miami,
FL 33176 © 2021 Mad Cave Studios, Inc. All rights reserved.
Nightmare in Savannah™ characters and the distinctive likeness(es) thereof are Trademarks
and Copyrights © 2021 Mad Cave Studios, Inc. ALL RIGHTS RESERVED. No portion of this
publication may be reproduced or transmitted in any form or by any means, without the express
written permission of Mad Cave Studios, Inc. Names, characters, places, and incidents featured in
this publication are the product of the author's imaginations or are used fictitiously. Any resemblance
to actual persons (living or dead), events, institutions, or locales, without satiric intent, is coincidental.

Printed in Canada
ISBN: 978-1-952303-26-5

Nightmare in Savannah

LELA GWENN
WRITER

ROWAN MACCOLL
ARTIST

MICAH MYERS
LETTERER

CHRIS SANCHEZ
EDITOR

DIANA BERMÚDEZ
LOGO & BOOK DESIGNER

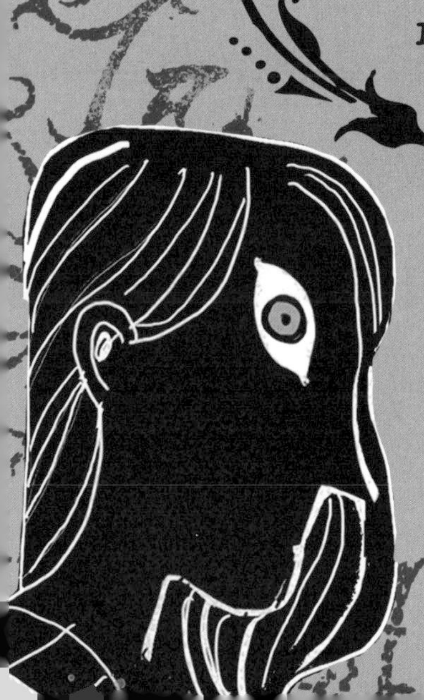

MAVERICK

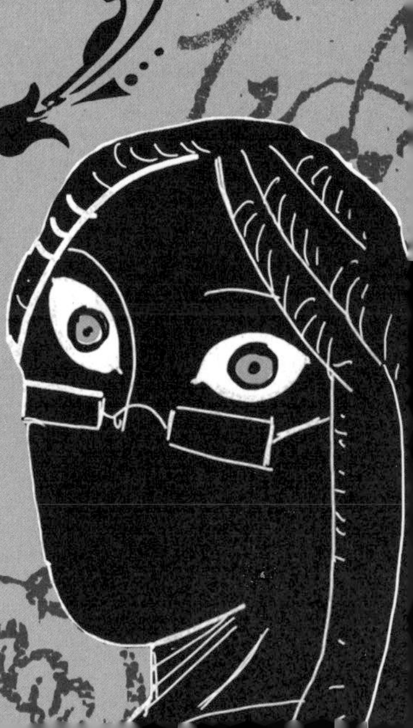

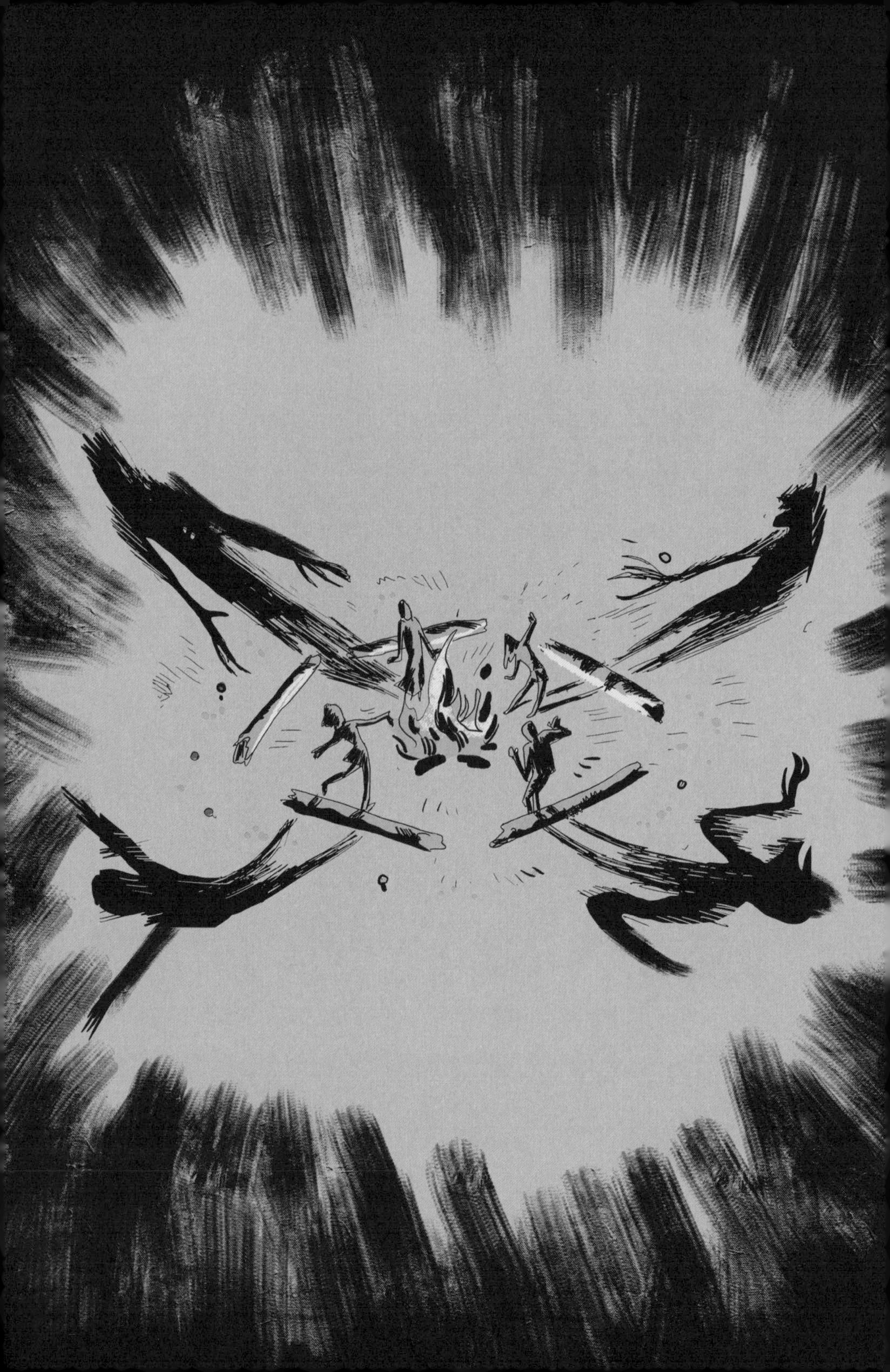

A Fairy Hunter's Diary

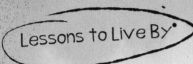

Lessons to Live By

Fairies are dangerous creatures.
They enjoy causing trouble.
If a Fairy is offended, thinks a person deserves to be punished,
or is simply bored...
they will exact painful revenge.

If you meet a fairy, be polite.
Any rude behavior is all the excuse they need.

Important:
The fairies are stealing children
and leaving fairy look-alikes in their place.

These ersatz children are Changelings.
Waiting for the day they mature into their powers.
They bring only death and destruction.

All Fairies must be DESTROYED!!

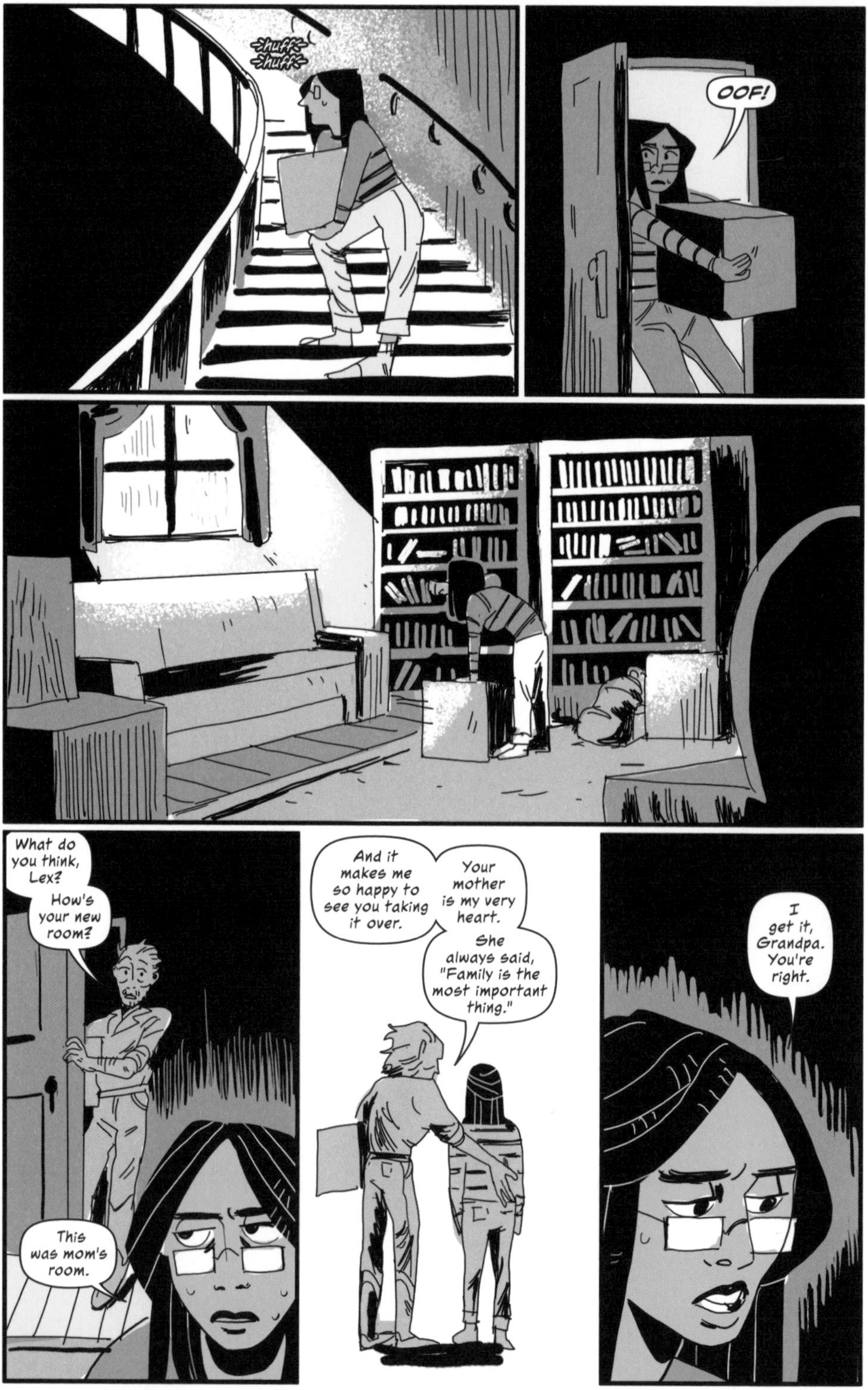

huff huff
OOF!
What do you think, Lex?
How's your new room?
This was mom's room.
And it makes me so happy to see you taking it over.
Your mother is my very heart.
She always said, "Family is the most important thing."
I get it, Grandpa. You're right.

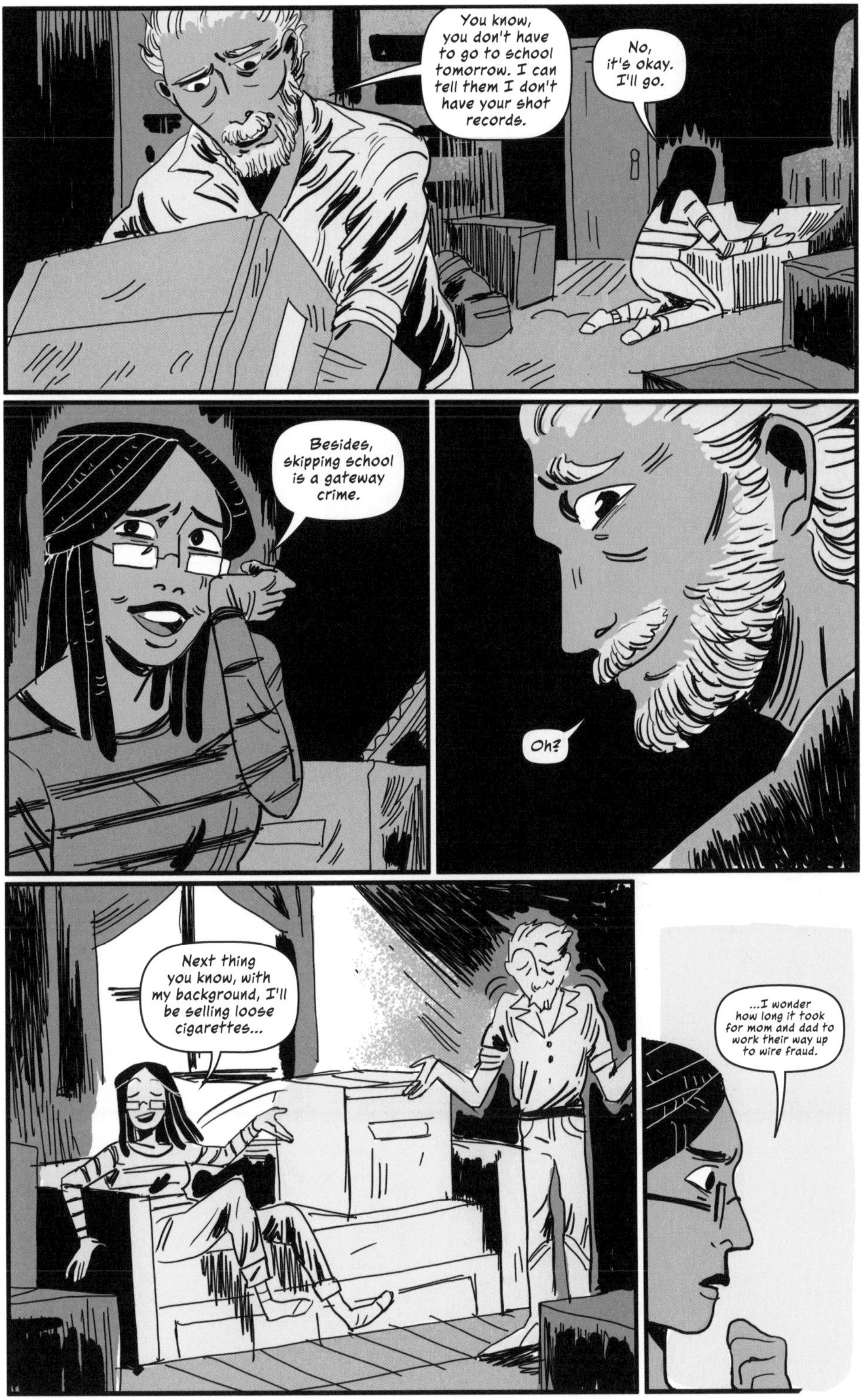
You know, you don't have to go to school tomorrow. I can tell them I don't have your shot records.
No, it's okay. I'll go.
Besides, skipping school is a gateway crime.
Oh?
Next thing you know, with my background, I'll be selling loose cigarettes...
...I wonder how long it took for mom and dad to work their way up to wire fraud.

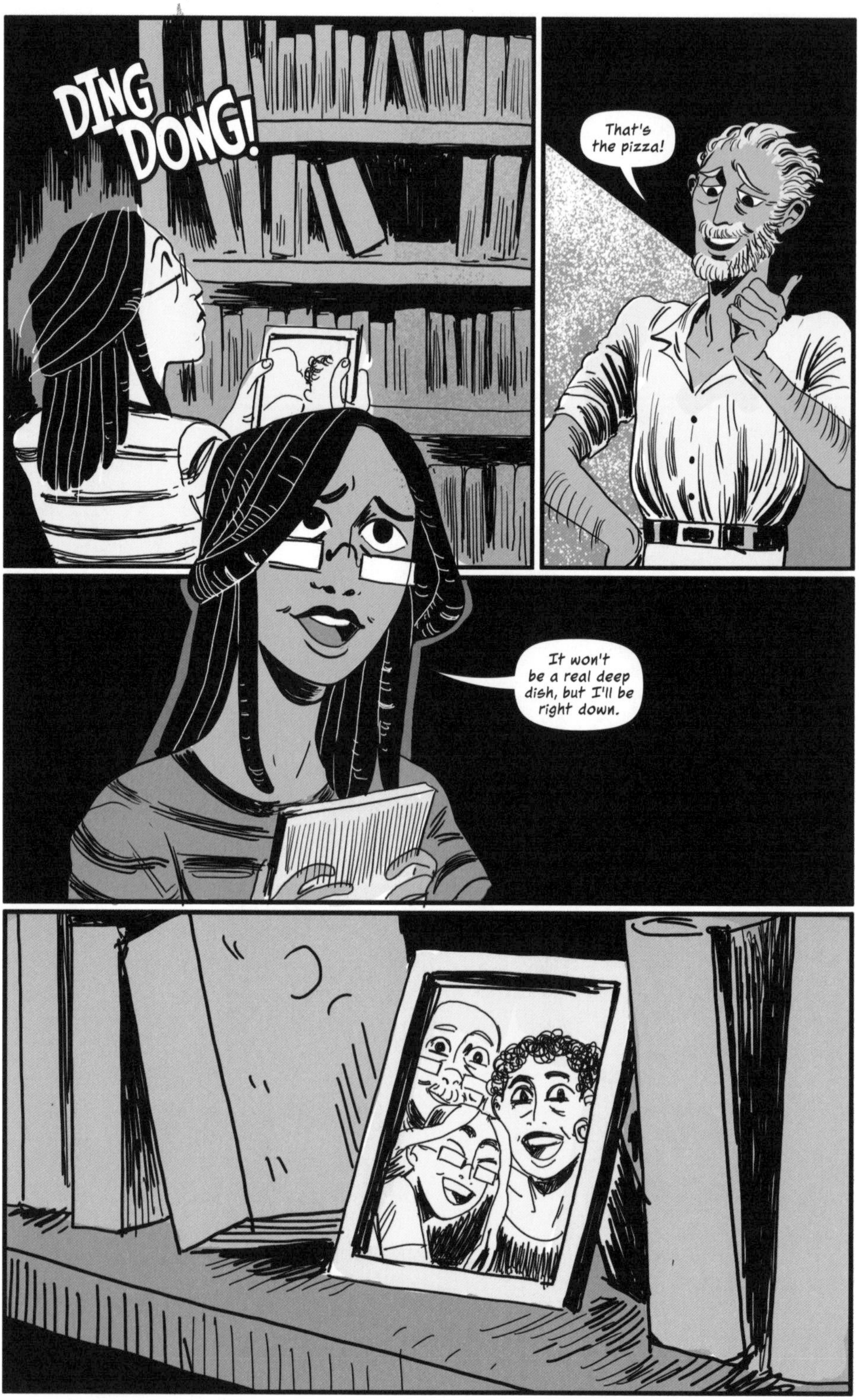
DING DONG!
That's the pizza!
It won't be a real deep dish, but I'll be right down.

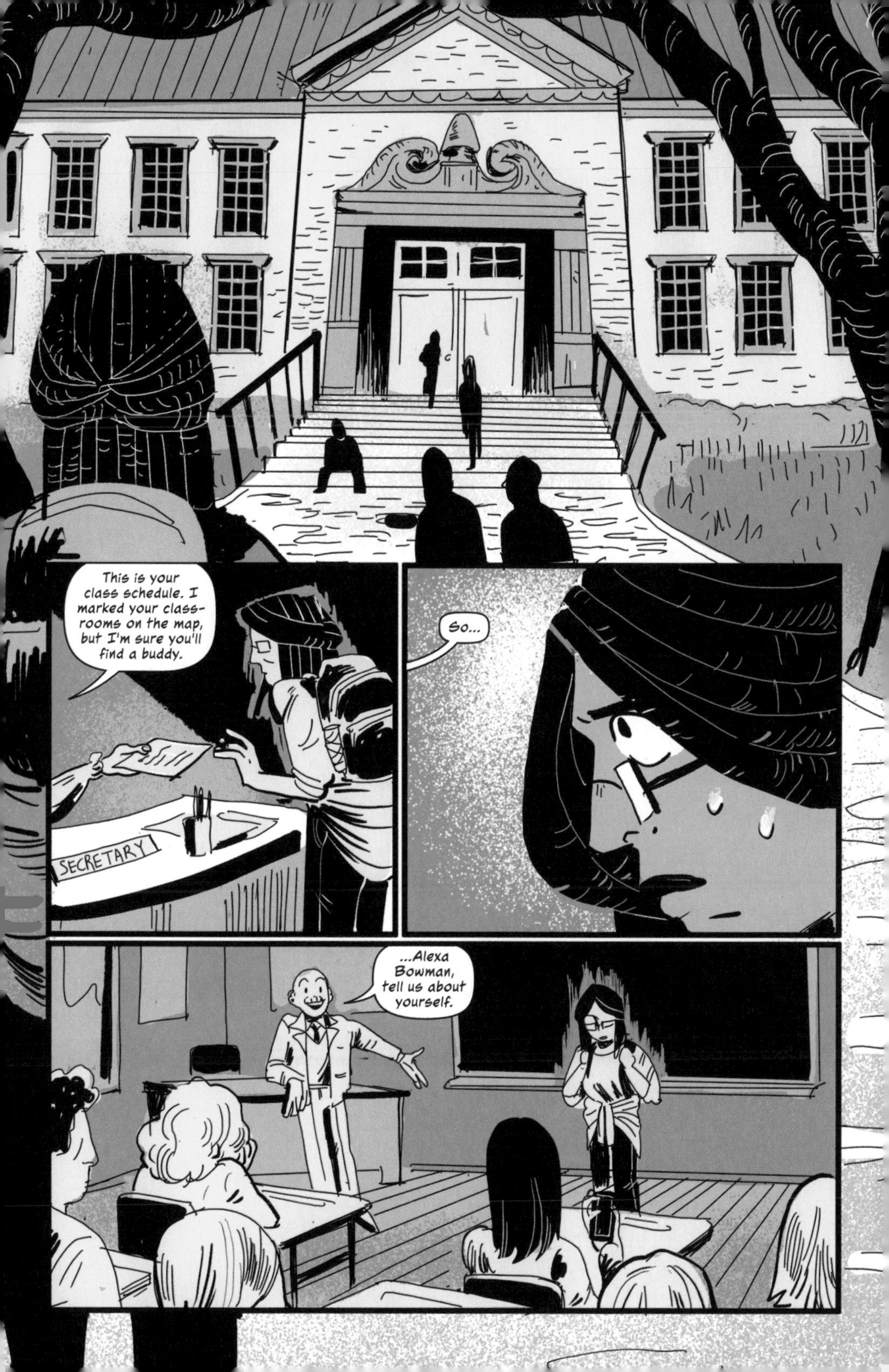
This is your class schedule. I marked your class-rooms on the map, but I'm sure you'll find a buddy.
SECRETARY
So...
...Alexa Bowman, tell us about yourself.

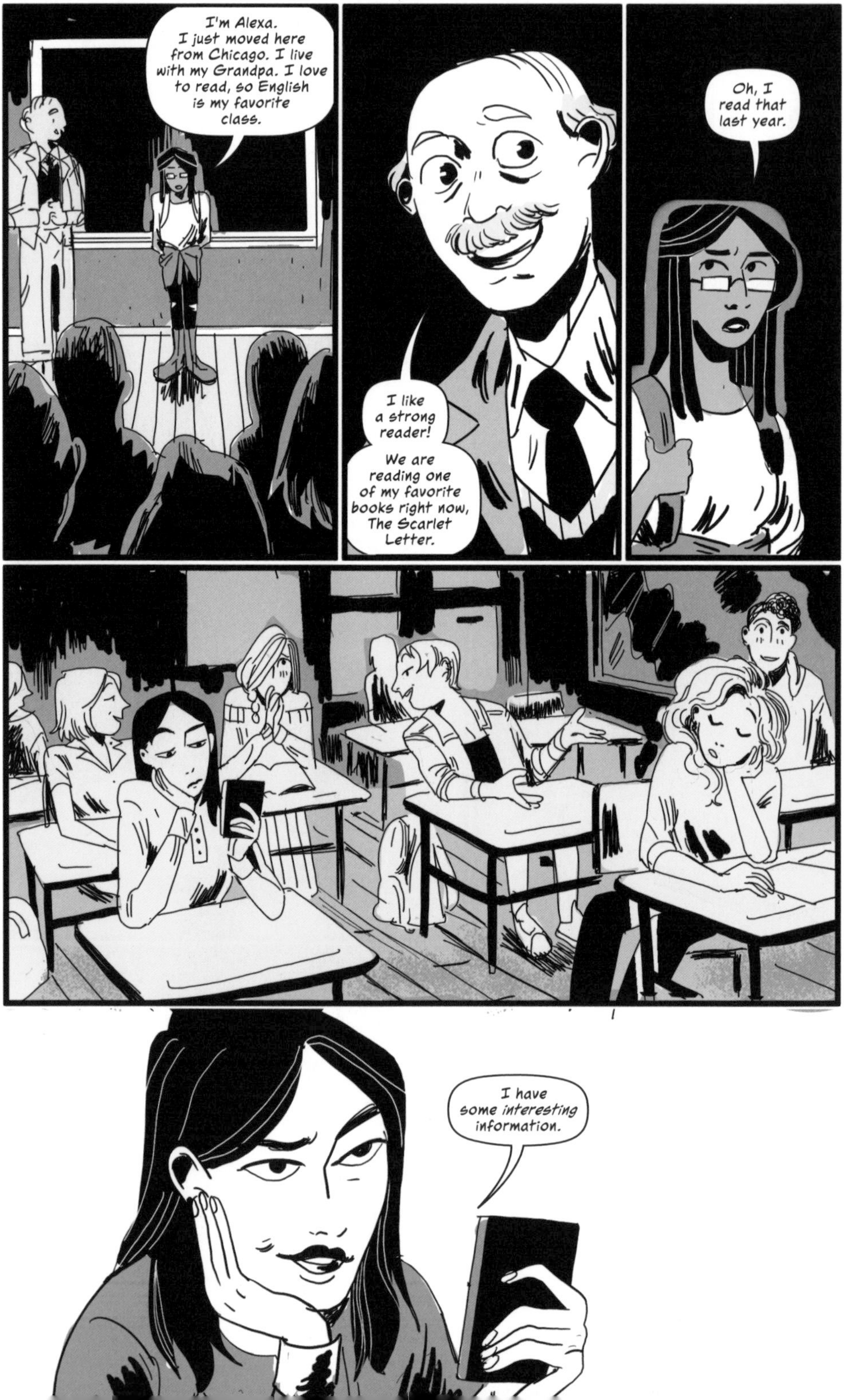

I'm Alexa. I just moved here from Chicago. I live with my Grandpa. I love to read, so English is my favorite class.
I like a strong reader!
We are reading one of my favorite books right now, The Scarlet Letter.
Oh, I read that last year.
I have some *interesting* information.

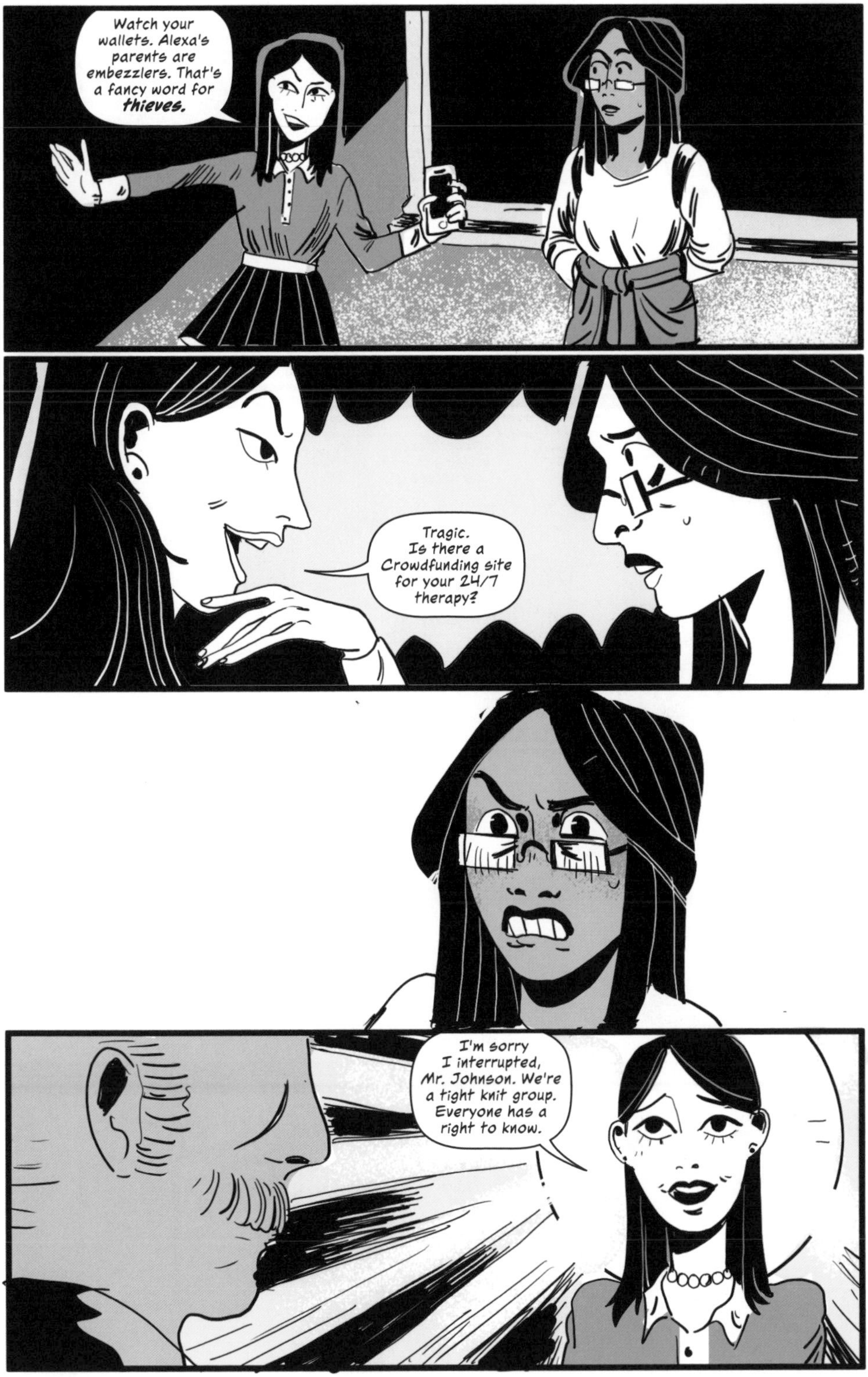
Watch your wallets. Alexa's parents are embezzlers. That's a fancy word for ***thieves.***
Tragic. Is there a Crowdfunding site for your 24/7 therapy?
I'm sorry I interrupted, Mr. Johnson. We're a tight knit group. Everyone has a right to know.

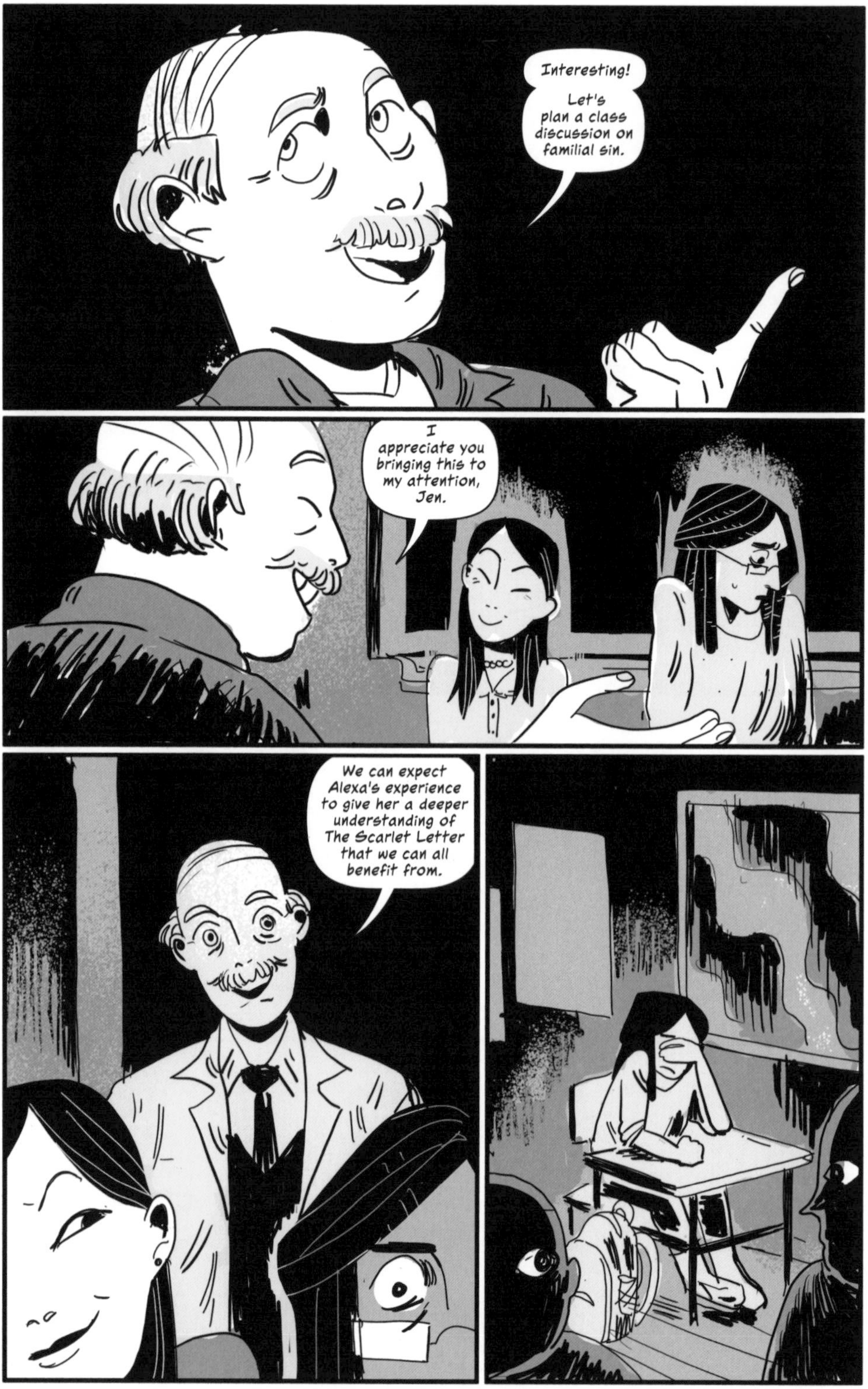
Interesting!
Let's plan a class discussion on familial sin.
I appreciate you bringing this to my attention, Jen.
We can expect Alexa's experience to give her a deeper understanding of The Scarlet Letter that we can all benefit from.

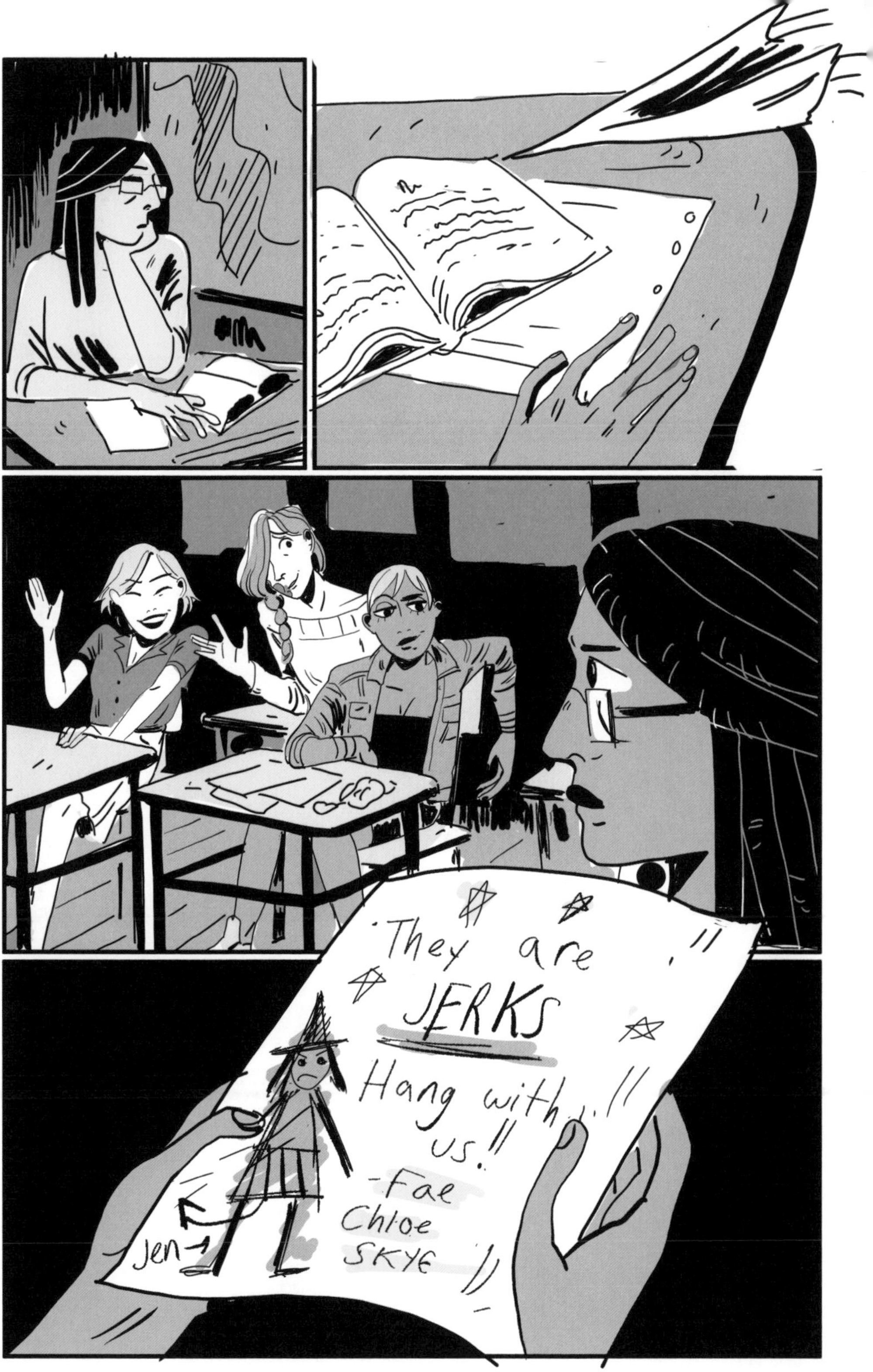
They are
JERKS
Hang with us!!
-Fae
Chloe
SKYE
Jen

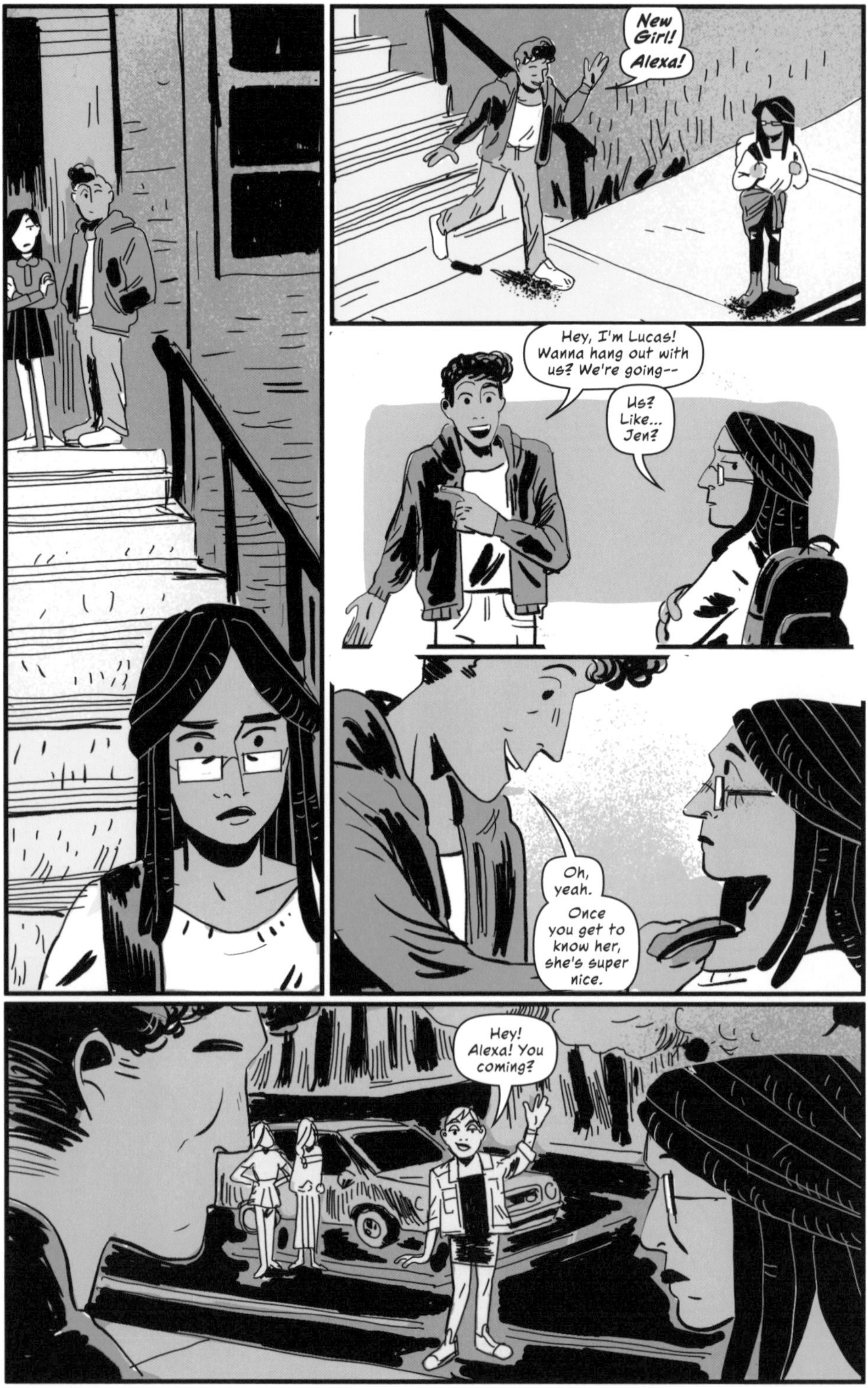
New Girl! Alexa!
Hey, I'm Lucas! Wanna hang out with us? We're going--
Us? Like... Jen?
Oh, yeah.
Once you get to know her, she's super nice.
Hey! Alexa! You coming?

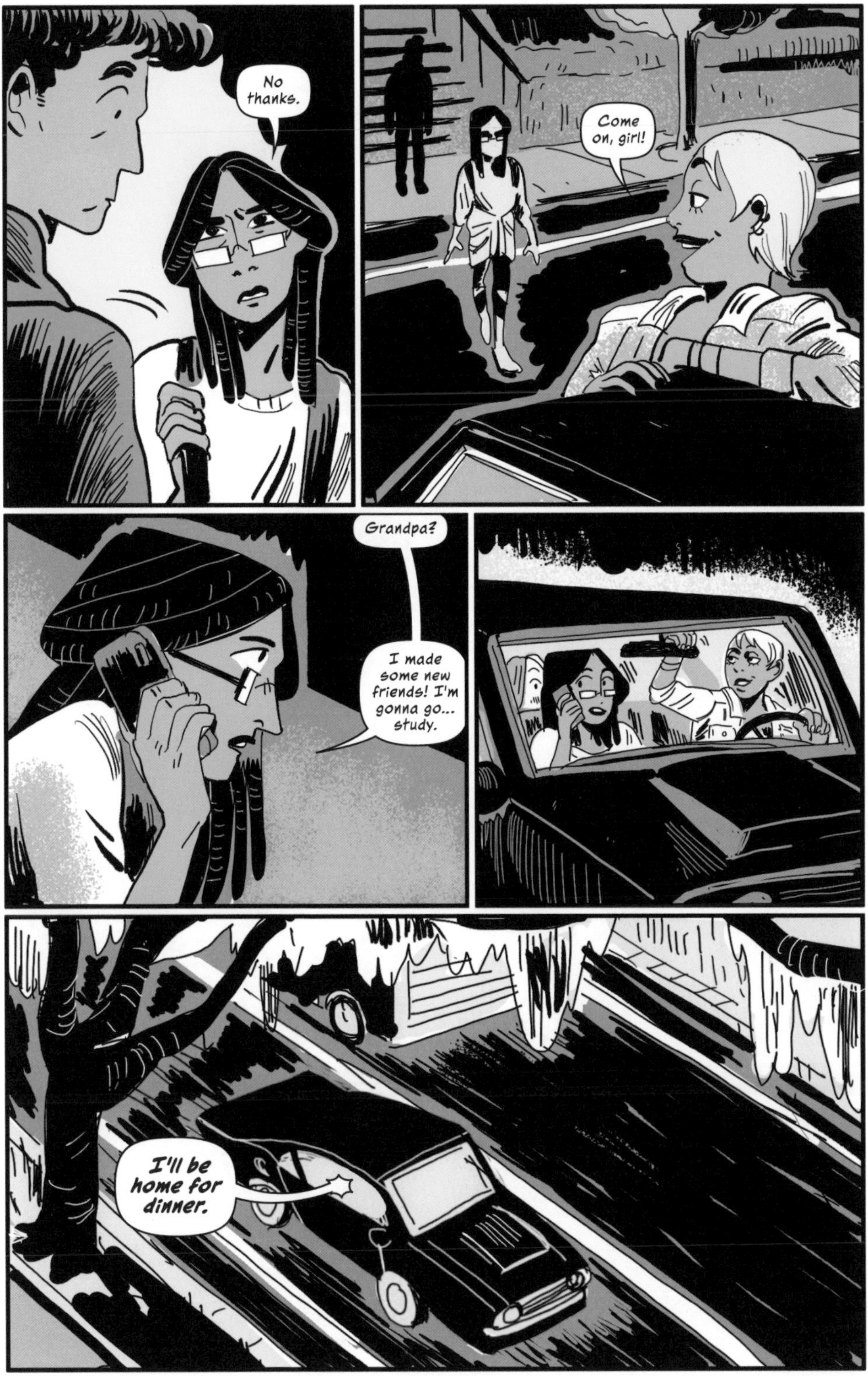
No thanks.
Come on, girl!
Grandpa?
I made some new friends! I'm gonna go... study.
I'll be home for dinner.

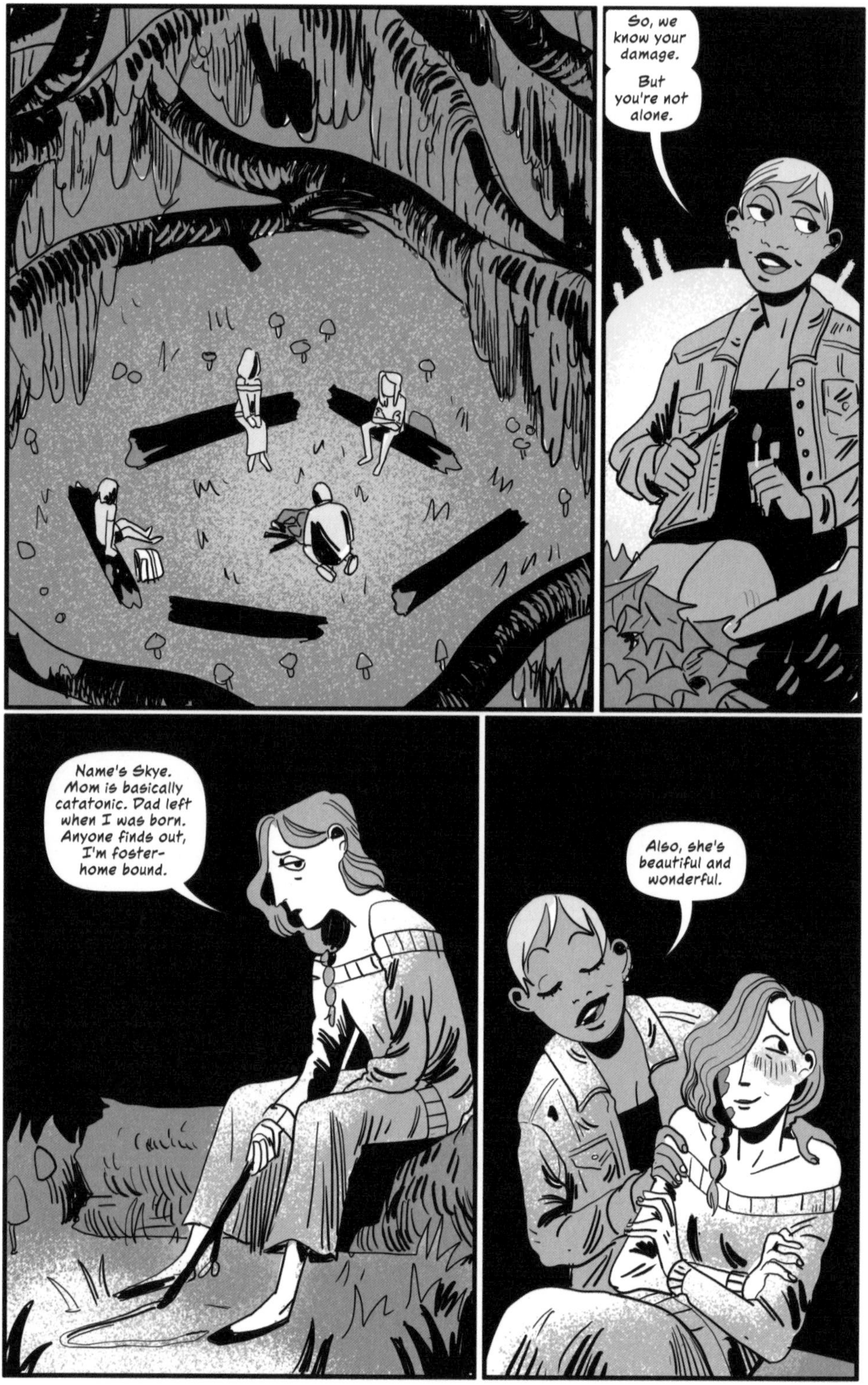
So, we know your damage.
But you're not alone.
Name's Skye. Mom is basically catatonic. Dad left when I was born. Anyone finds out, I'm foster-home bound.
Also, she's beautiful and wonderful.

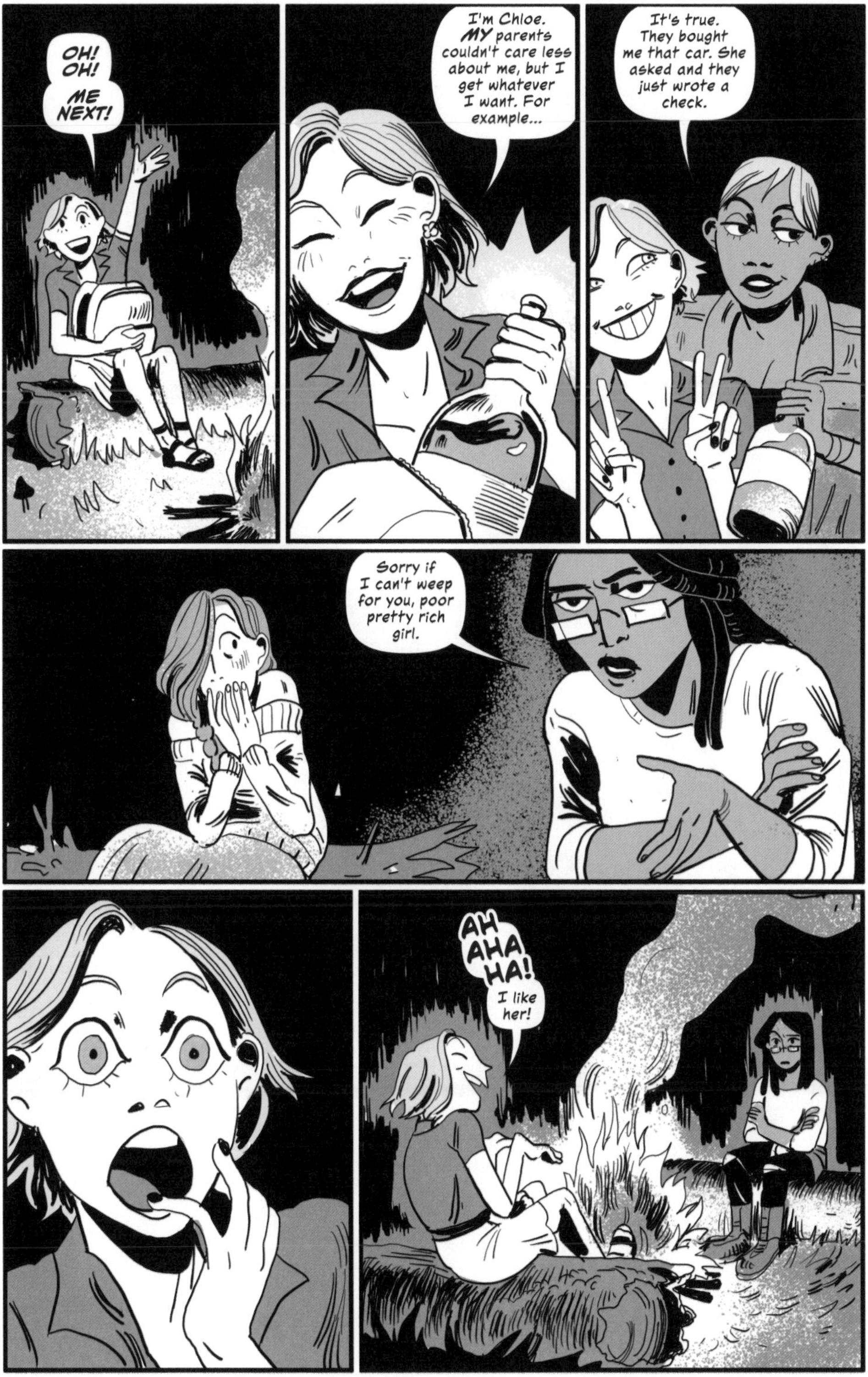
OH! OH! ME NEXT!
I'm Chloe. MY parents couldn't care less about me, but I get whatever I want. For example...
It's true. They bought me that car. She asked and they just wrote a check.
Sorry if I can't weep for you, poor pretty rich girl.
AH AHA HA!
I like her!

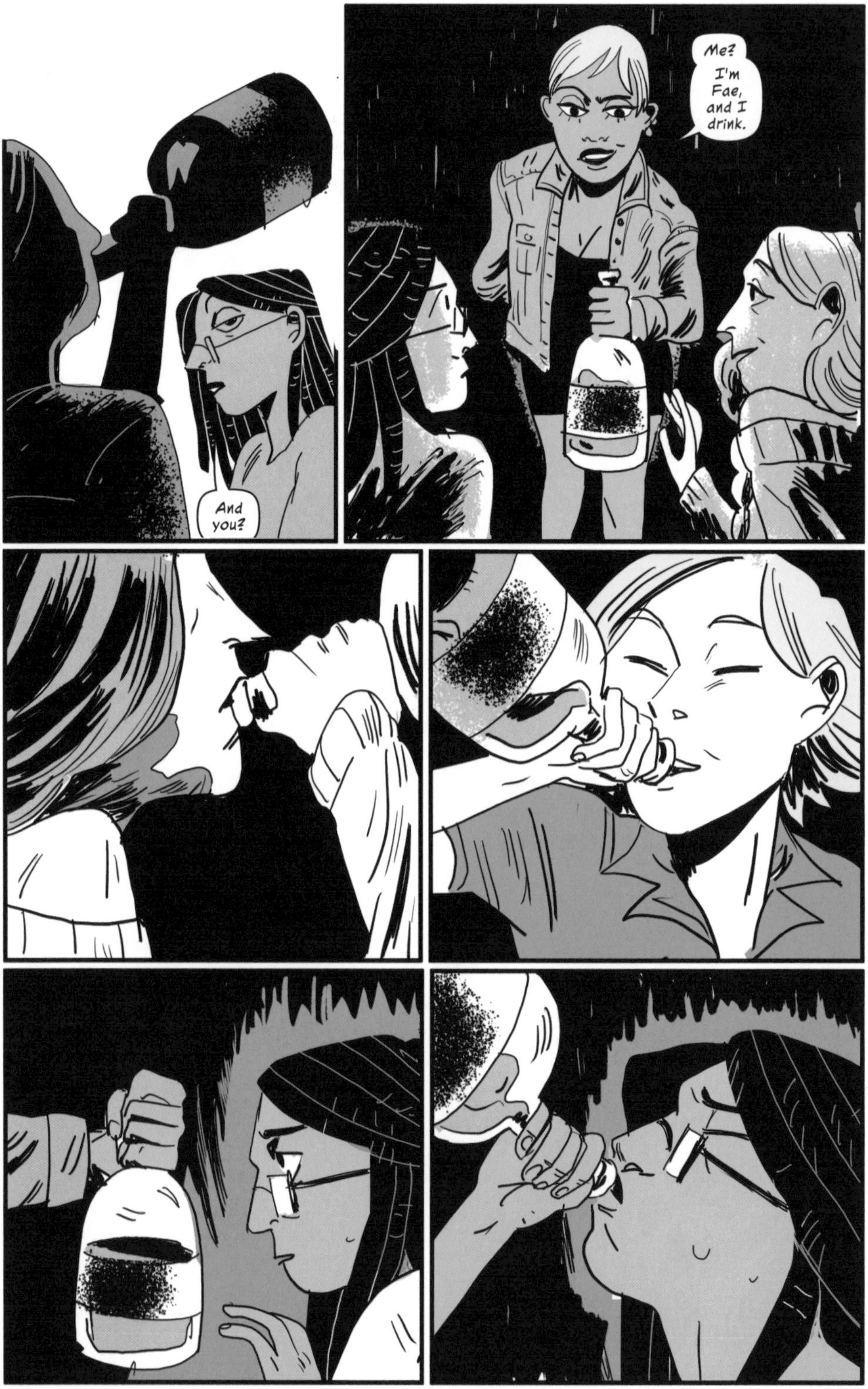
And you?
Me?
I'm Fae, and I drink.

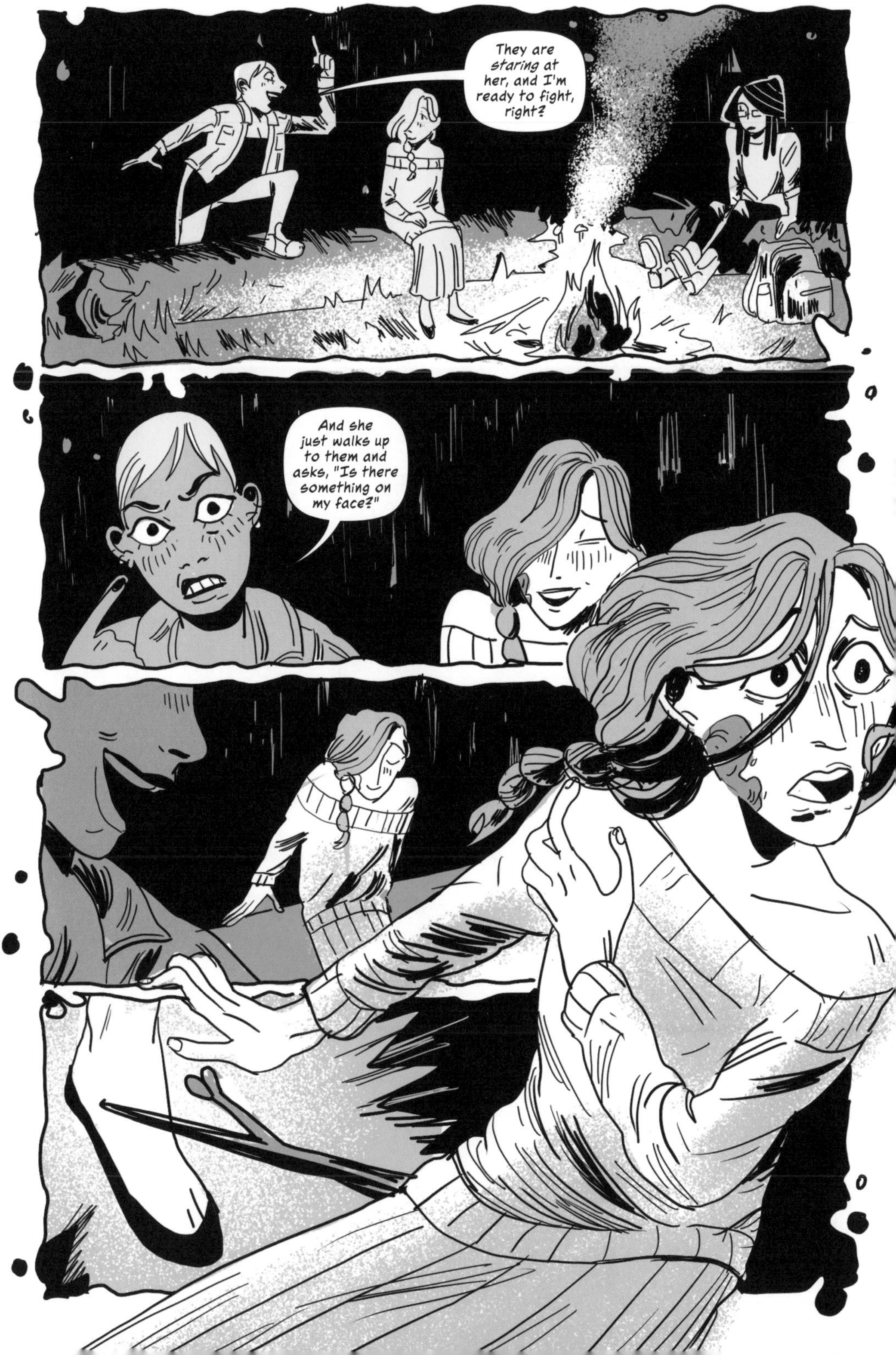
They are staring at her, and I'm ready to fight, right?
And she just walks up to them and asks, "Is there something on my face?"

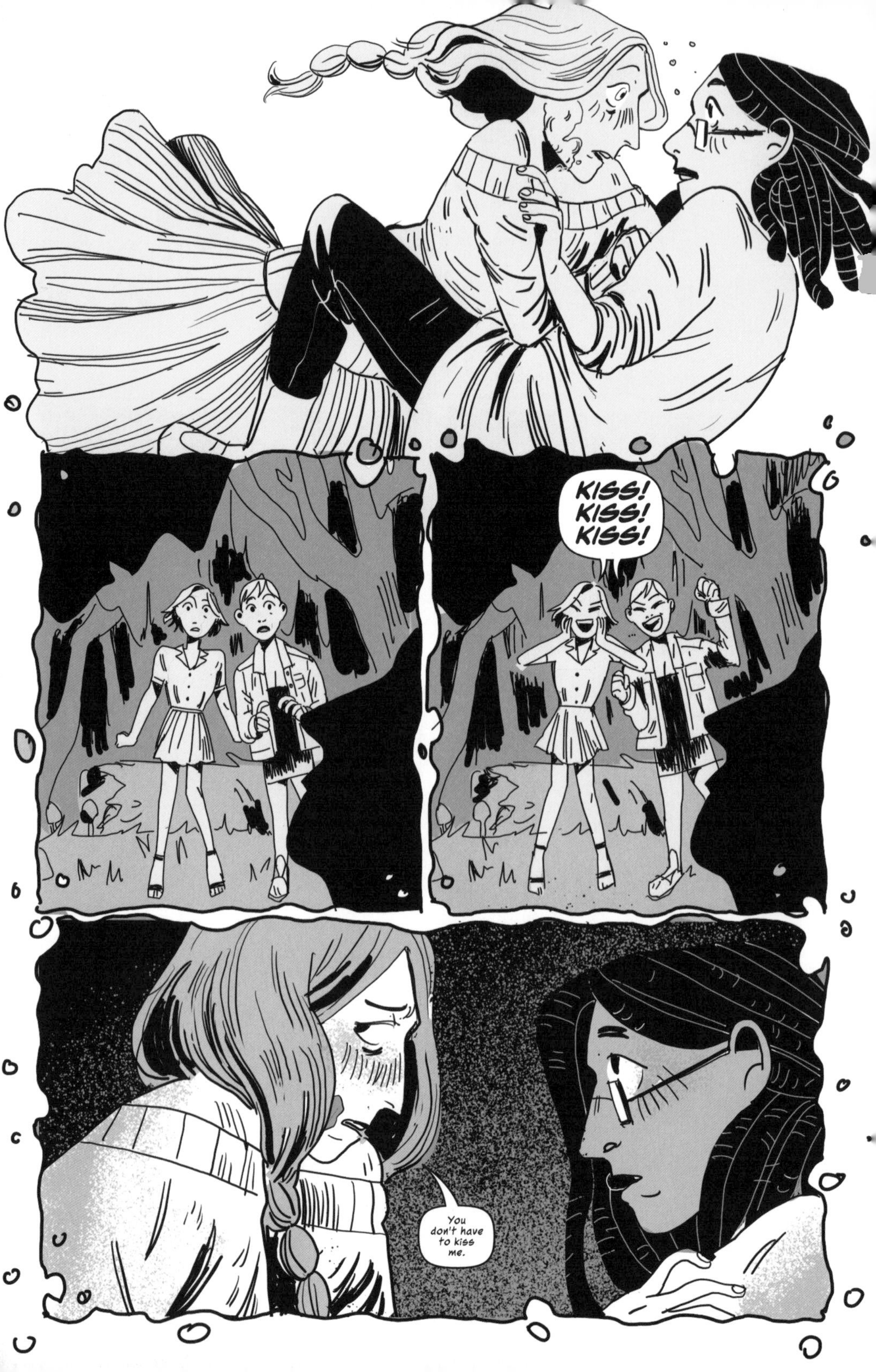
KISS! KISS! KISS!
You don't have to kiss me.

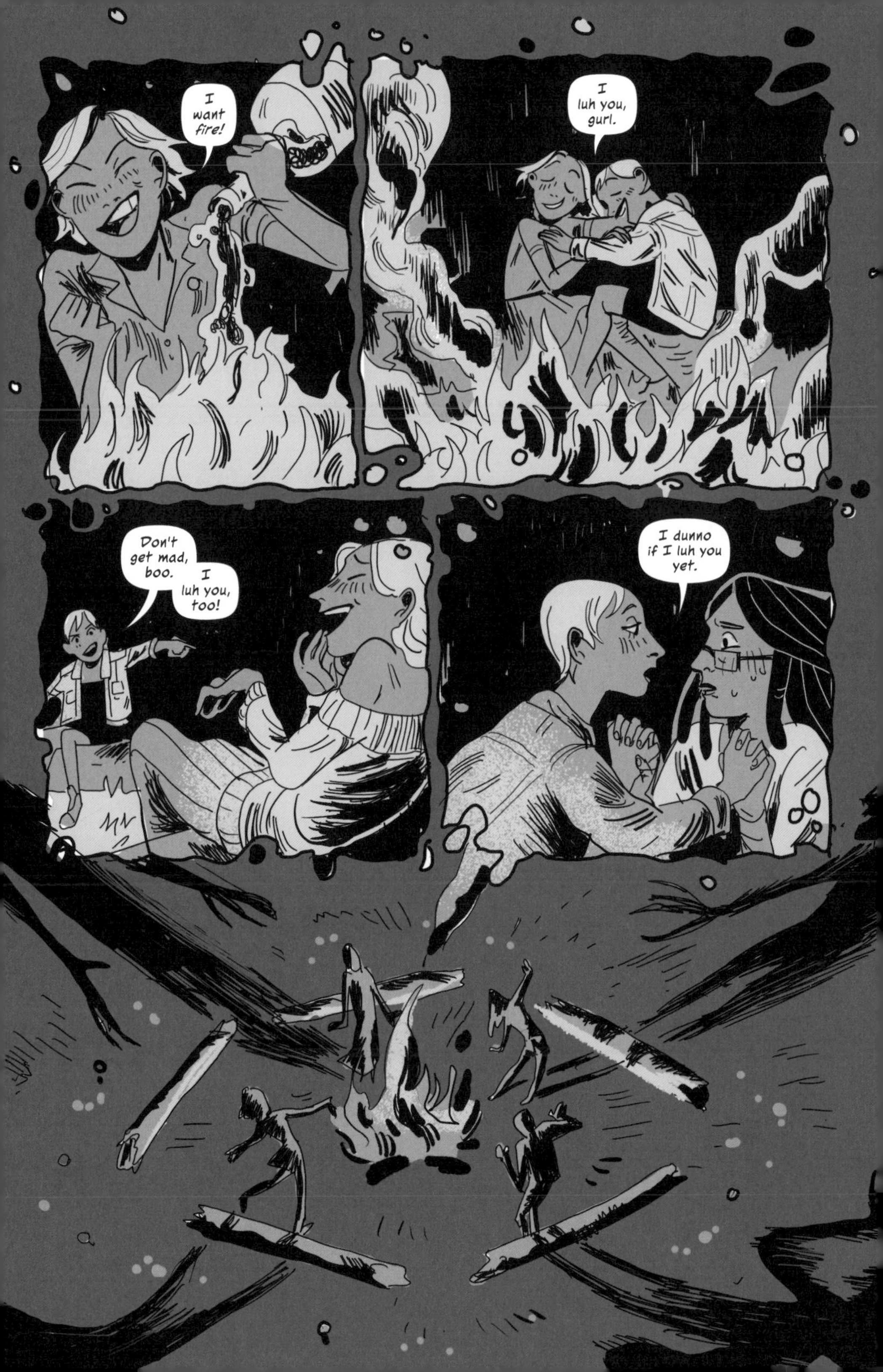
I want fire!
I luh you, gurl.
Don't get mad, boo.
I luh you, too!
I dunno if I luh you yet.

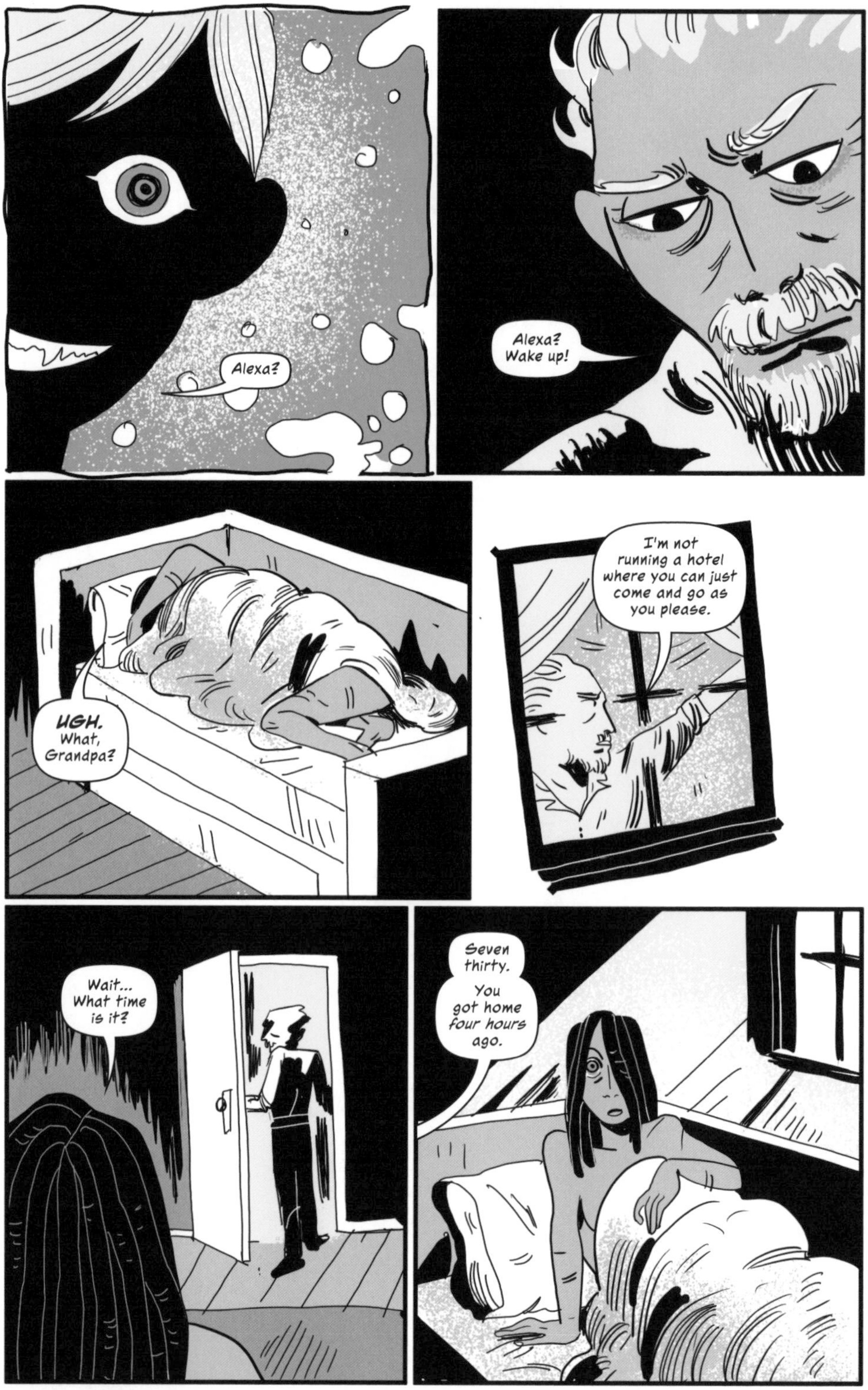
Alexa?
Alexa? Wake up!
UGH. What, Grandpa?
I'm not running a hotel where you can just come and go as you please.
Wait... What time is it?
Seven thirty.
You got home four hours ago.

What the hell?
How did I get home?
Where are my clothes?
What happened to me?

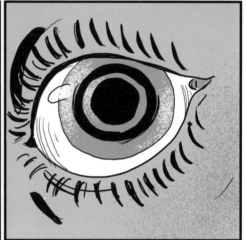

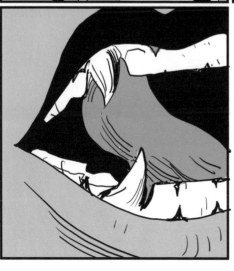

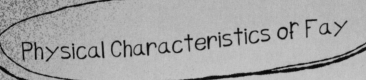

Physical Characteristics of Fay

Once a Changeling matures, they develop changes to their anatomy.

Hidden under powerful illusions to the untrained eye, these changes mark the beginning of control and when they truly should be feared.

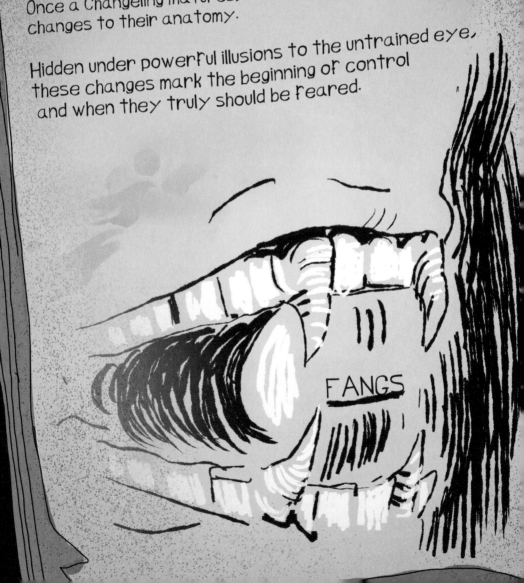

FANGS

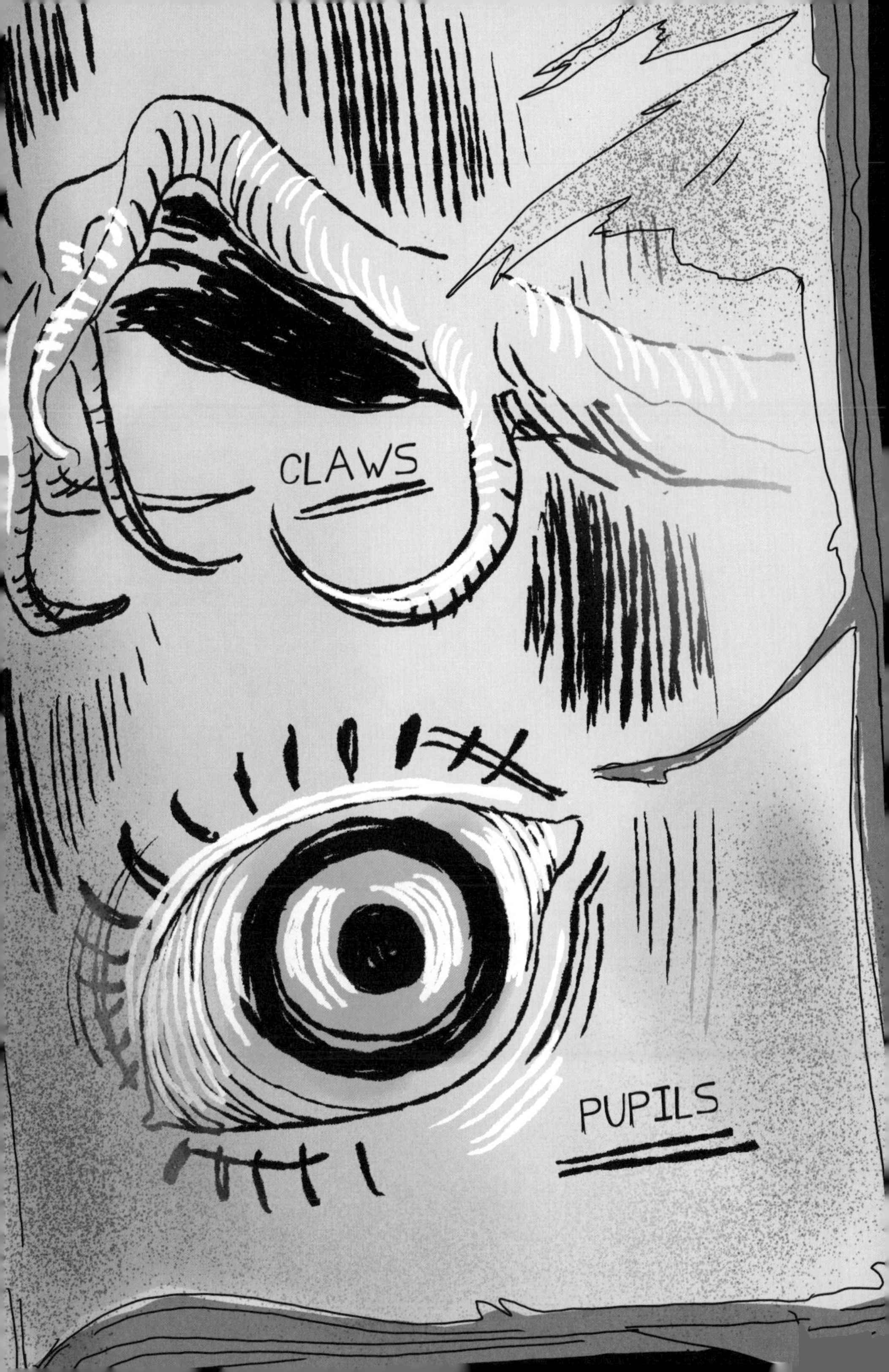
CLAWS
PUPILS

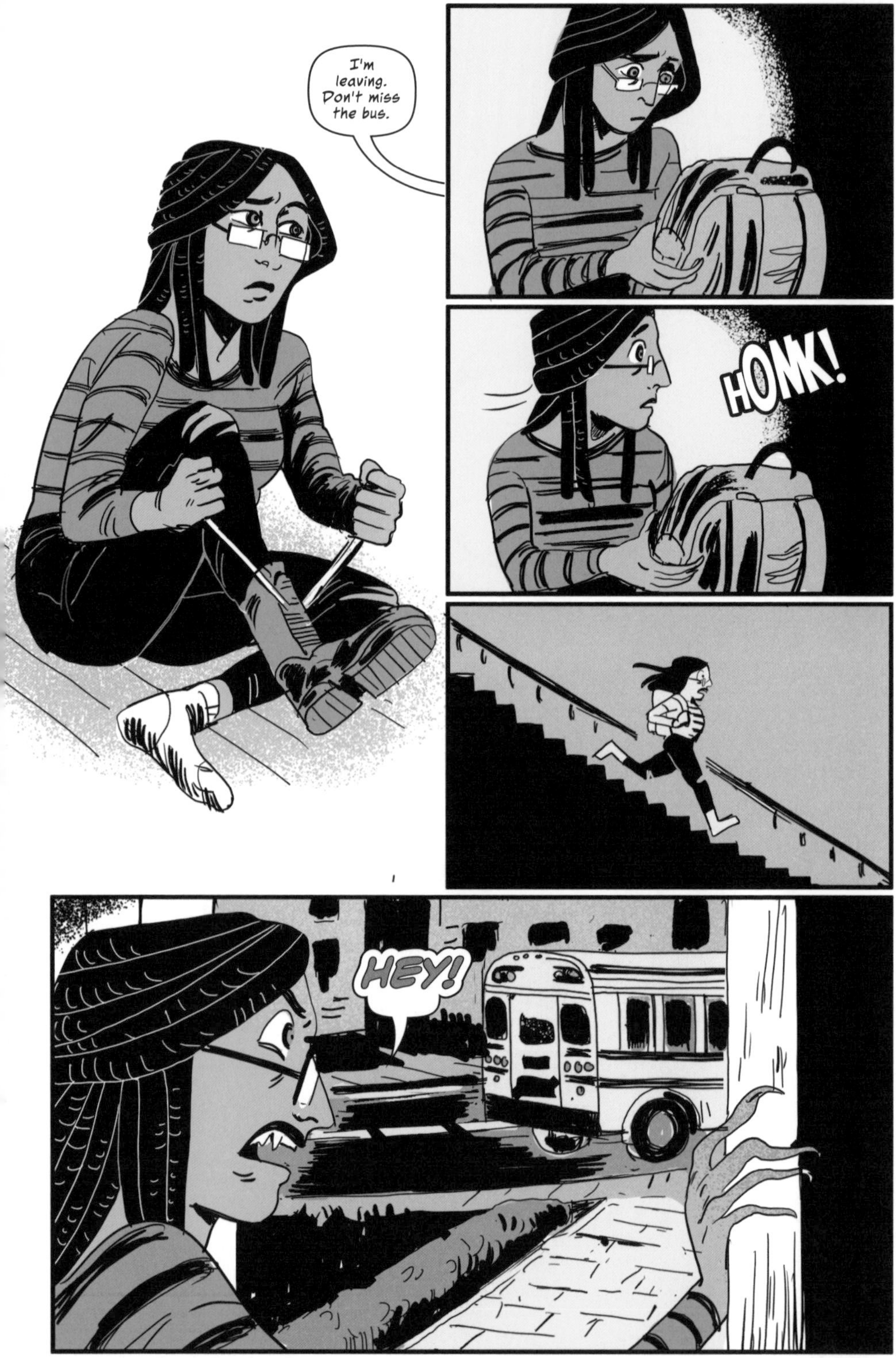
I'm leaving. Don't miss the bus.
HONK!
HEY!

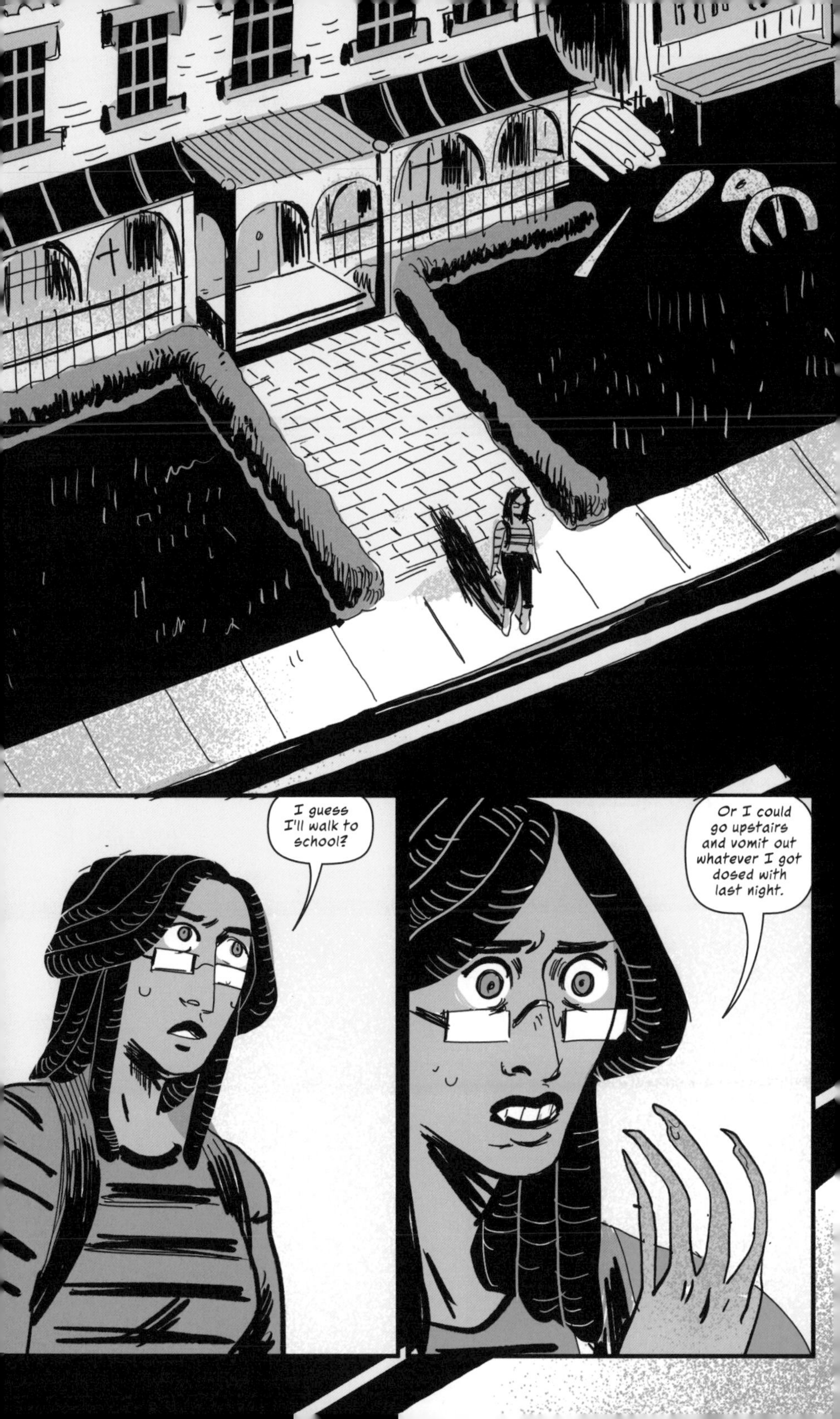
I guess I'll walk to school?
Or I could go upstairs and vomit out whatever I got dosed with last night.

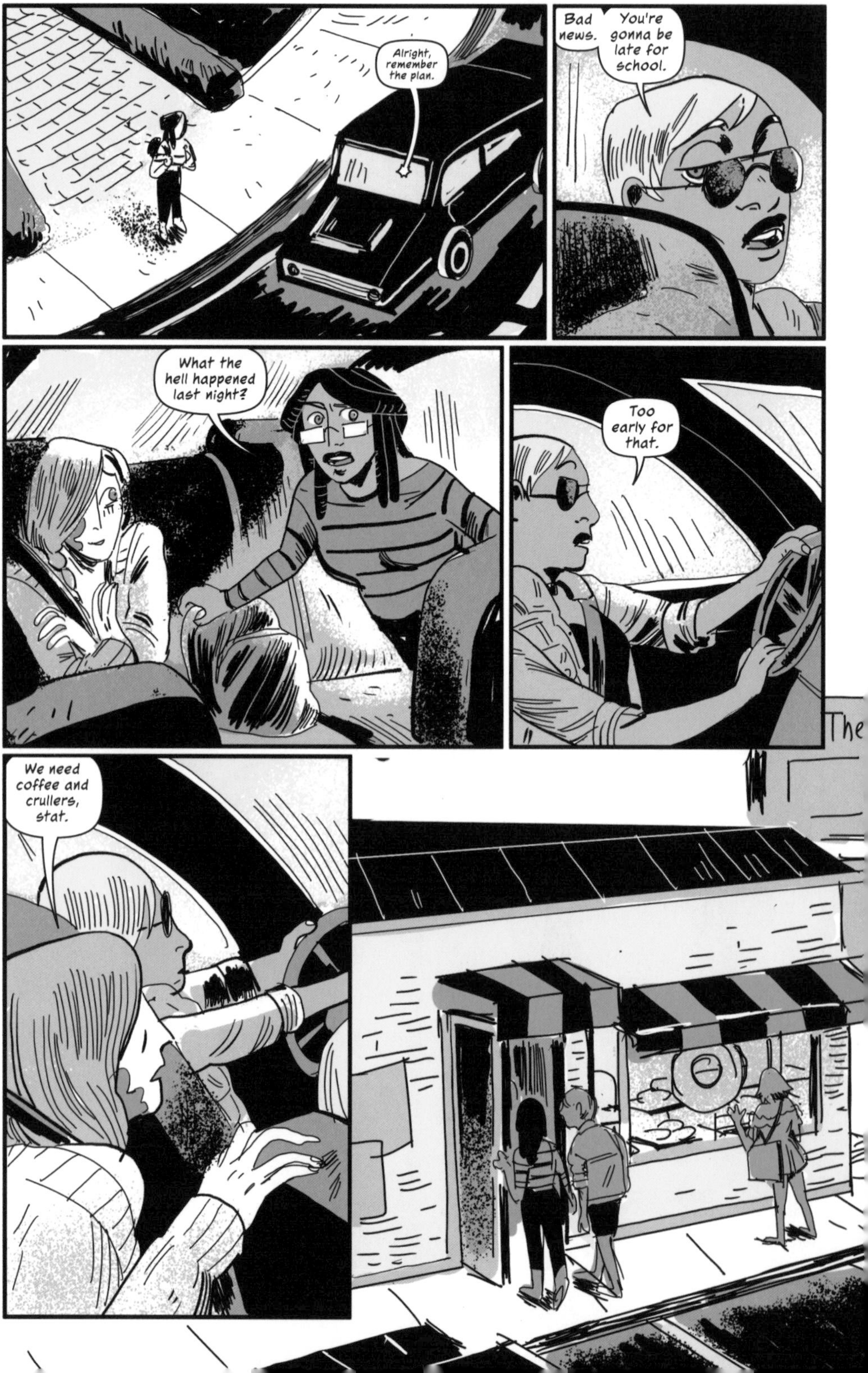

Alright, remember the plan.
Bad news.
You're gonna be late for school.
What the hell happened last night?
Too early for that.
We need coffee and crullers, stat.
The

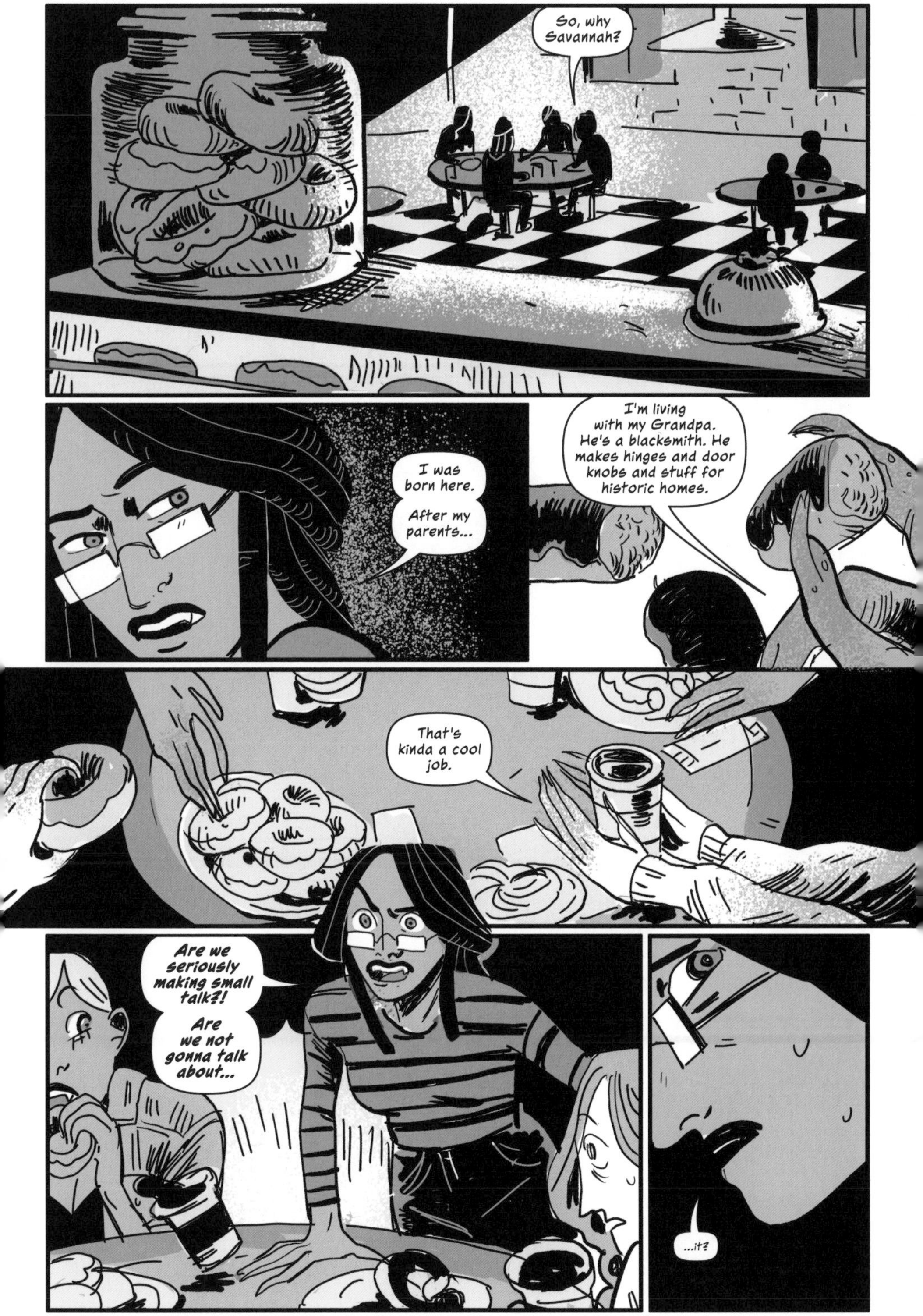
So, why Savannah?
I was born here.
After my parents...
I'm living with my Grandpa. He's a blacksmith. He makes hinges and door knobs and stuff for historic homes.
That's kinda a cool job.
Are we seriously making small talk?!
Are we not gonna talk about...
...it?

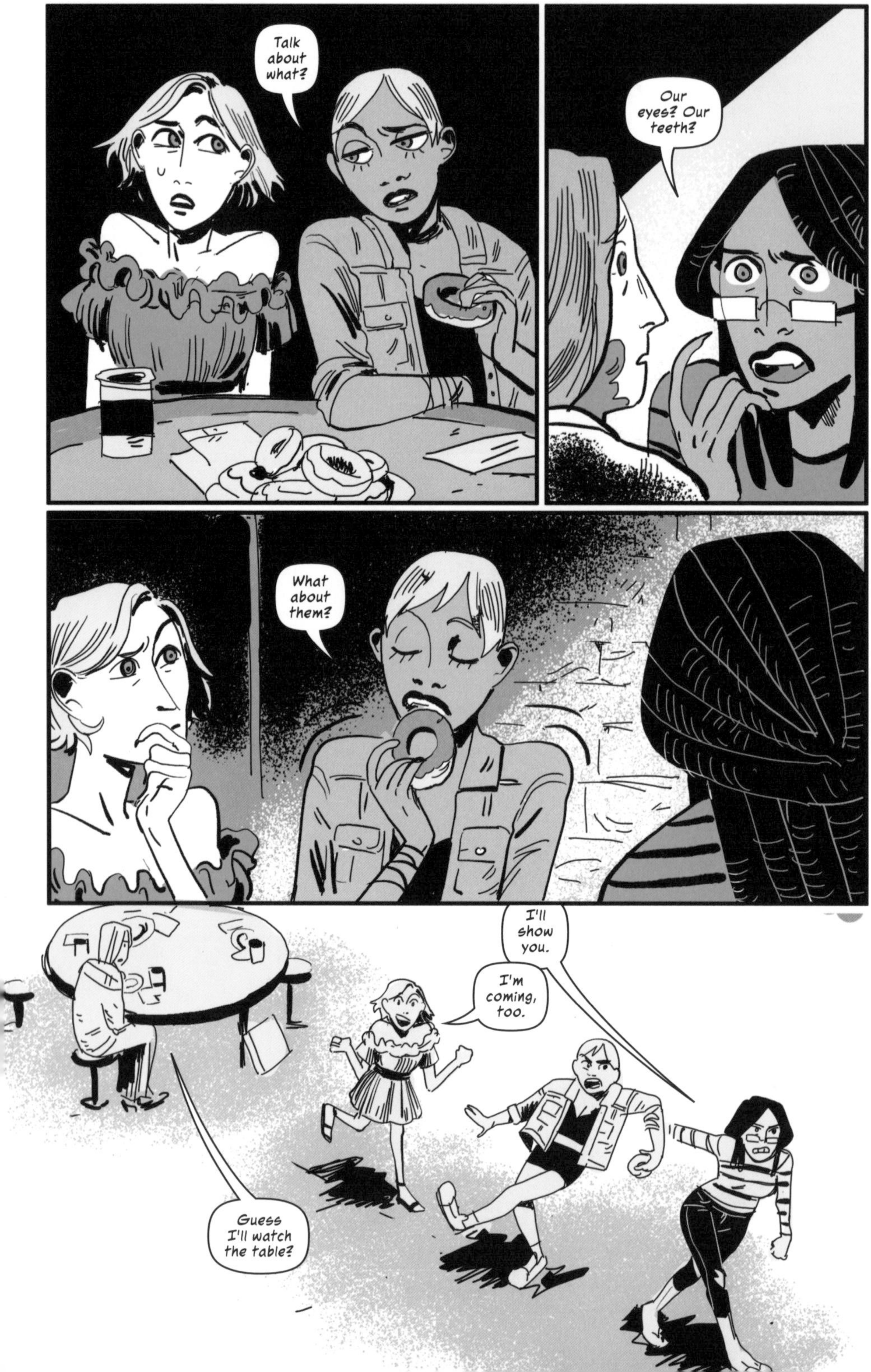
Talk about what?
Our eyes? Our teeth?
What about them?
I'll show you.
I'm coming, too.
Guess I'll watch the table?

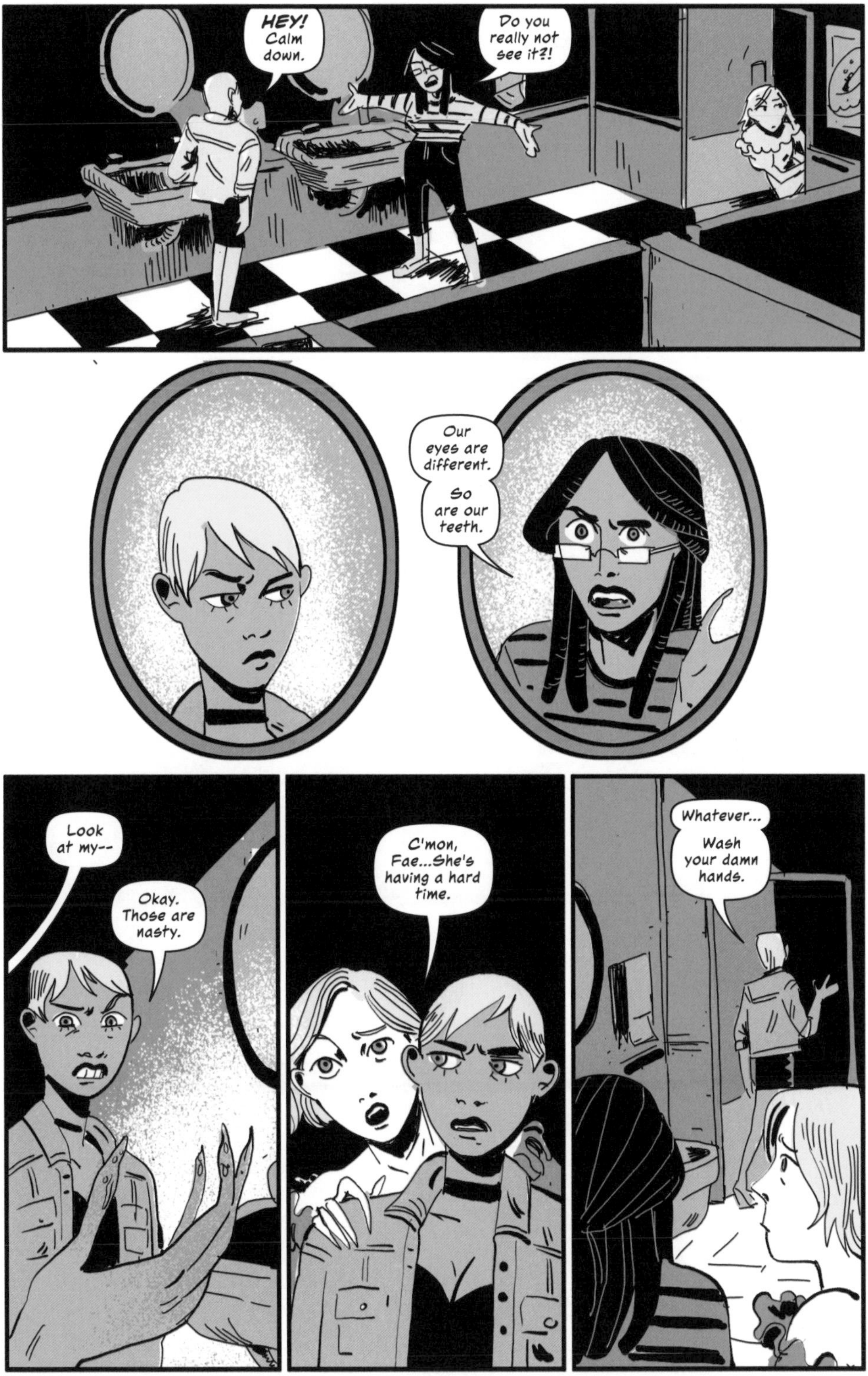

HEY! Calm down.
Do you really not see it?!
Our eyes are different.
So are our teeth.
Look at my--
Okay. Those are nasty.
C'mon, Fae...She's having a hard time.
Whatever...
Wash your damn hands.

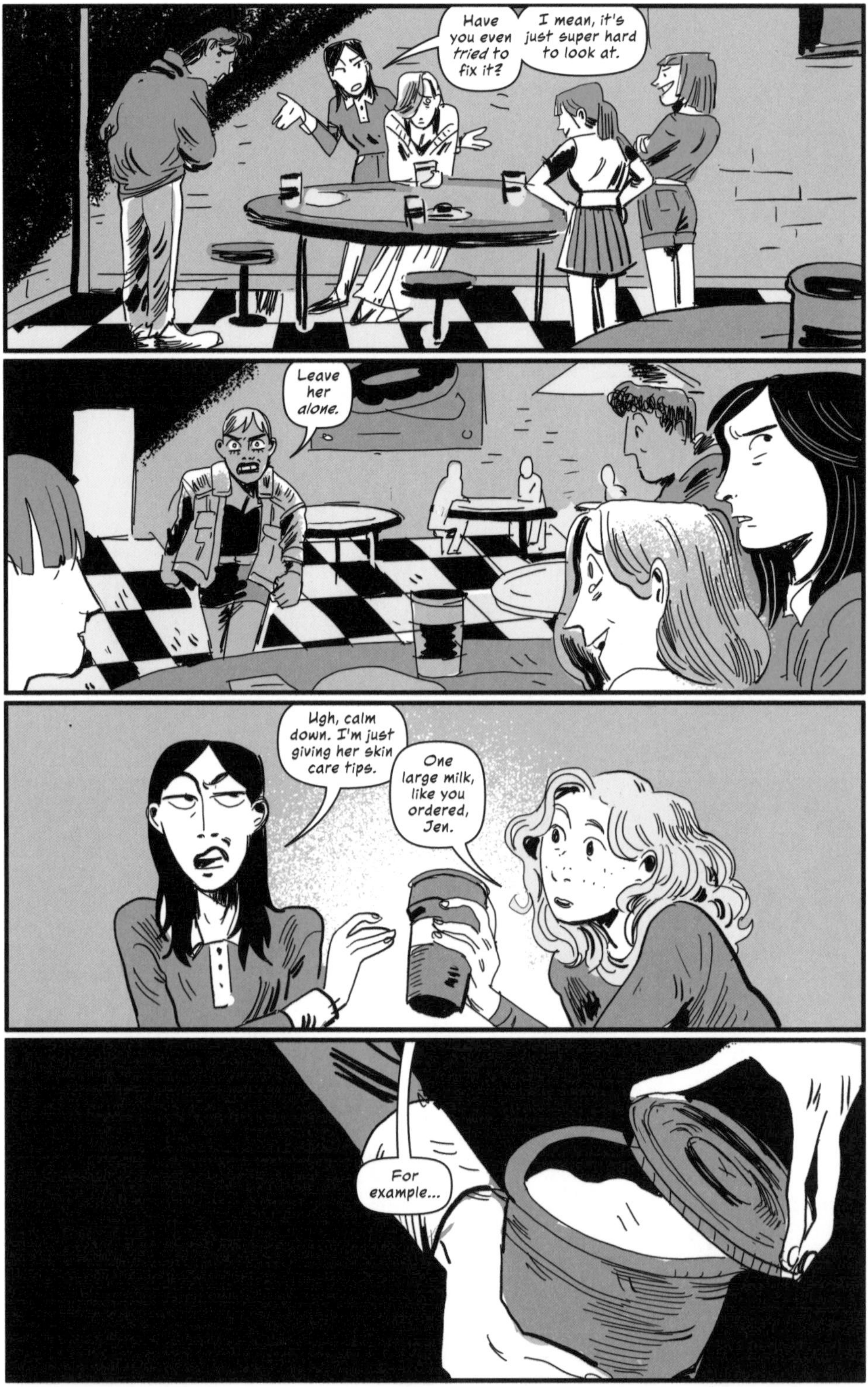
Have you even *tried* to fix it?
I mean, it's just super hard to look at.
Leave her alone.
Ugh, calm down. I'm just giving her skin care tips.
One large milk, like you ordered, Jen.
For example...

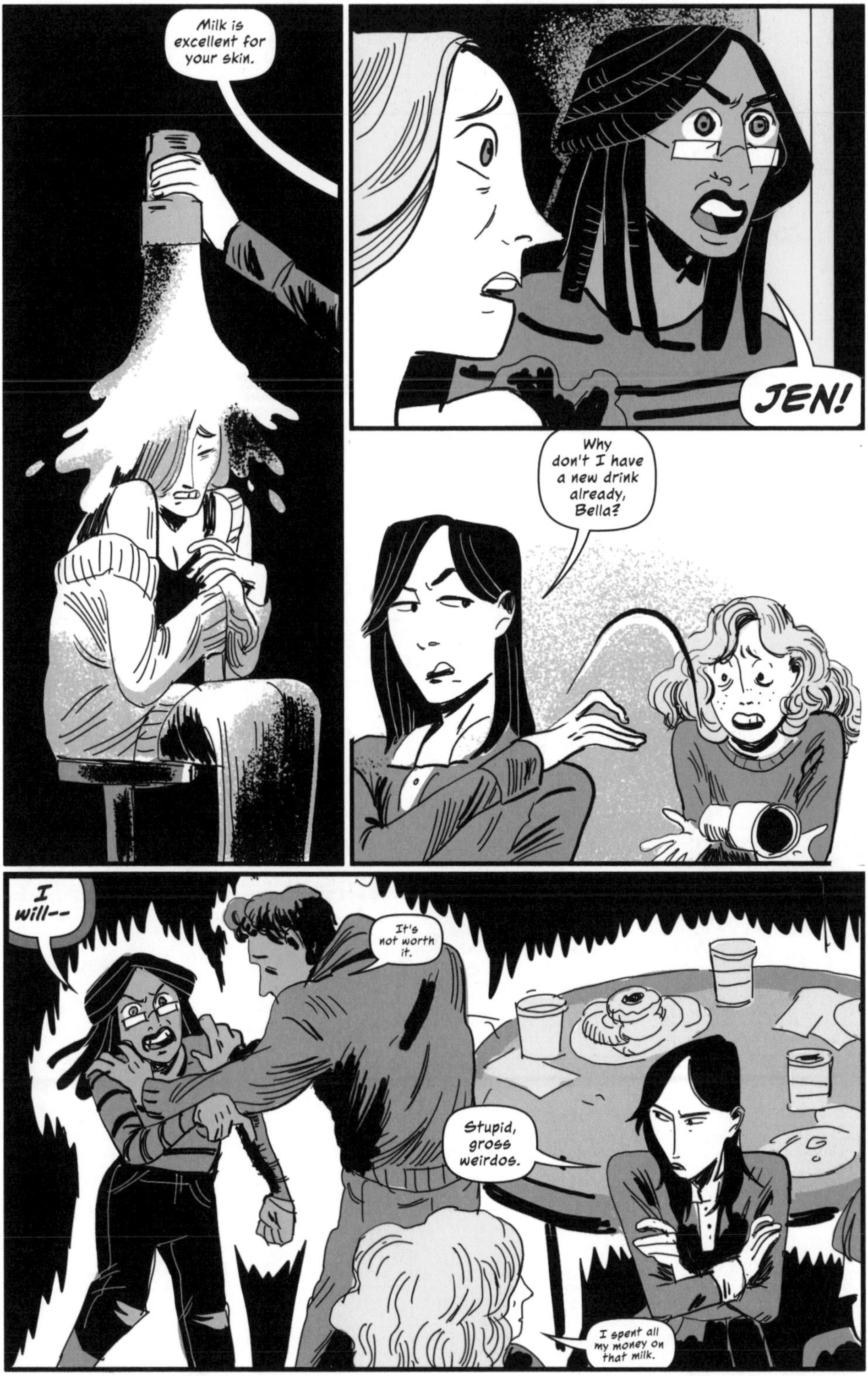
Milk is excellent for your skin.
JEN!
Why don't I have a new drink already, Bella?
I will--
It's not worth it.
Stupid, gross weirdos.
I spent all my money on that milk.

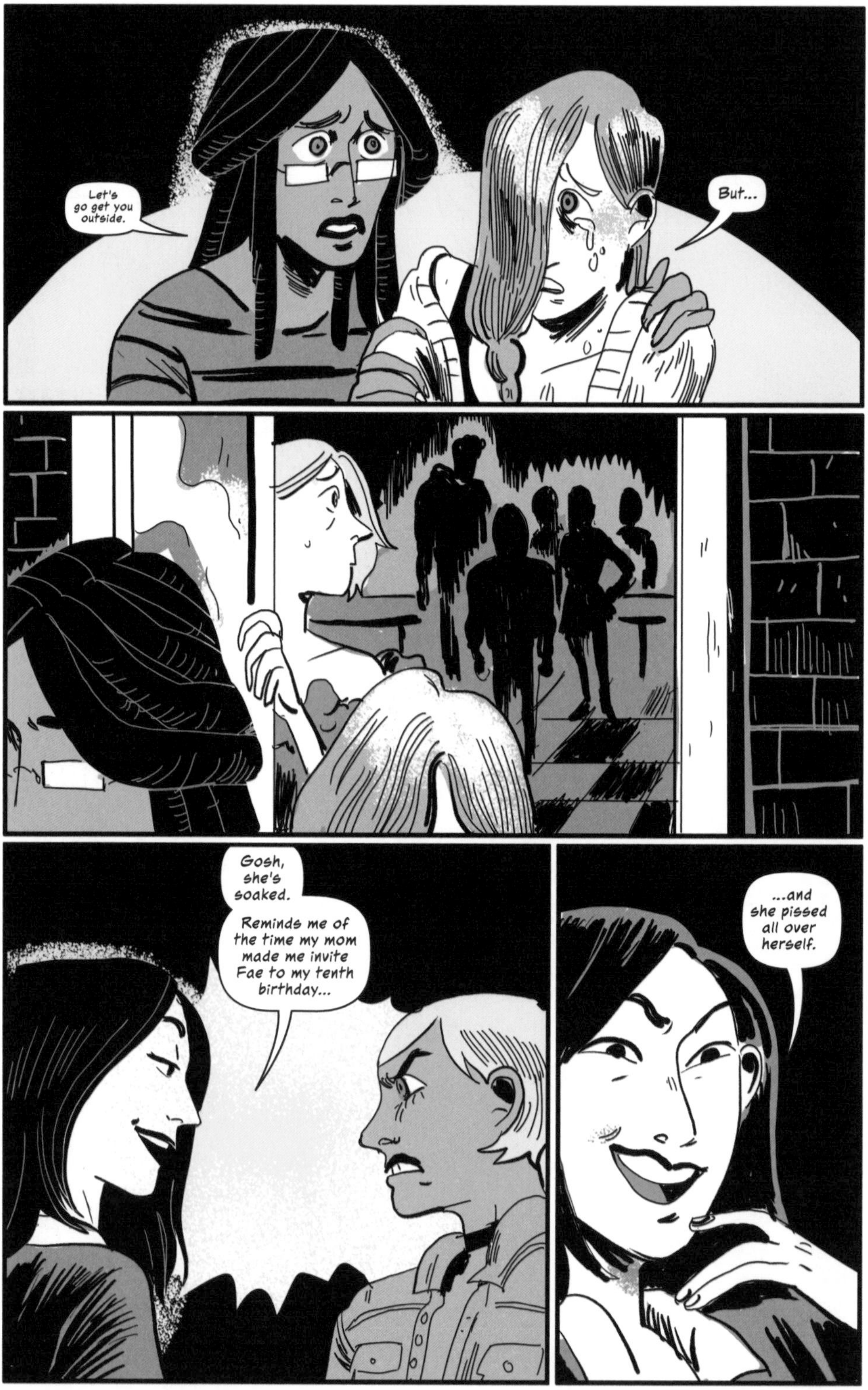
Let's go get you outside.
But...
Gosh, she's soaked.
Reminds me of the time my mom made me invite Fae to my tenth birthday...
...and she pissed all over herself.

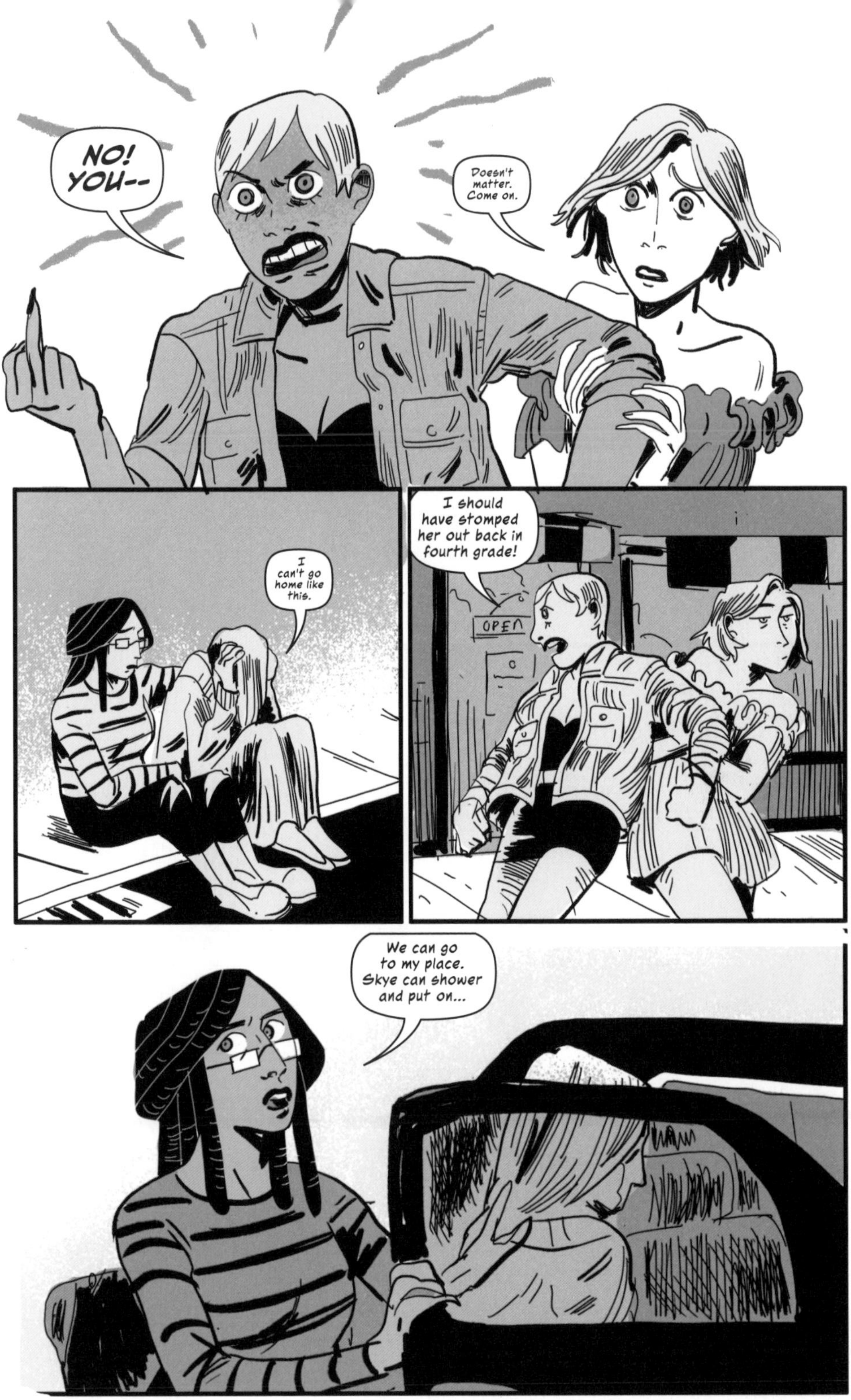
NO! YOU--
Doesn't matter. Come on.
I can't go home like this.
I should have stomped her out back in fourth grade!
OPEN
We can go to my place. Skye can shower and put on...

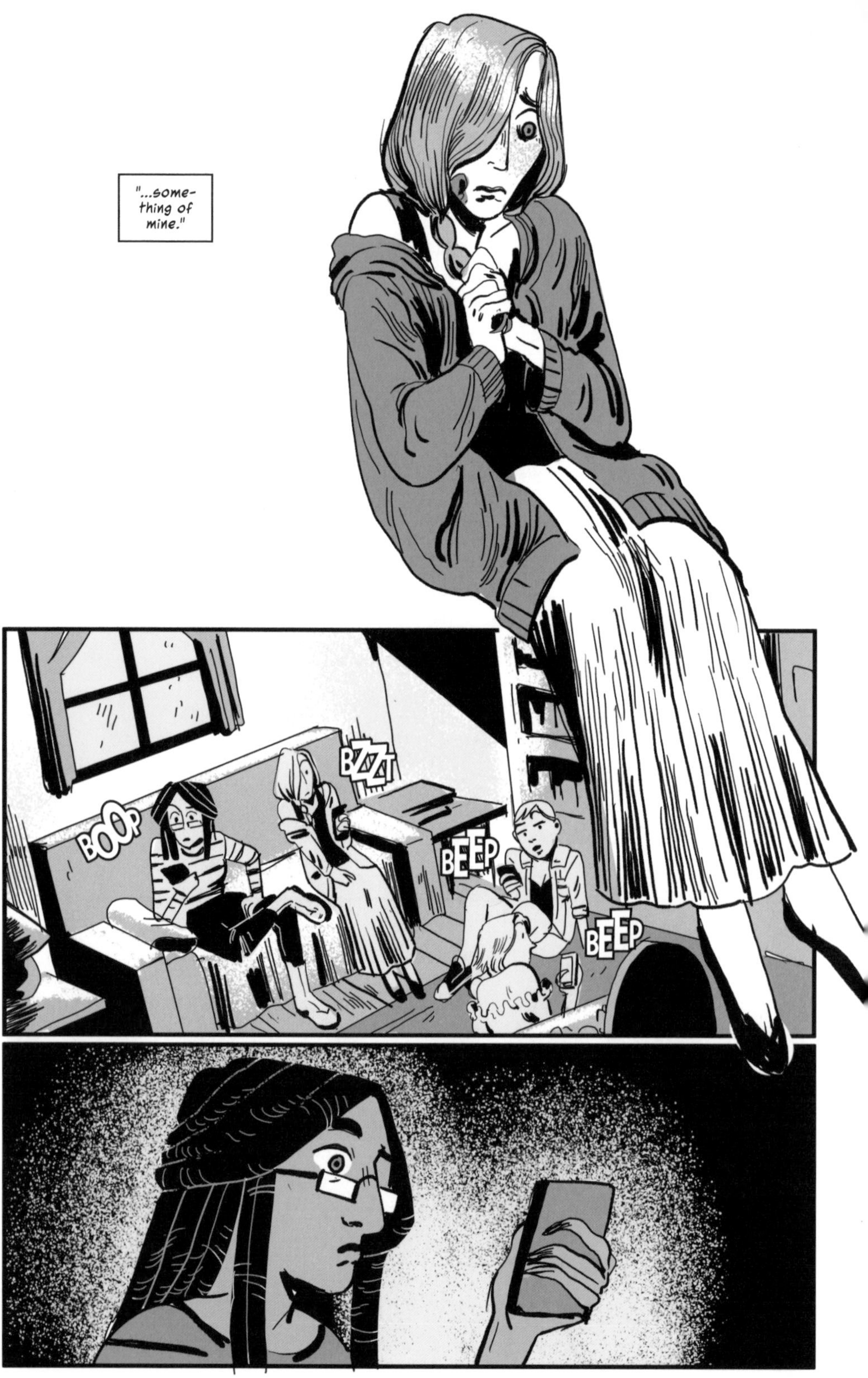
"...some-
thing of
mine."
BOOP
BZZZT
BEEP
BEEP

FROM: MR. E. JOHNSON <ejohnson@summerlandhs.edu>
to: BCC

SUBJECT: If you fail to plan, you plan to fail.

Girls,

Each of you chose to miss my class today and each of you failed to turn in your reading journals.

As you may know, reading journals are 30% of you're overall grade. You are all in danger of failure due to your poor choices.

Actually, that isn't true. Due to the fact that Ms. Bowman has no other grades in my book, and she has a zero for this, she is not in danger of failing. She is failing.

Take Care,
Mr. E. Johnson
English and Language Arts Facilitator
Summerland High School

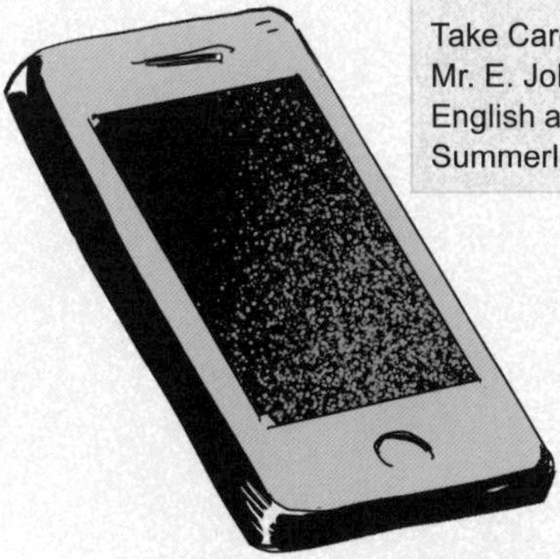

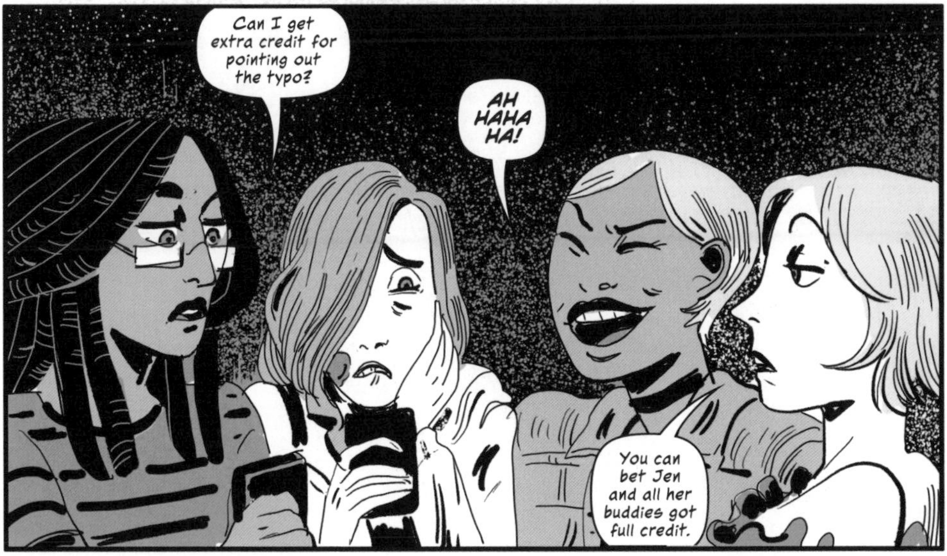
Can I get extra credit for pointing out the typo?
AH HAHA HA!
You can bet Jen and all her buddies got full credit.

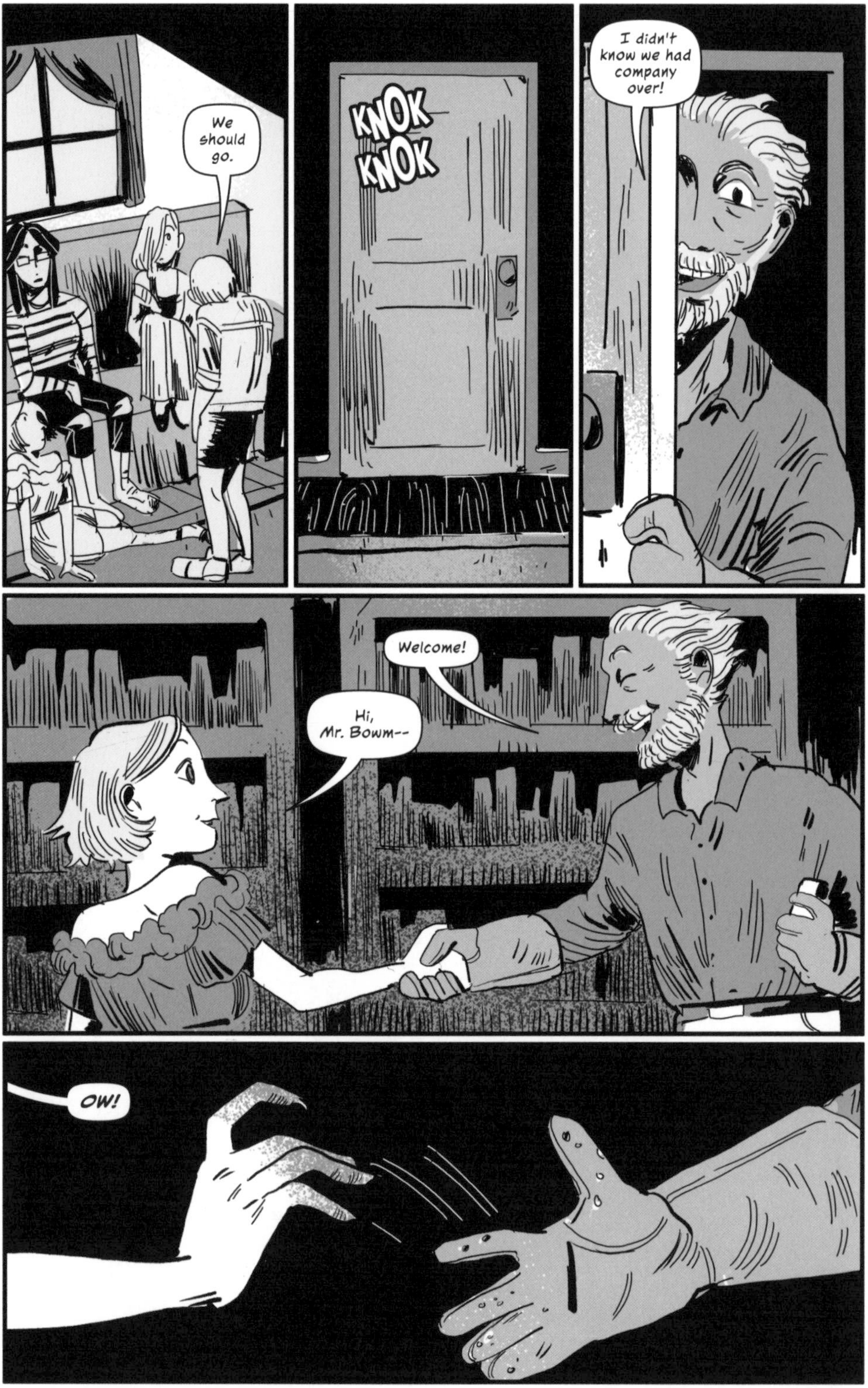
We should go.
KNOK KNOK
I didn't know we had company over!
Welcome!
Hi, Mr. Bowm--
OW!

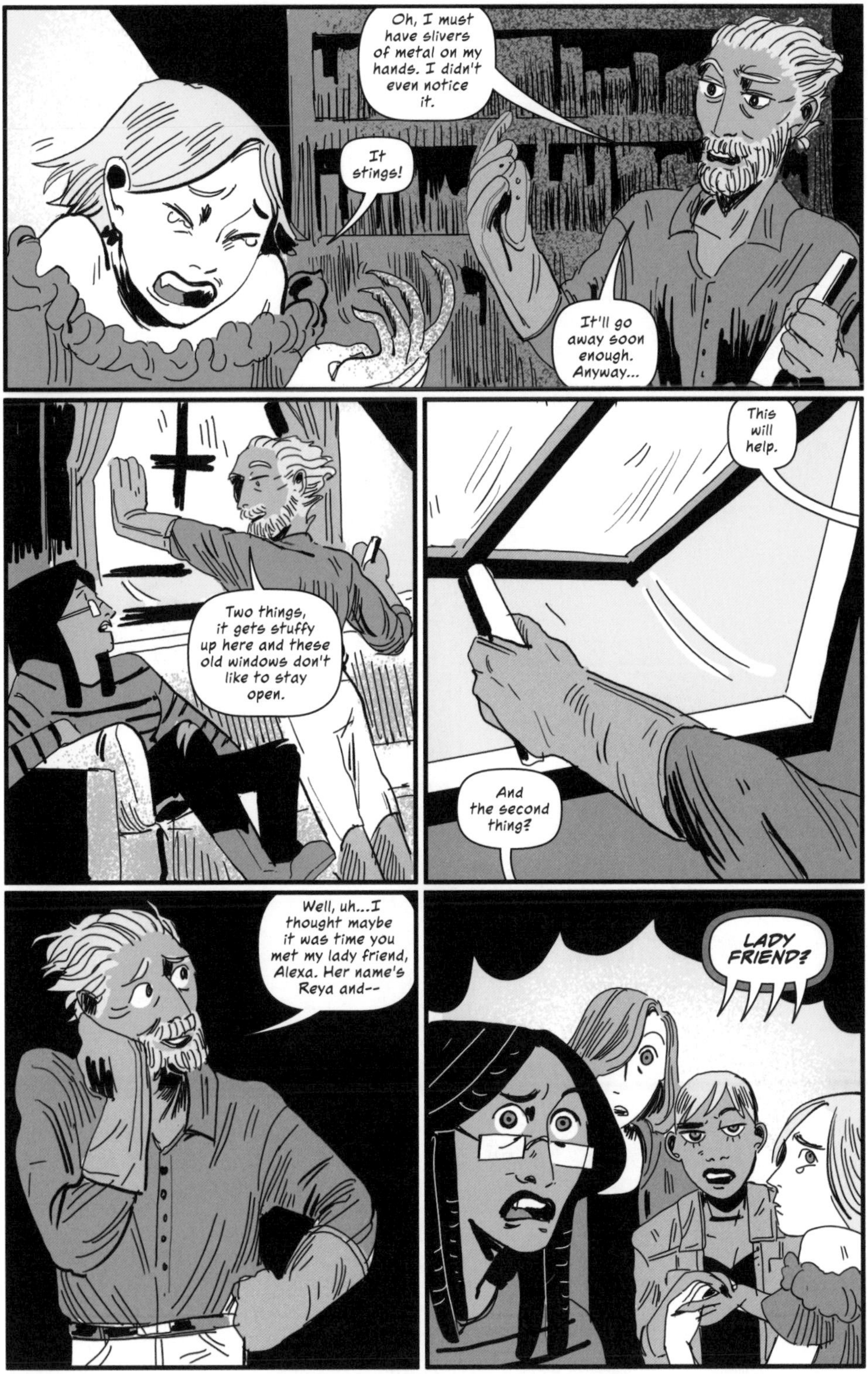
Oh, I must have slivers of metal on my hands. I didn't even notice it.
It stings!
It'll go away soon enough. Anyway...
Two things, it gets stuffy up here and these old windows don't like to stay open.
This will help.
And the second thing?
Well, uh...I thought maybe it was time you met my lady friend, Alexa. Her name's Reya and--
LADY FRIEND?

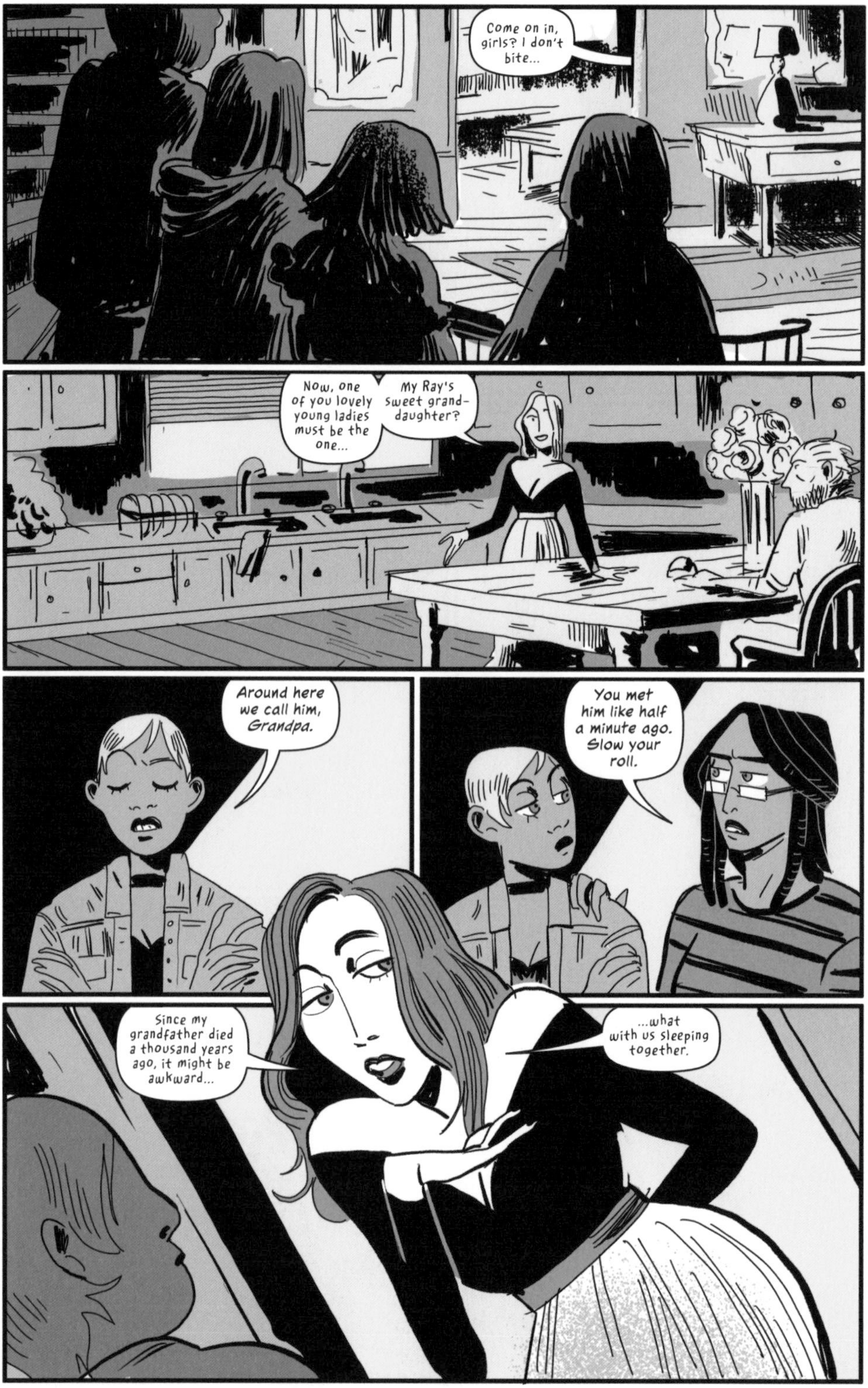
Come on in, girls? I don't bite...
Now, one of you lovely young ladies must be the one...
My Ray's sweet grand-daughter?
Around here we call him, Grandpa.
You met him like half a minute ago. Slow your roll.
Since my grandfather died a thousand years ago, it might be awkward...
...what with us sleeping together.

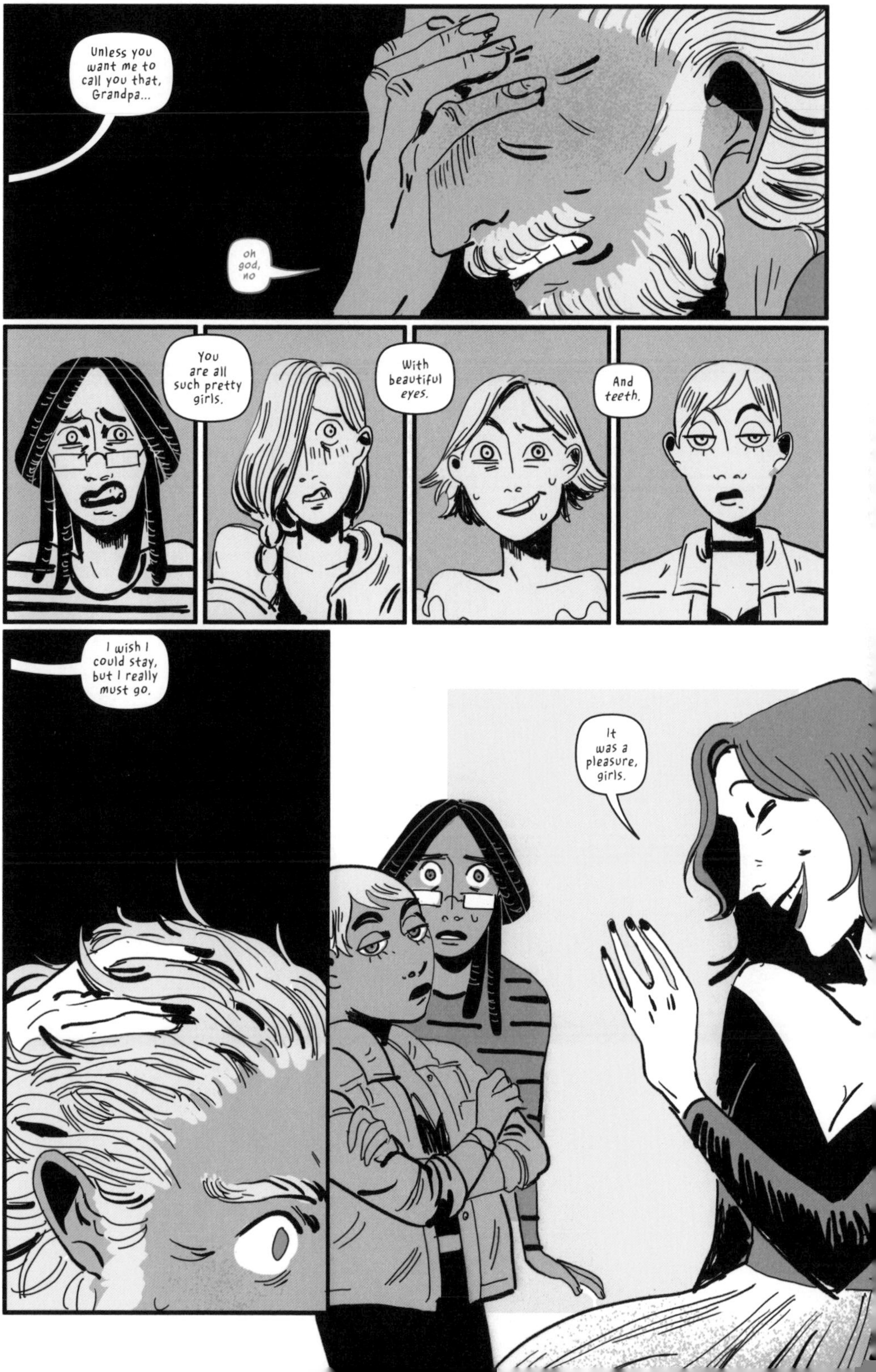

Unless you want me to call you that, Grandpa...
oh god, no
You are all such pretty girls.
With beautiful *eyes.*
And *teeth.*
I wish I could stay, but I really must go.
It was a pleasure, girls.

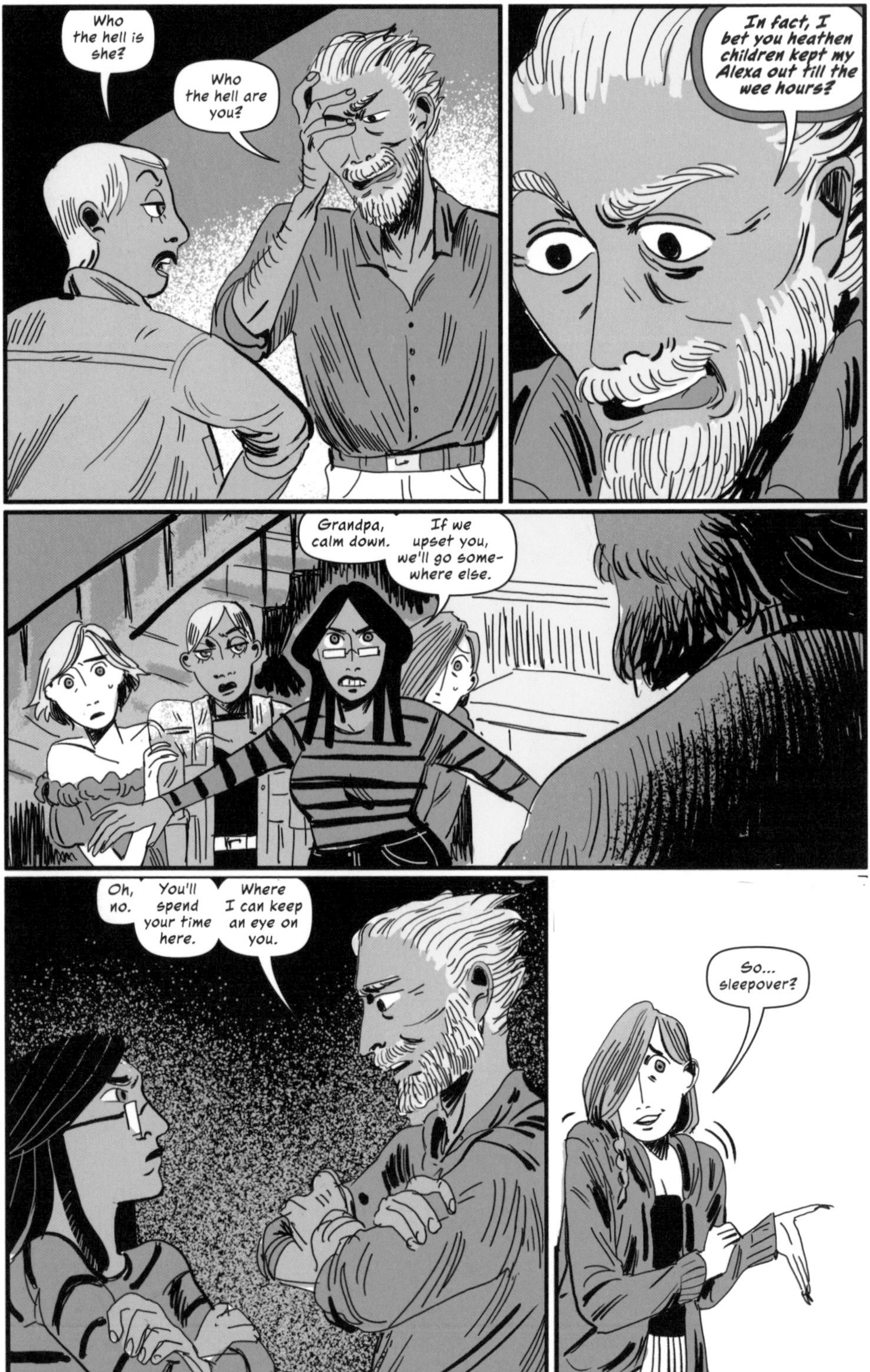
Who the hell is she?
Who the hell are you?
In fact, I bet you heathen children kept my Alexa out till the wee hours?
Grandpa, calm down.
If we upset you, we'll go somewhere else.
Oh, no.
You'll spend your time here.
Where I can keep an eye on you.
So... sleepover?

Fay Social Structures

Fairies are social creatures,
often building close-knit relationships with their kind.
These Frolics find a territory, stake their claim,
and begin to corrupt those around them.

These groups are prone to jealousy and
can be broken up with the right words
from an experienced Hunter.

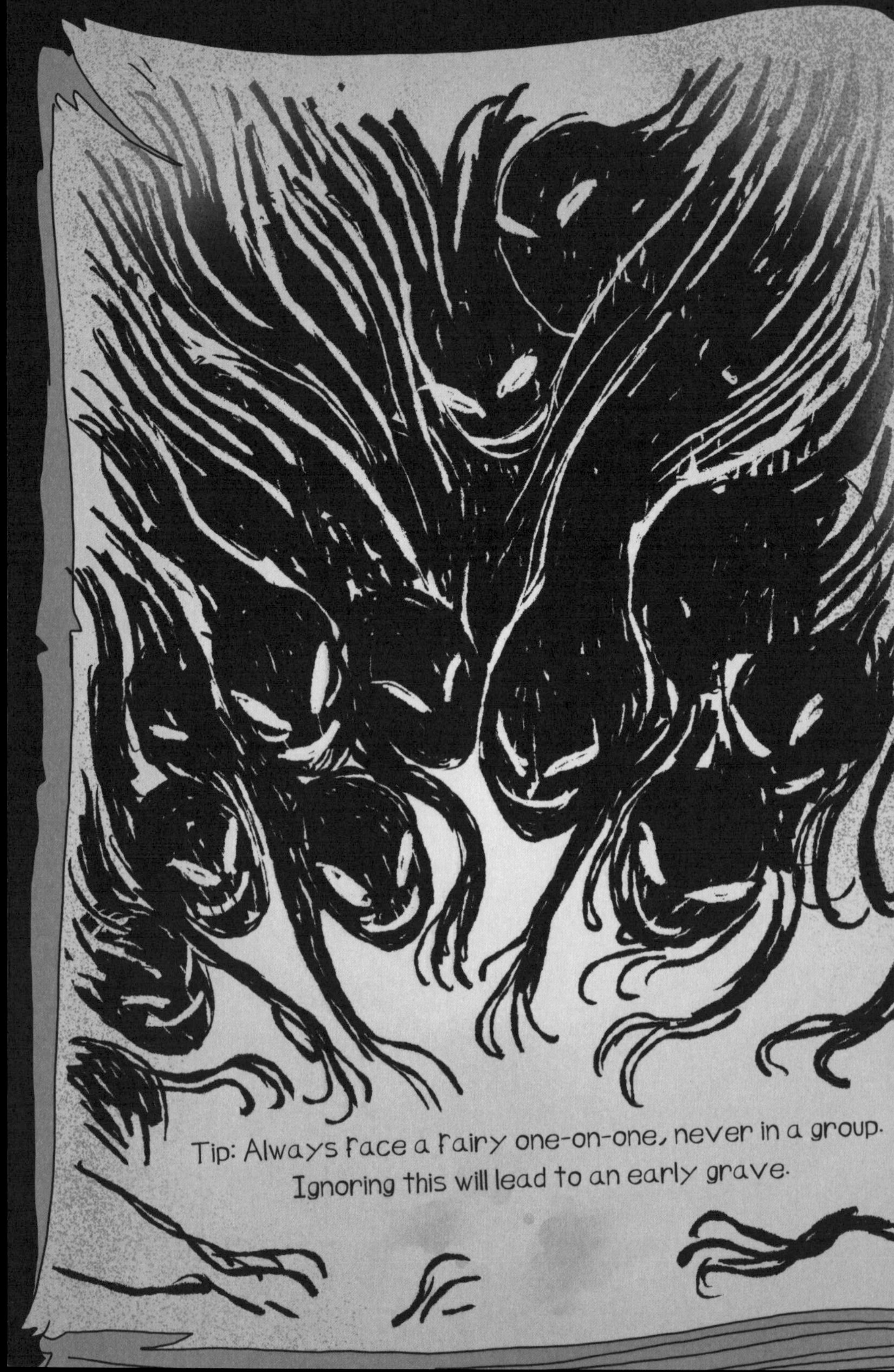
Tip: Always face a fairy one-on-one, never in a group.
Ignoring this will lead to an early grave.

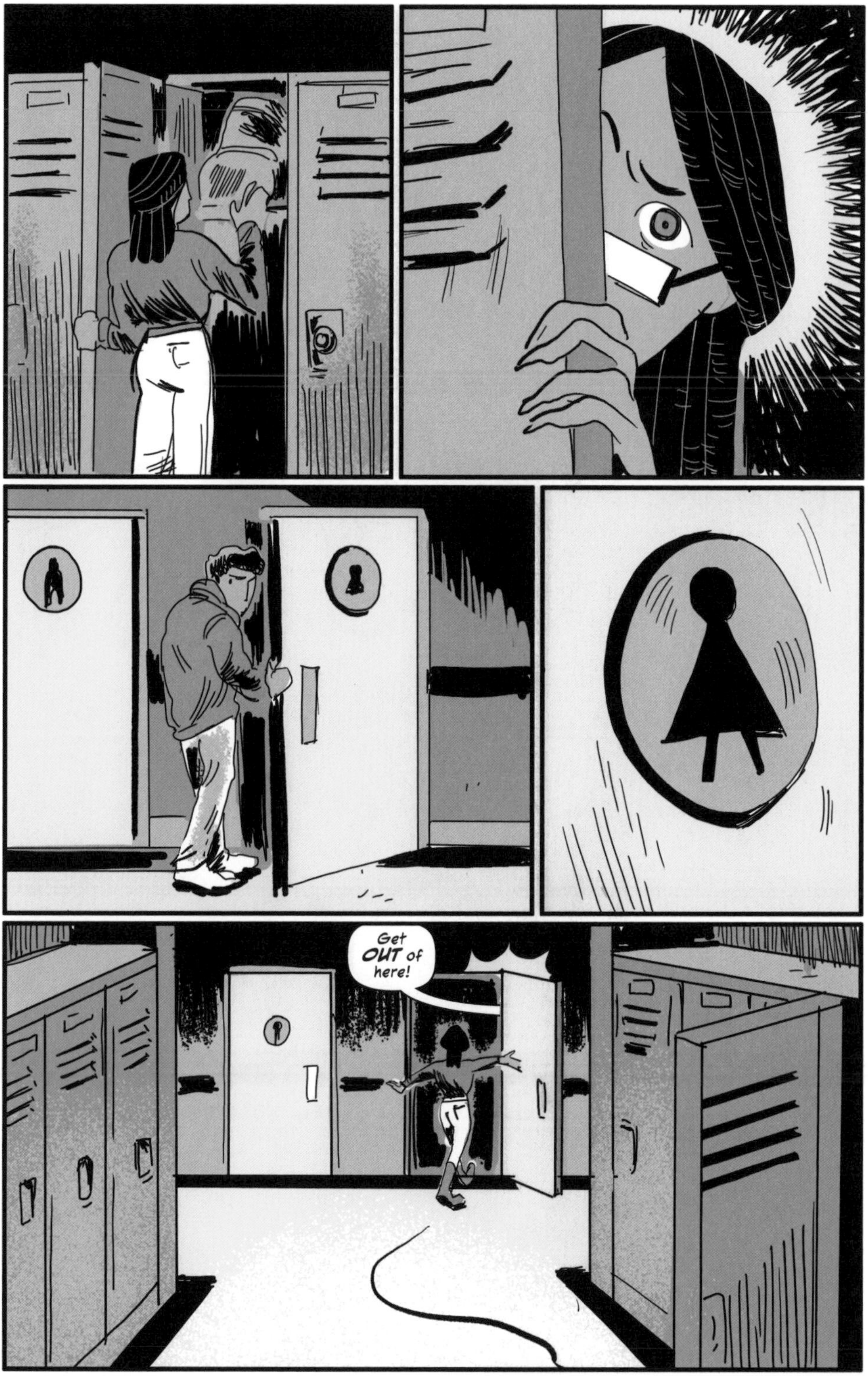
Get OUT of here!

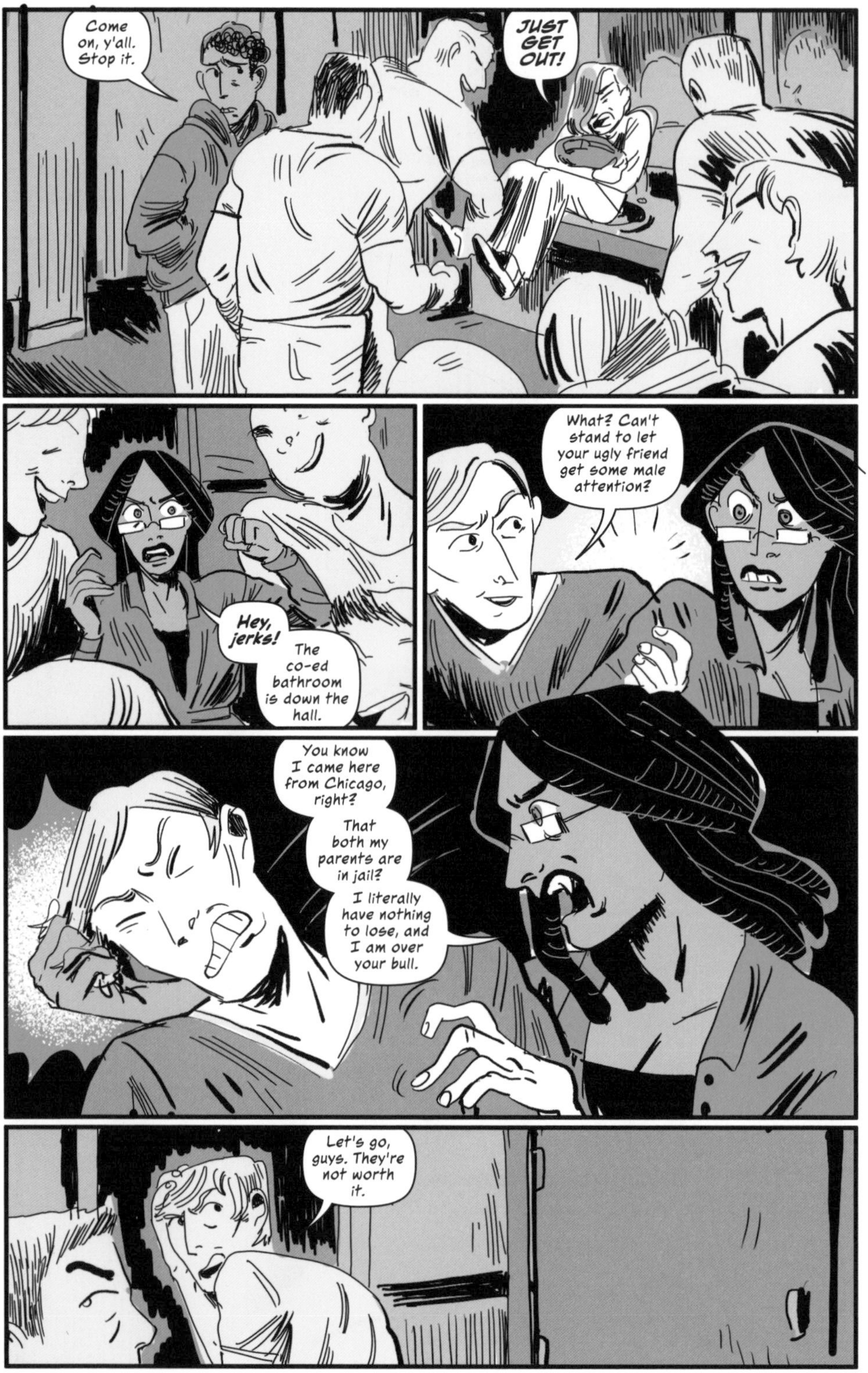
Come on, y'all. Stop it.
JUST GET OUT!
Hey, jerks!
The co-ed bathroom is down the hall.
What? Can't stand to let your ugly friend get some male attention?
You know I came here from Chicago, right?
That both my parents are in jail?
I literally have nothing to lose, and I am over your bull.
Let's go, guys. They're not worth it.

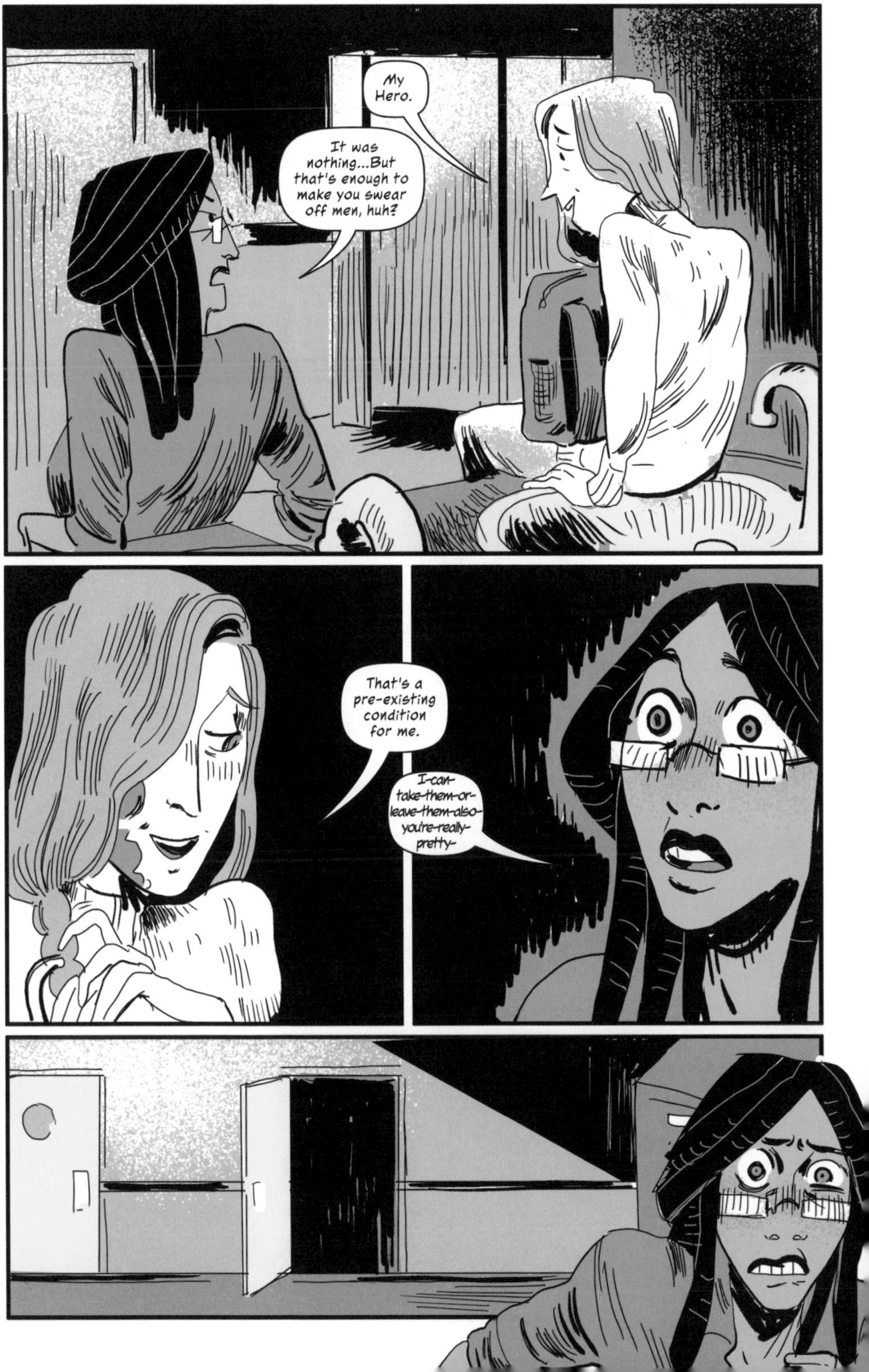

My Hero.
It was nothing...But that's enough to make you swear off men, huh?
That's a pre-existing condition for me.
I-can-take-them-or-leave-them-also-you're-really-pretty-

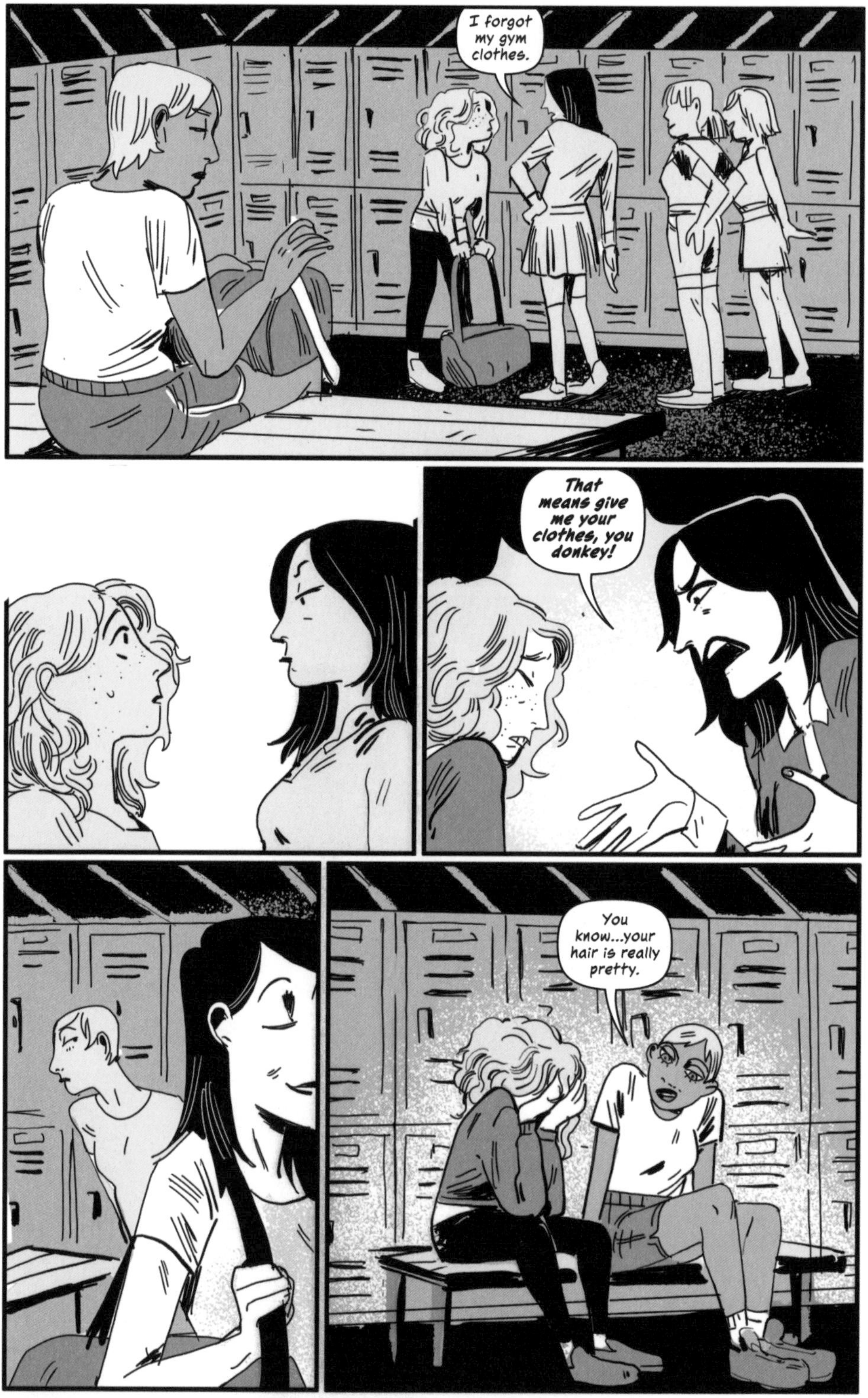
I forgot my gym clothes.
That means give me your clothes, you donkey!
You know...your hair is really pretty.

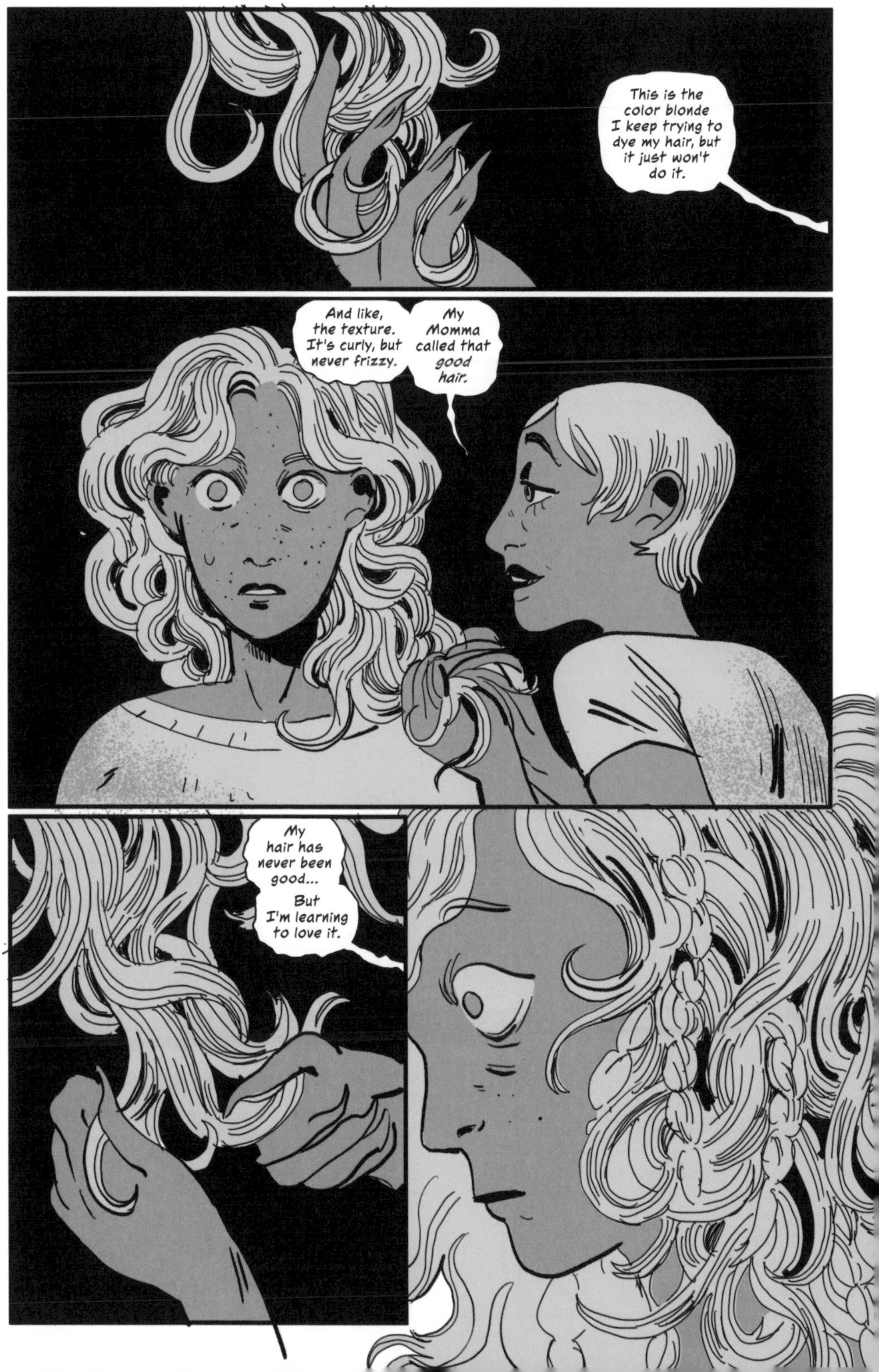
This is the color blonde I keep trying to dye my hair, but it just won't do it.
And like, the texture. It's curly, but never frizzy.
My Momma called that good hair.
My hair has never been good...
But I'm learning to love it.

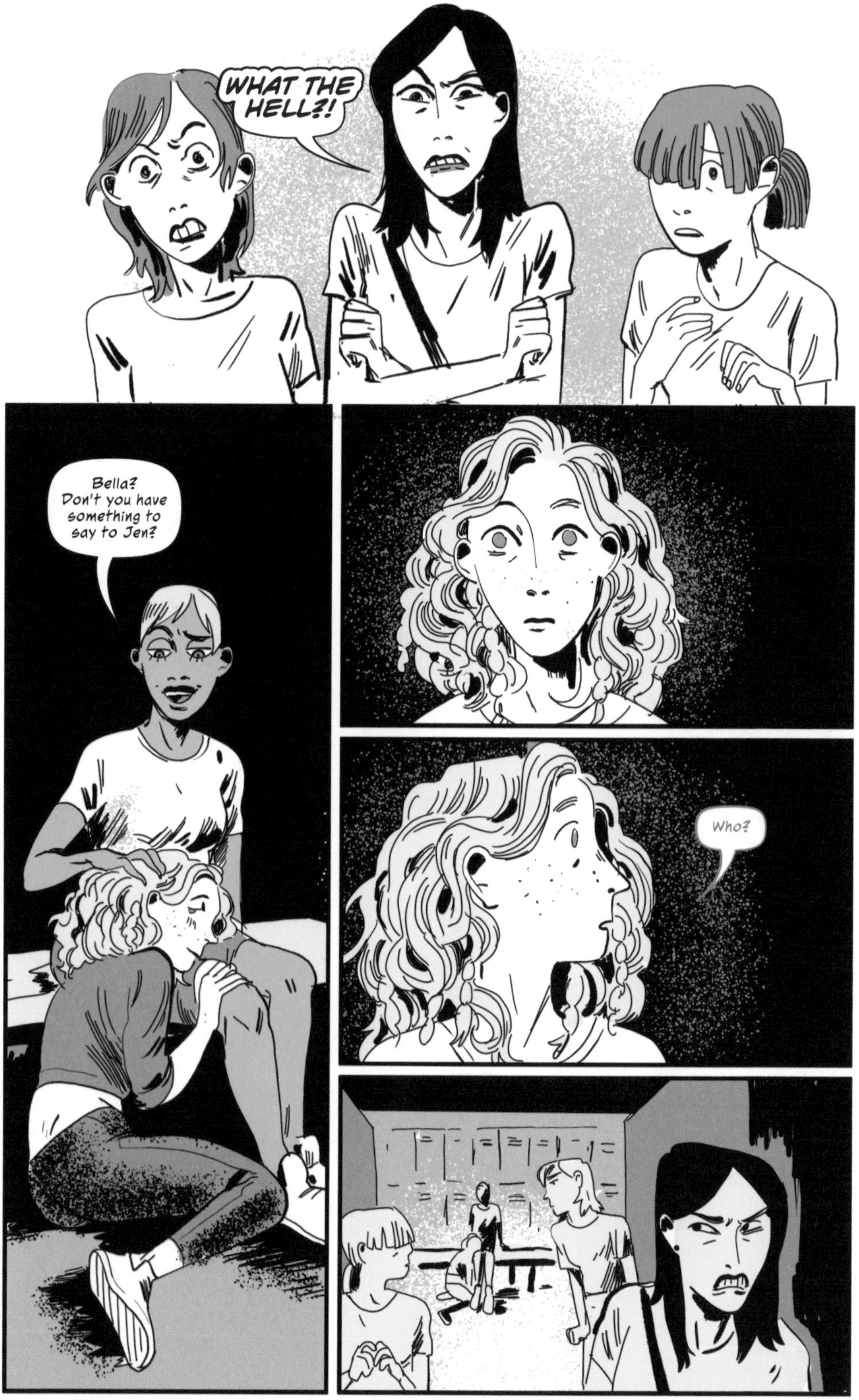
WHAT THE HELL?!
Bella? Don't you have something to say to Jen?
Who?

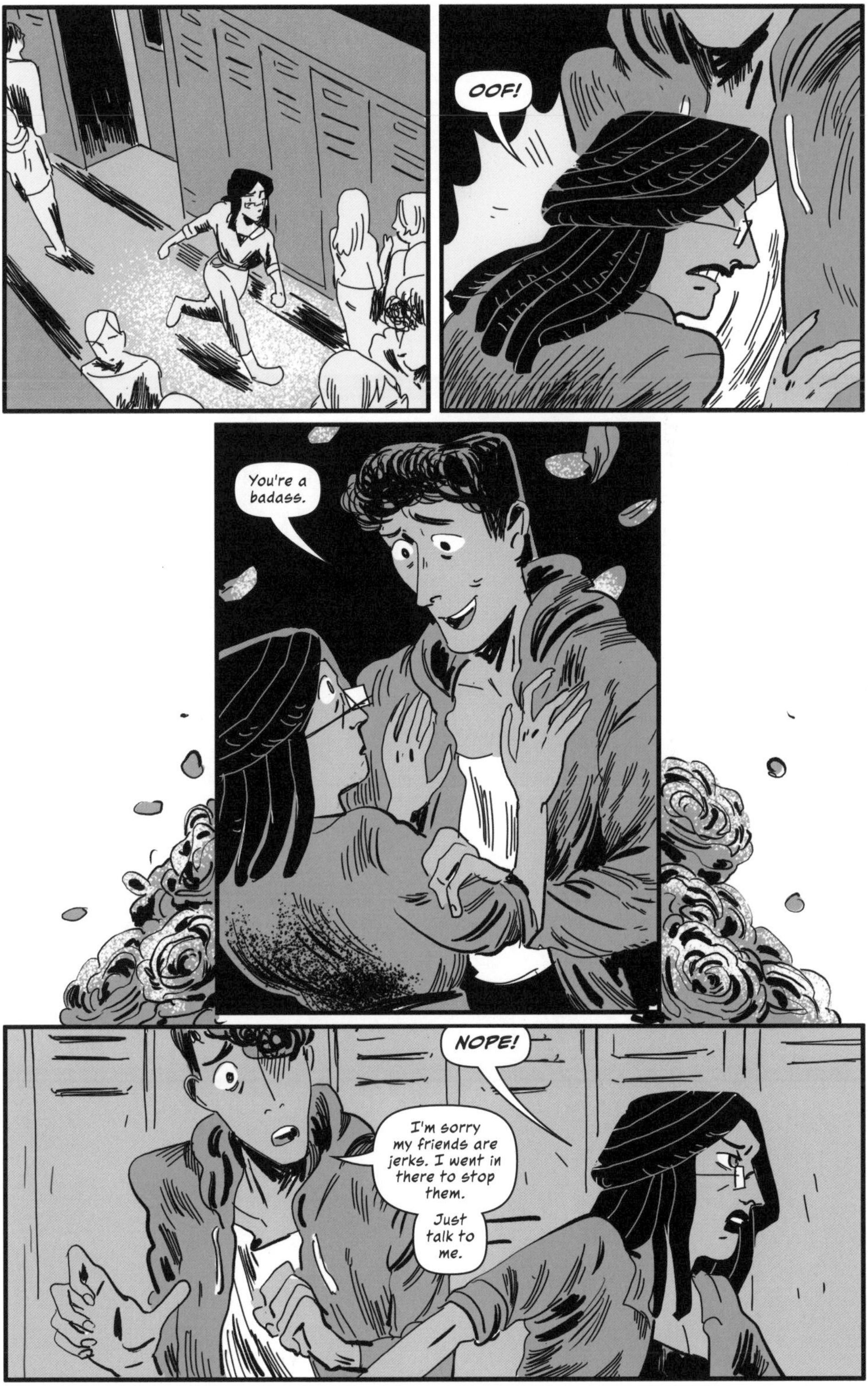
OOF!
You're a badass.
NOPE!
I'm sorry my friends are jerks. I went in there to stop them.
Just talk to me.

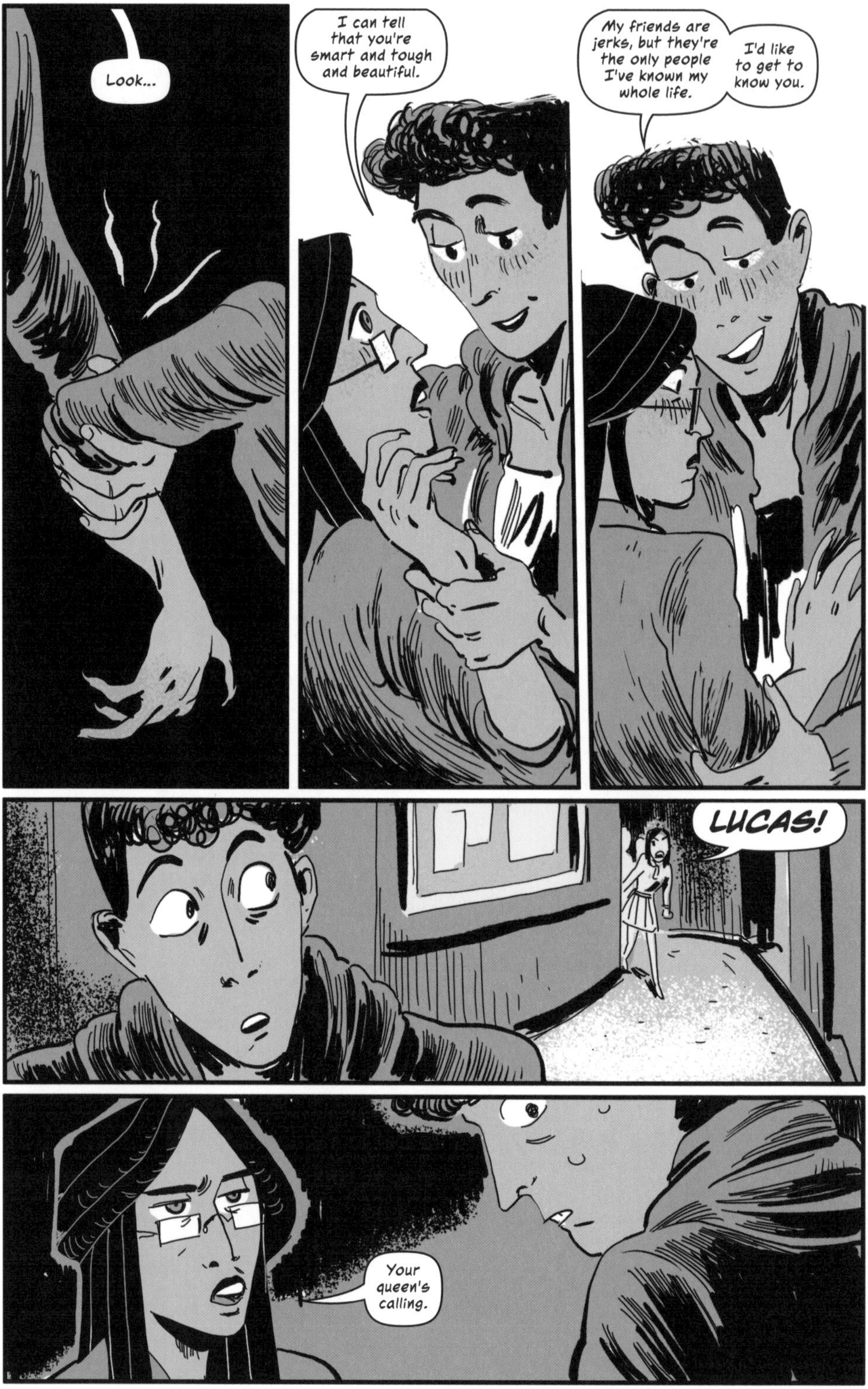
Look...
I can tell that you're smart and tough and beautiful.
My friends are jerks, but they're the only people I've known my whole life.
I'd like to get to know you.
LUCAS!
Your queen's calling.

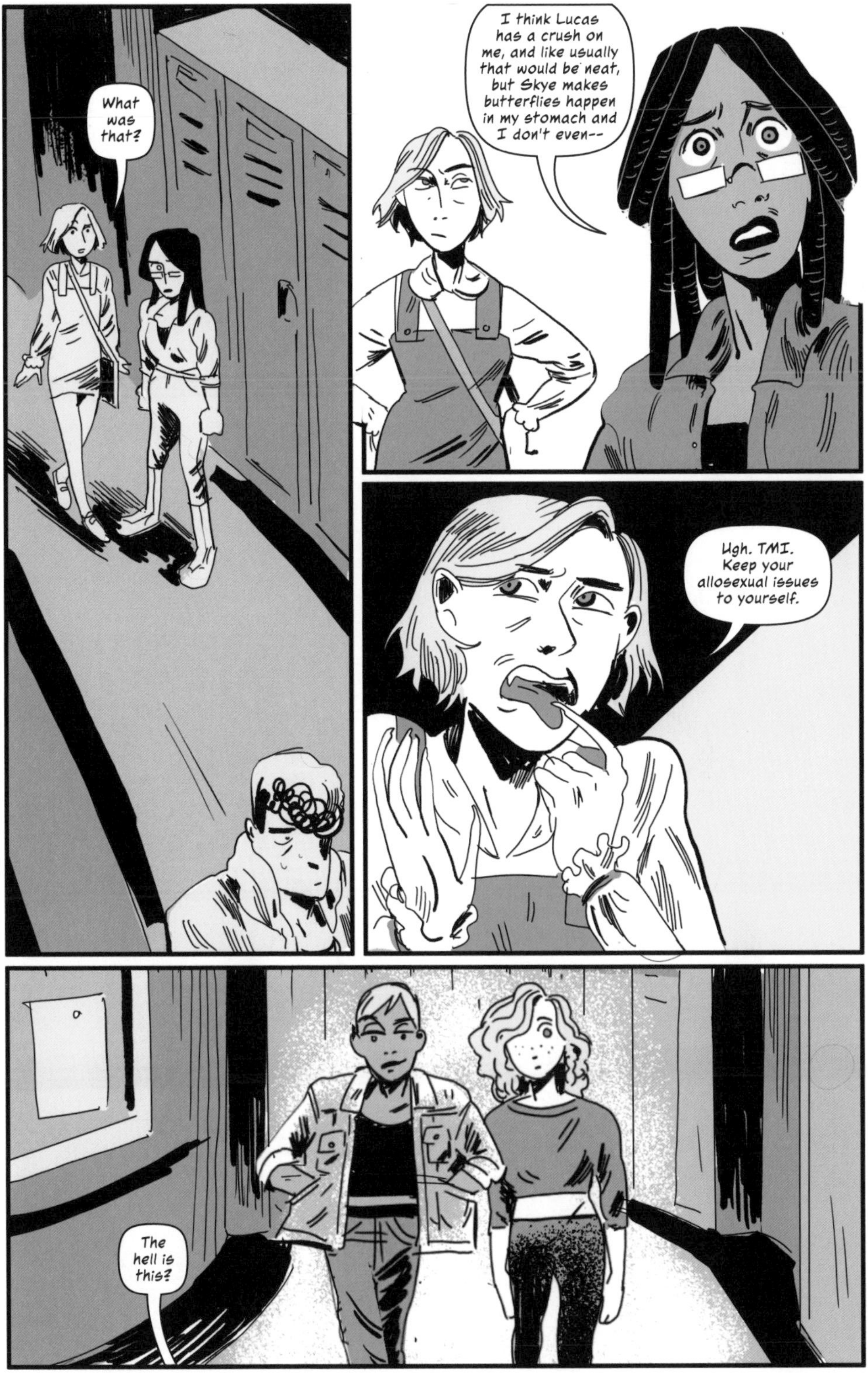
What was that?
I think Lucas has a crush on me, and like usually that would be neat, but Skye makes butterflies happen in my stomach and I don't even--
Ugh. TMI. Keep your allosexual issues to yourself.
The hell is this?

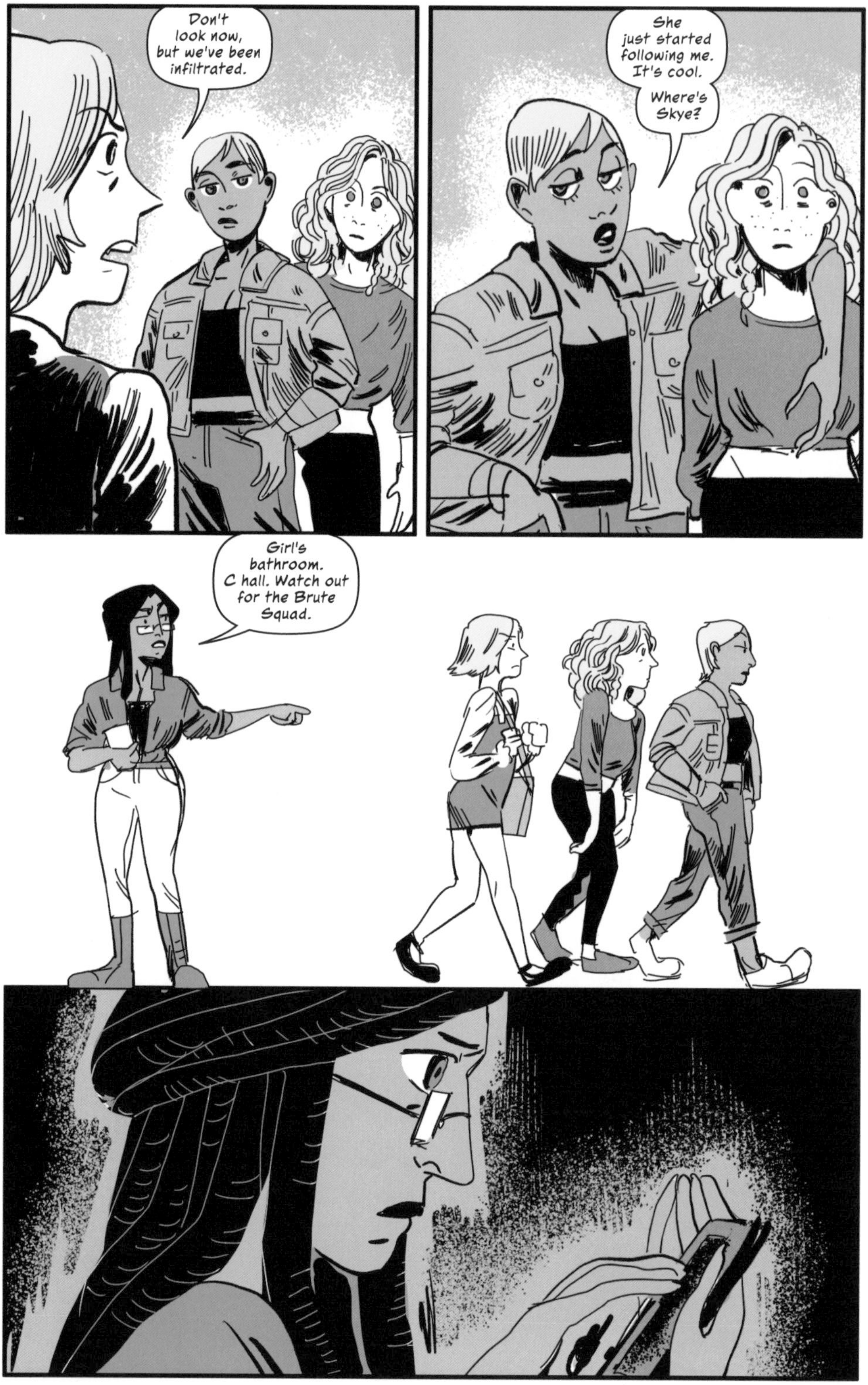
Don't look now, but we've been infiltrated.
She just started following me. It's cool.
Where's Skye?
Girl's bathroom. C hall. Watch out for the Brute Squad.

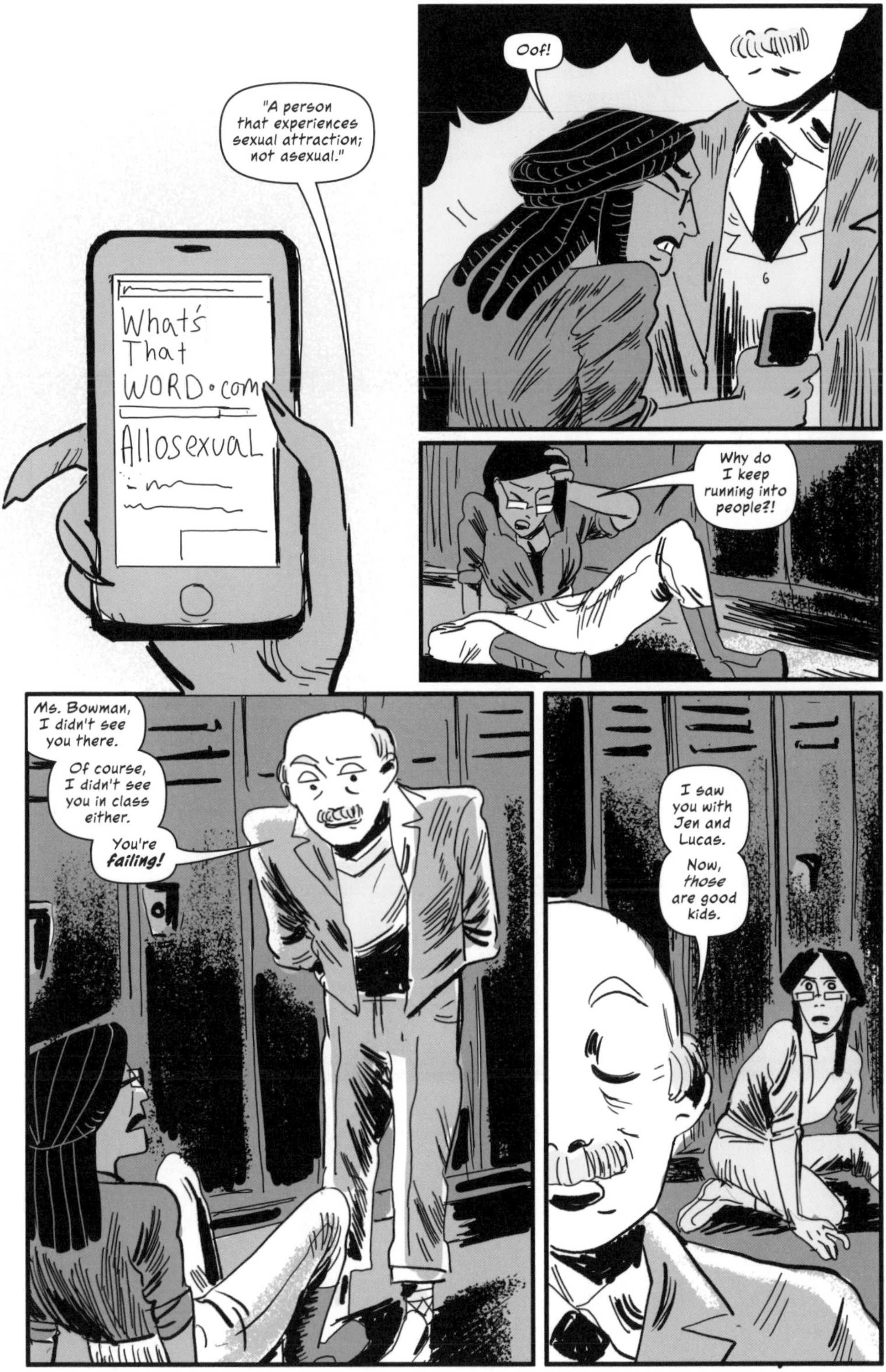
"A person that experiences sexual attraction; not asexual."
What's That WORD•com
Allosexual
Oof!
Why do I keep running into people?!
Ms. Bowman, I didn't see you there.
Of course, I didn't see you in class either.
You're **failing!**
I saw you with Jen and Lucas.
Now, *those* are good kids.

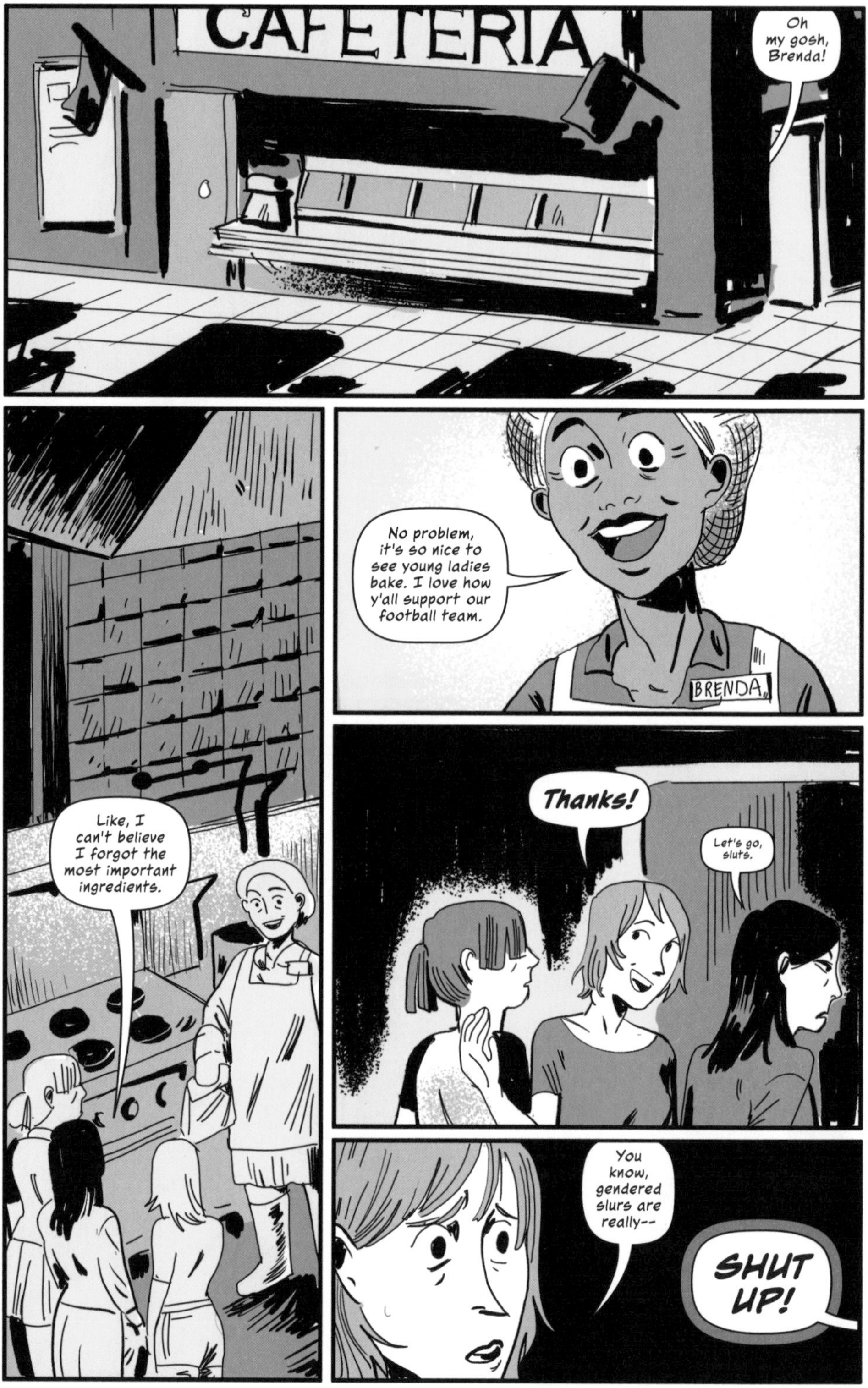
CAFETERIA
Oh my gosh, Brenda!
Like, I can't believe I forgot the most important ingredients.
No problem, it's so nice to see young ladies bake. I love how y'all support our football team.
BRENDA
Thanks!
Let's go, sluts.
You know, gendered slurs are really--
SHUT UP!

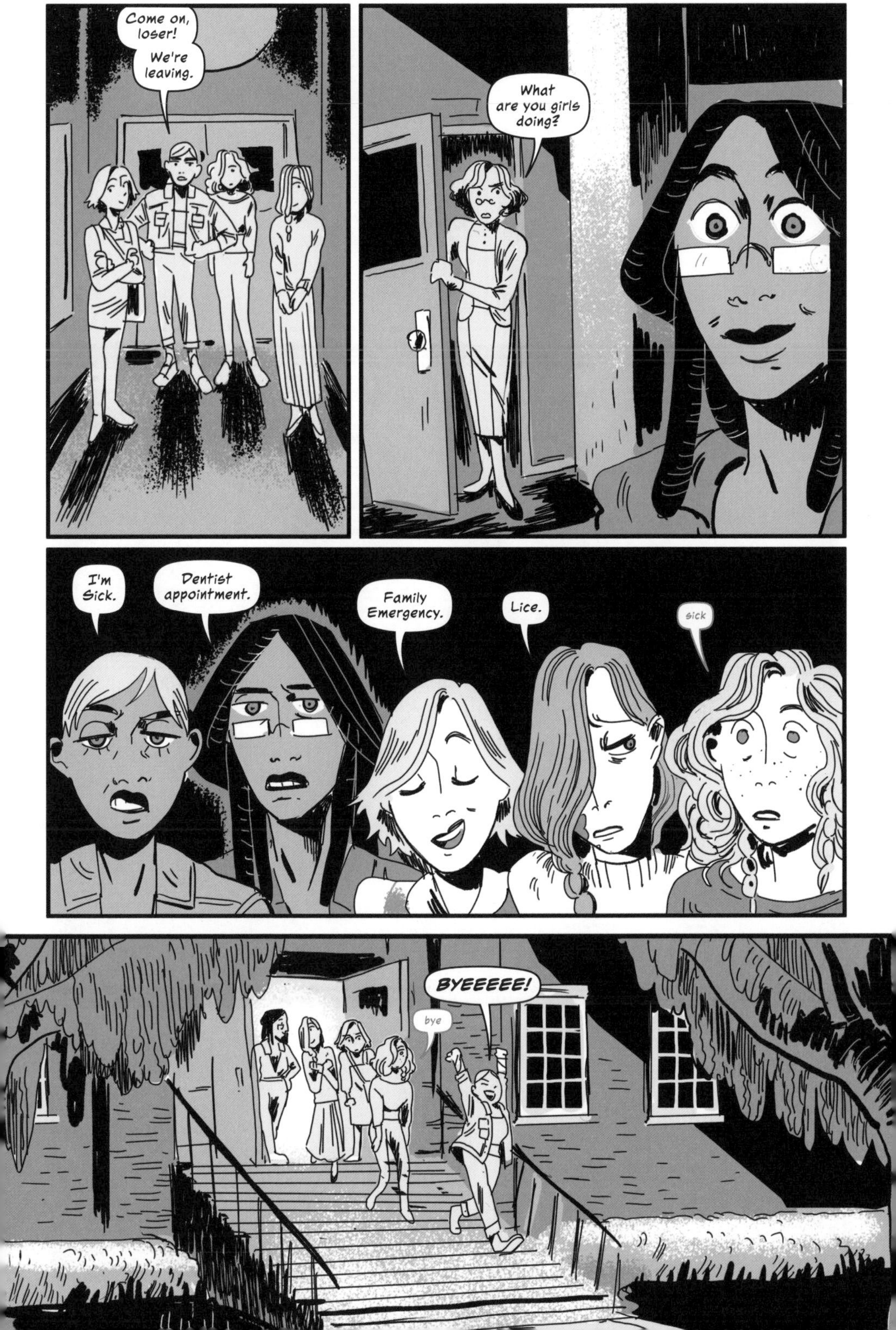
Come on, loser!
We're leaving.
What are you girls doing?
I'm Sick.
Dentist appointment.
Family Emergency.
Lice.
sick
BYEEEEE!
bye

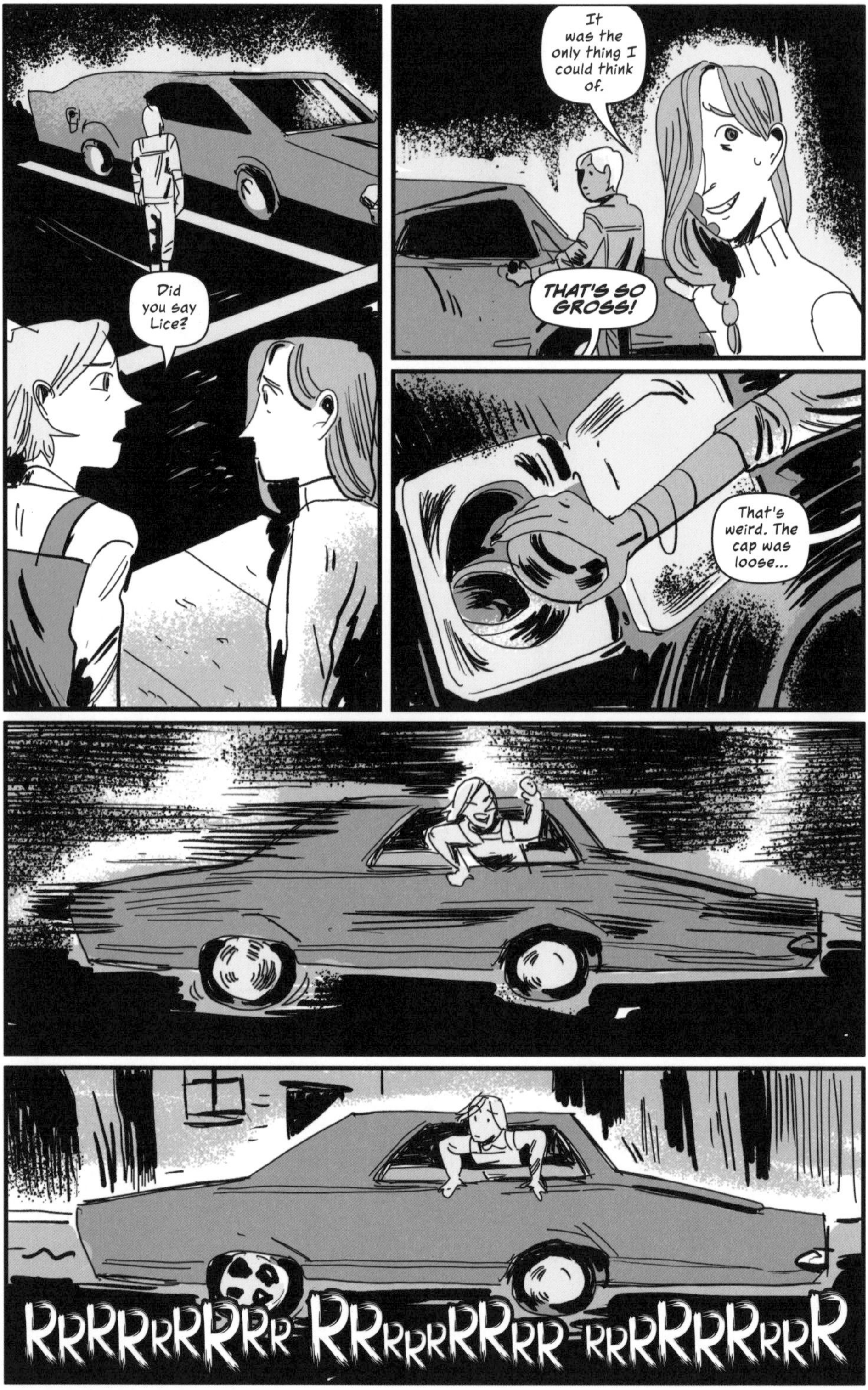
Did you say Lice?
It was the only thing I could think of.
THAT'S SO GROSS!
That's weird. The cap was loose...
RRRRRRRRRR-RRRRRRRRRR-RRRRRRRRRR

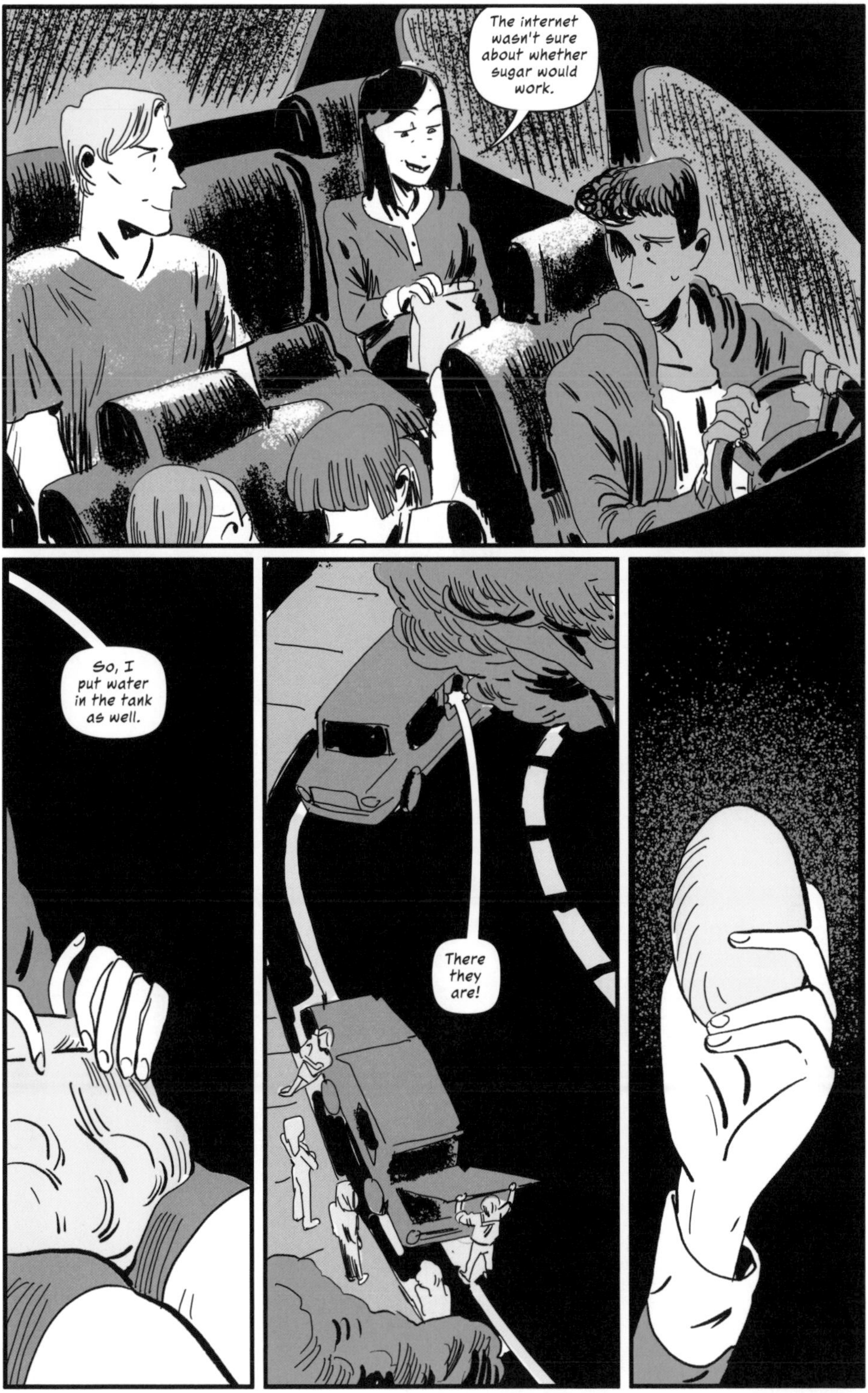
The internet wasn't sure about whether sugar would work.
So, I put water in the tank as well.
There they are!

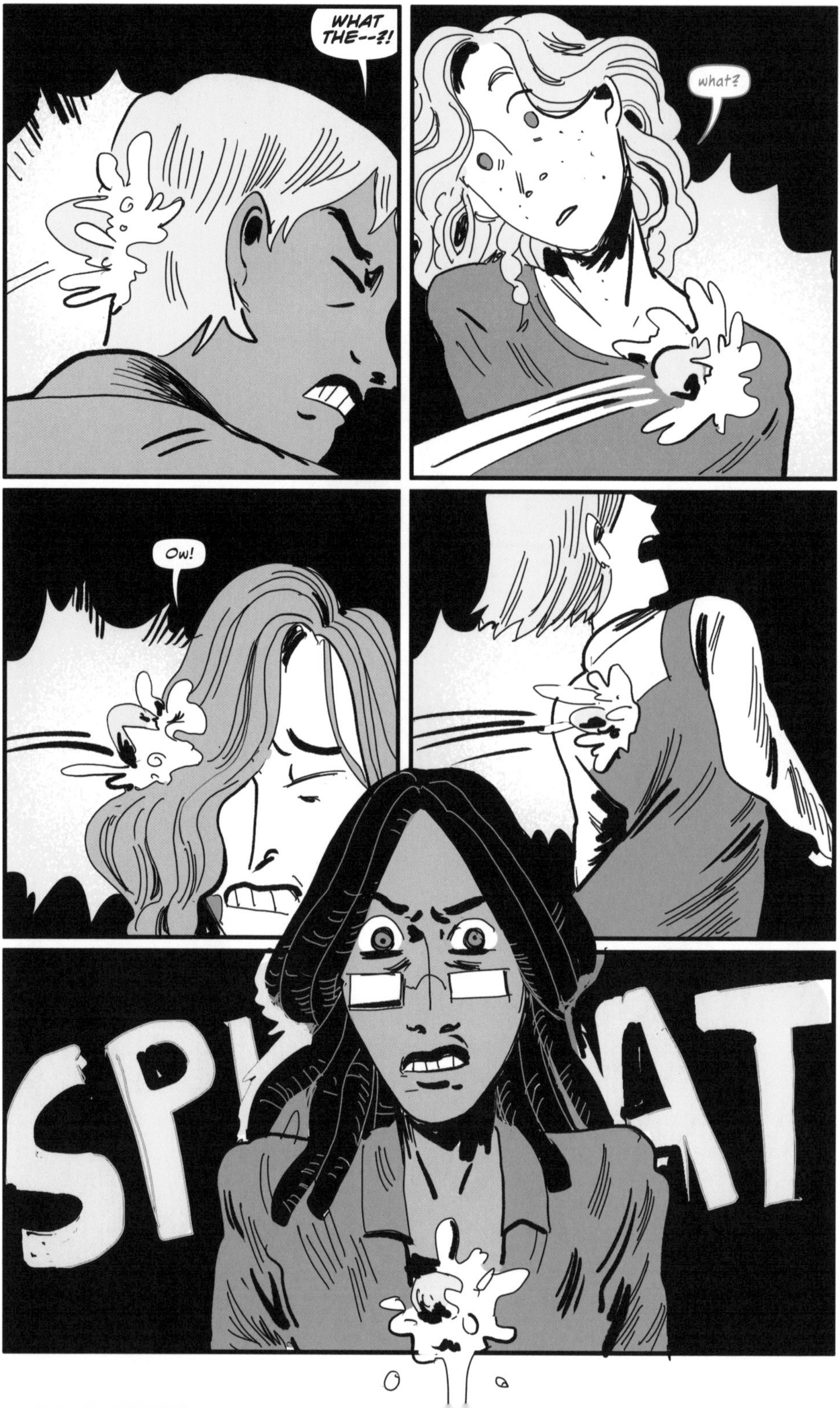
WHAT THE--?!
what?
Ow!
SPLAT

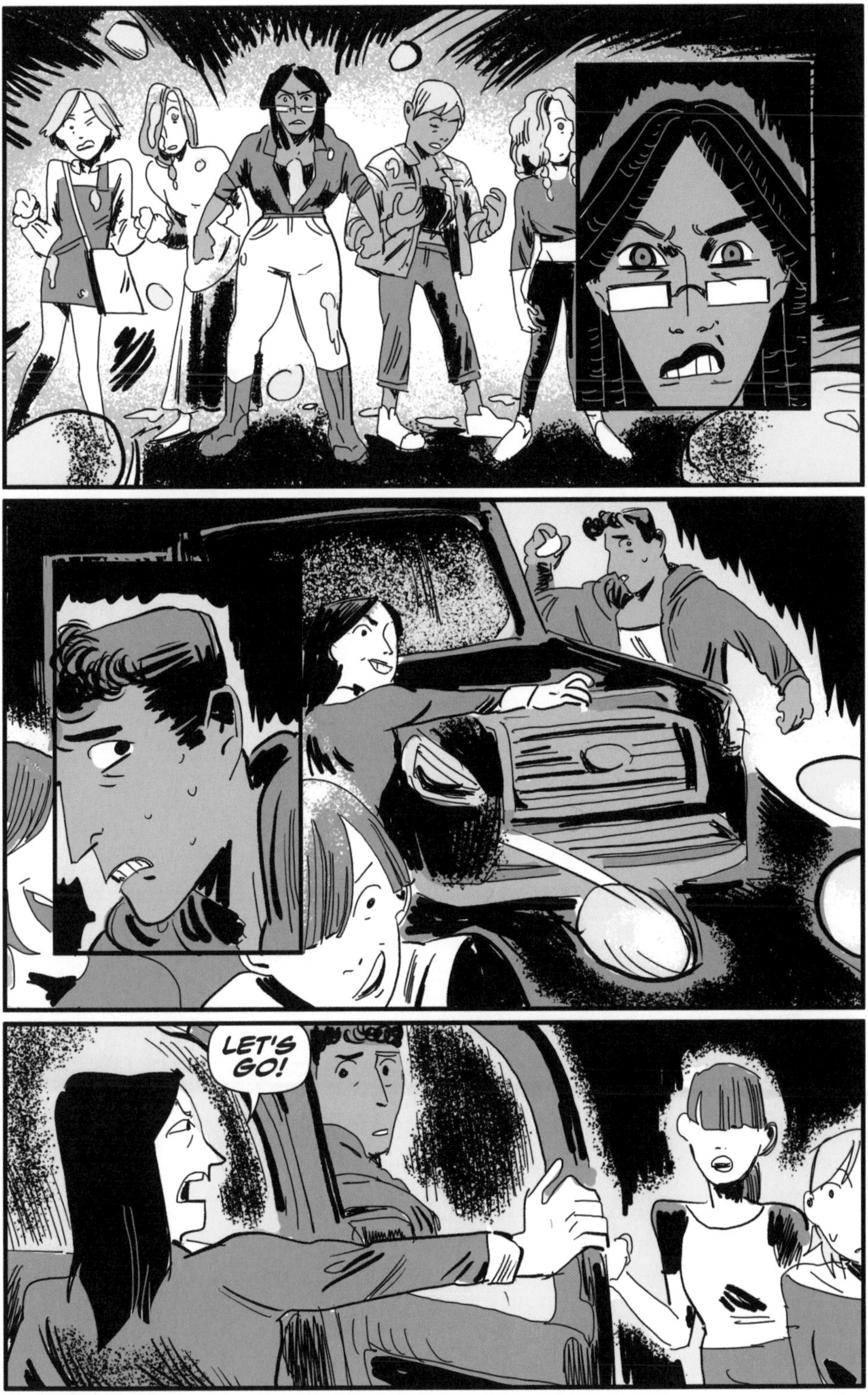
LET'S GO!

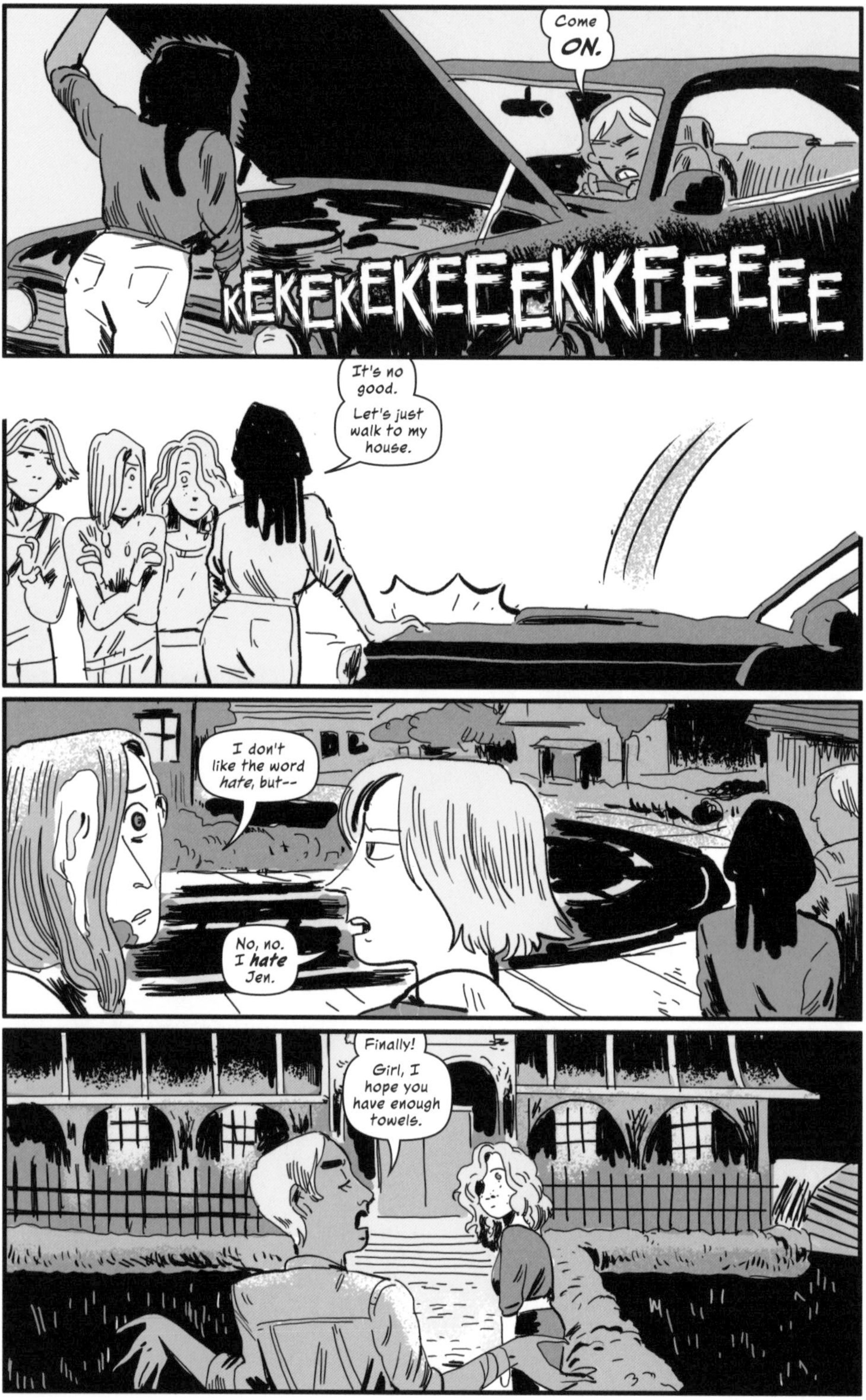
Come ON.
KEKEKEKEEEEKKEEEEE
It's no good.
Let's just walk to my house.
I don't like the word hate, but--
No, no. I hate Jen.
Finally!
Girl, I hope you have enough towels.

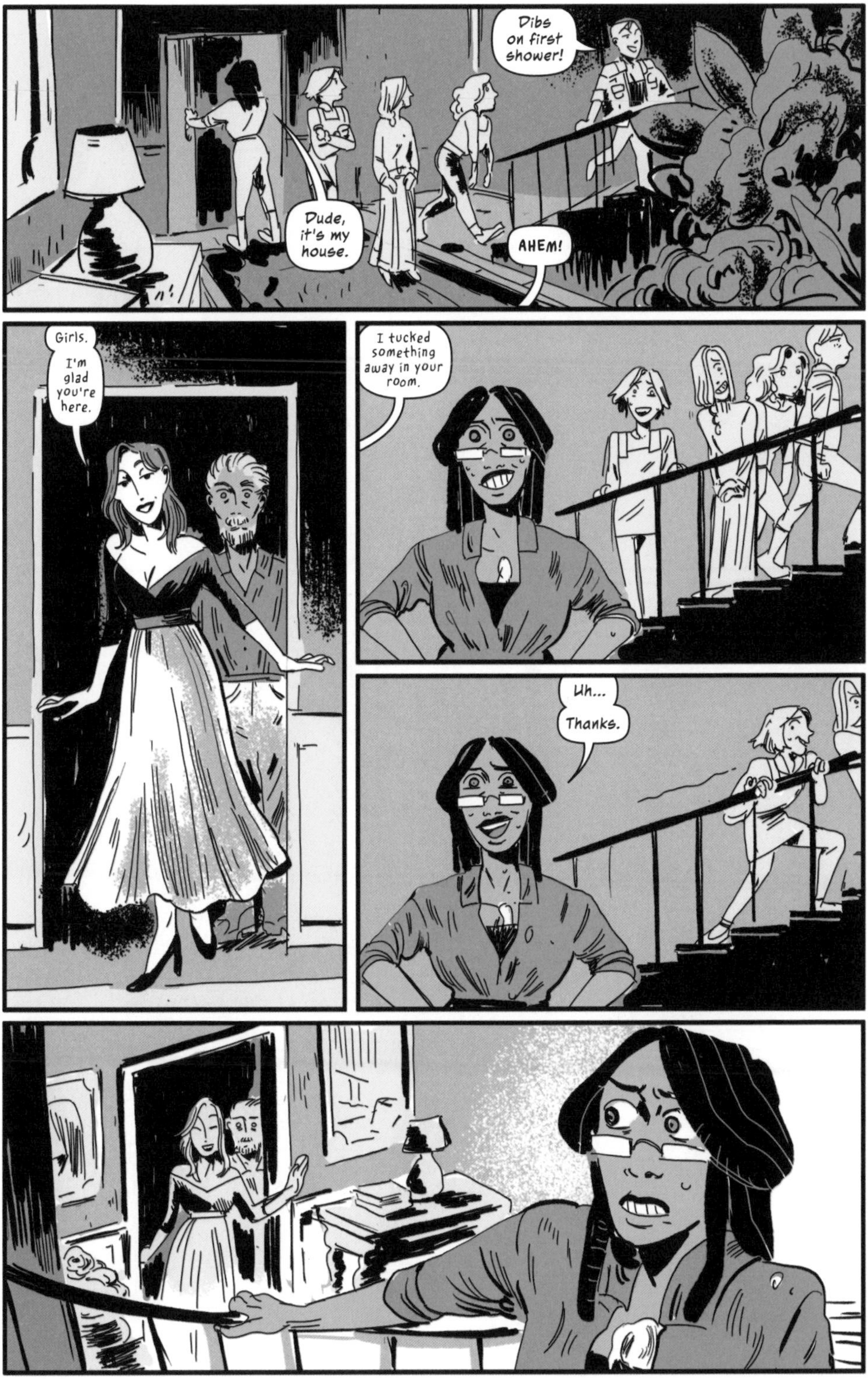
Dibs on first shower!
Dude, it's my house.
AHEM!
Girls.
I'm glad you're here.
I tucked something away in your room.
Uh...
Thanks.

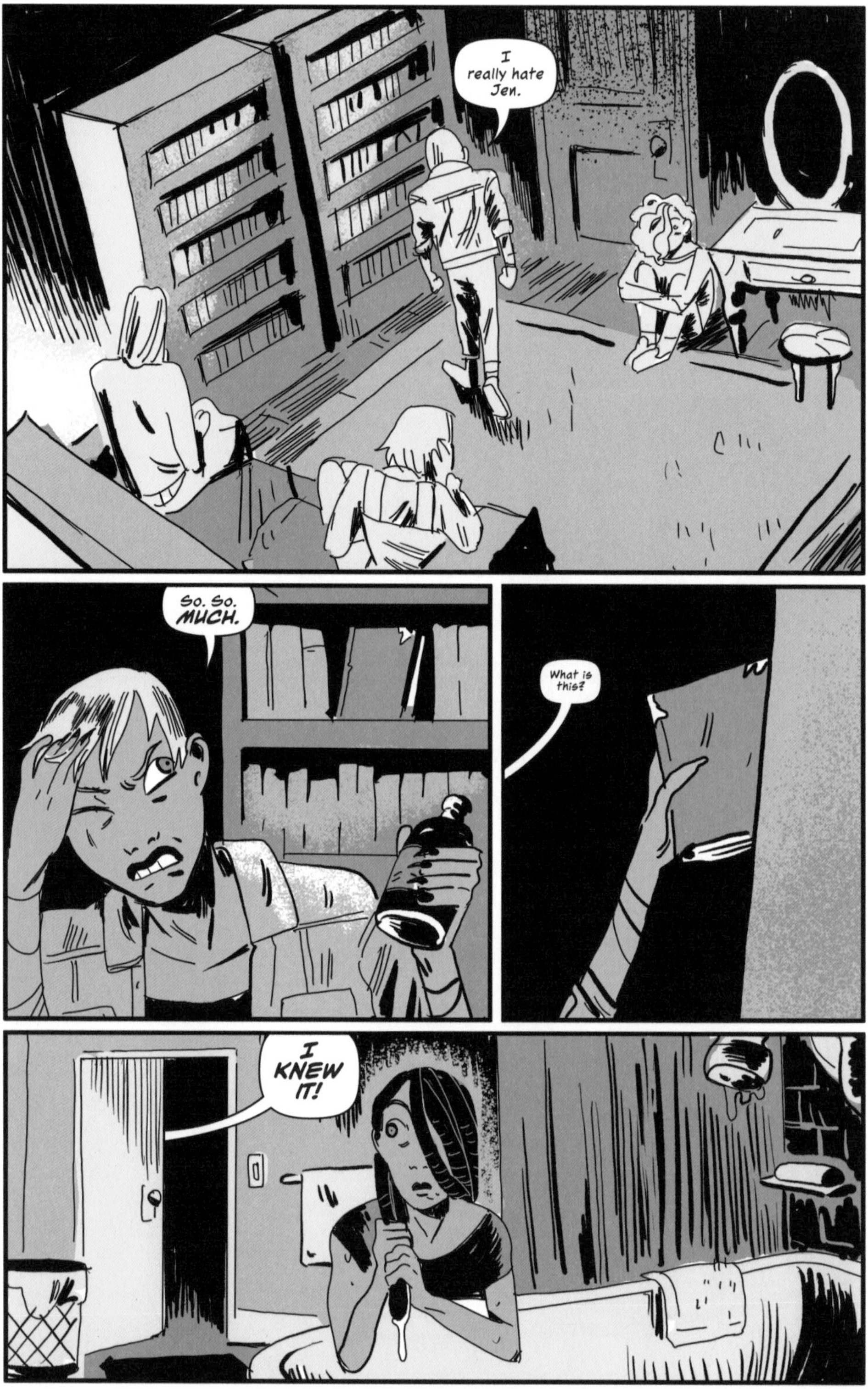
I really hate Jen.
So. So. MUCH.
What is this?
I KNEW IT!

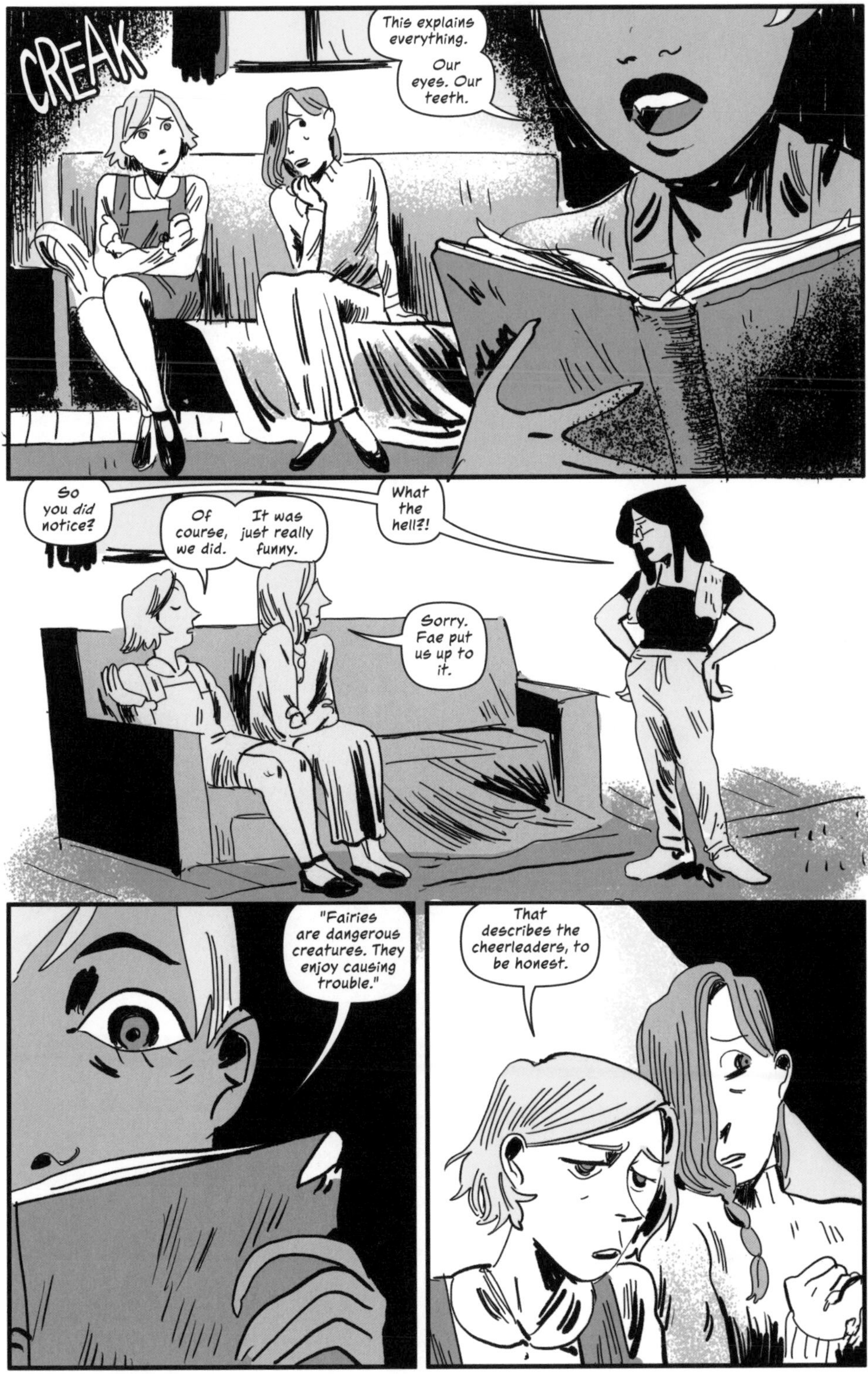
CREAK
This explains everything.
Our eyes. Our teeth.
So you *did* notice?
Of course, we did.
It was just really funny.
What the hell?!
Sorry. Fae put us up to it.
"Fairies are dangerous creatures. They enjoy causing trouble."
That describes the cheerleaders, to be honest.

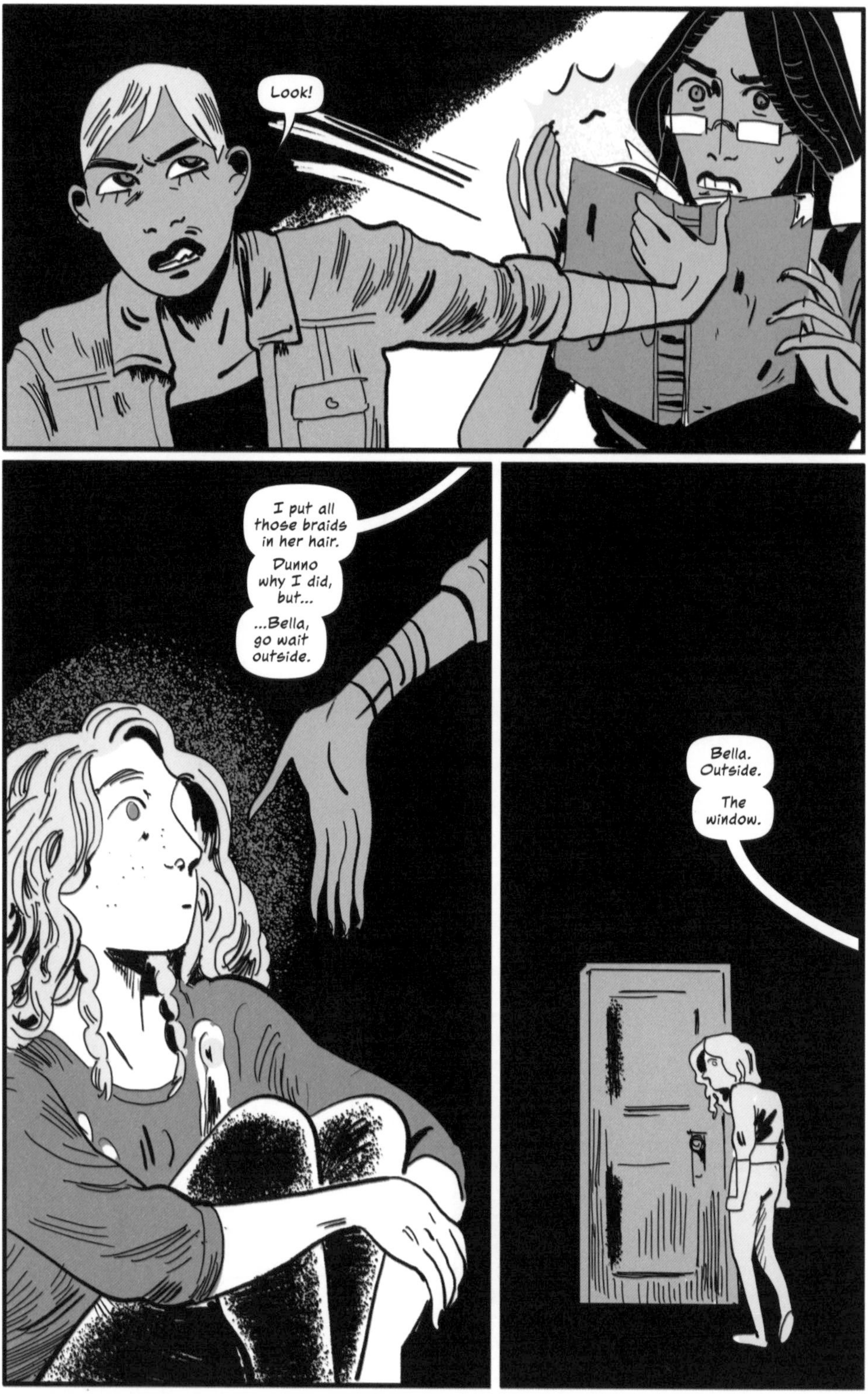
Look!
I put all those braids in her hair.
Dunno why I did, but...
...Bella, go wait outside.
Bella. Outside.
The window.

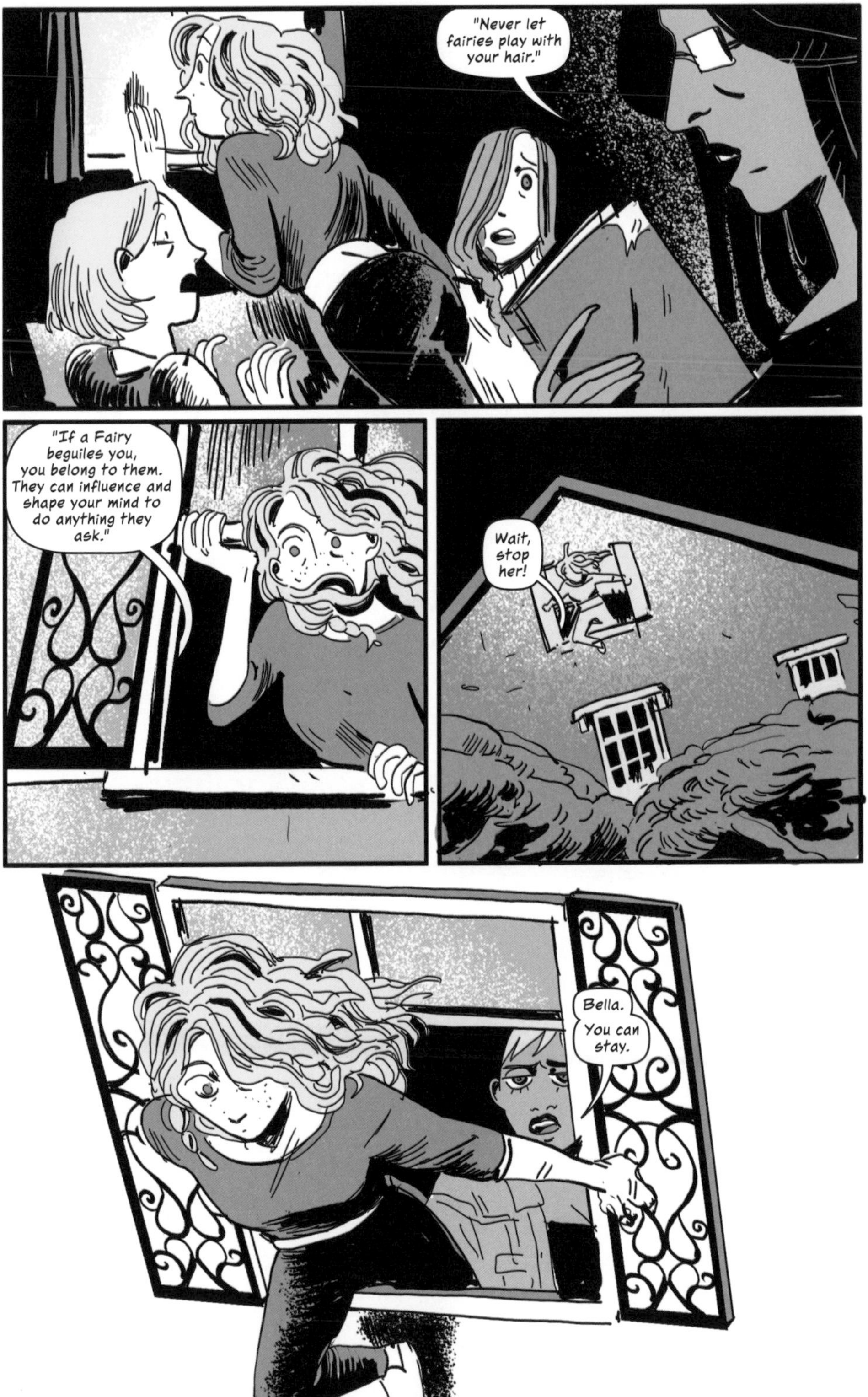
"Never let fairies play with your hair."
"If a Fairy beguiles you, you belong to them. They can influence and shape your mind to do anything they ask."
Wait, stop her!
Bella.
You can stay.

As is my duty, I went to check the newborns.
I touched each of their precious feet with a cold-forged iron rod.

Four children screamed at the touch.
One of them, my beloved granddaughter.

They were all gone and replaced.

Never has there been this many Changelings at once...
I will try to get my granddaughter back, by any means.
I may have to go to darker sources to investigate.

Do not be fooled by their innocent faces.
Changeling magic is untethered by tradition
and therefore more dangerous.
They will find their powers through intuition.

The darkness inside of them speaks more loudly to some than others

Together they are too powerful,
I must separate those that I can...

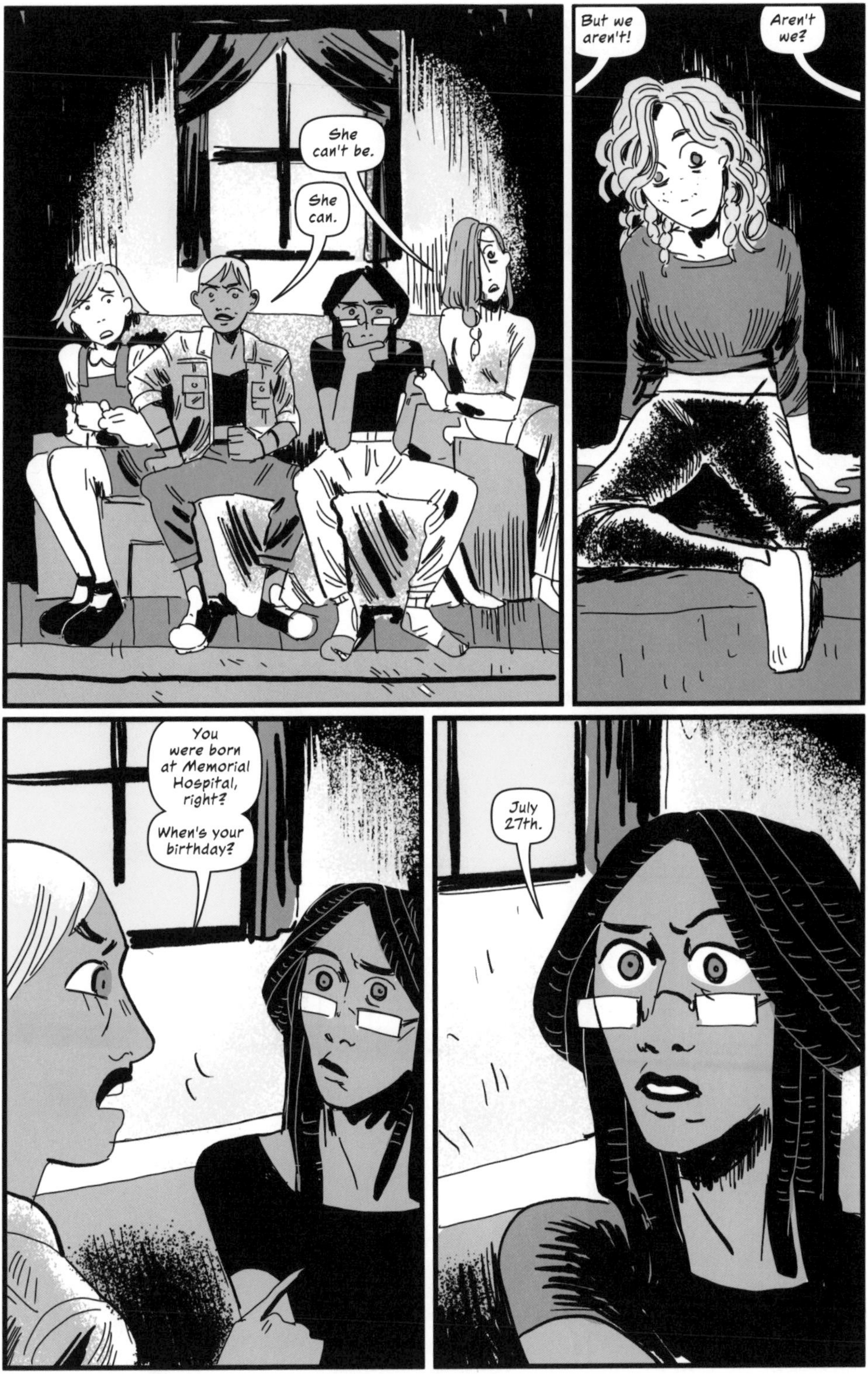

She can't be.
She can.
But we aren't!
Aren't we?
You were born at Memorial Hospital, right?
When's your birthday?
July 27th.

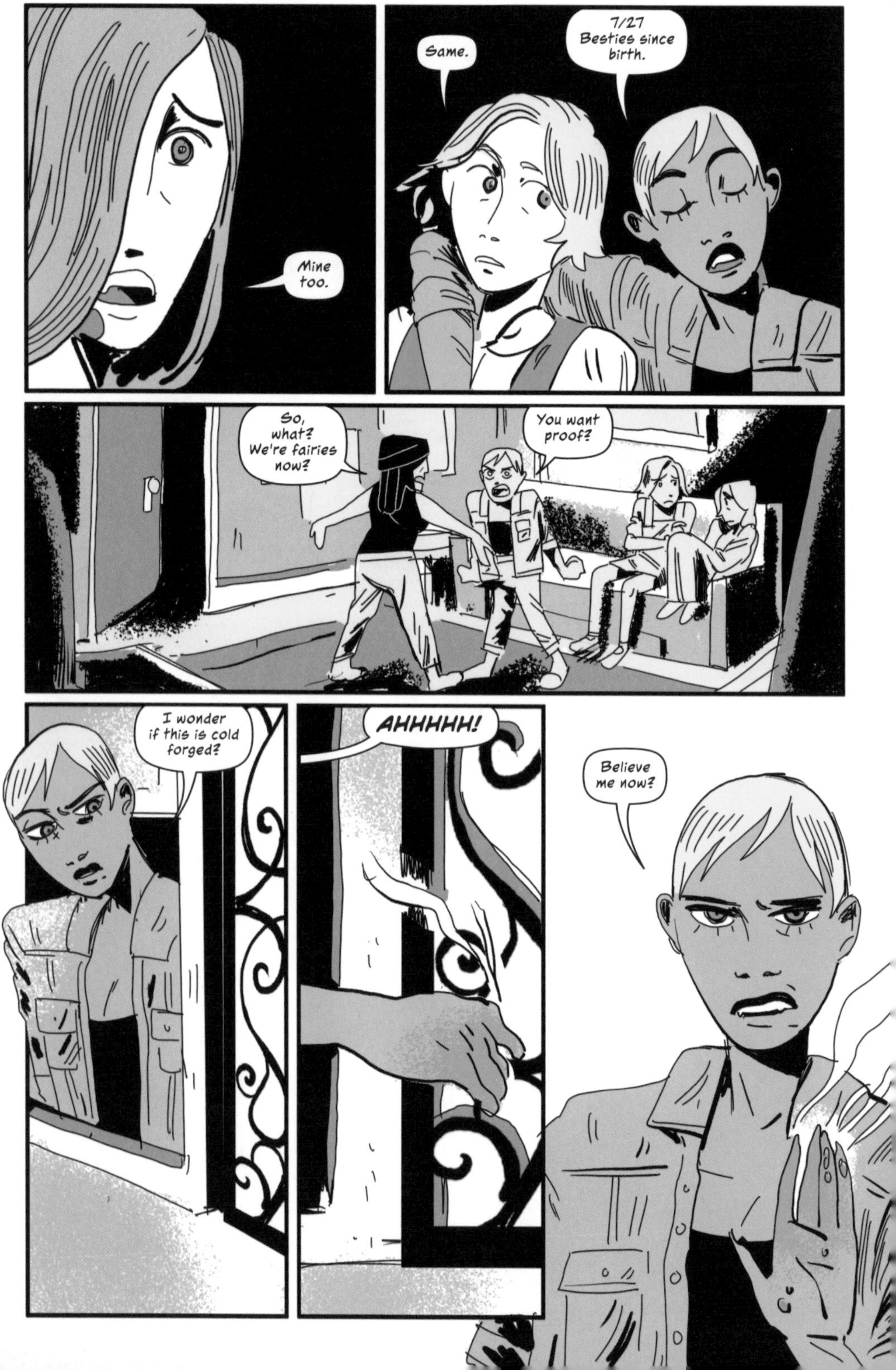
Mine too.
Same.
7/27 Besties since birth.
So, what? We're fairies now?
You want proof?
I wonder if this is cold forged?
AHHHHH!
Believe me now?

I've spoken to the Outcast
and she has told me many things.

War among the fairies is what drives
the great number of Changelings.
Some are parents wishing to spare their children
at the cost of human lives.
Others are kidnapped fairies of highborn families.

The Outcast says that the most highborn,
the future queen of all the fairies,
has been taken.
That does not bode well.

A Fairy Queen would be a
force of immeasurable destructive power.

Note for Future Hunters:
The Outcast is never to be trusted.
She is still a fairy and prone to all their capricious evil.
Ply her with gifts, but take precautions.
A salt tablet under the tongue is a good start.

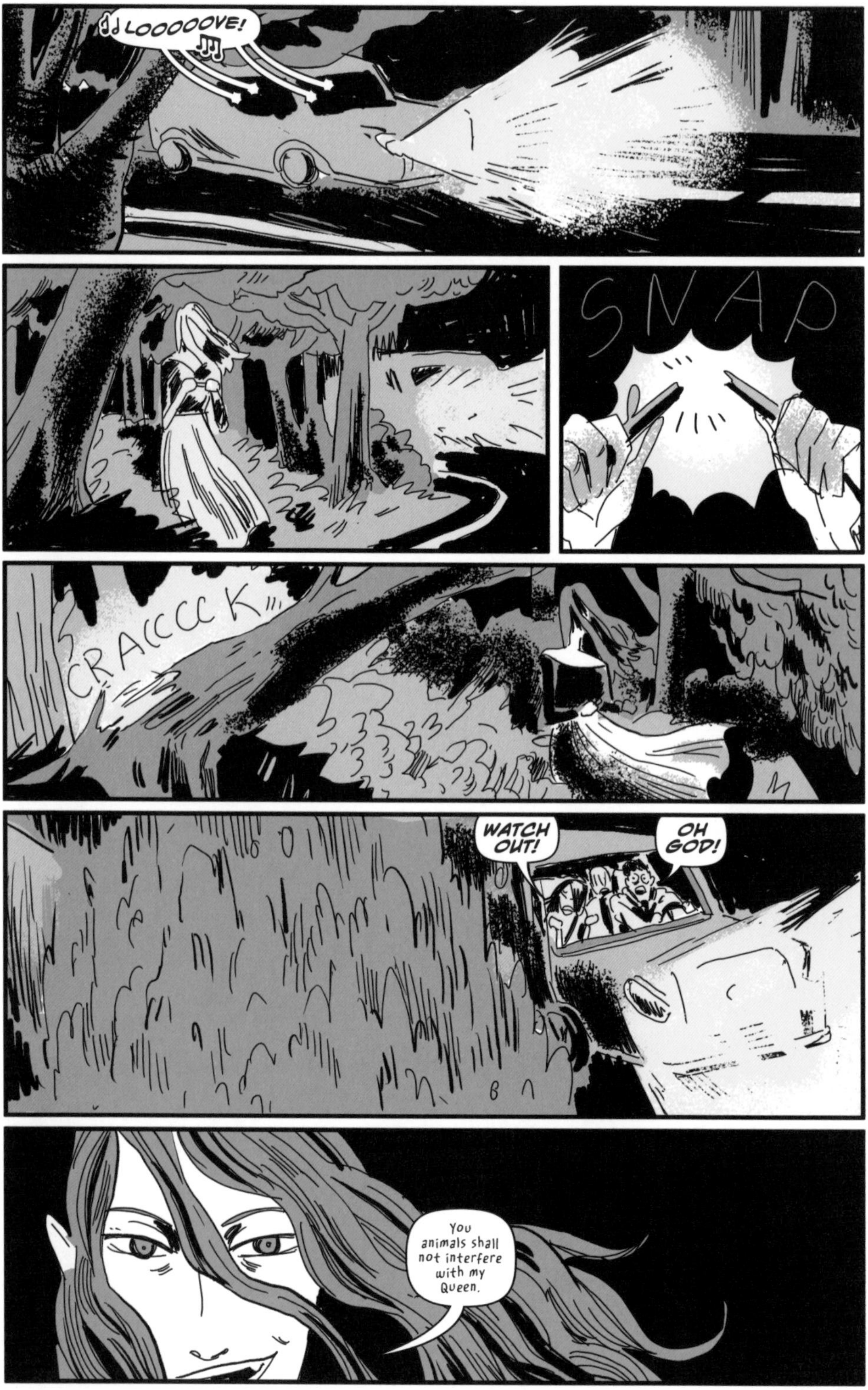
LOOOOOVE!
SNAP
CRACCCCK
WATCH OUT!
OH GOD!
You animals shall not interfere with my Queen.

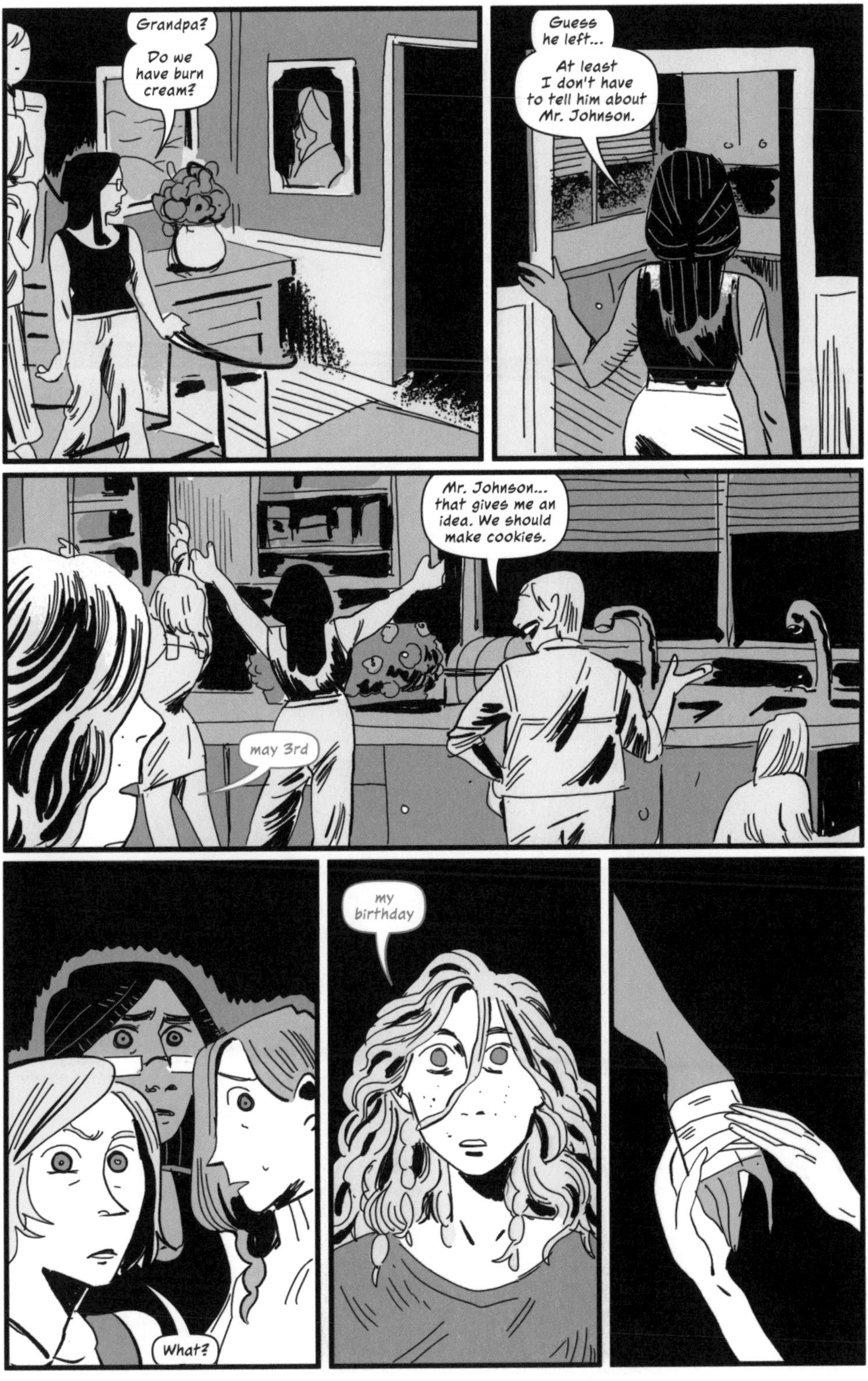
Grandpa?
Do we have burn cream?
Guess he left...
At least I don't have to tell him about Mr. Johnson.
Mr. Johnson... that gives me an idea. We should make cookies.
may 3rd
What?
my birthday

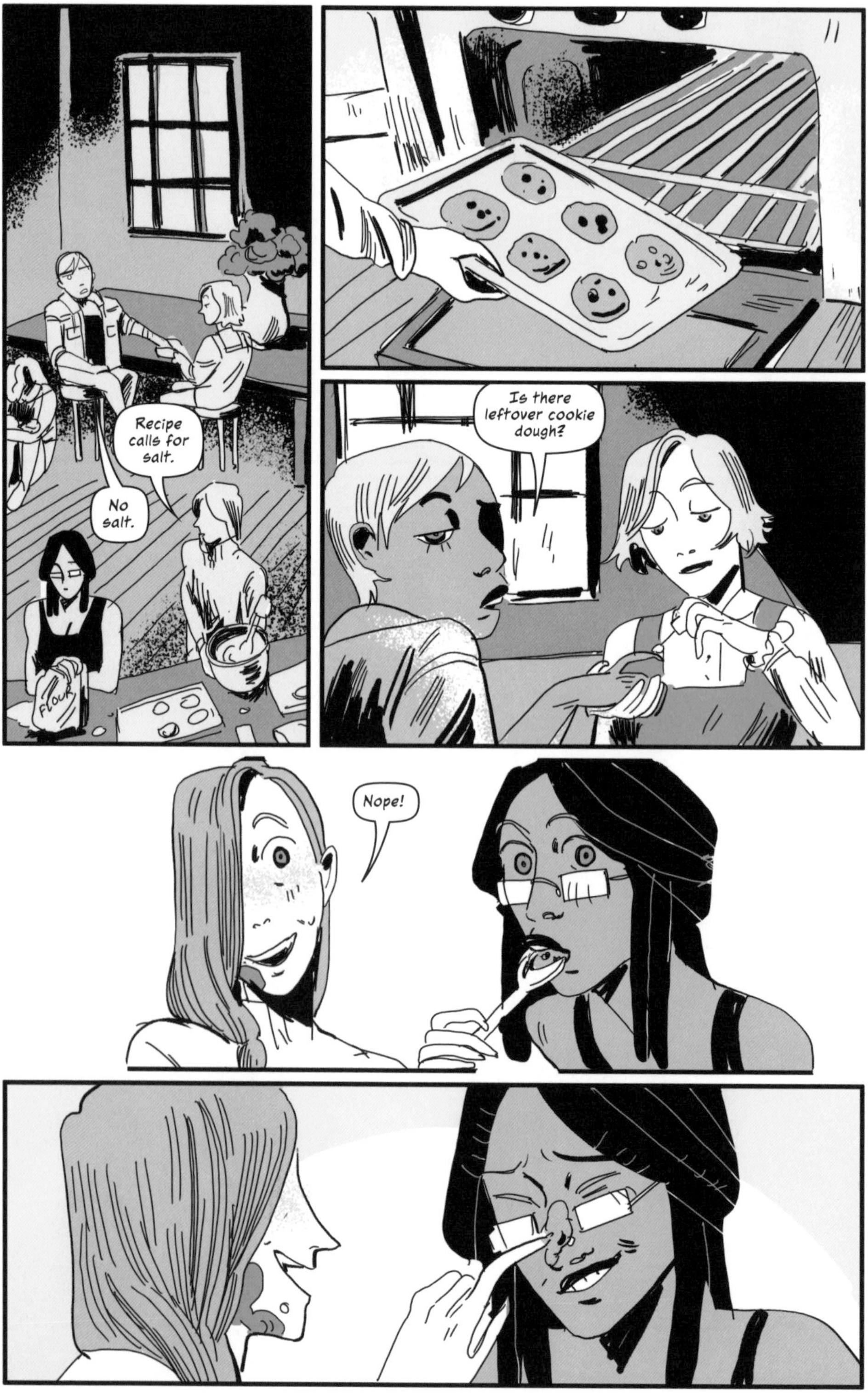
Recipe calls for salt.
No salt.
Is there leftover cookie dough?
Nope!

Beguilement:
A Fairy's Greatest Weapon

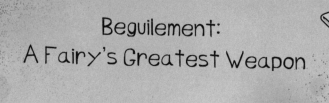

NEVER

Dance with fairies
Eat food prepared by fairies
Let fairies play with your hair
Make any type of deal with fairies

All of these can lead to *beguilement*.

If a Fairy beguiles you, you belong to them.
They can influence and shape your mind to do anything they ask.
In extreme cases, you can end up lost in the space
between our world and theirs.

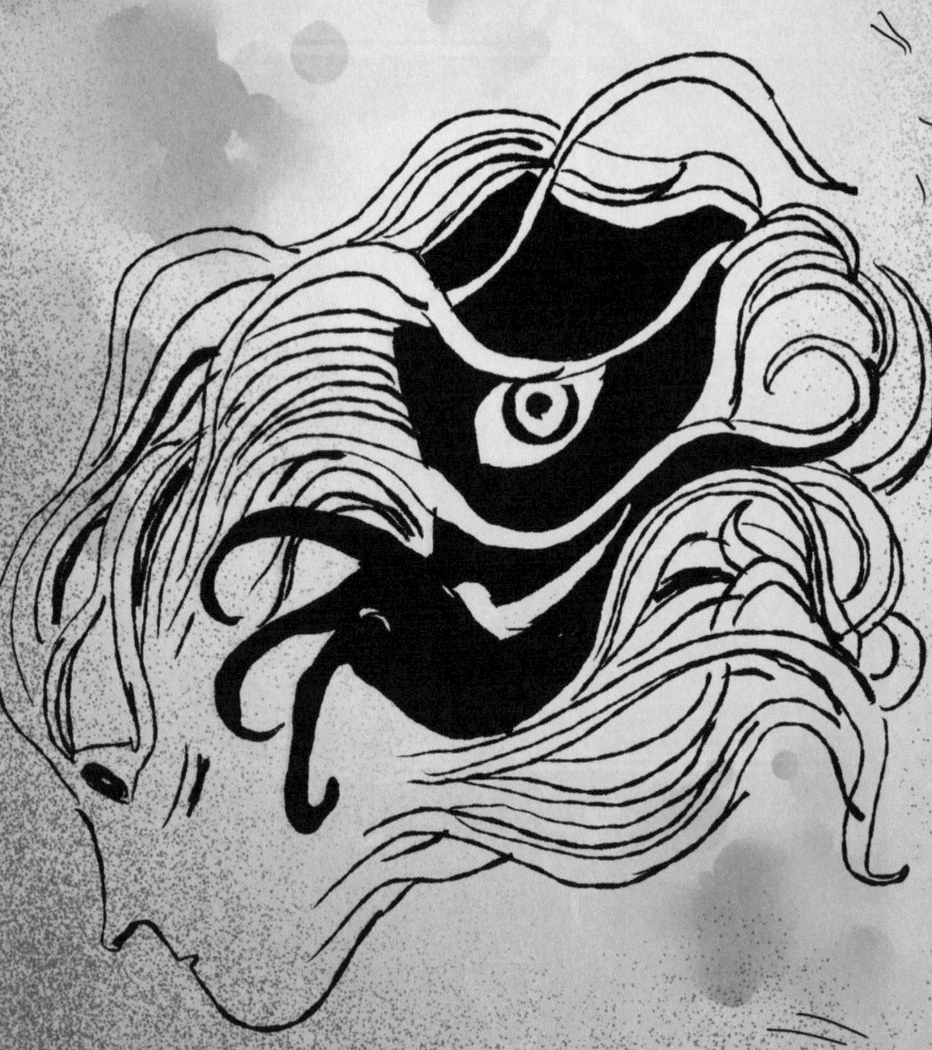

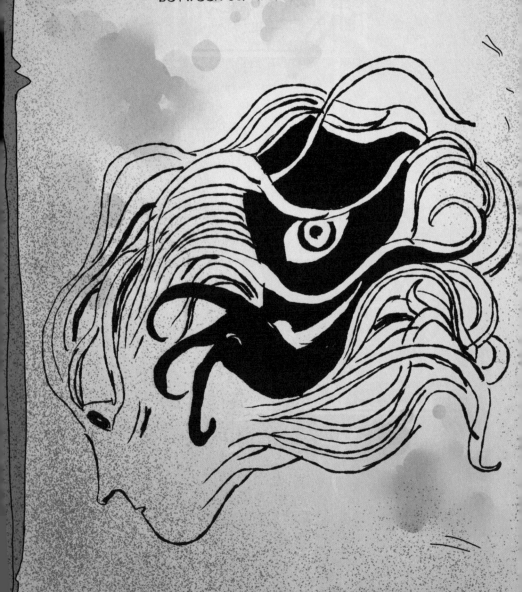

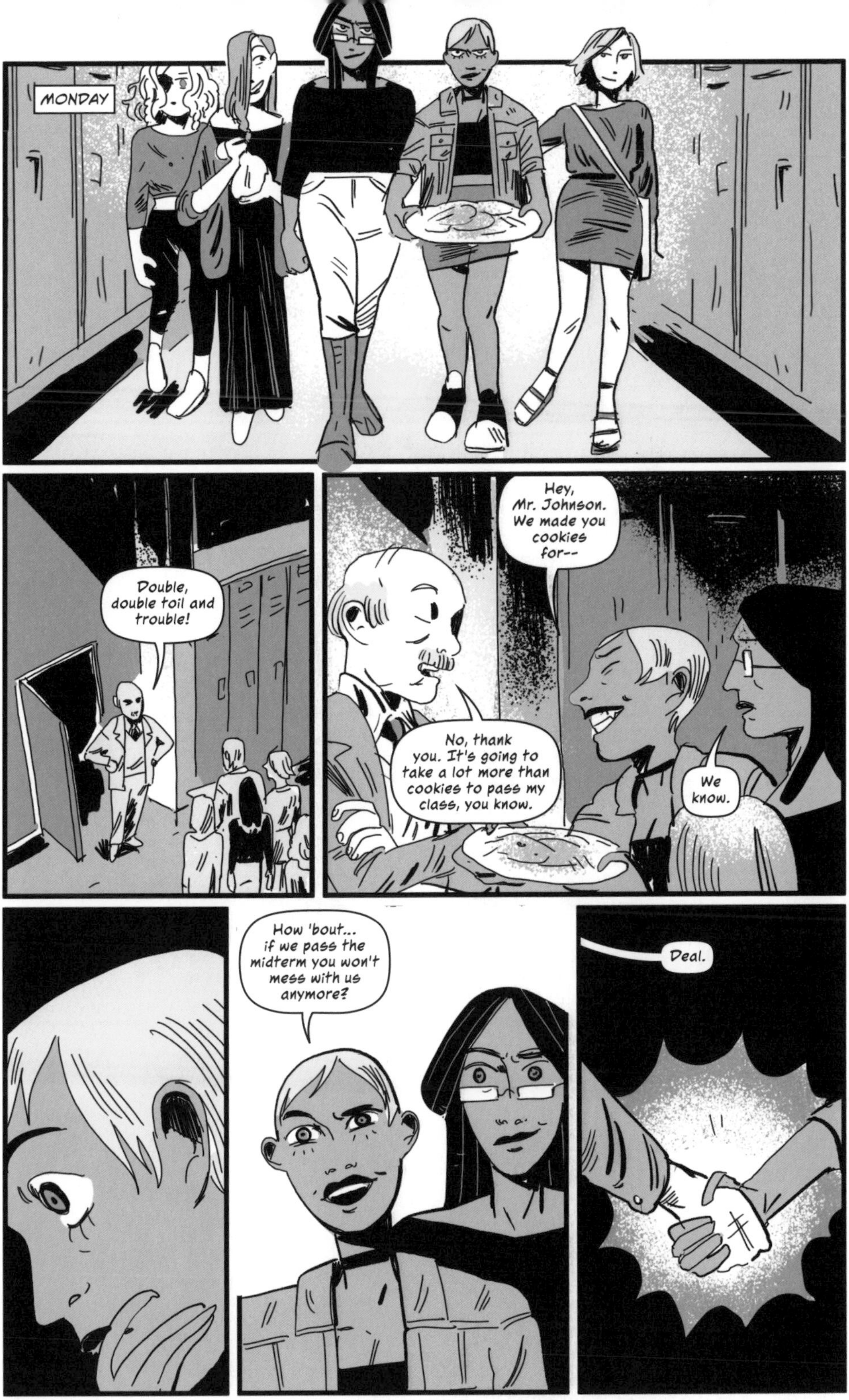
MONDAY
Double, double toil and trouble!
Hey, Mr. Johnson. We made you cookies for--
No, thank you. It's going to take a lot more than cookies to pass my class, you know.
We know.
How 'bout... if we pass the midterm you won't mess with us anymore?
Deal.

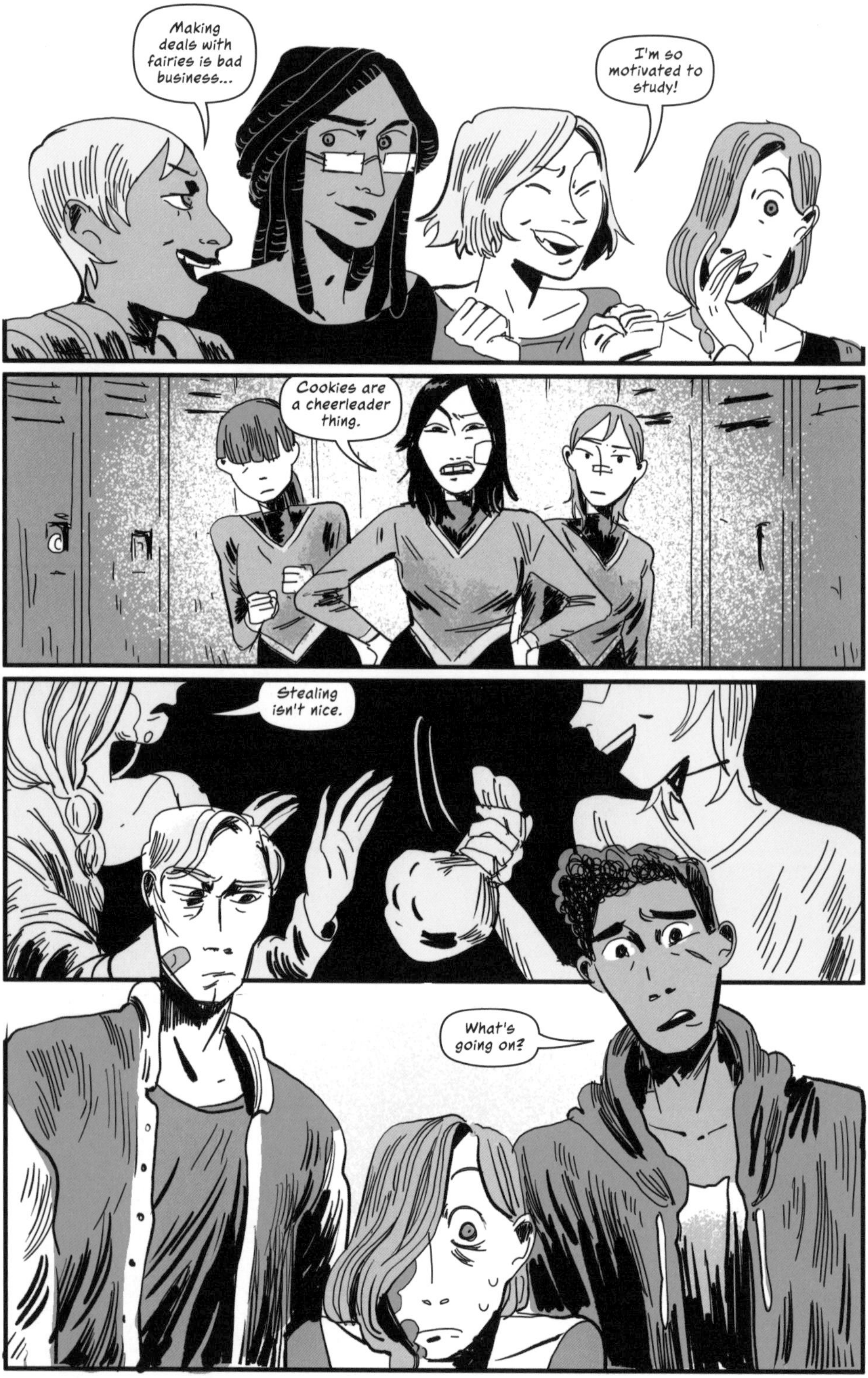
Making deals with fairies is bad business...
I'm so motivated to study!
Cookies are a cheerleader thing.
Stealing isn't nice.
What's going on?

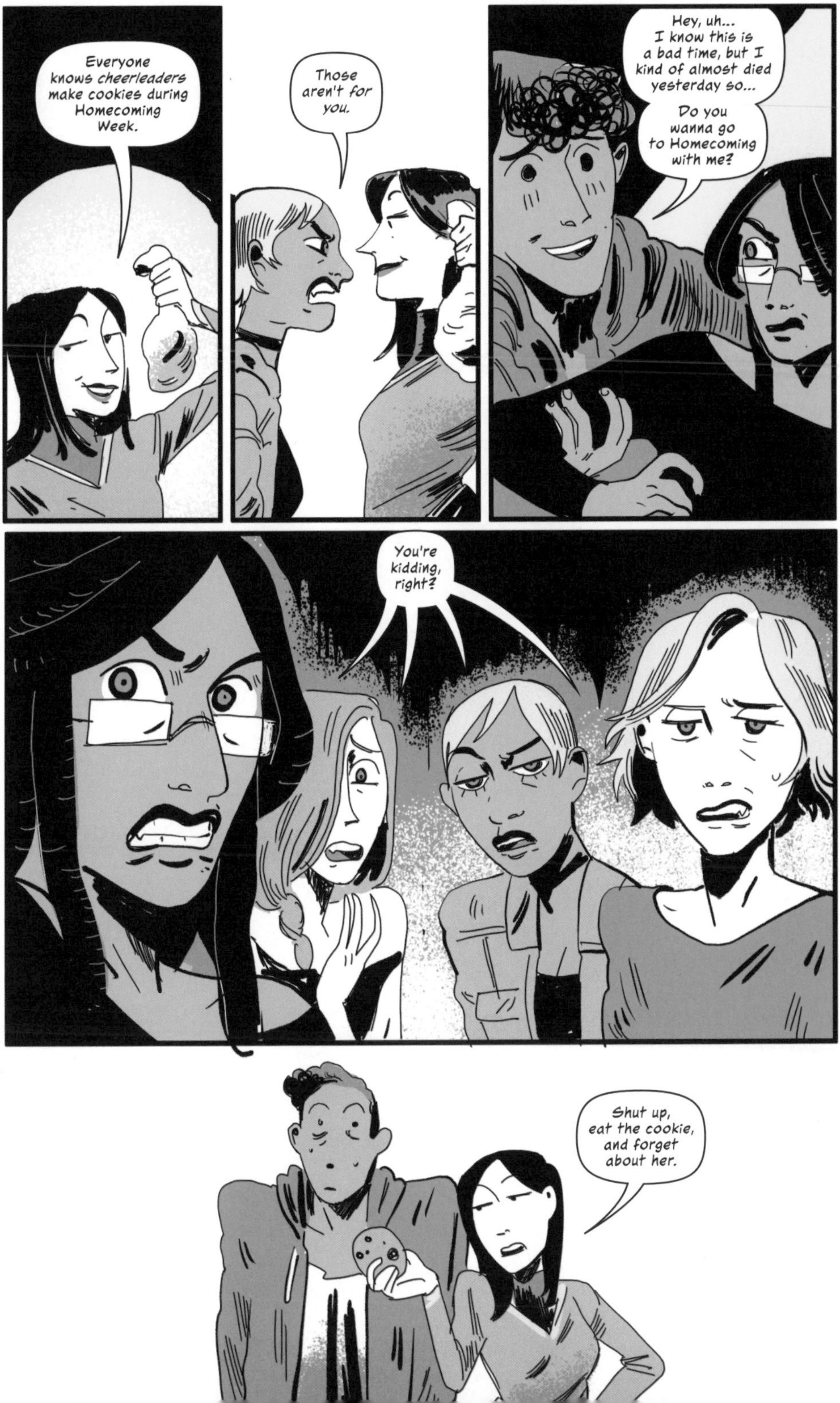
Everyone knows cheerleaders make cookies during Homecoming Week.
Those aren't for you.
Hey, uh... I know this is a bad time, but I kind of almost died yesterday so...
Do you wanna go to Homecoming with me?
You're kidding, right?
Shut up, eat the cookie, and forget about her.

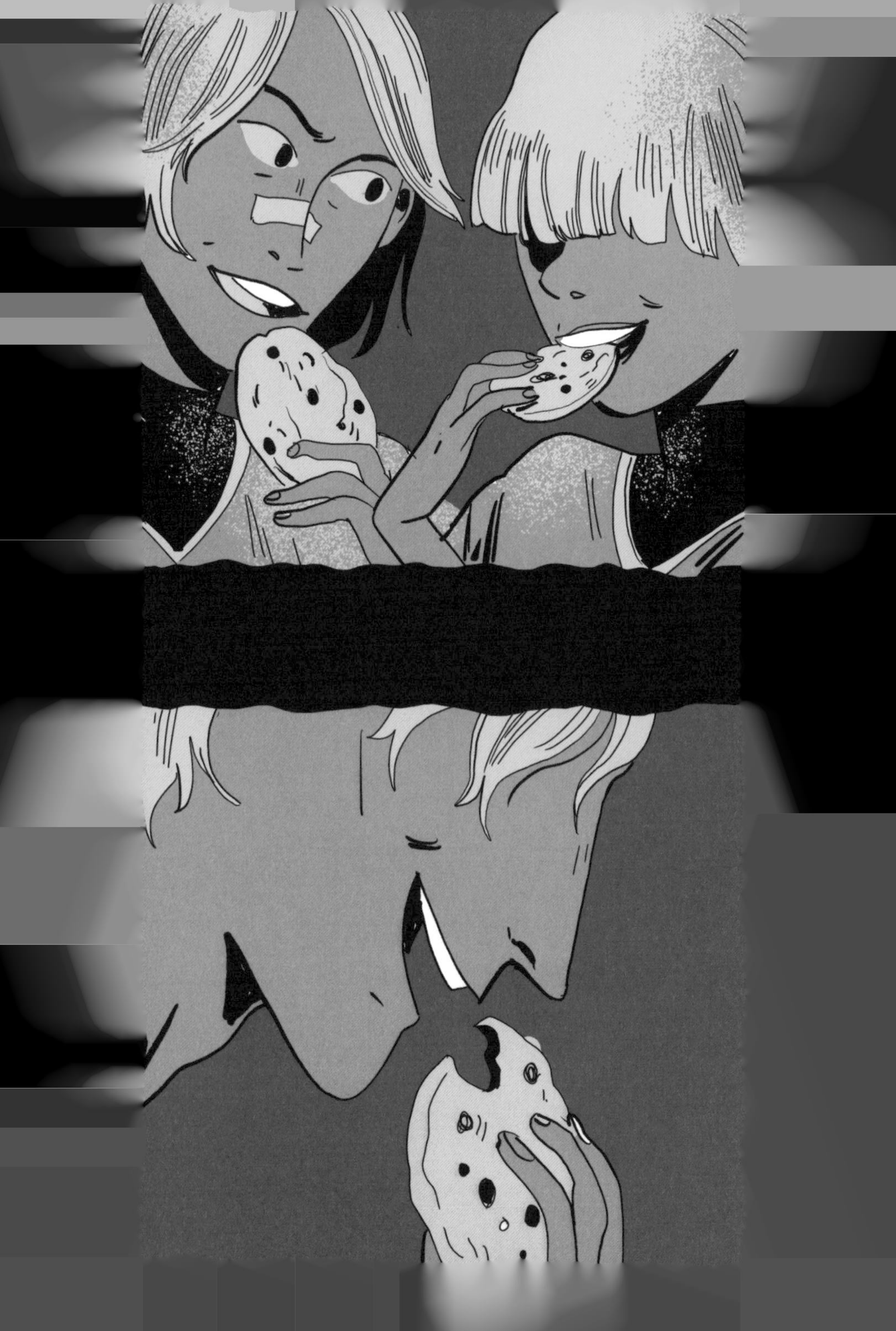

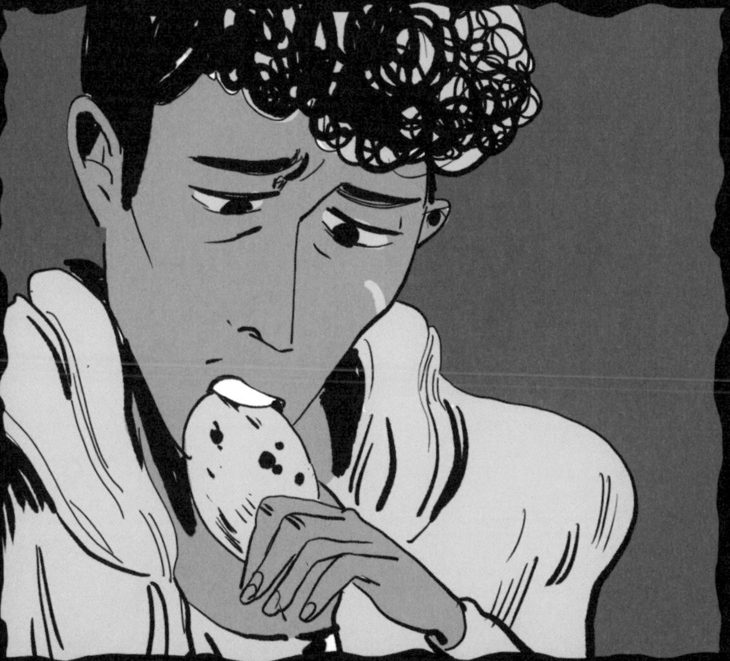

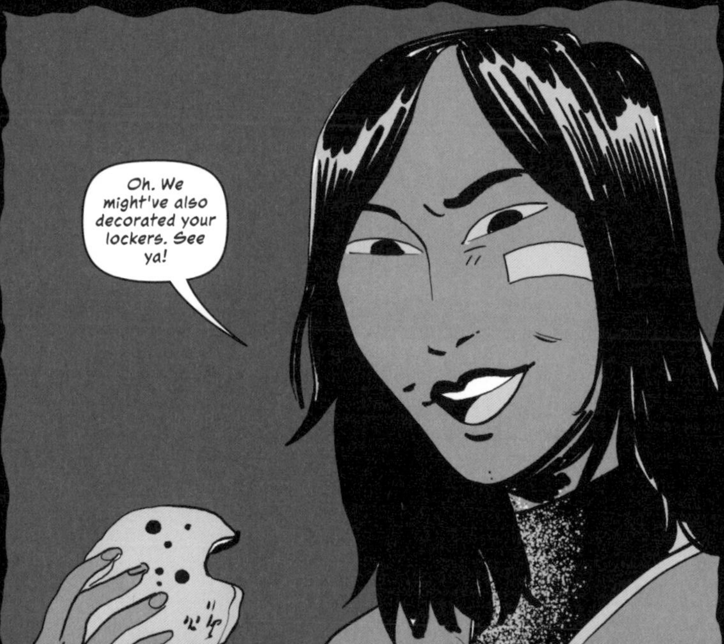
Oh. We might've also decorated your lockers. See ya!

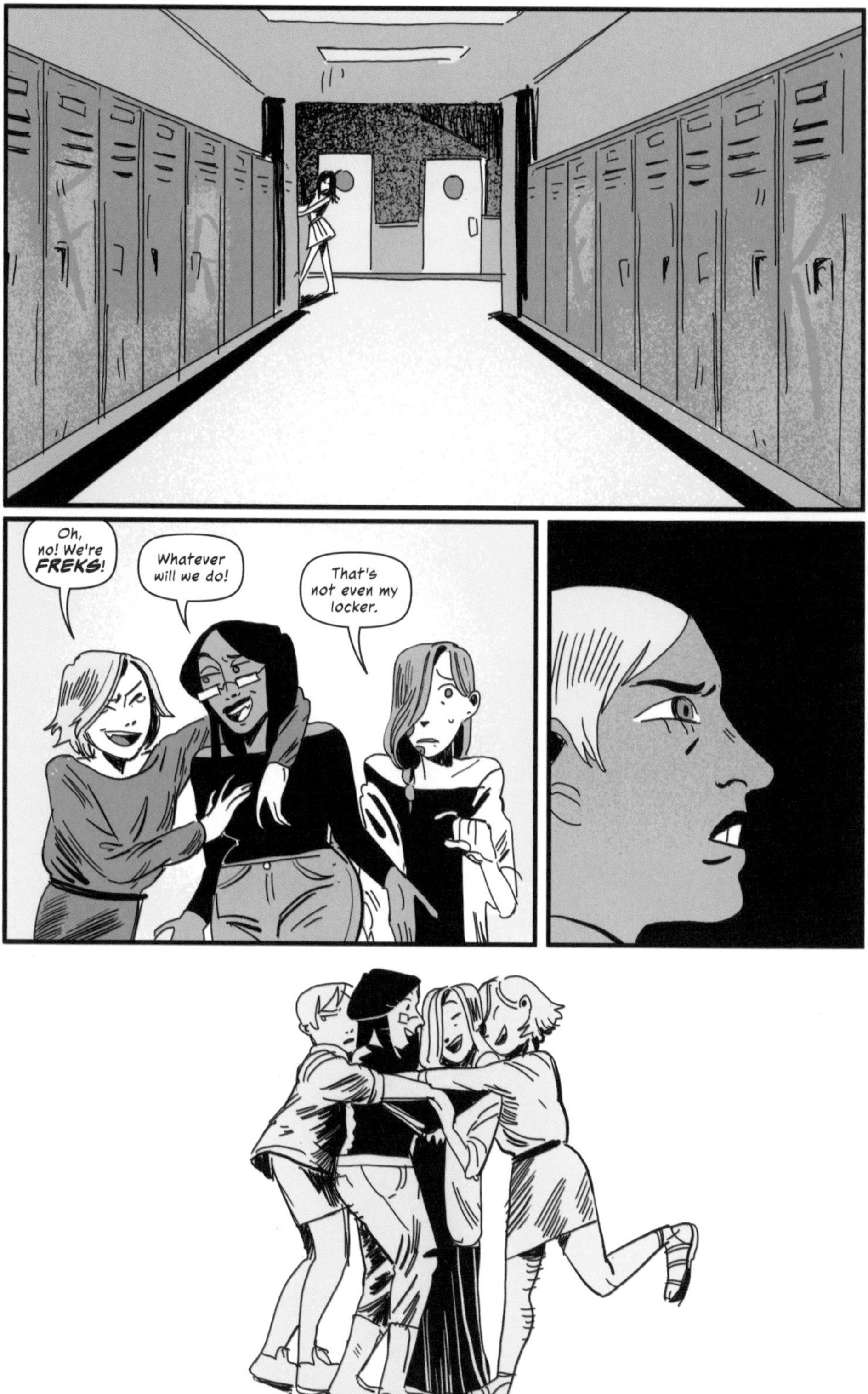
Oh, no! We're FREKS!
Whatever will we do!
That's not even my locker.

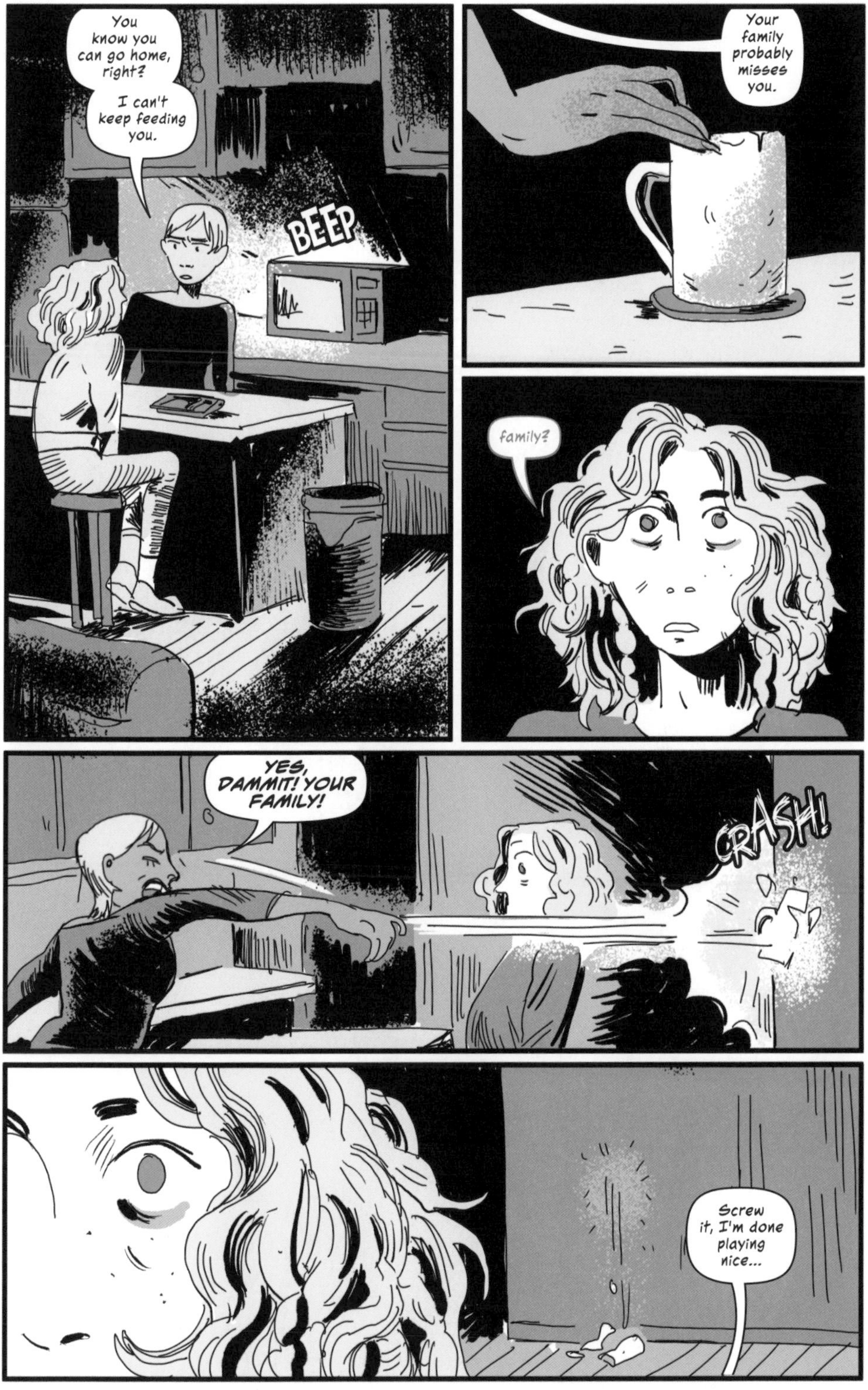
You know you can go home, right?
I can't keep feeding you.
BEEP
Your family probably misses you.
family?
YES, DAMMIT! YOUR FAMILY!
CRASH!
Screw it, I'm done playing nice...

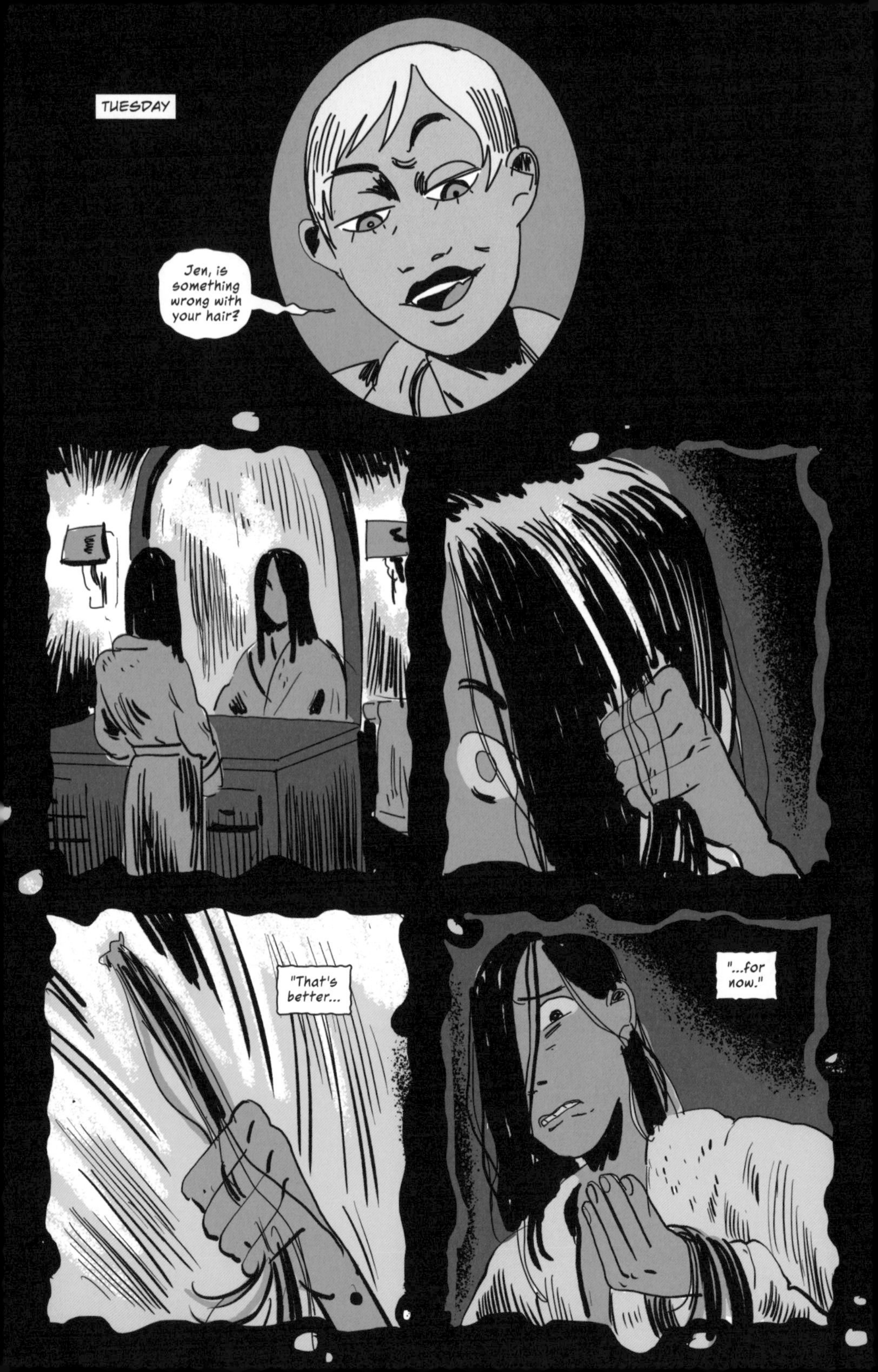
TUESDAY
Jen, is something wrong with your hair?
"That's better...
"...for now."

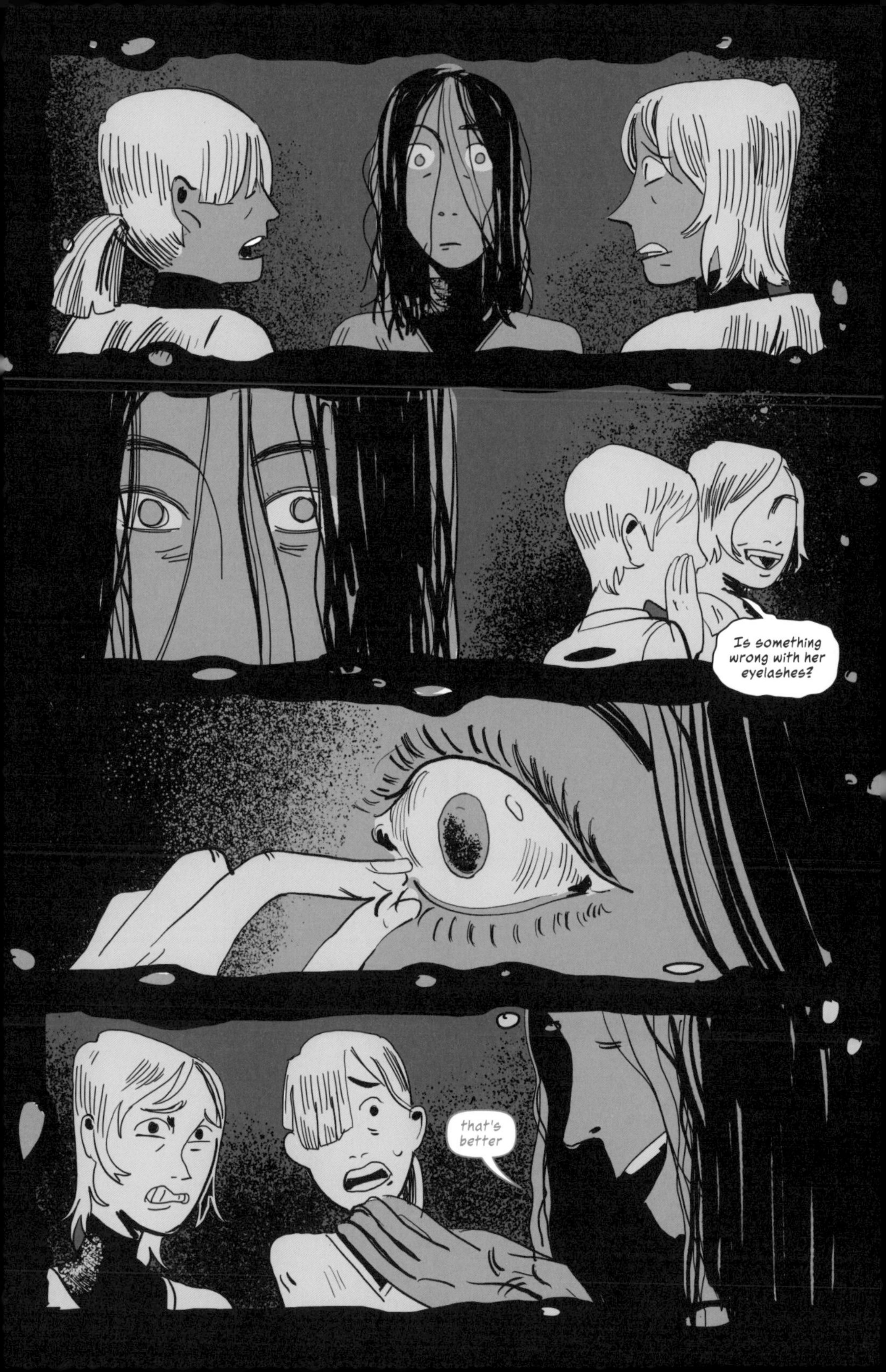
Is something wrong with her eyelashes?
that's better

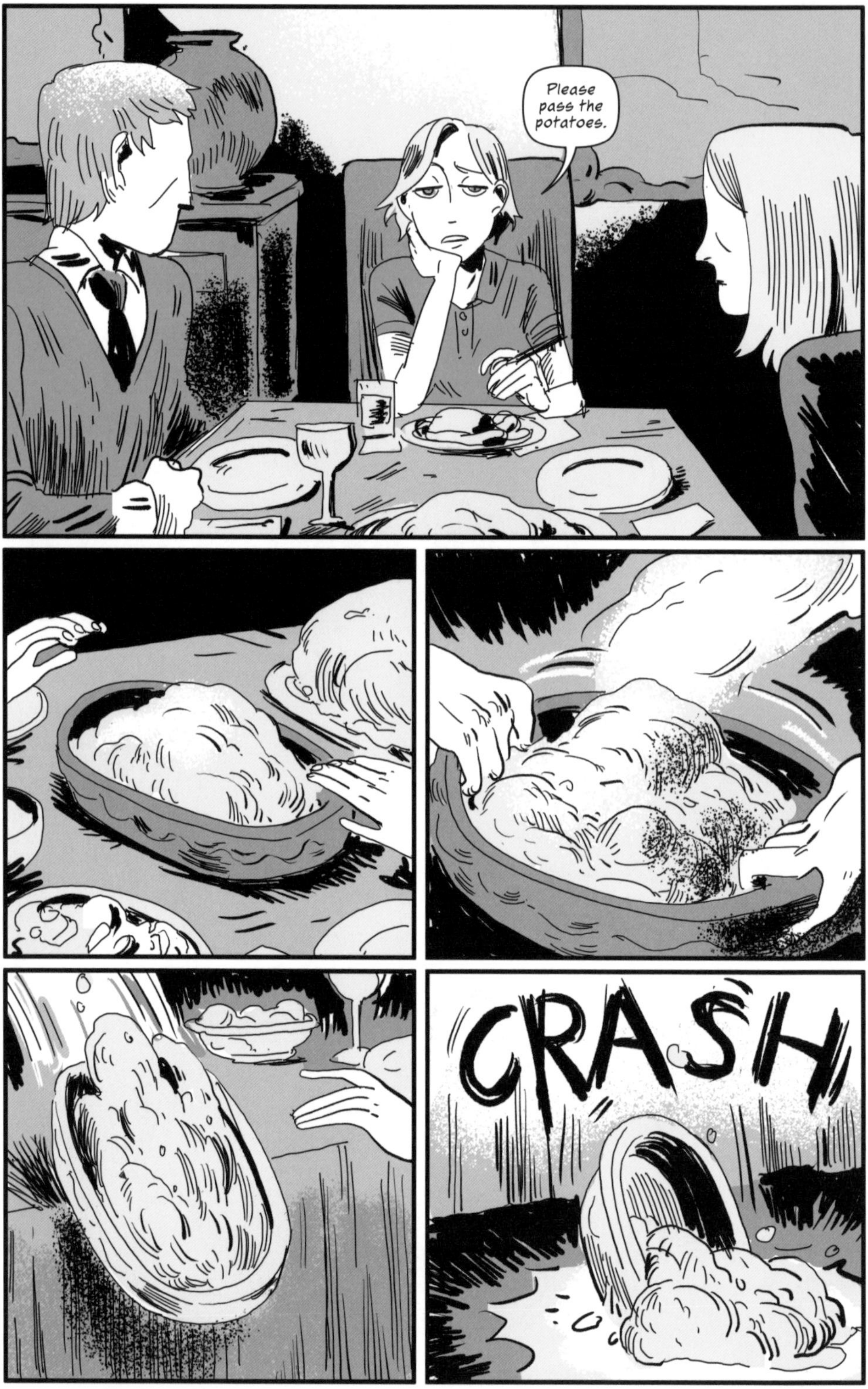
Please pass the potatoes.
CRASH

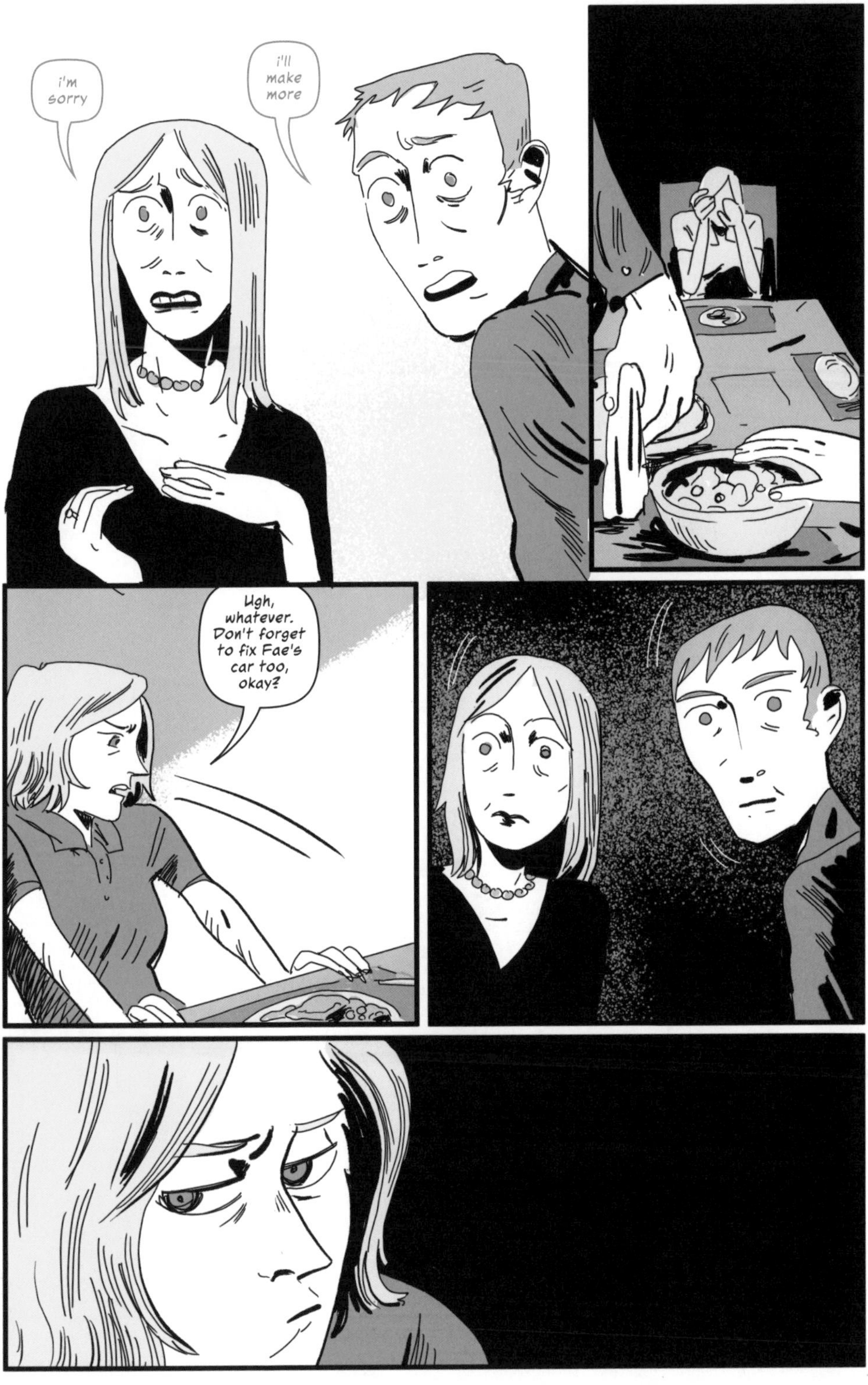

i'm sorry
i'll make more
Ugh, whatever. Don't forget to fix Fae's car too, okay?

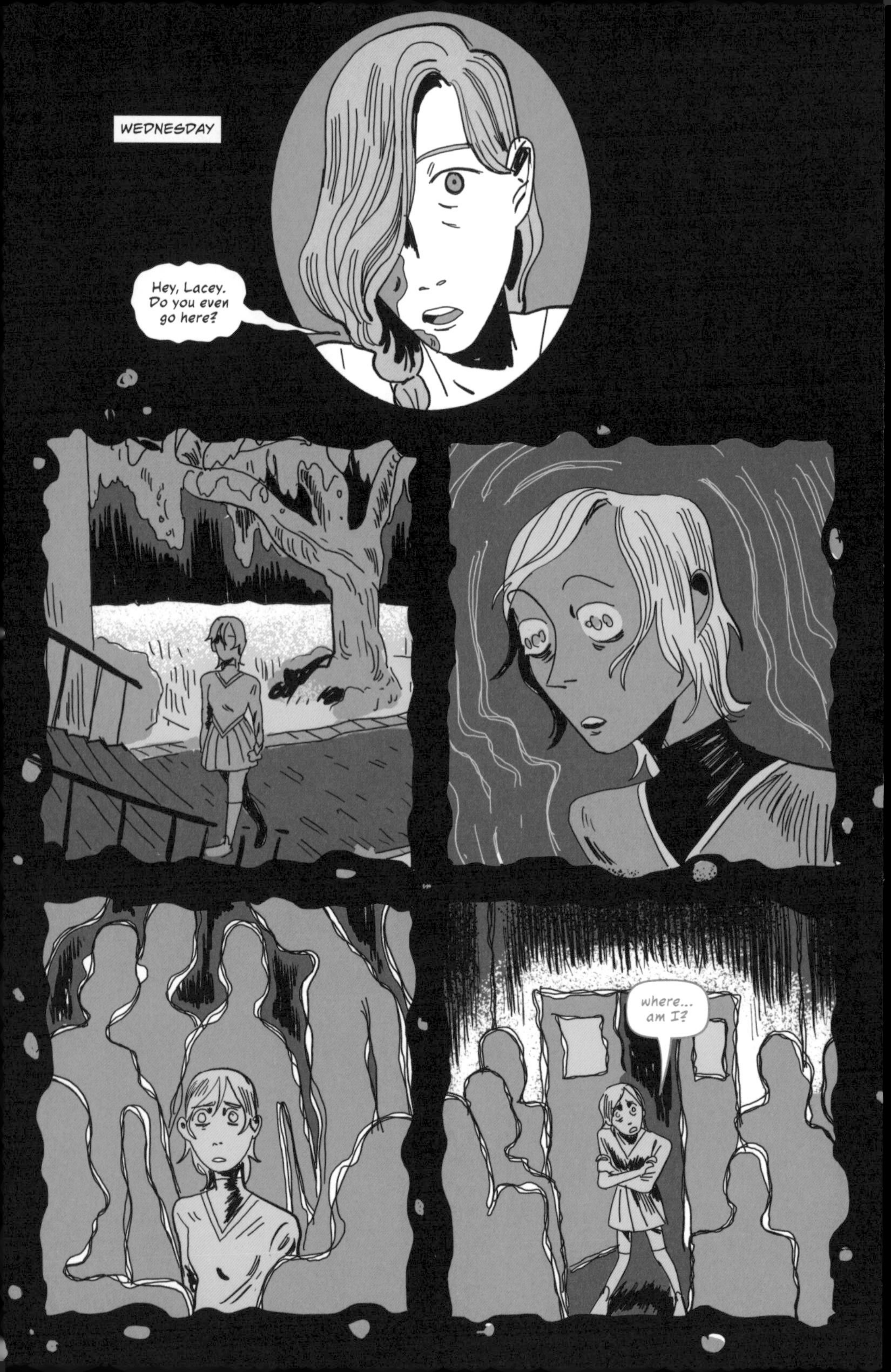
WEDNESDAY
Hey, Lacey.
Do you even
go here?
where...
am I?

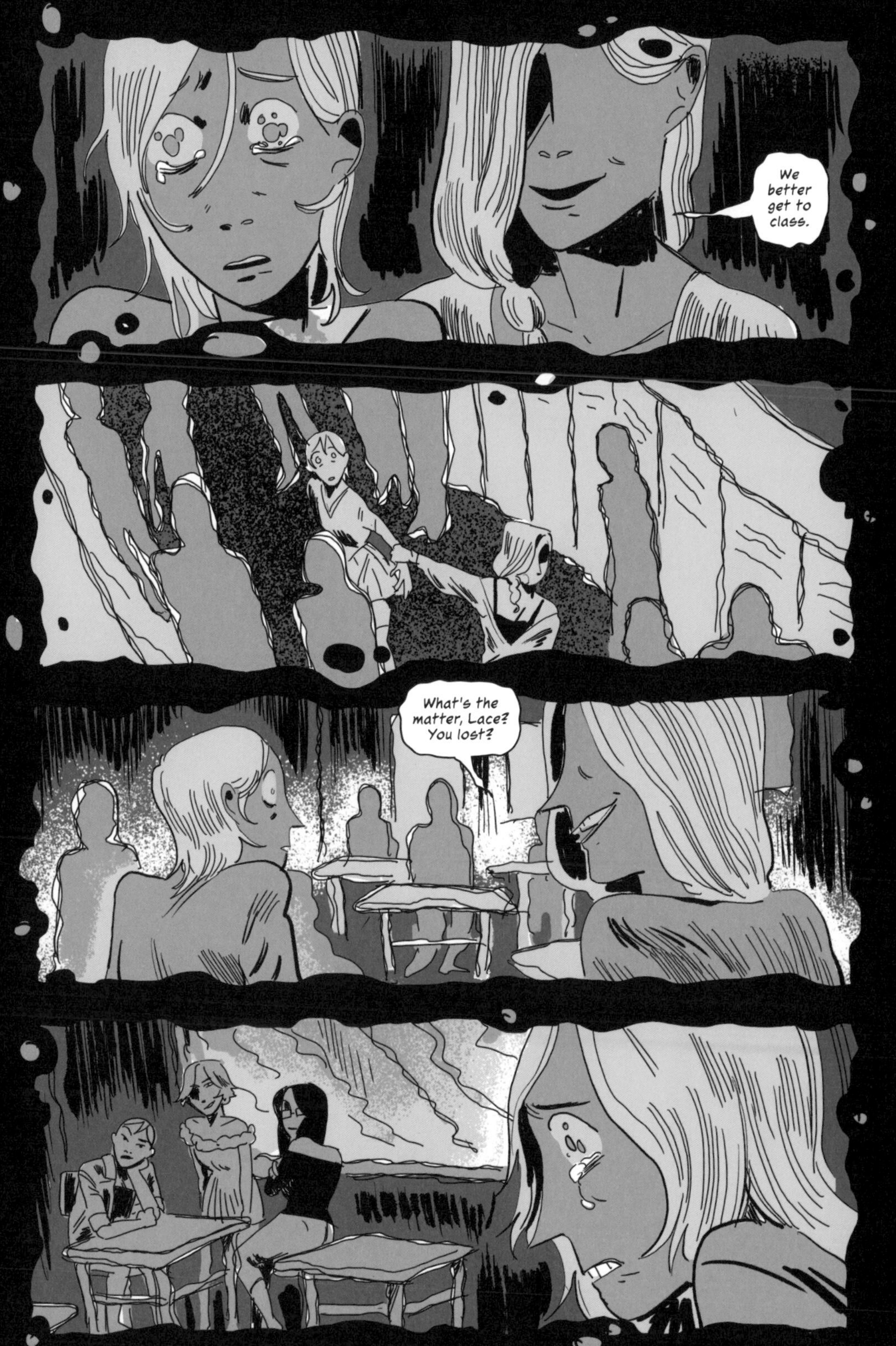
We better get to class.
What's the matter, Lace? You lost?

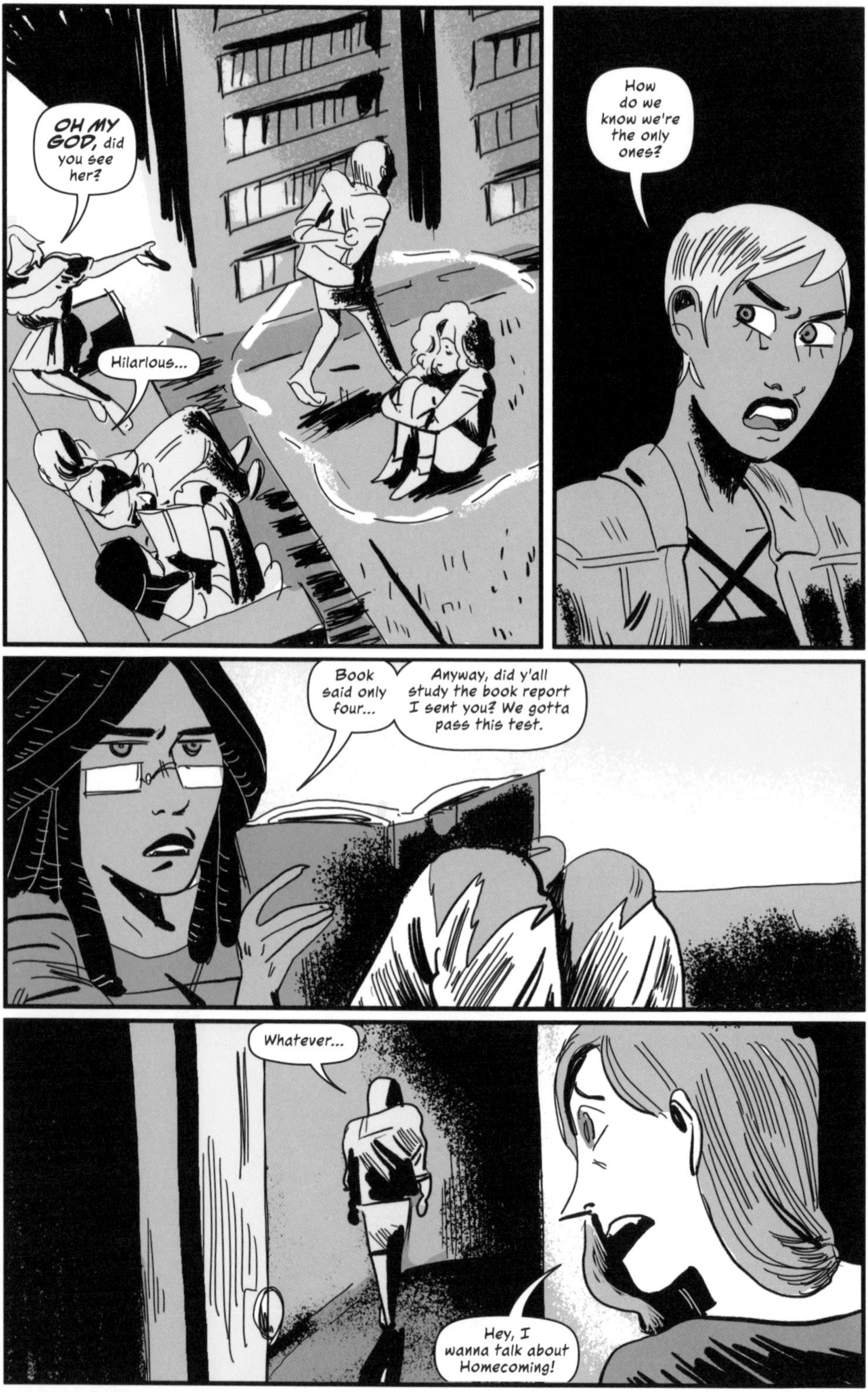

OH MY GOD, did you see her?
Hilarious...
How do we know we're the only ones?
Book said only four...
Anyway, did y'all study the book report I sent you? We gotta pass this test.
Whatever...
Hey, I wanna talk about Homecoming!

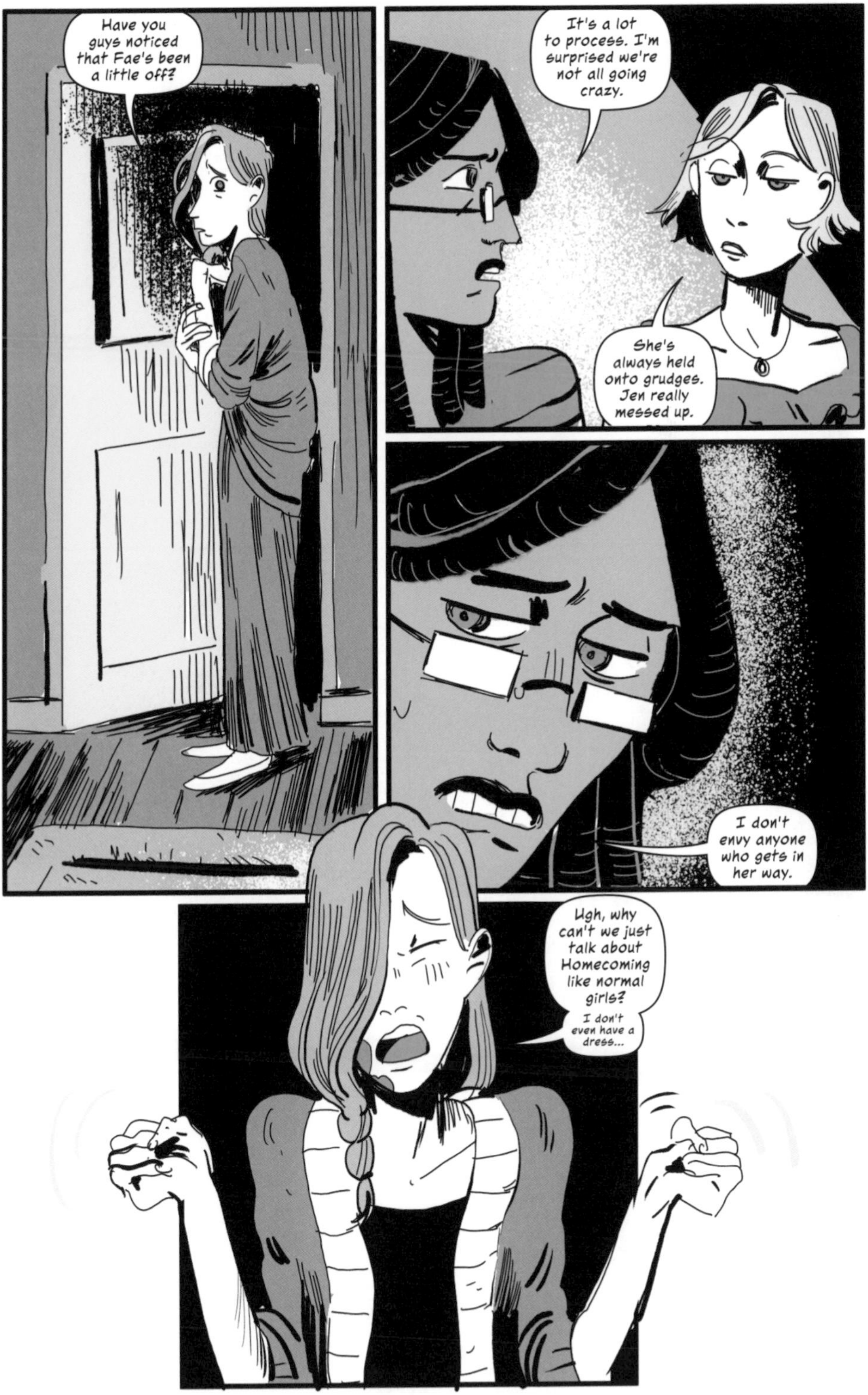
Have you guys noticed that Fae's been a little off?
It's a lot to process. I'm surprised we're not all going crazy.
She's always held onto grudges. Jen really messed up.
I don't envy anyone who gets in her way.
Ugh, why can't we just talk about Homecoming like normal girls?
I don't even have a dress...

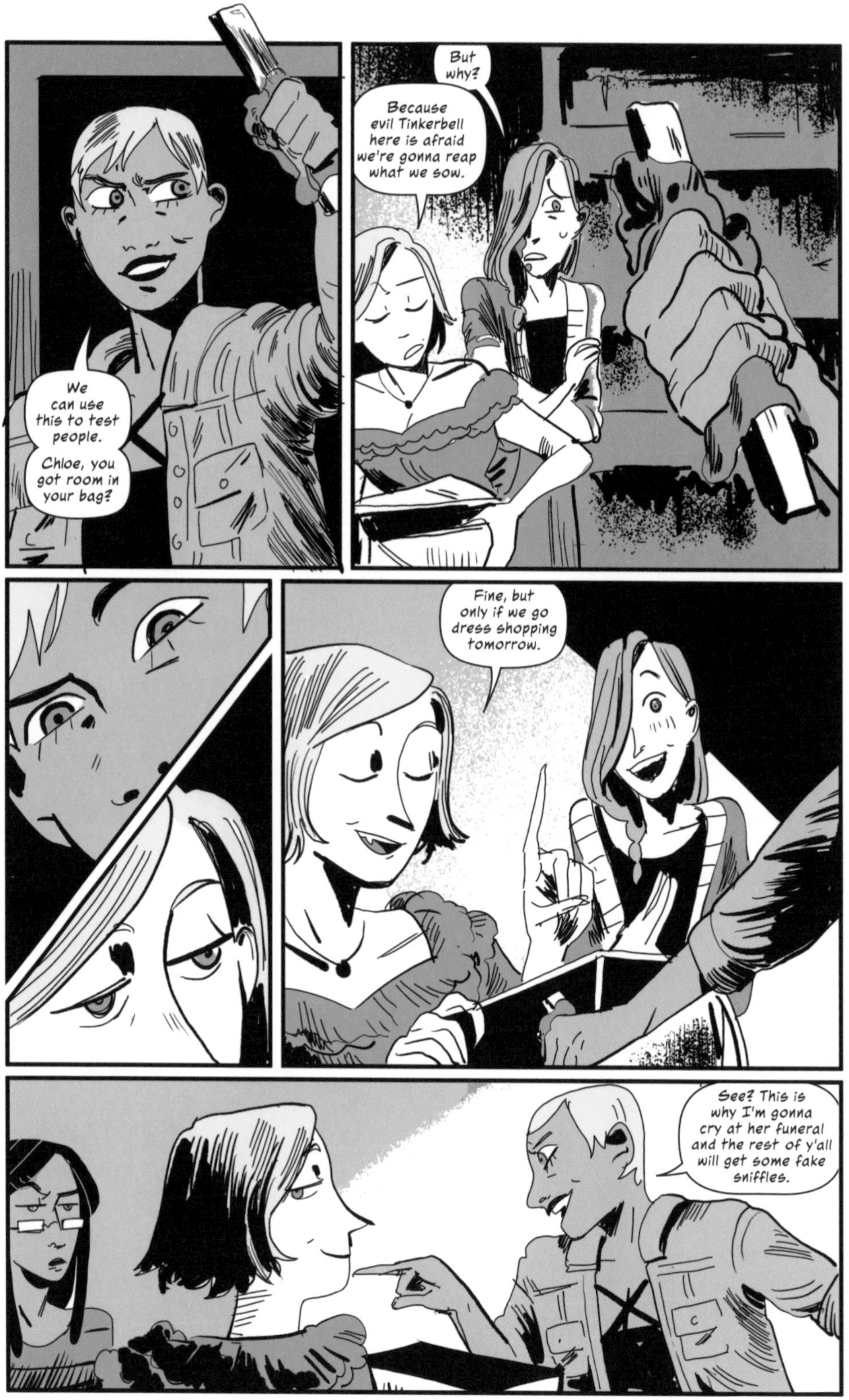
We can use this to test people.
Chloe, you got room in your bag?
But why?
Because evil Tinkerbell here is afraid we're gonna reap what we sow.
Fine, but only if we go dress shopping tomorrow.
See? This is why I'm gonna cry at her funeral and the rest of y'all will get some fake sniffles.

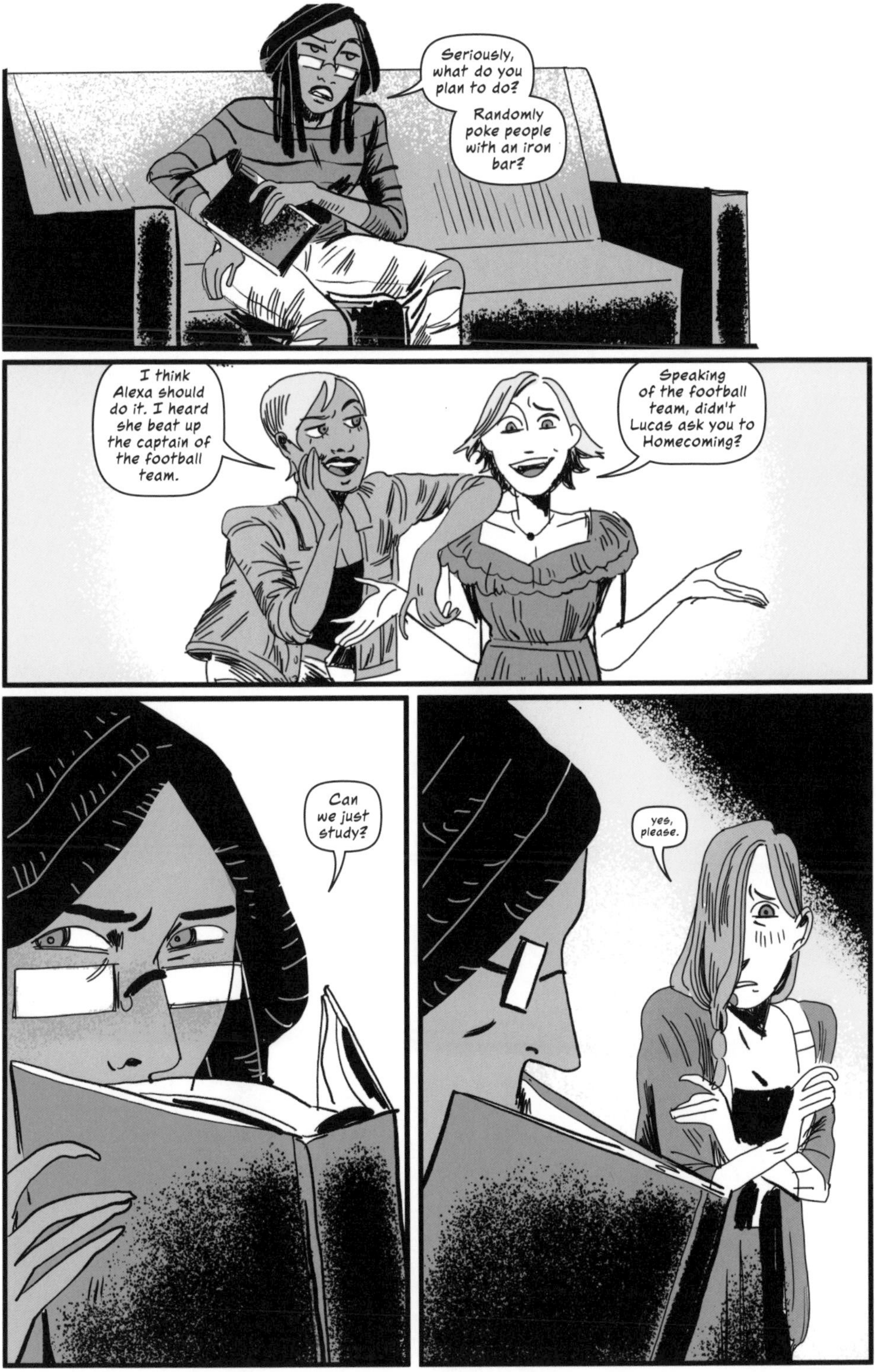
Seriously, what do you plan to do?
Randomly poke people with an iron bar?
I think Alexa should do it. I heard she beat up the captain of the football team.
Speaking of the football team, didn't Lucas ask you to Homecoming?
Can we just study?
yes, please.

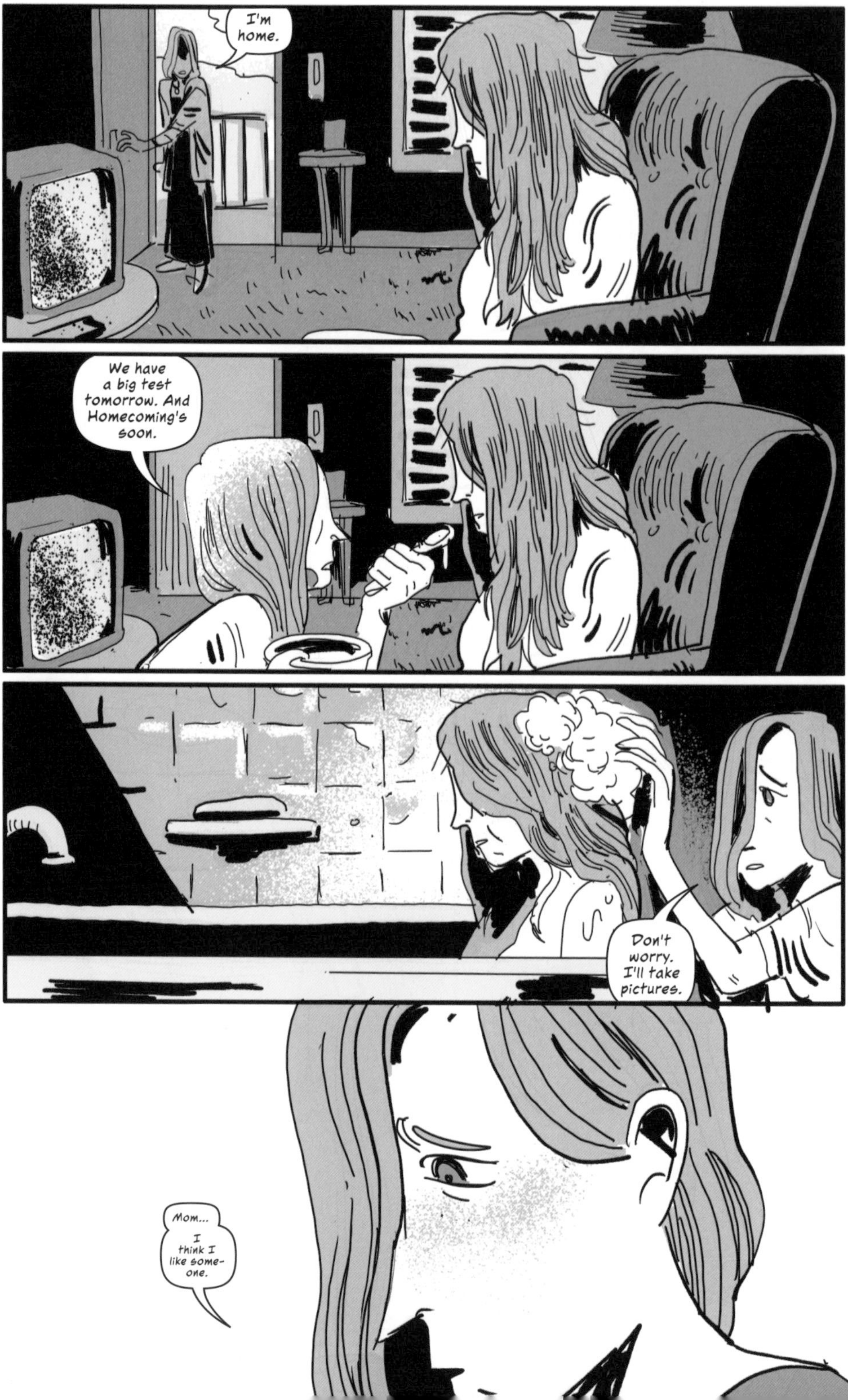
I'm home.
We have a big test tomorrow. And Homecoming's soon.
Don't worry. I'll take pictures.
Mom...
I think I like some-one.

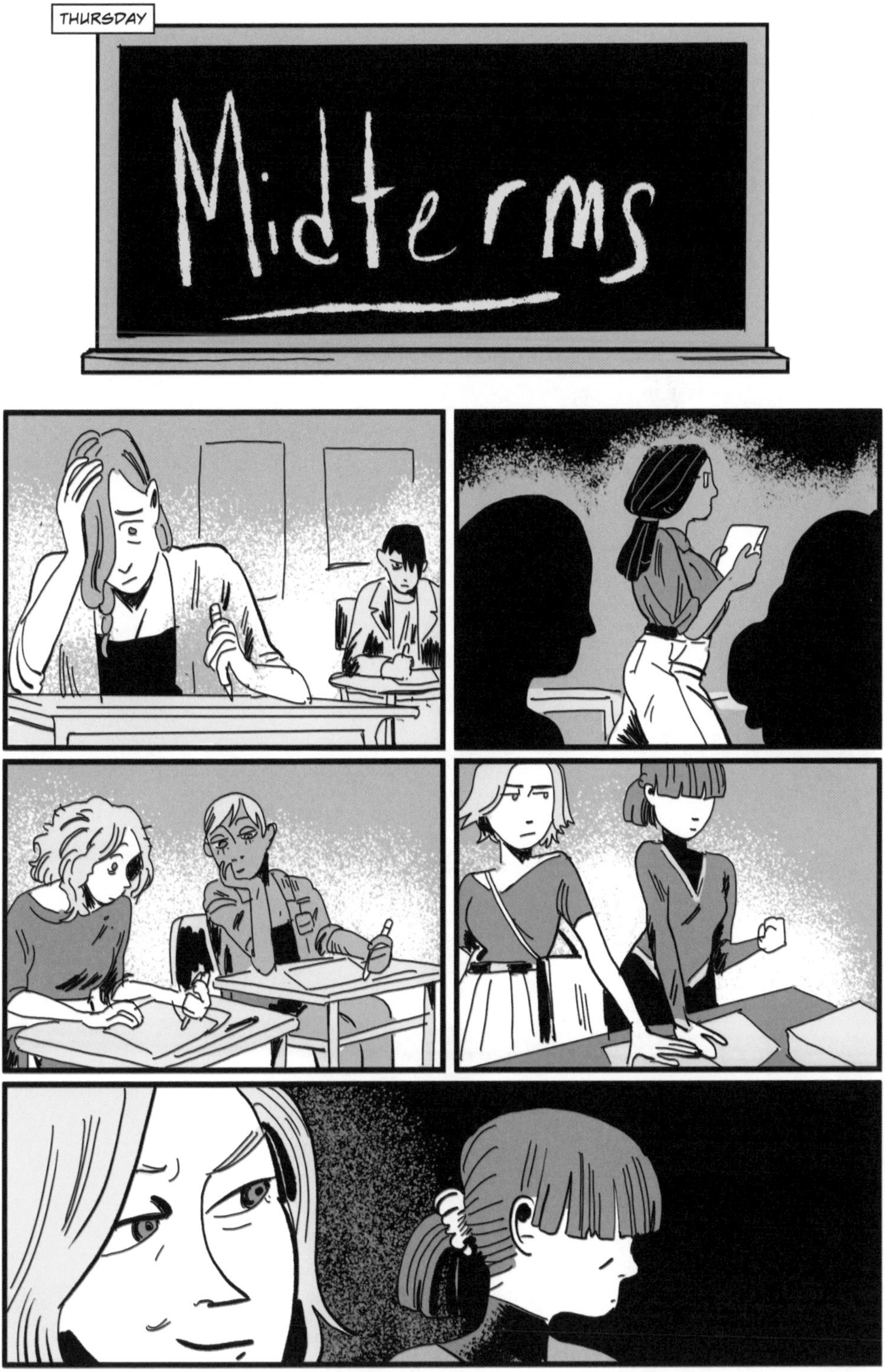
THURSDAY
Midterms

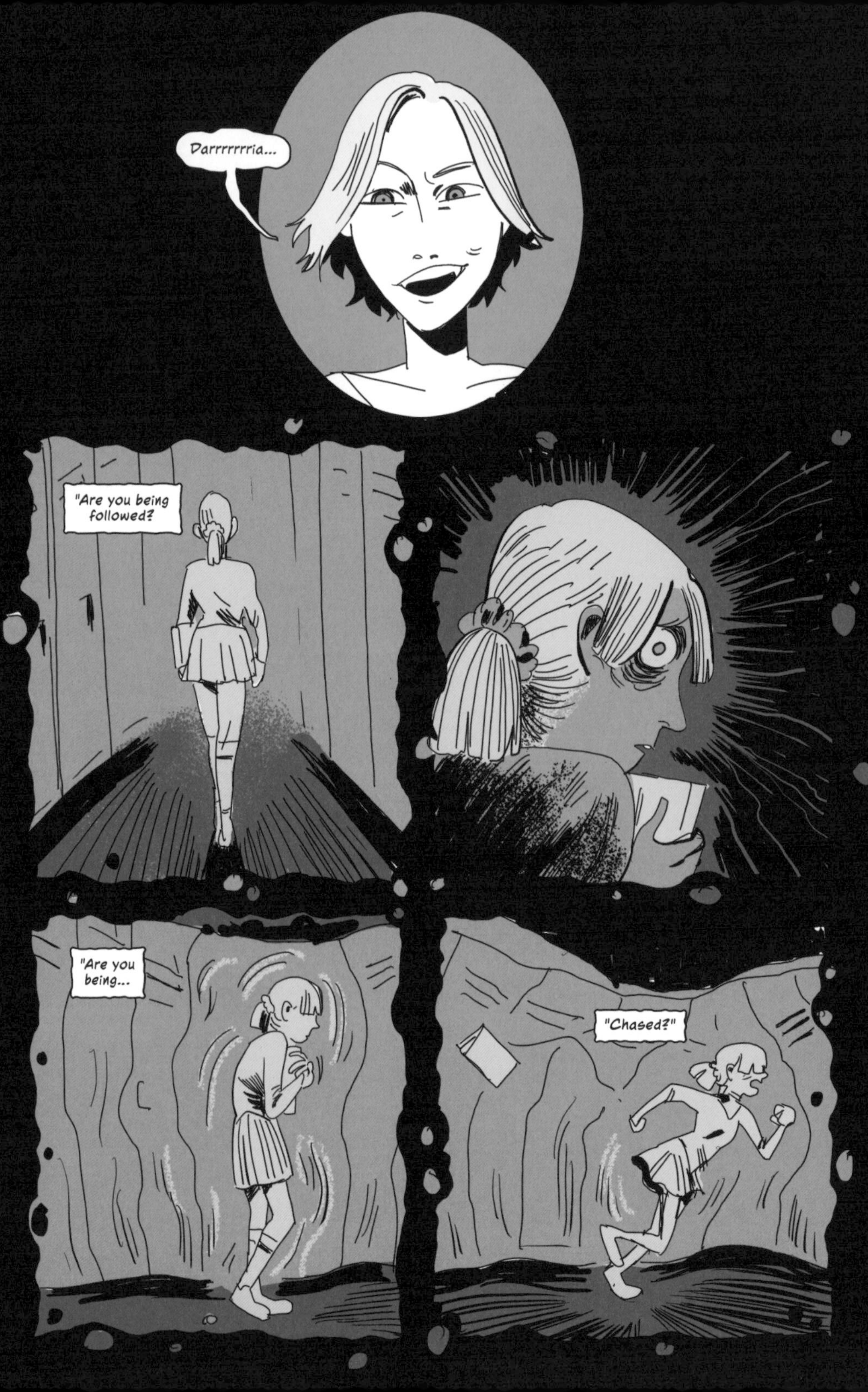
Darrrrrrria...
"Are you being followed?
"Are you being...
"Chased?"

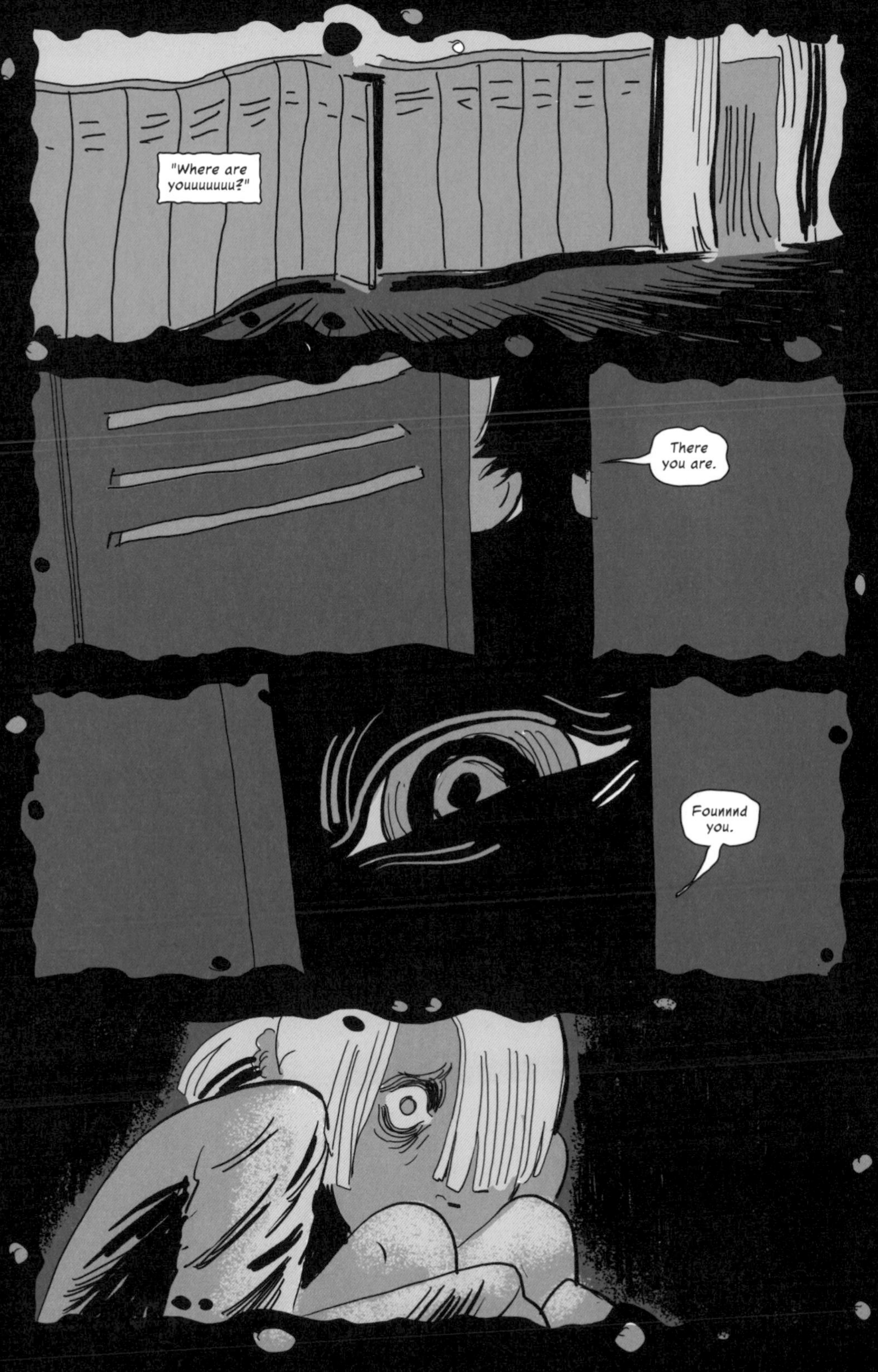
"Where are youuuuuuu?"
There you are.
Founnnd you.

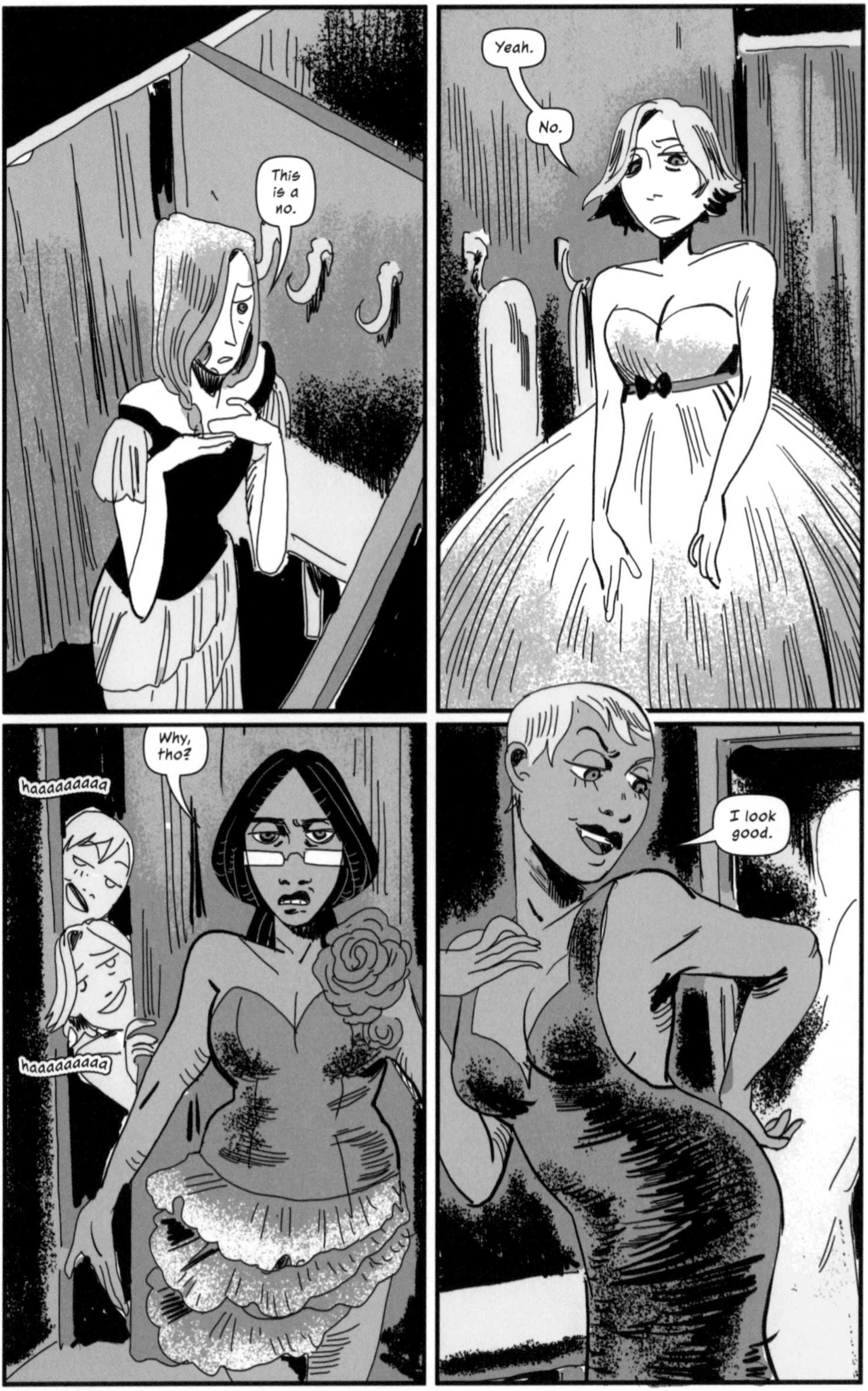
This is a no.
Yeah.
No.
haaaaaaaaa
haaaaaaaaa
Why, tho?
I look good.

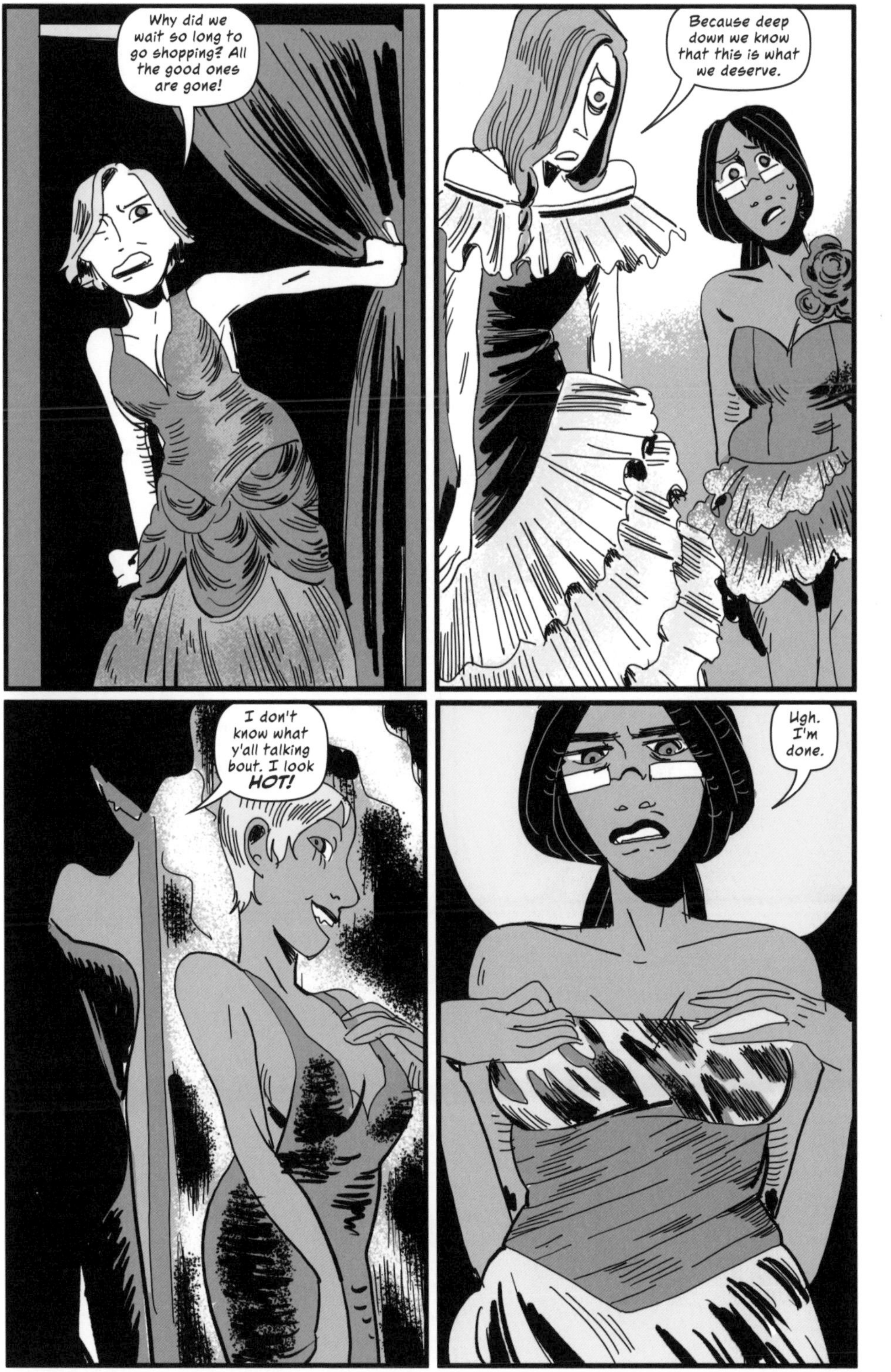
Why did we wait so long to go shopping? All the good ones are gone!
Because deep down we know that this is what we deserve.
I don't know what y'all talking bout. I look **HOT!**
Ugh. I'm done.

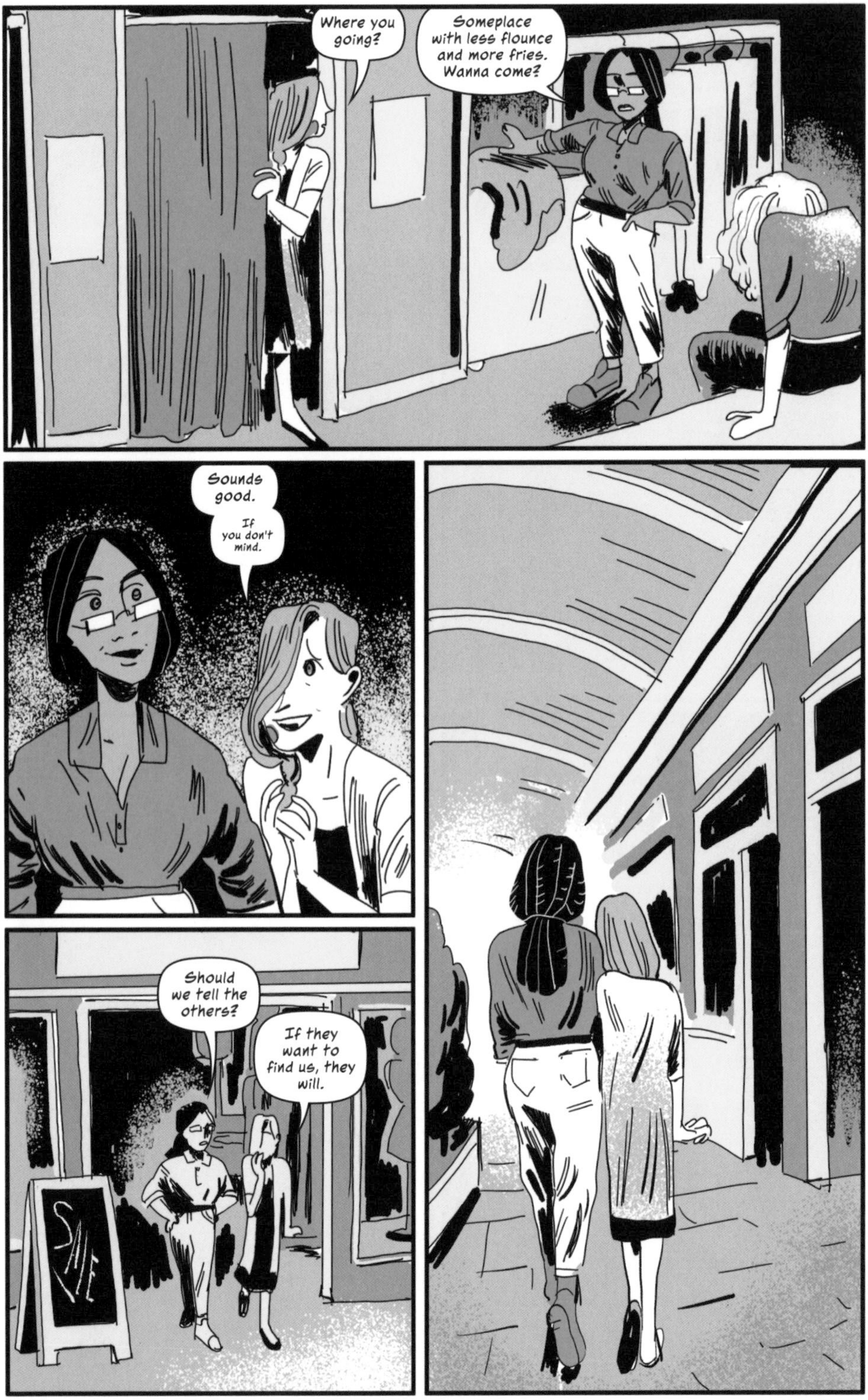
Where you going?
Someplace with less flounce and more fries. Wanna come?
Sounds good.
If you don't mind.
Should we tell the others?
If they want to find us, they will.
SALE

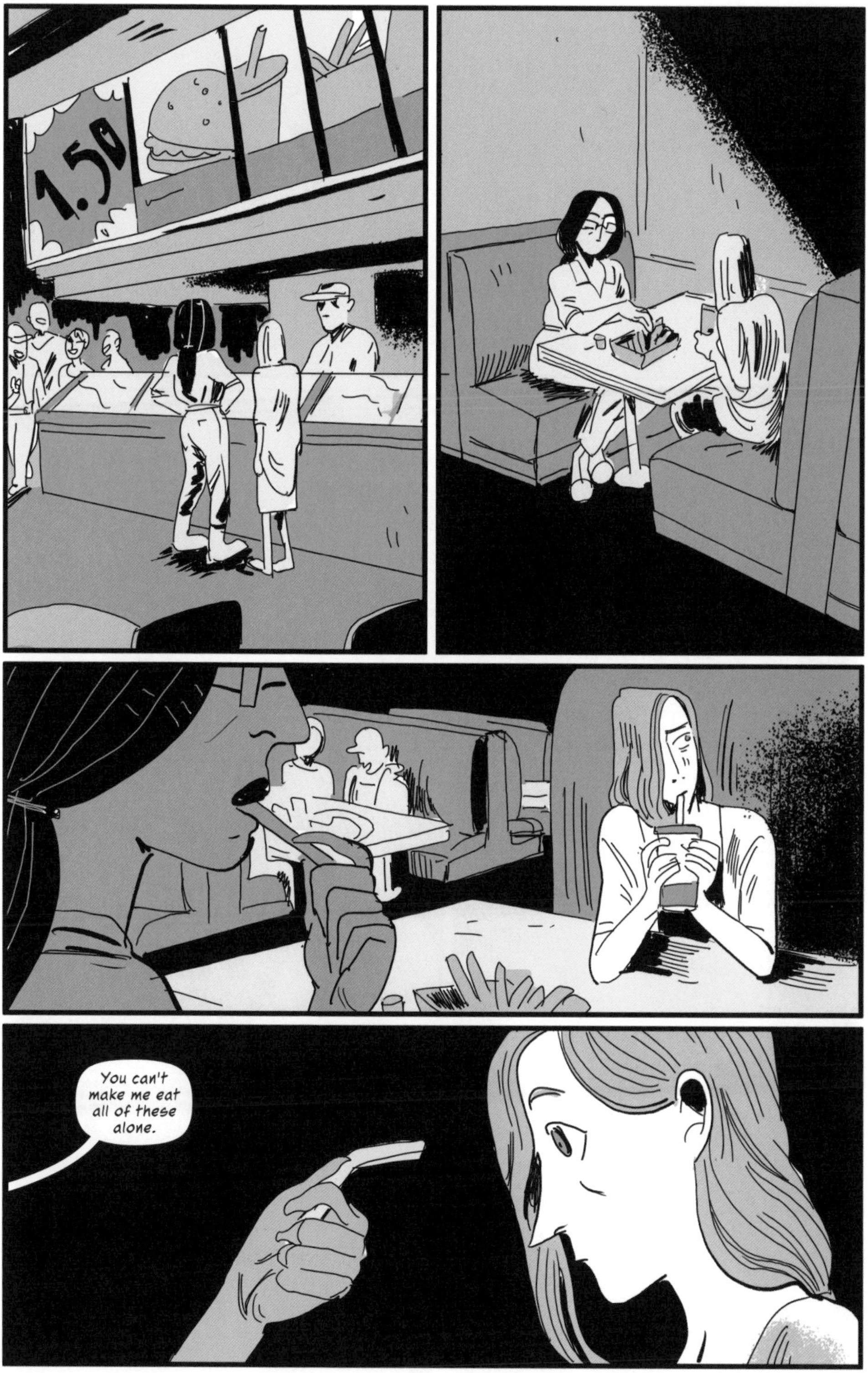
1.50
You can't make me eat all of these alone.

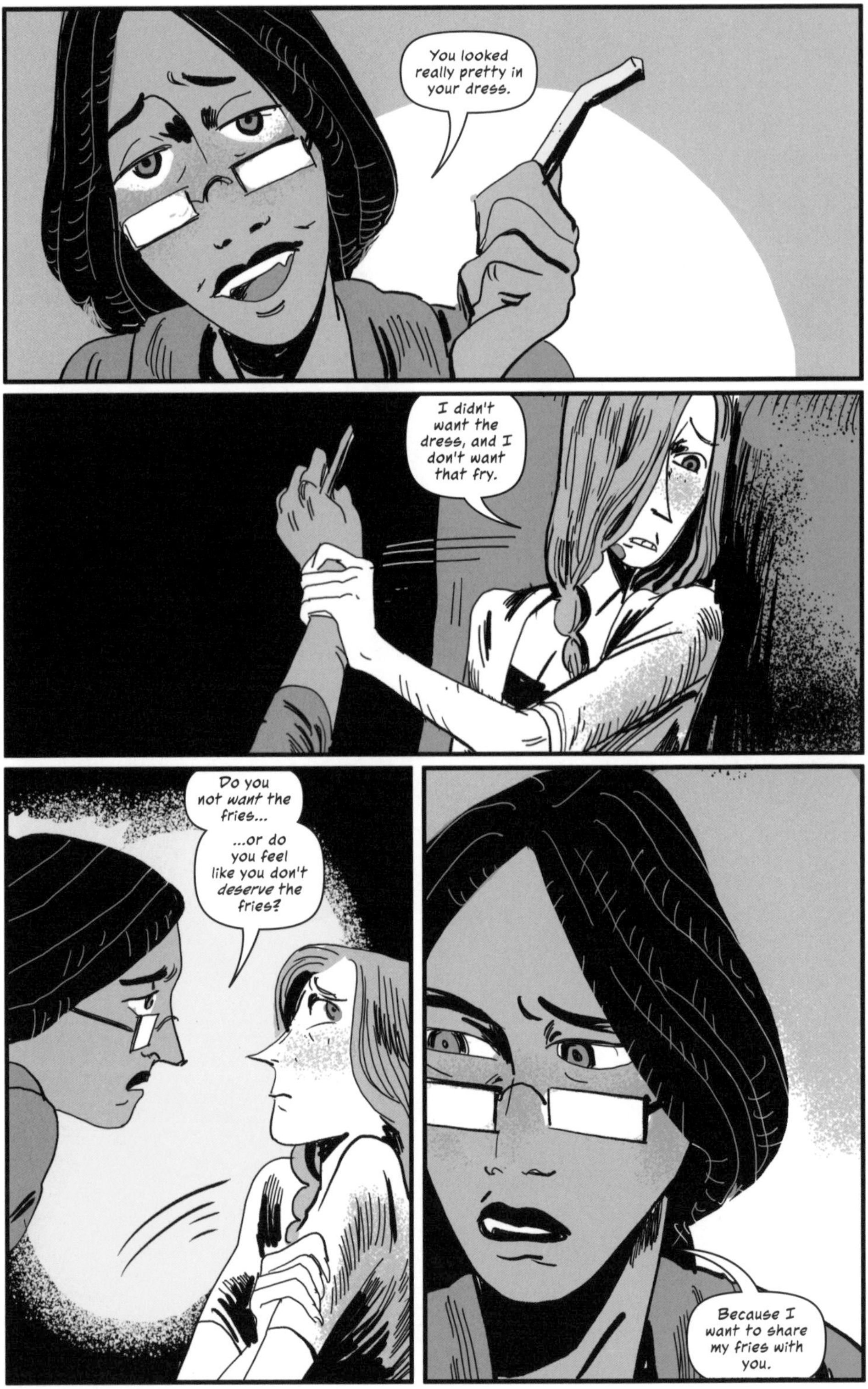
You looked really pretty in your dress.
I didn't want the dress, and I don't want that fry.
Do you not want the fries...
...or do you feel like you don't deserve the fries?
Because I want to share my fries with you.

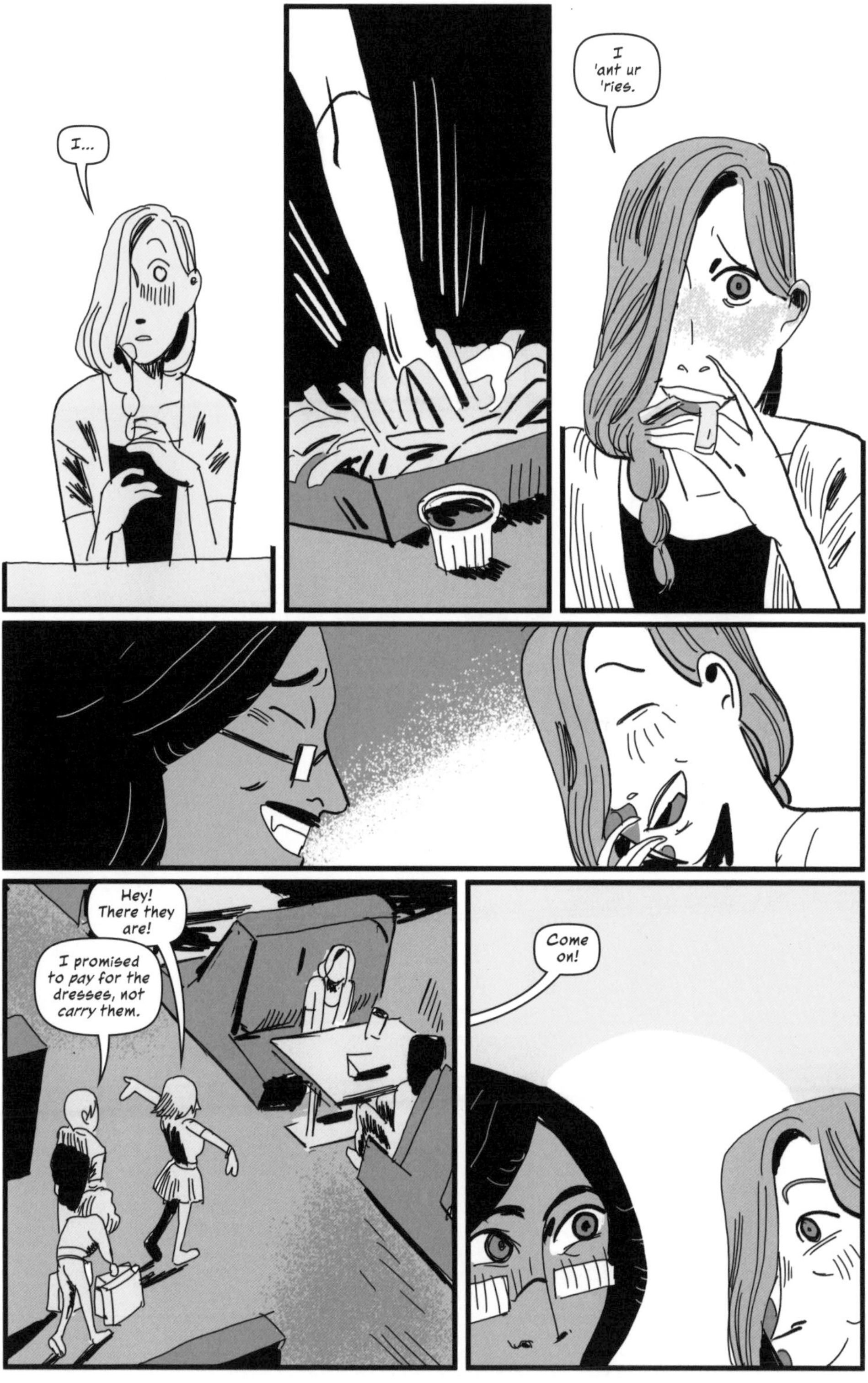
I...
I 'ant ur 'ries.
Hey! There they are!
I promised to pay for the dresses, not carry them.
Come on!

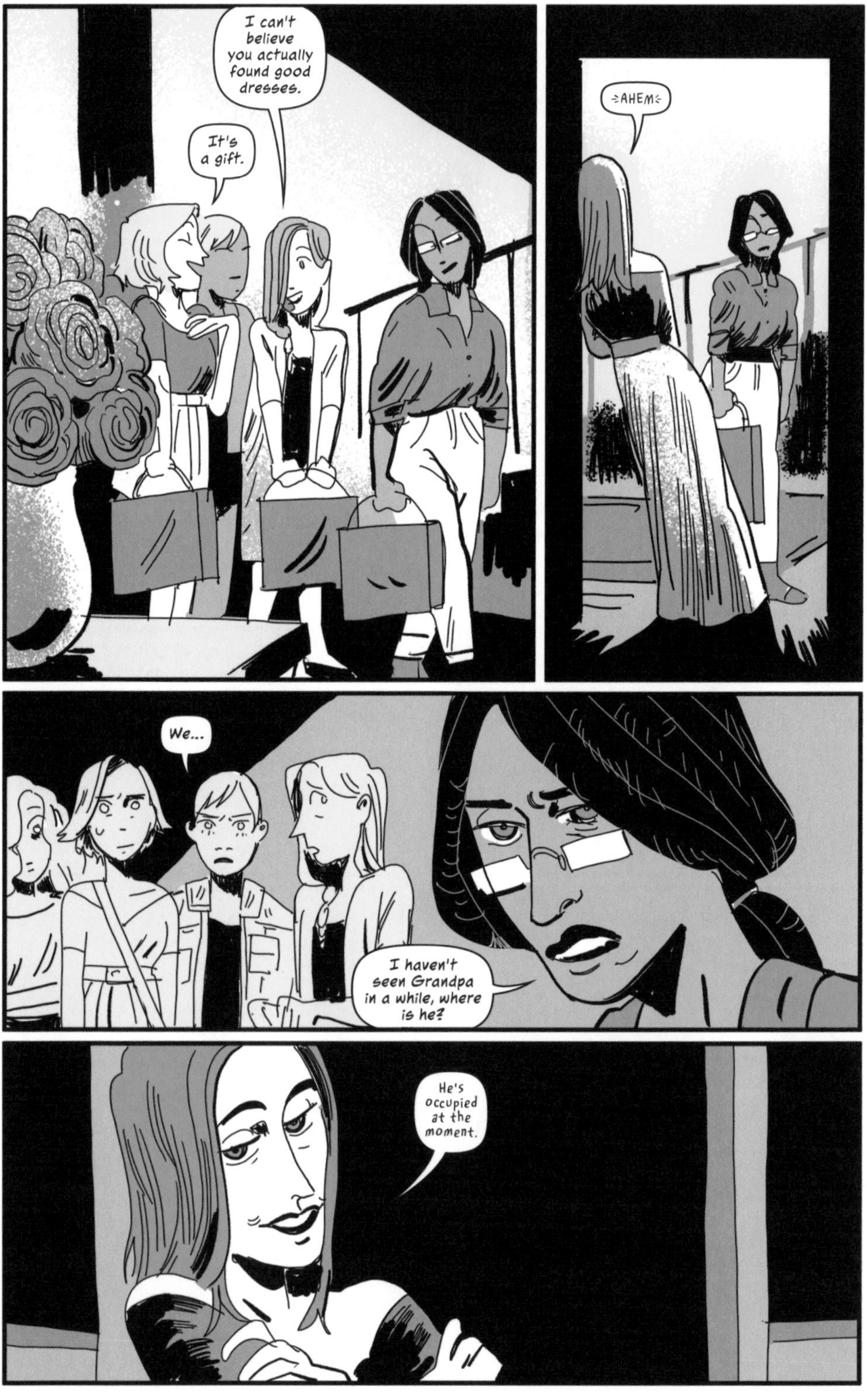
I can't believe you actually found good dresses.
It's a gift.
=AHEM=
We...
I haven't seen Grandpa in a while, where is he?
He's occupied at the moment.

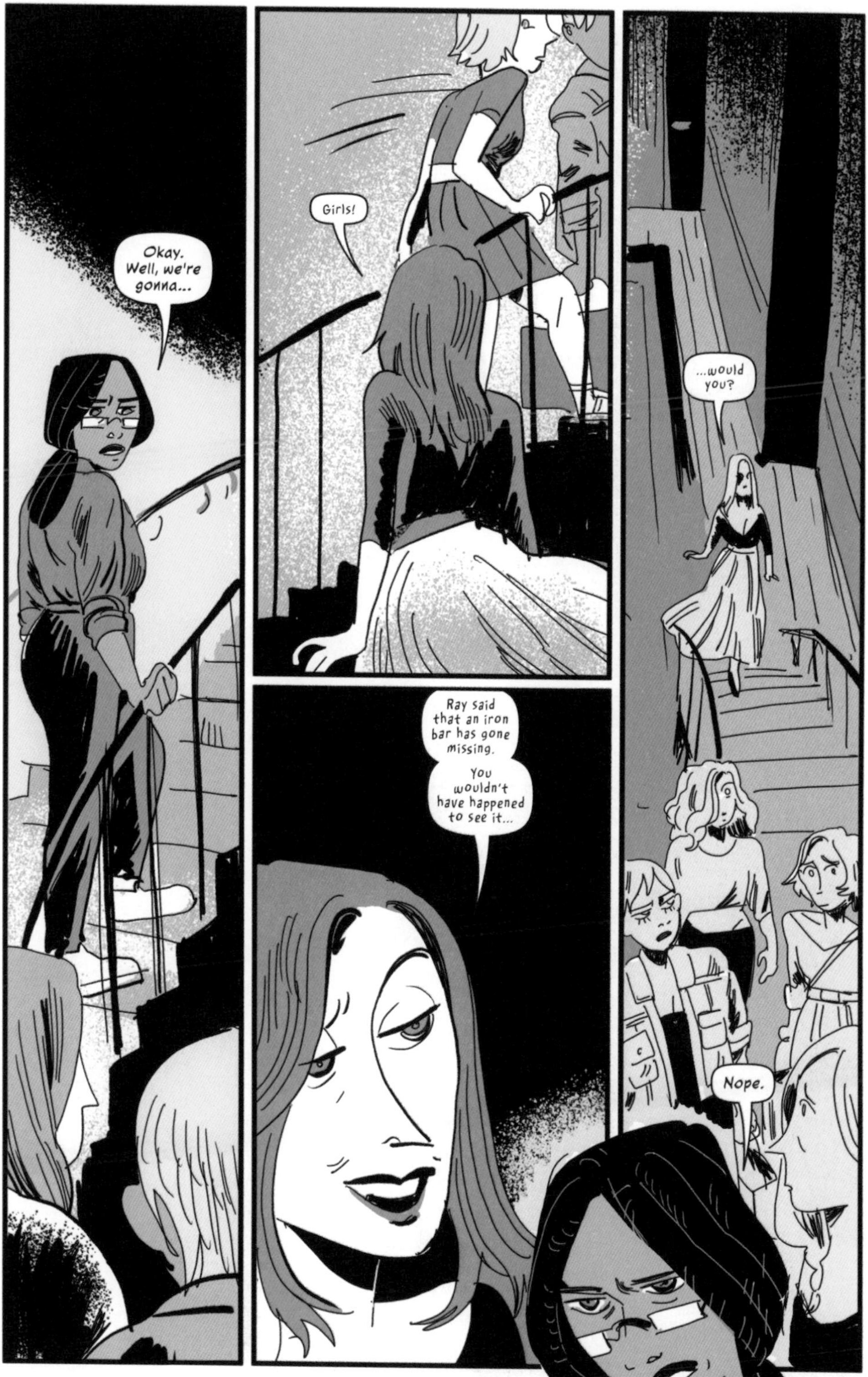
Okay. Well, we're gonna...
Girls!
...would you?
Ray said that an iron bar has gone missing.
You wouldn't have happened to see it...
Nope.

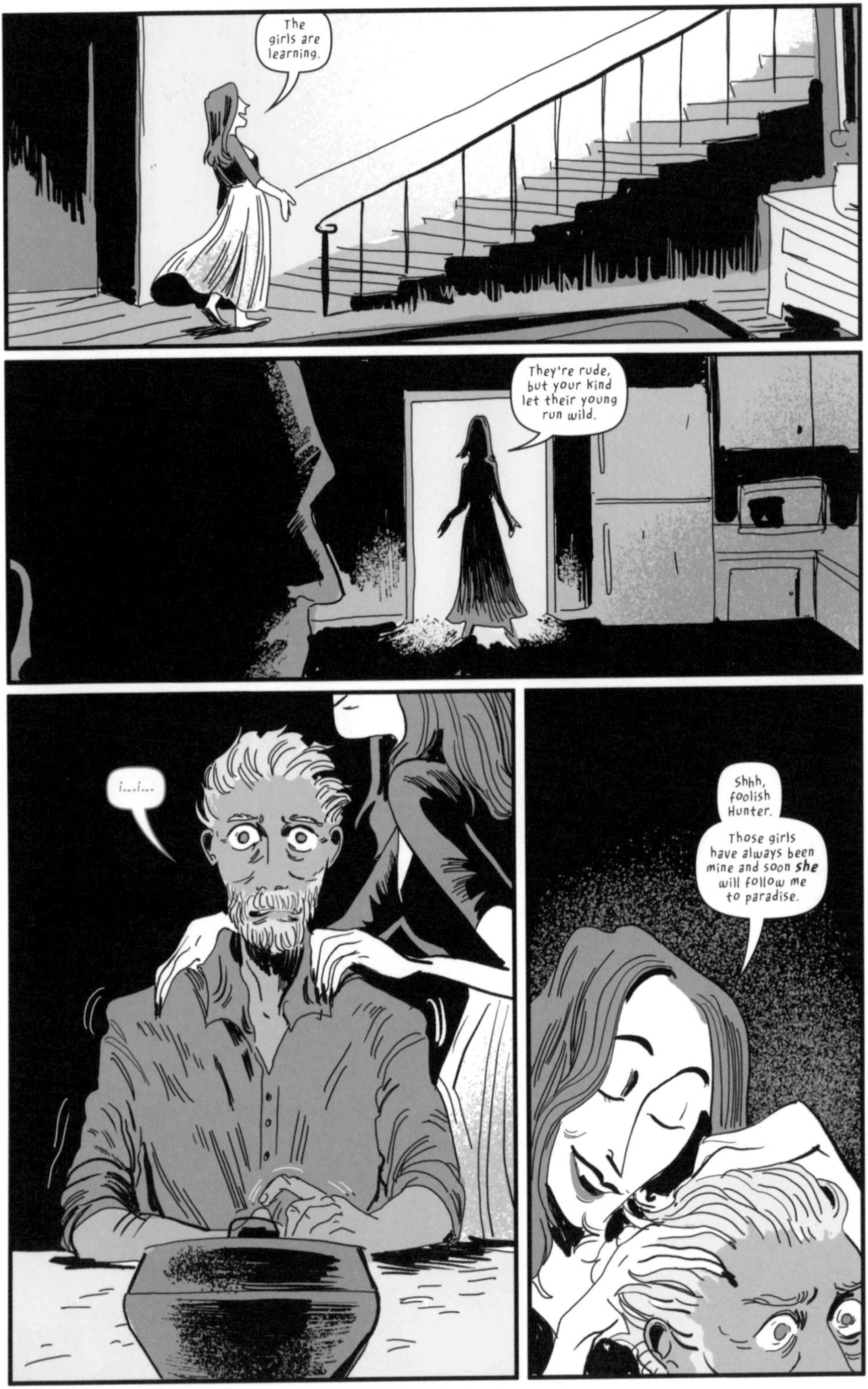
The girls are learning.
They're rude, but your kind let their young run wild.
I...I...
Shhh, foolish Hunter.
Those girls have always been mine and soon **she** will follow me to paradise.

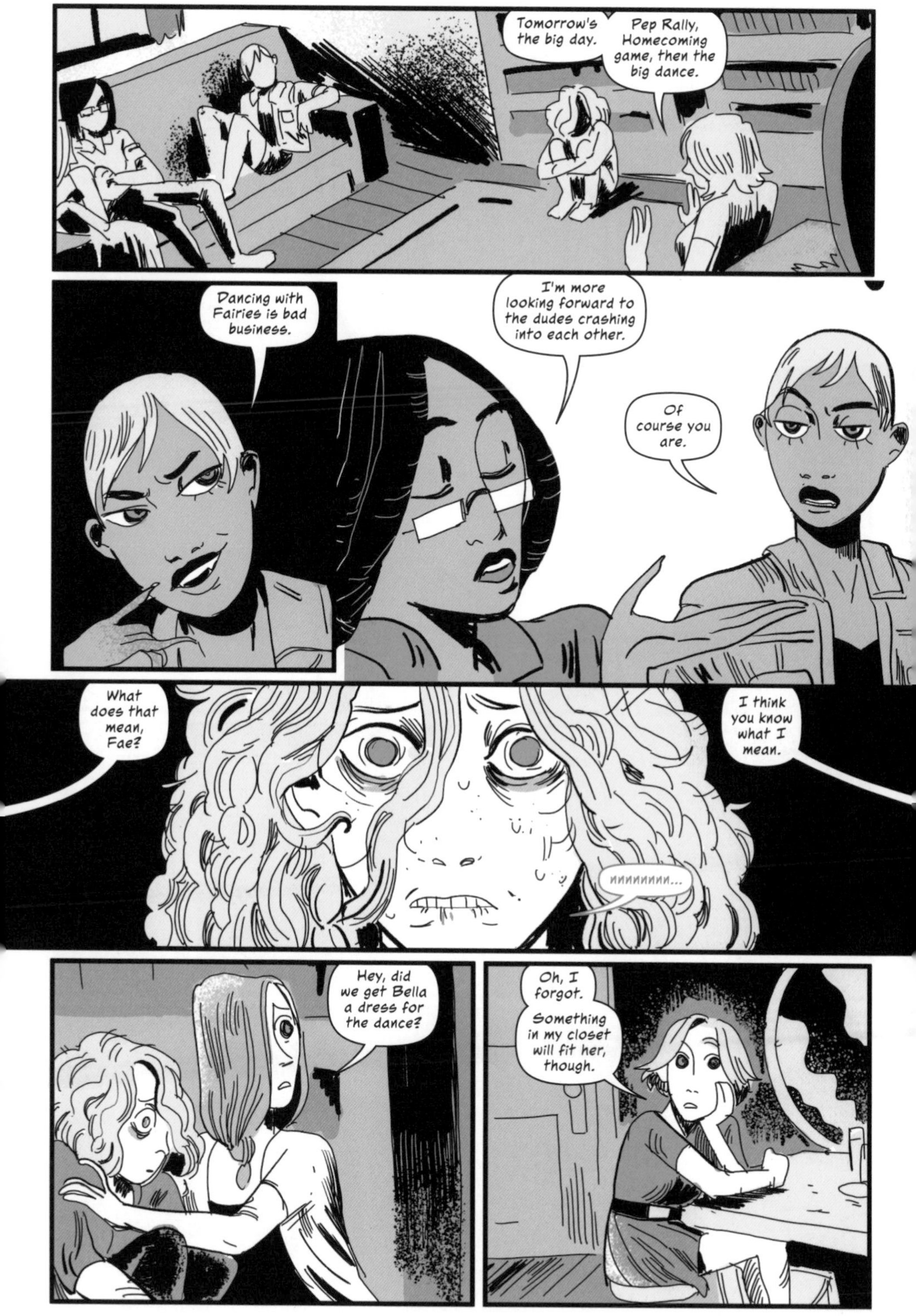

Tomorrow's the big day.
Pep Rally, Homecoming game, then the big dance.
Dancing with Fairies is bad business.
I'm more looking forward to the dudes crashing into each other.
Of course you are.
What does that mean, Fae?
I think you know what I mean.
nnnnnnnnn...
Hey, did we get Bella a dress for the dance?
Oh, I forgot.
Something in my closet will fit her, though.

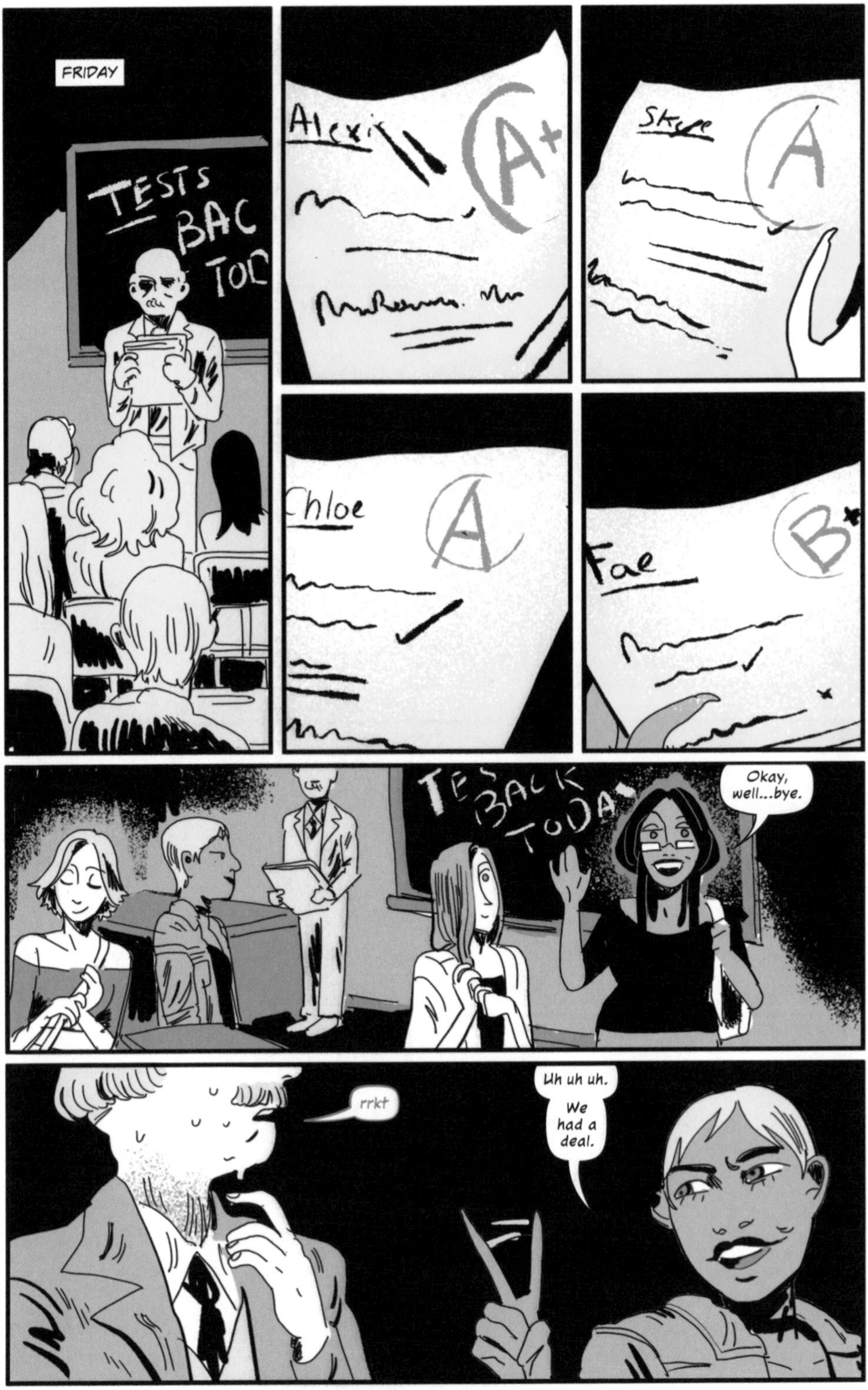
FRIDAY
TESTS BAC TOD
Alexis
A+
Skye
A
Chloe
A
Fae
B+
TES BACK TODA
Okay, well...bye.
rrkt
Uh uh uh.
We had a deal.

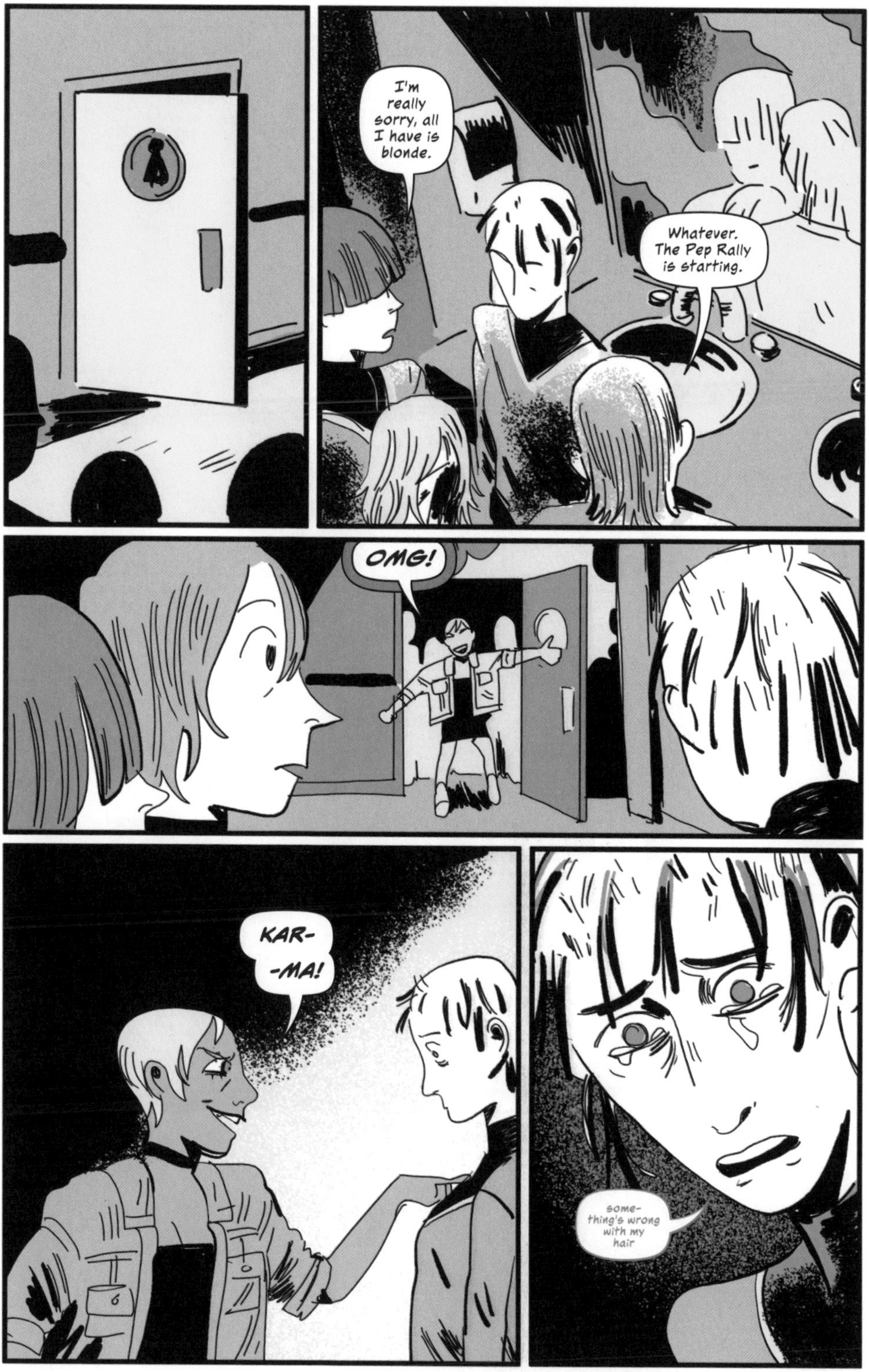
I'm really sorry, all I have is blonde.
Whatever. The Pep Rally is starting.
OMG!
KAR- -MA!
some-thing's wrong with my hair

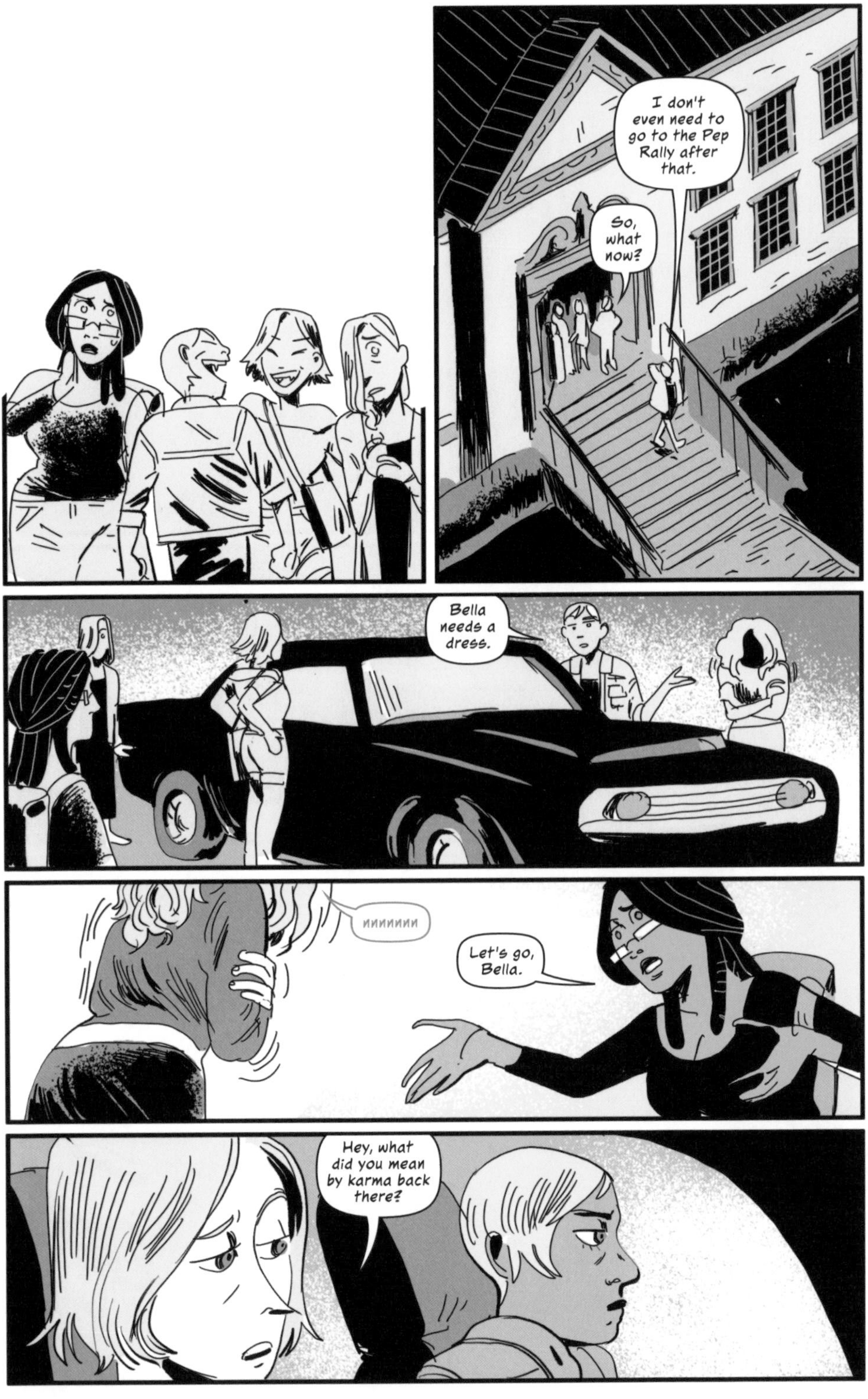
I don't even need to go to the Pep Rally after that.
So, what now?
Bella needs a dress.
NNNNNNN
Let's go, Bella.
Hey, what did you mean by karma back there?

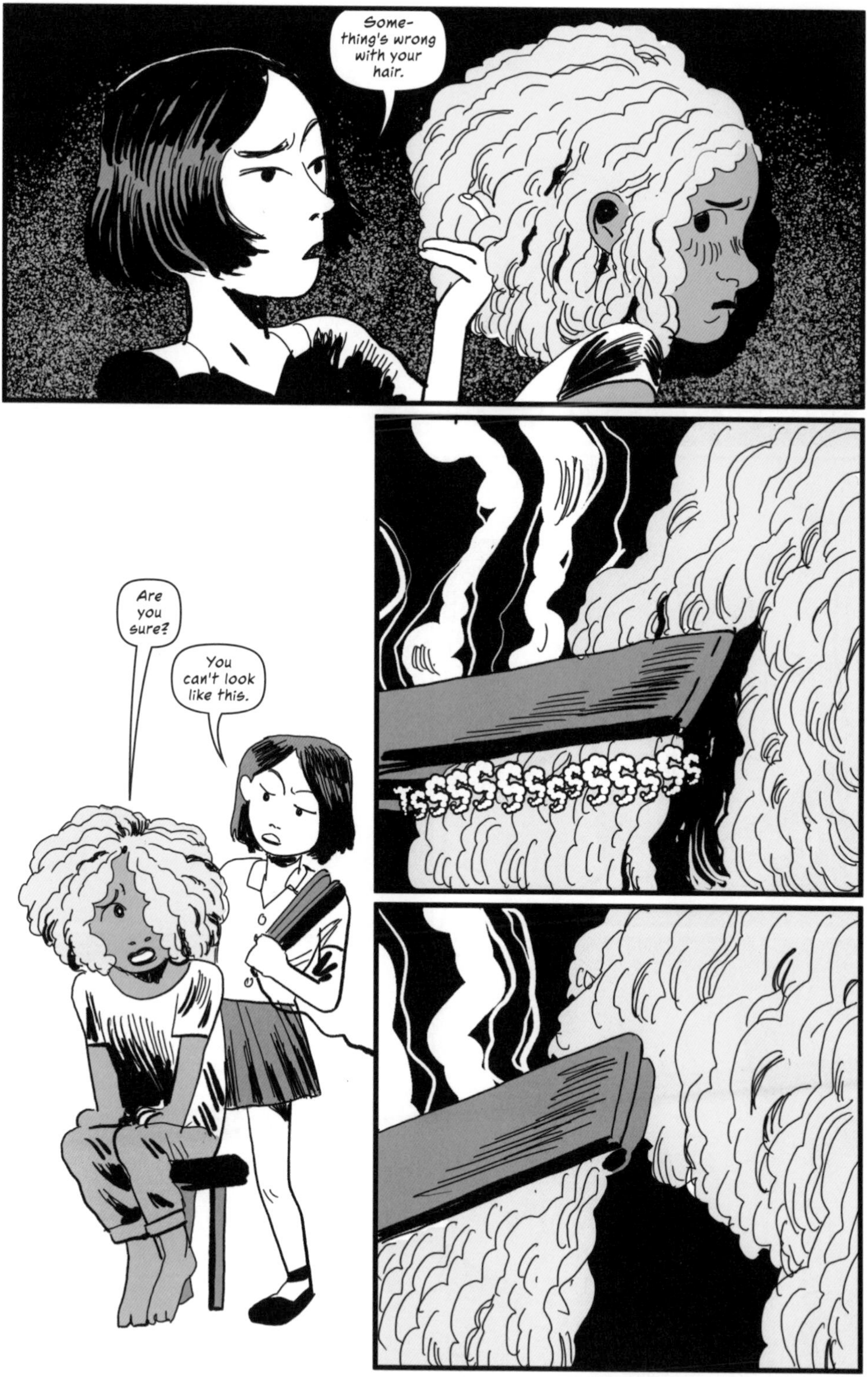
Something's wrong with your hair.
Are you sure?
You can't look like this.
TsSSSSSSSSSSSSs

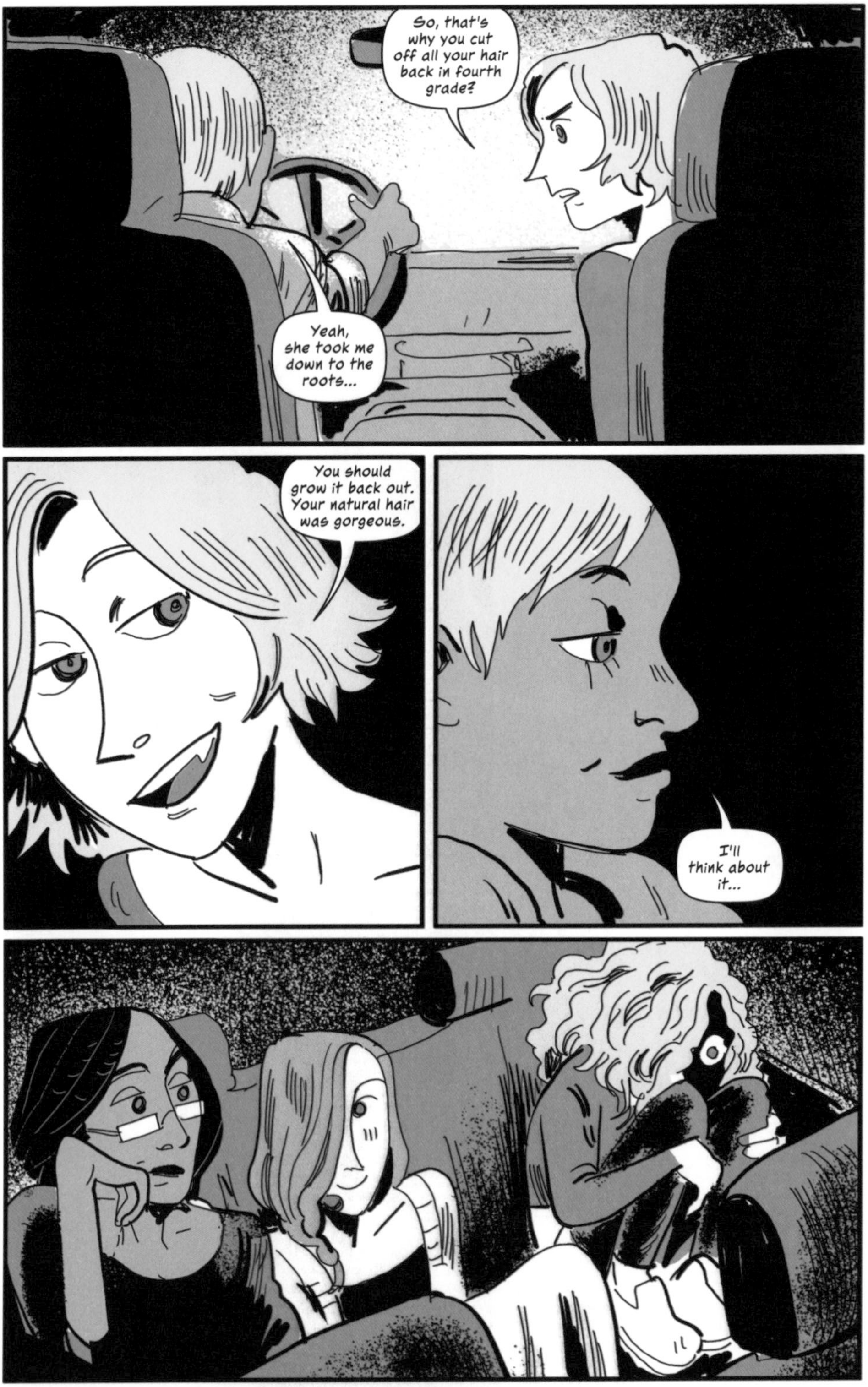
So, that's why you cut off all your hair back in fourth grade?
Yeah, she took me down to the roots...
You should grow it back out. Your natural hair was gorgeous.
I'll think about it...

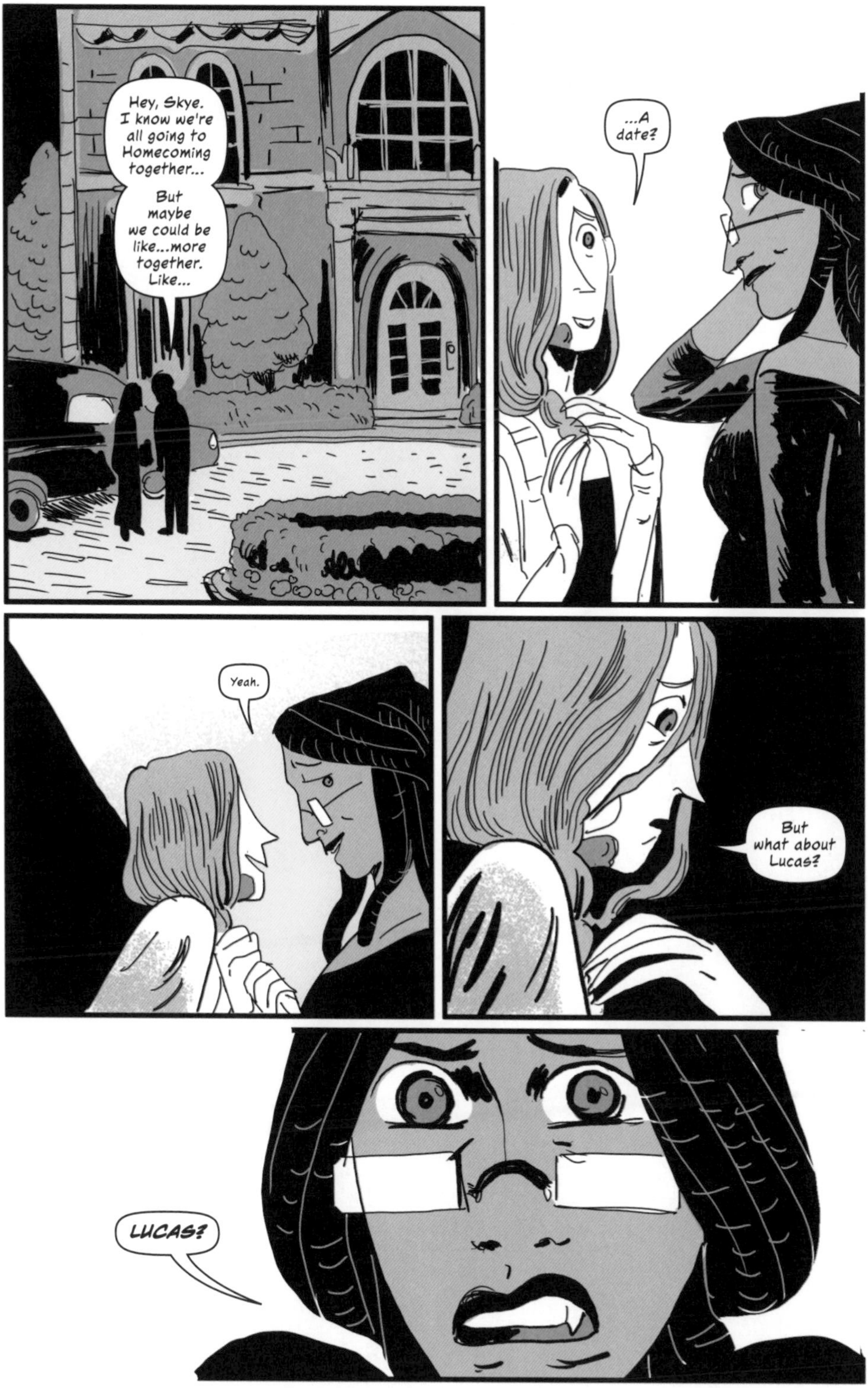
Hey, Skye. I know we're all going to Homecoming together...
But maybe we could be like...more together. Like...
...A date?
Yeah.
But what about Lucas?
LUCAS?

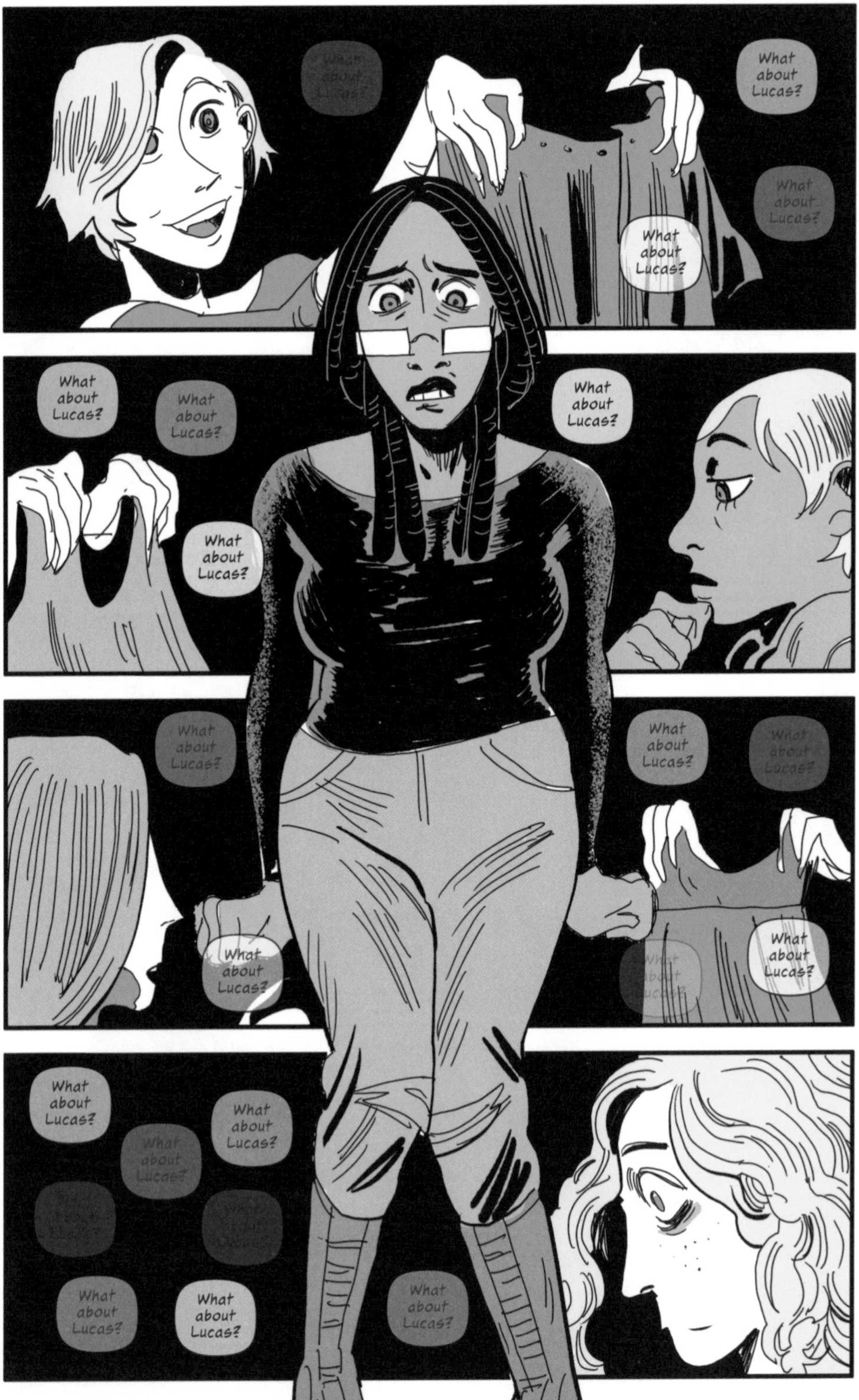

What about Lucas?
What about Lucas?
What about Lucas?
What about Lucas?
What about Lucas?
What about Lucas?
What about Lucas?
What about Lucas?
What about Lucas?
What about Lucas?
What about Lucas?
What about Lucas?
What about Lucas?
What about Lucas?
What about Lucas?
What about Lucas?
What about Lucas?
What about Lucas?
What about Lucas?
What about Lucas?

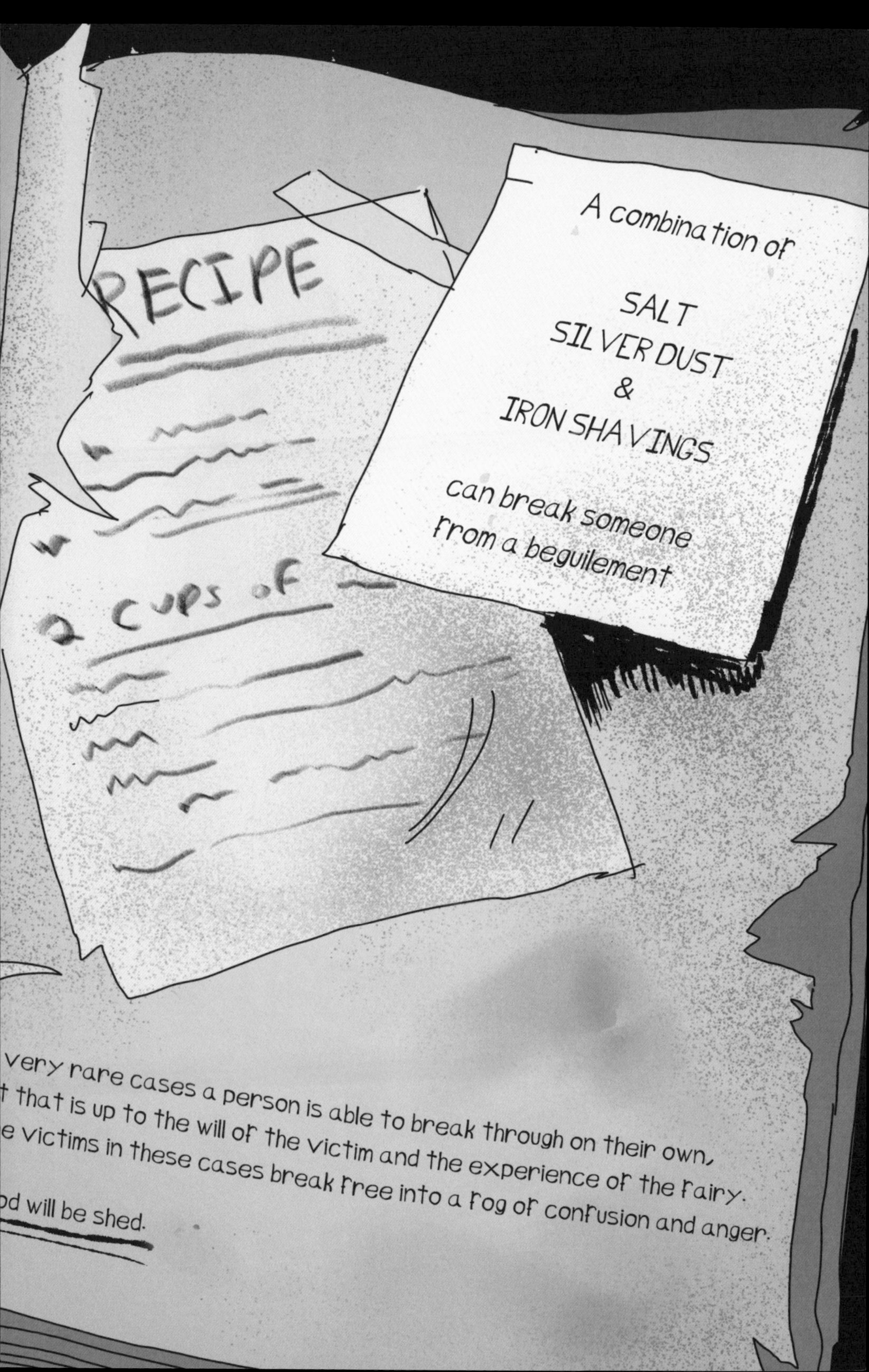
RECIPE
2 cups of
A combination of
SALT
SILVER DUST
&
IRON SHAVINGS
can break someone from a beguilement
very rare cases a person is able to break through on their own,
t that is up to the will of the victim and the experience of the fairy.
e victims in these cases break free into a fog of confusion and anger.
od will be shed.

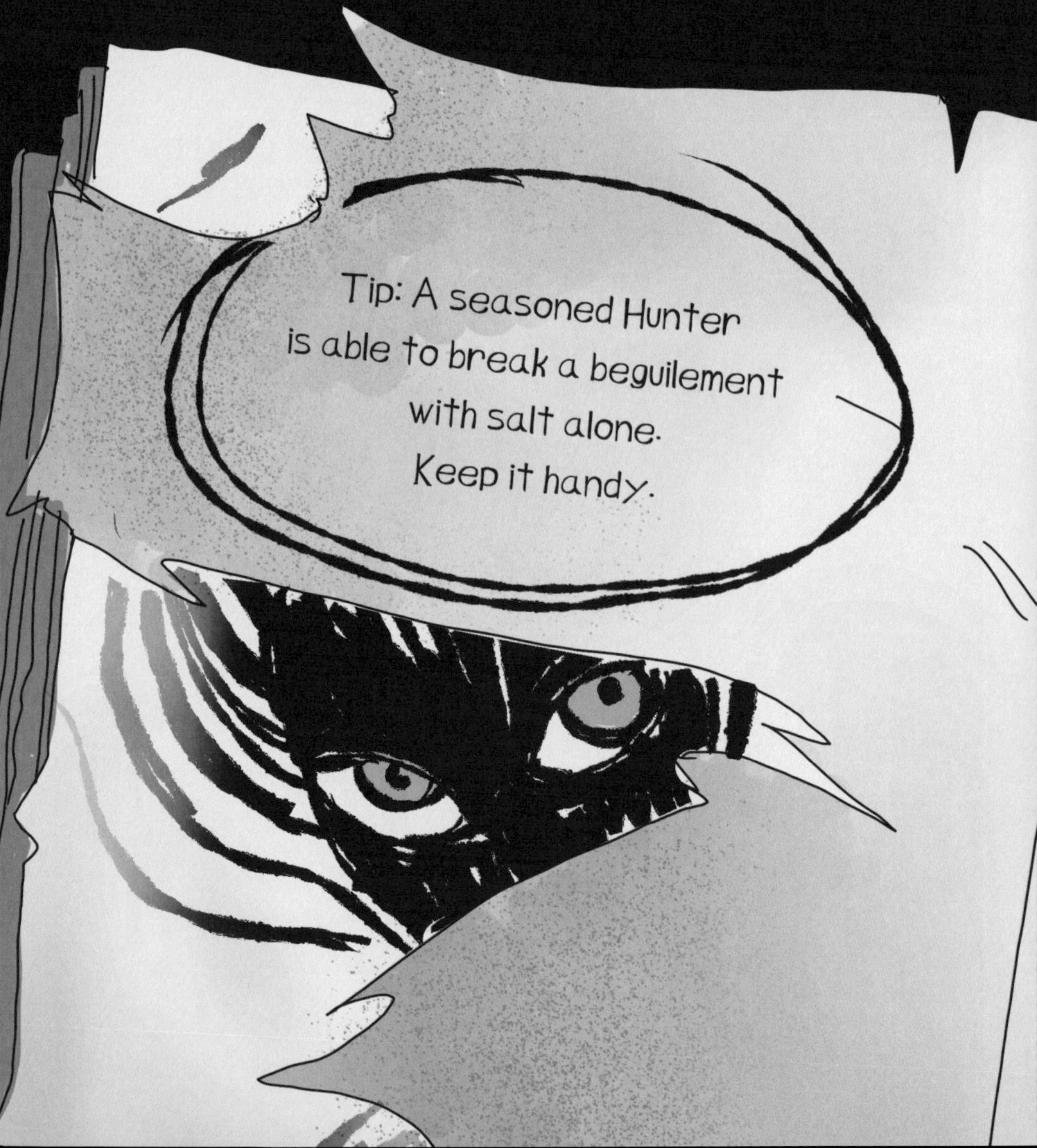
Tip: A seasoned Hunter is able to break a beguilement with salt alone. Keep it handy.

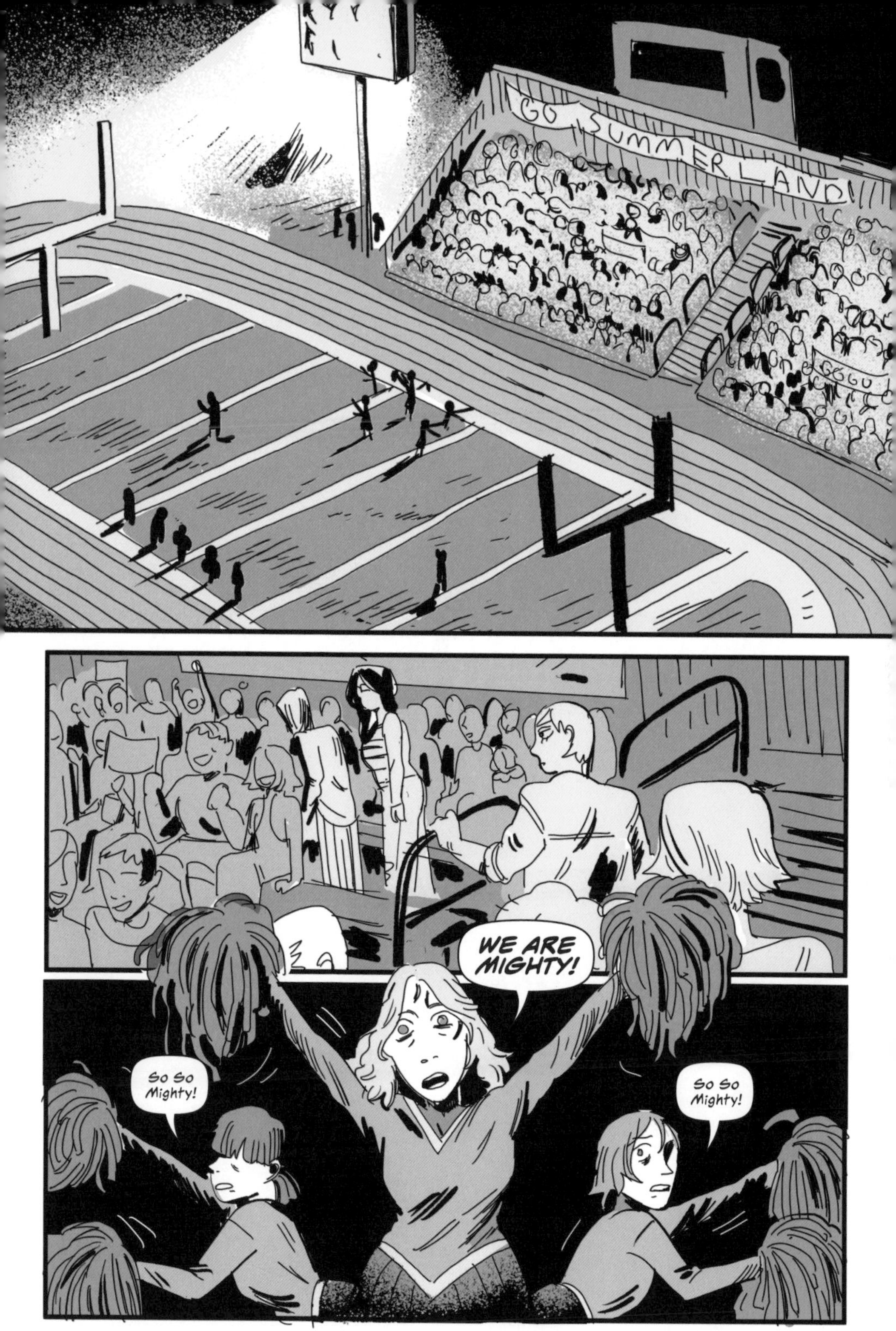
GO SUMMERLAND
WE ARE MIGHTY!
So So Mighty!
So So Mighty!

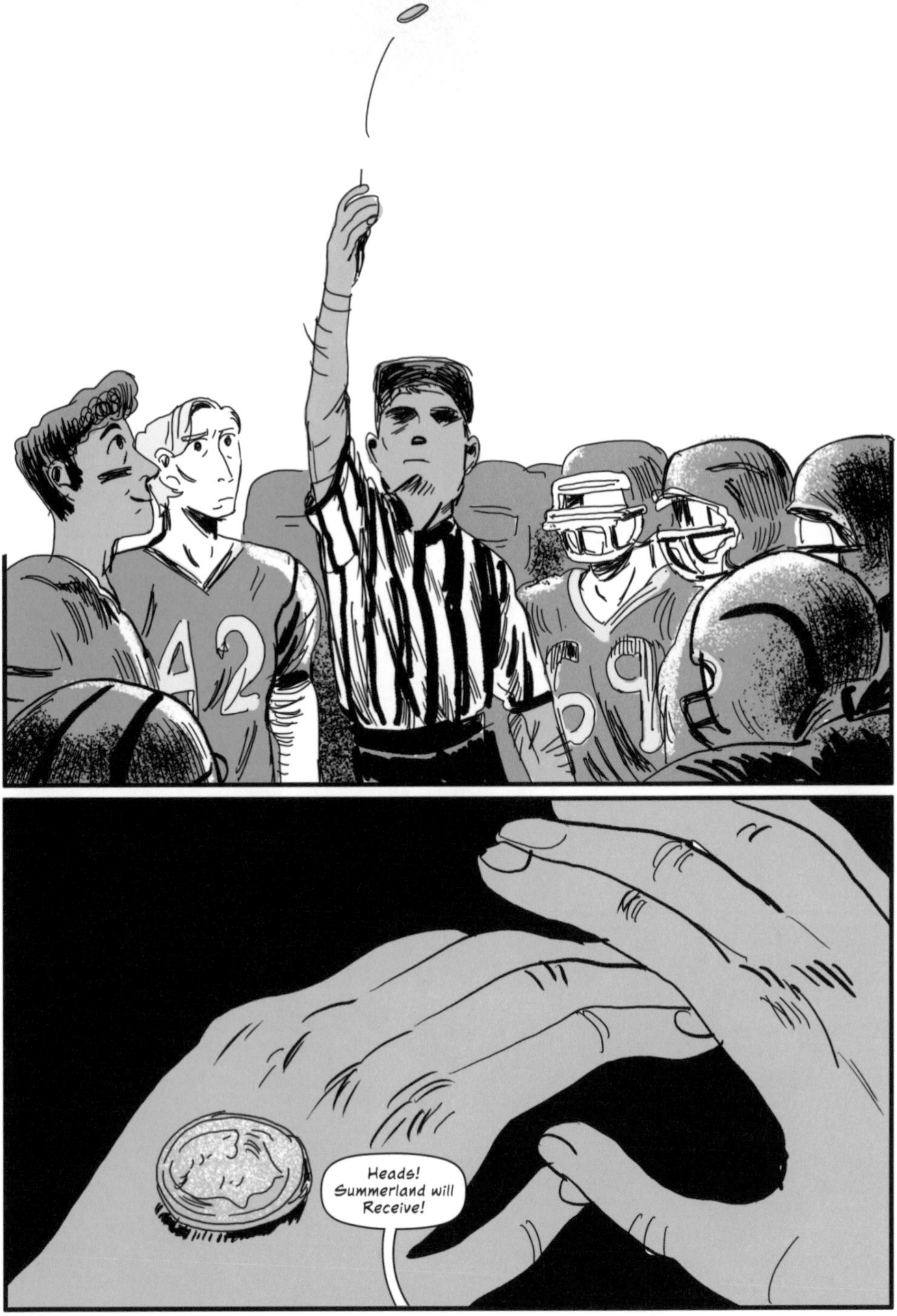
Heads! Summerland will Receive!

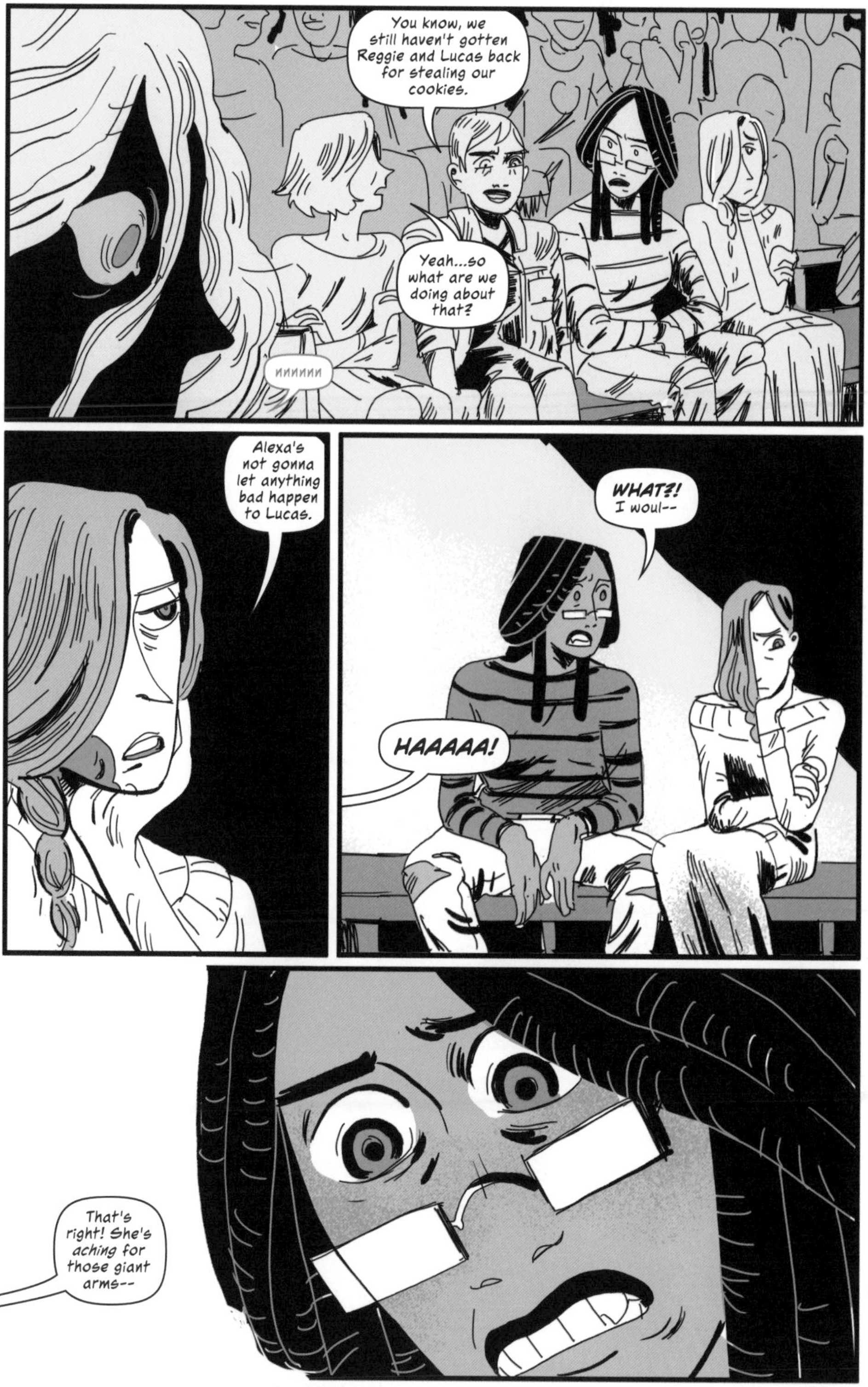
You know, we still haven't gotten Reggie and Lucas back for stealing our cookies.
Yeah...so what are we doing about that?
нинини
Alexa's not gonna let anything bad happen to Lucas.
WHAT?! I woul--
HAAAAA!
That's right! She's aching for those giant arms--

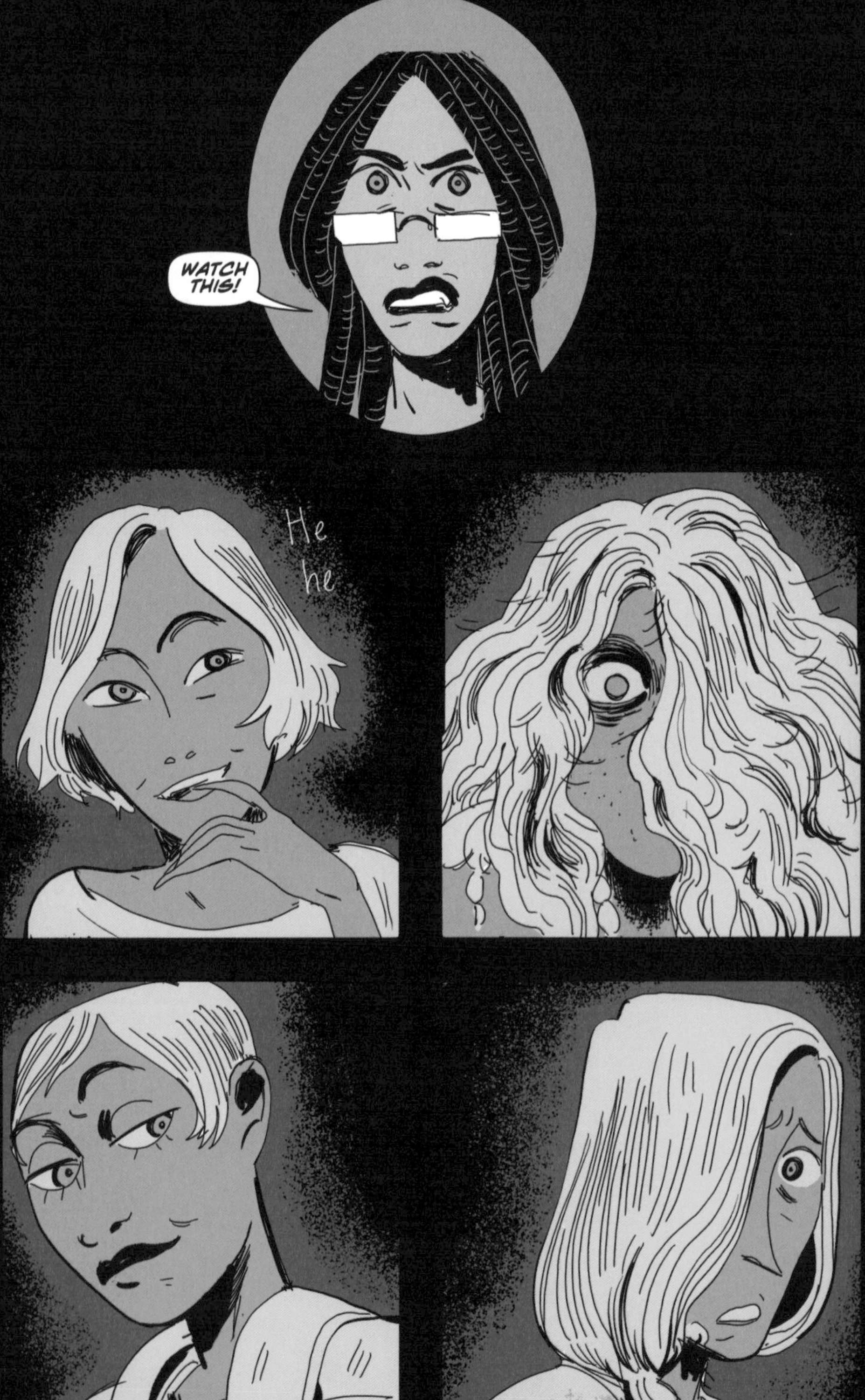
WATCH THIS!
He he

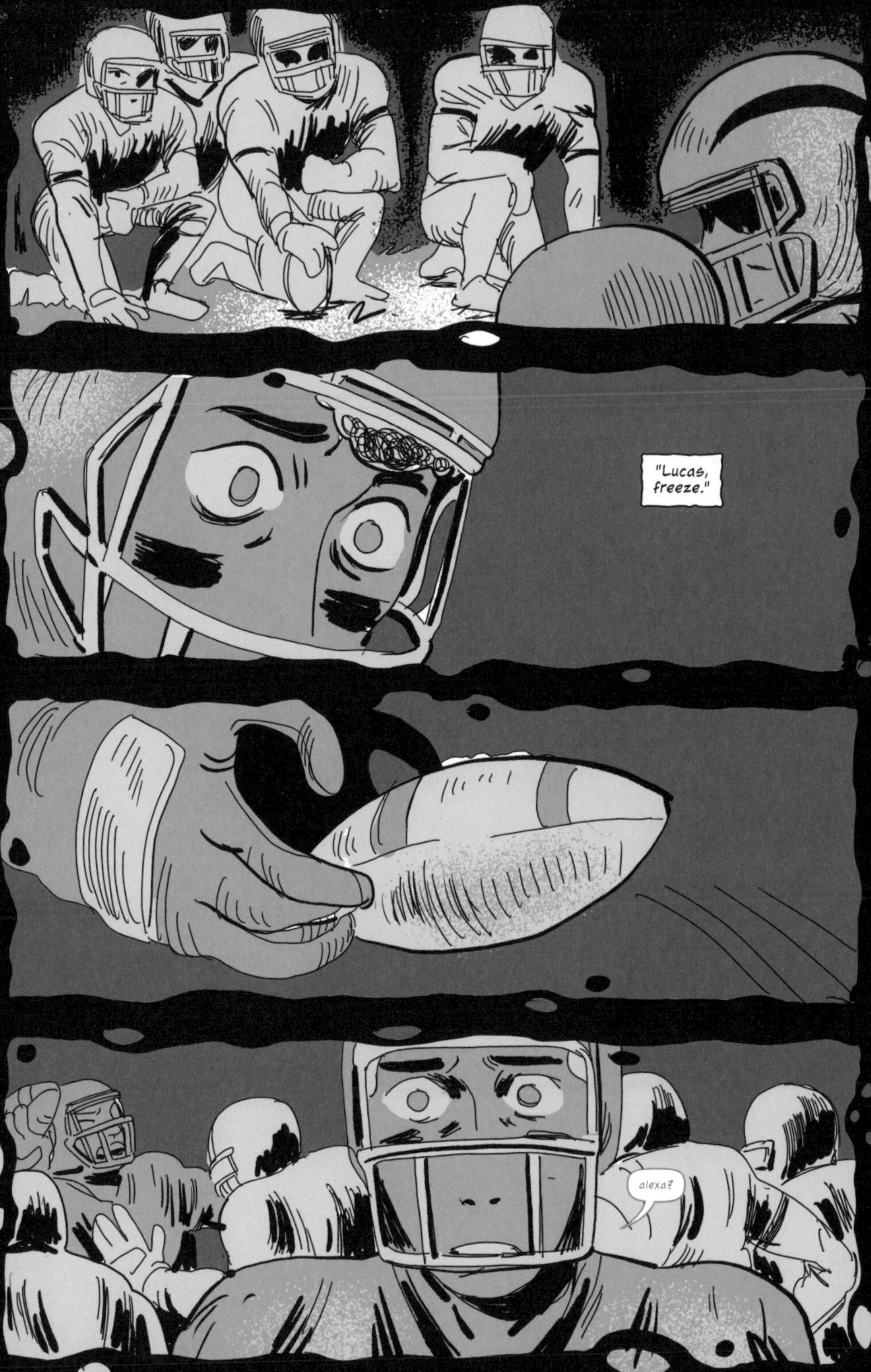
"Lucas, freeze."
alexa?

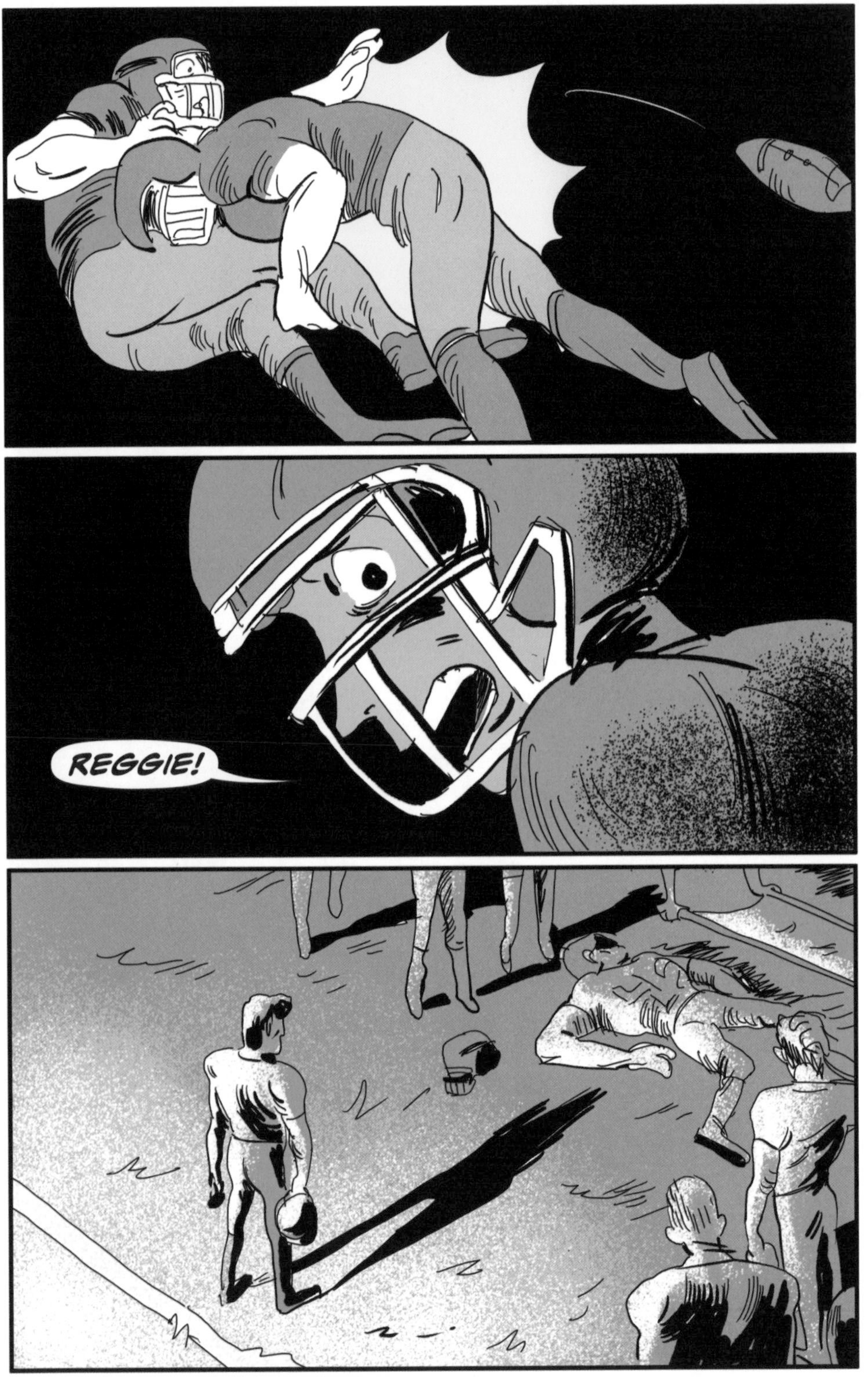
REGGIE!

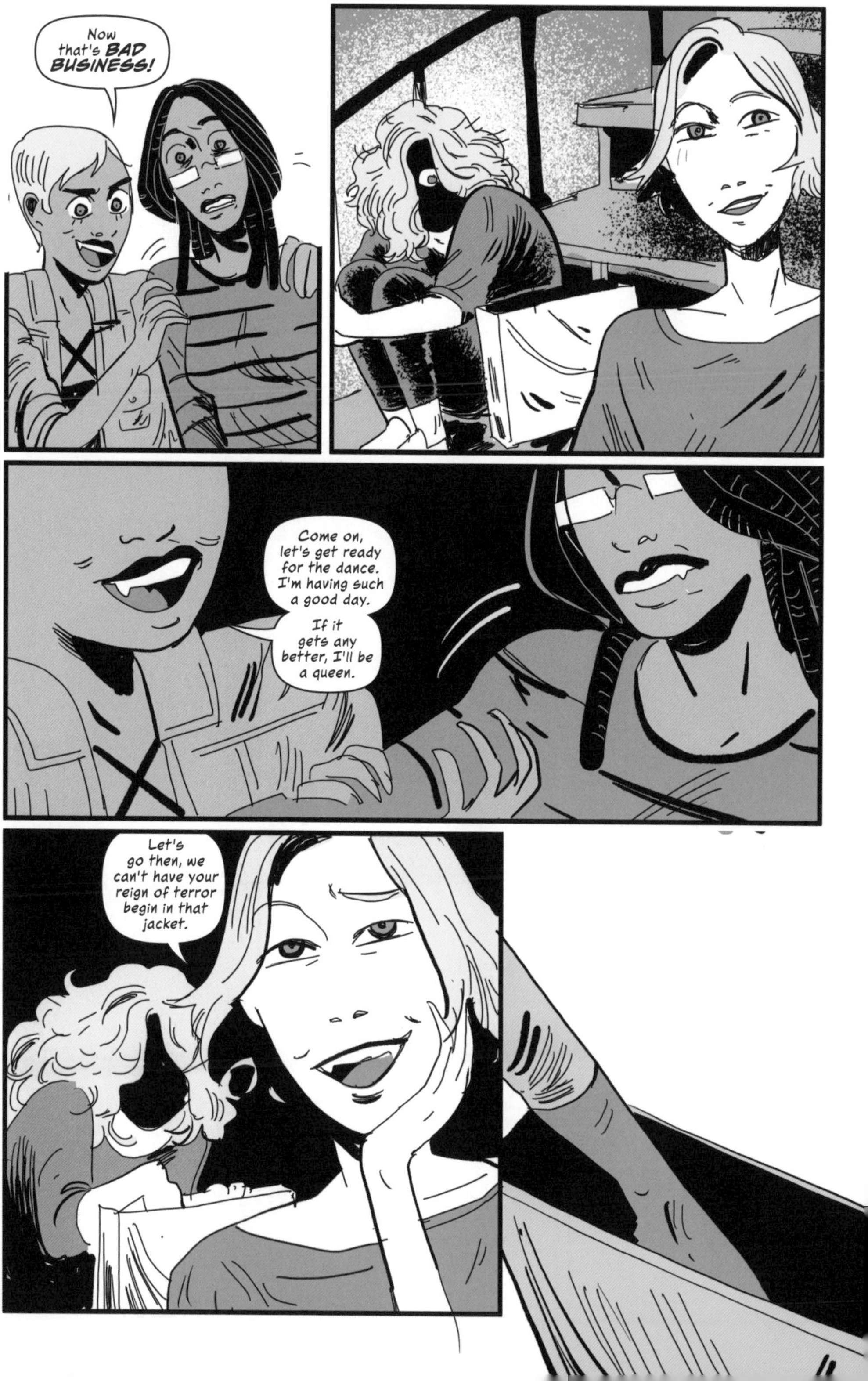
Now that's BAD BUSINESS!
Come on, let's get ready for the dance. I'm having such a good day.
If it gets any better, I'll be a queen.
Let's go then, we can't have your reign of terror begin in that jacket.

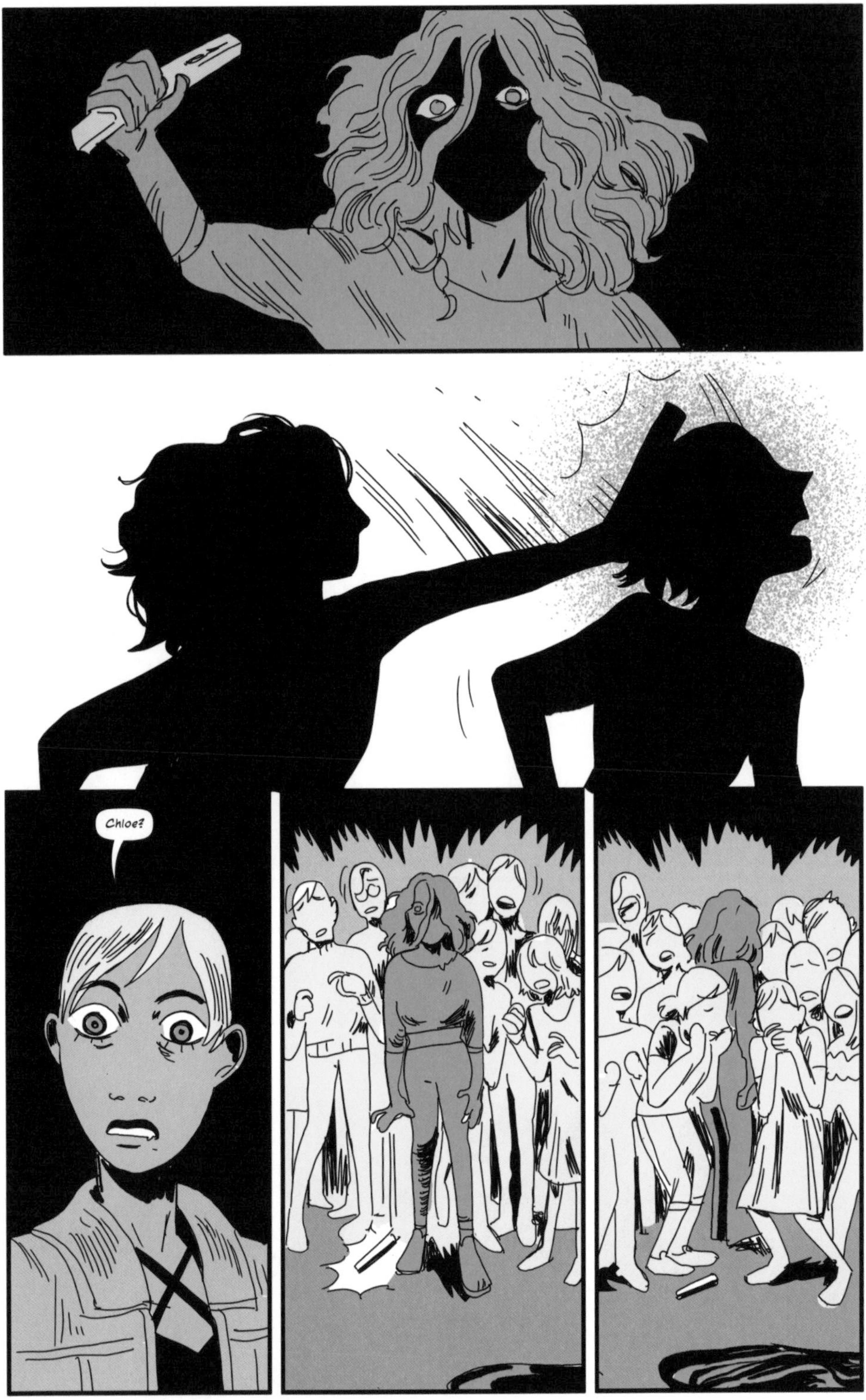
Chloe?

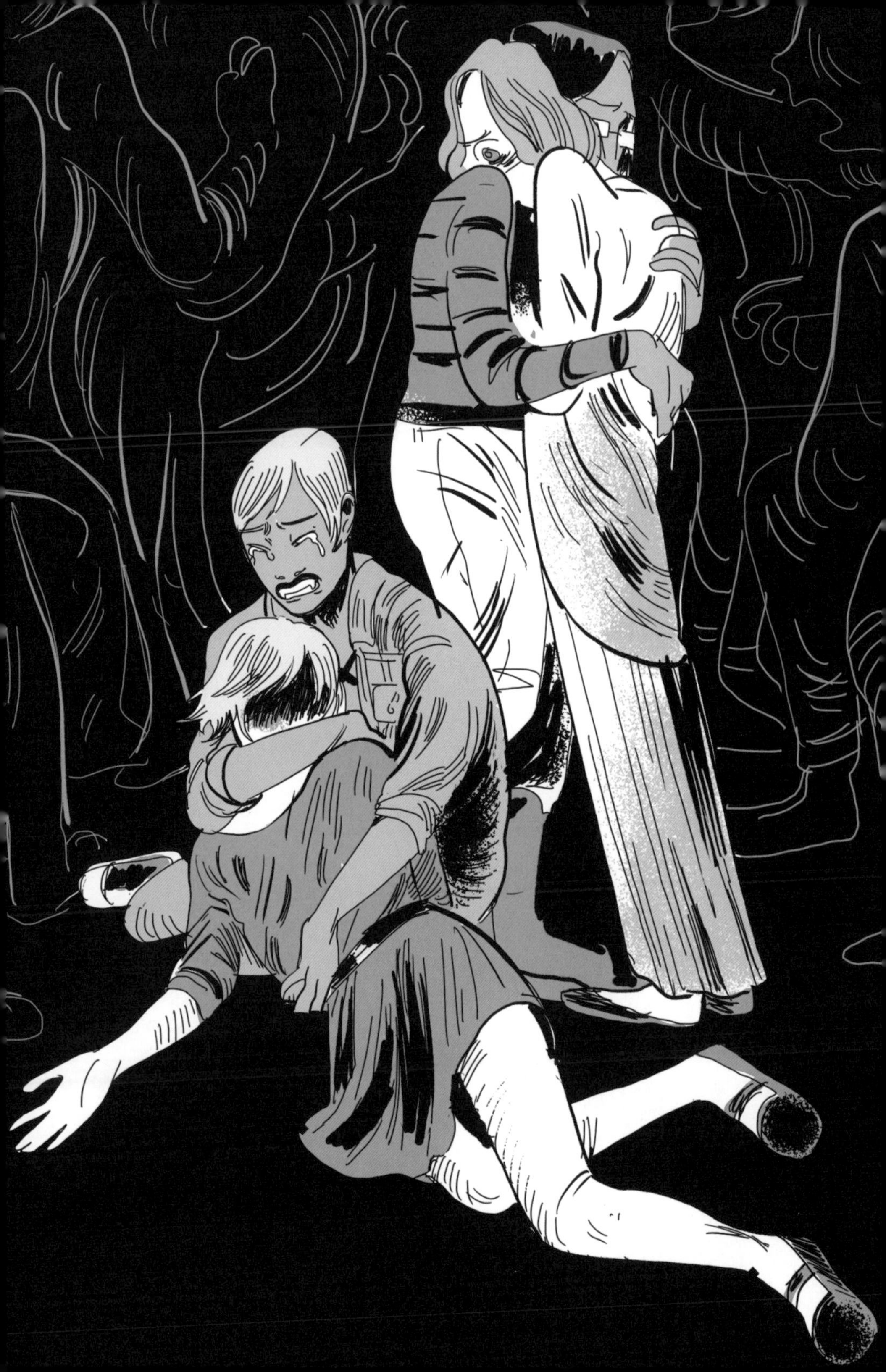

Fay; And Their Mindstate

Faires get what they want from birth.
Through magic and influence, they are rarely told no.
Filling their days with joy and merriment.

...Which makes the fallout of their wrath
that much more dangerous.
Fay hold grudges for lifetimes,
and if you have particularly harmed their kin,
nothing can save you.

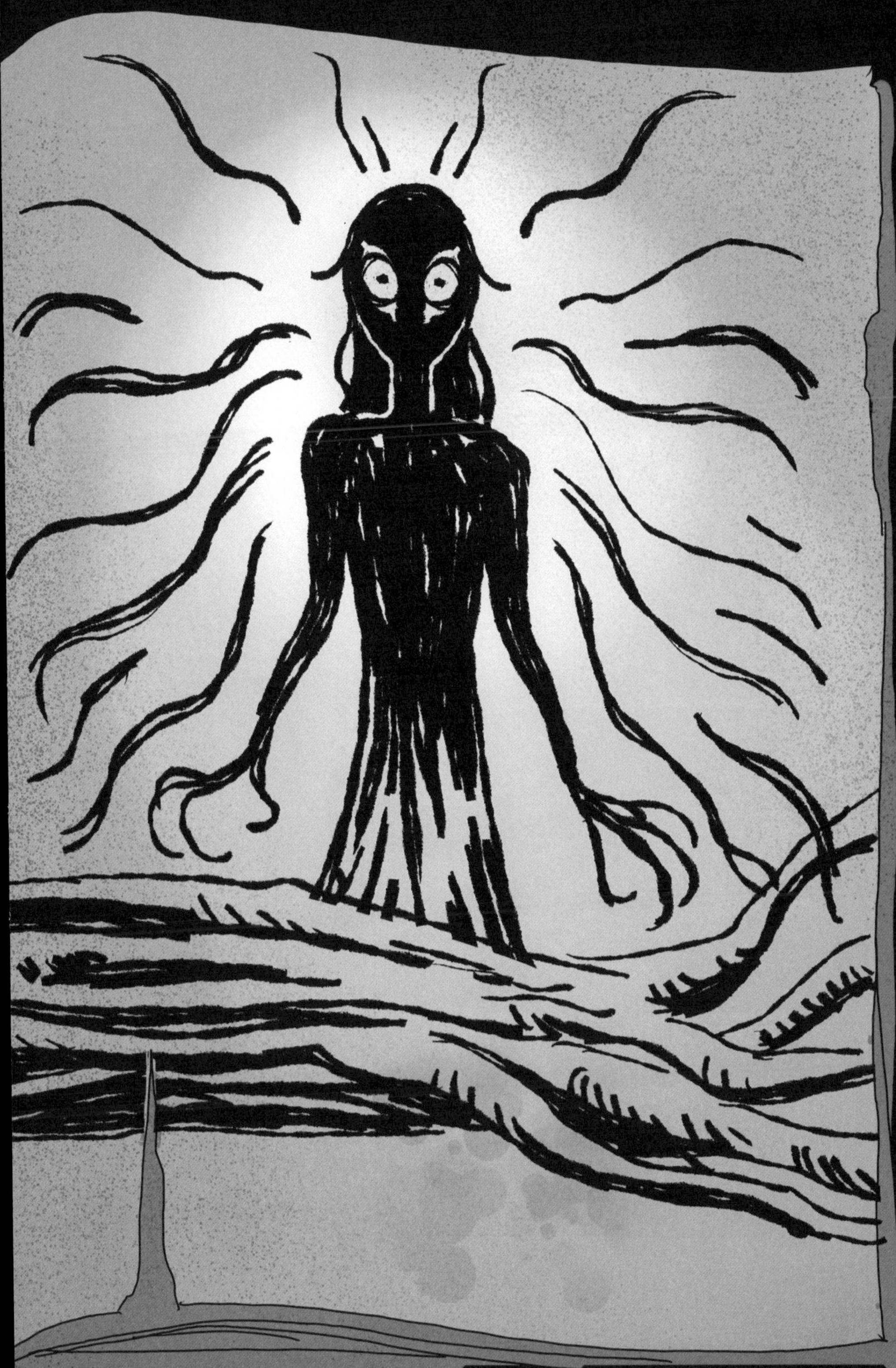

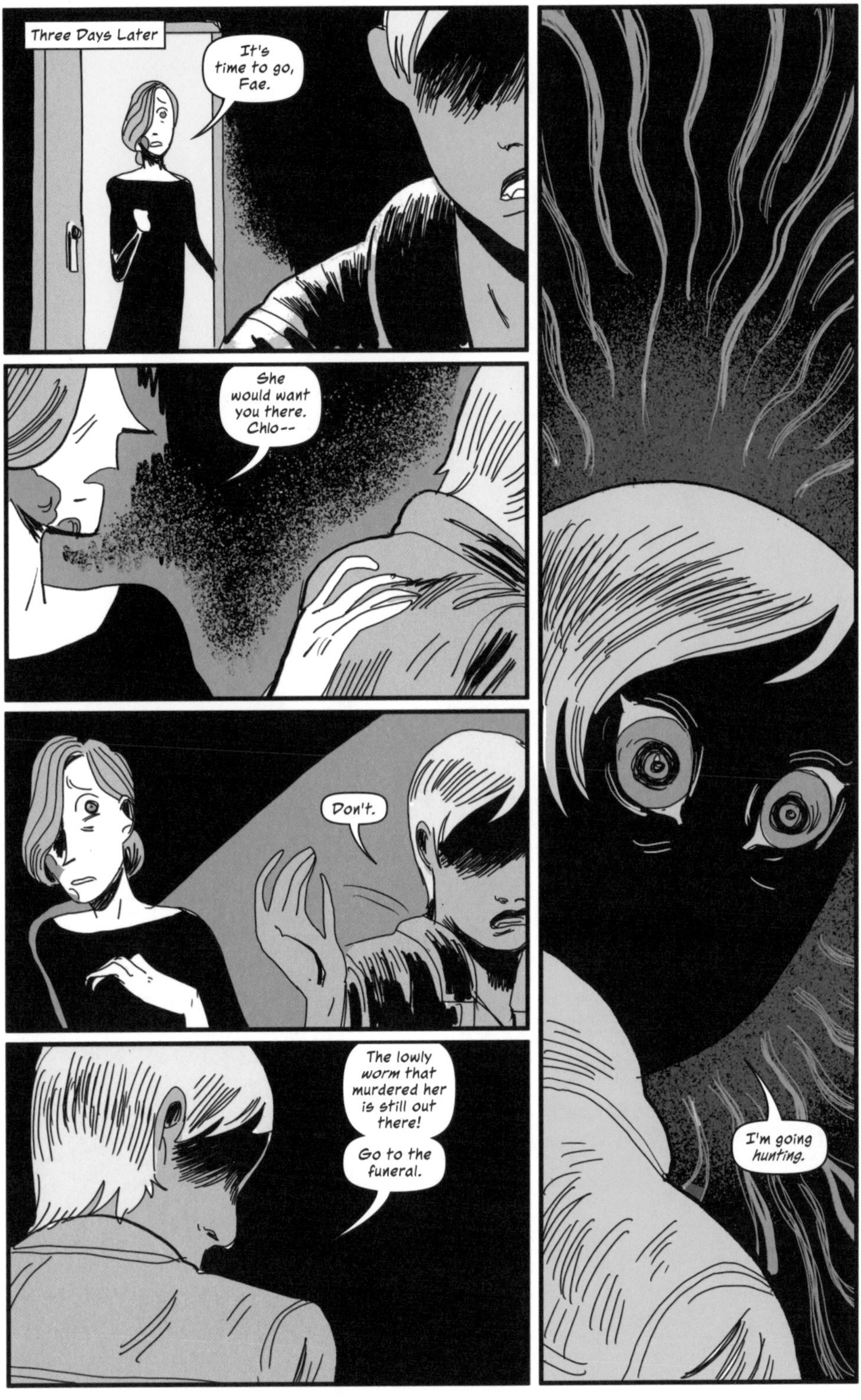
Three Days Later
It's time to go, Fae.
She would want you there. Chlo--
Don't.
The lowly *worm* that murdered her is still out there!
Go to the funeral.
I'm going *hunting.*

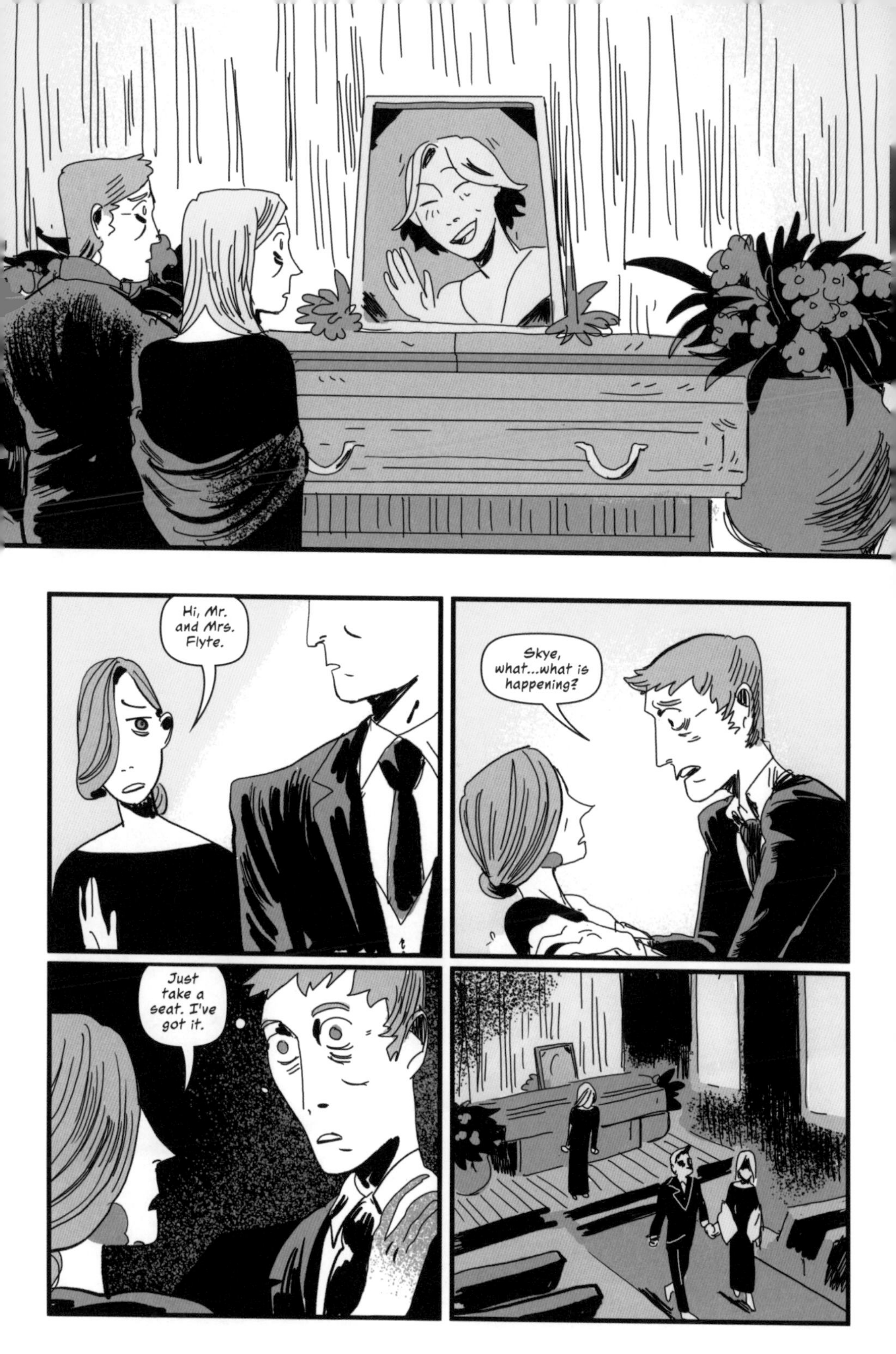
Hi, Mr. and Mrs. Flyte.
Skye, what...what is happening?
Just take a seat. I've got it.

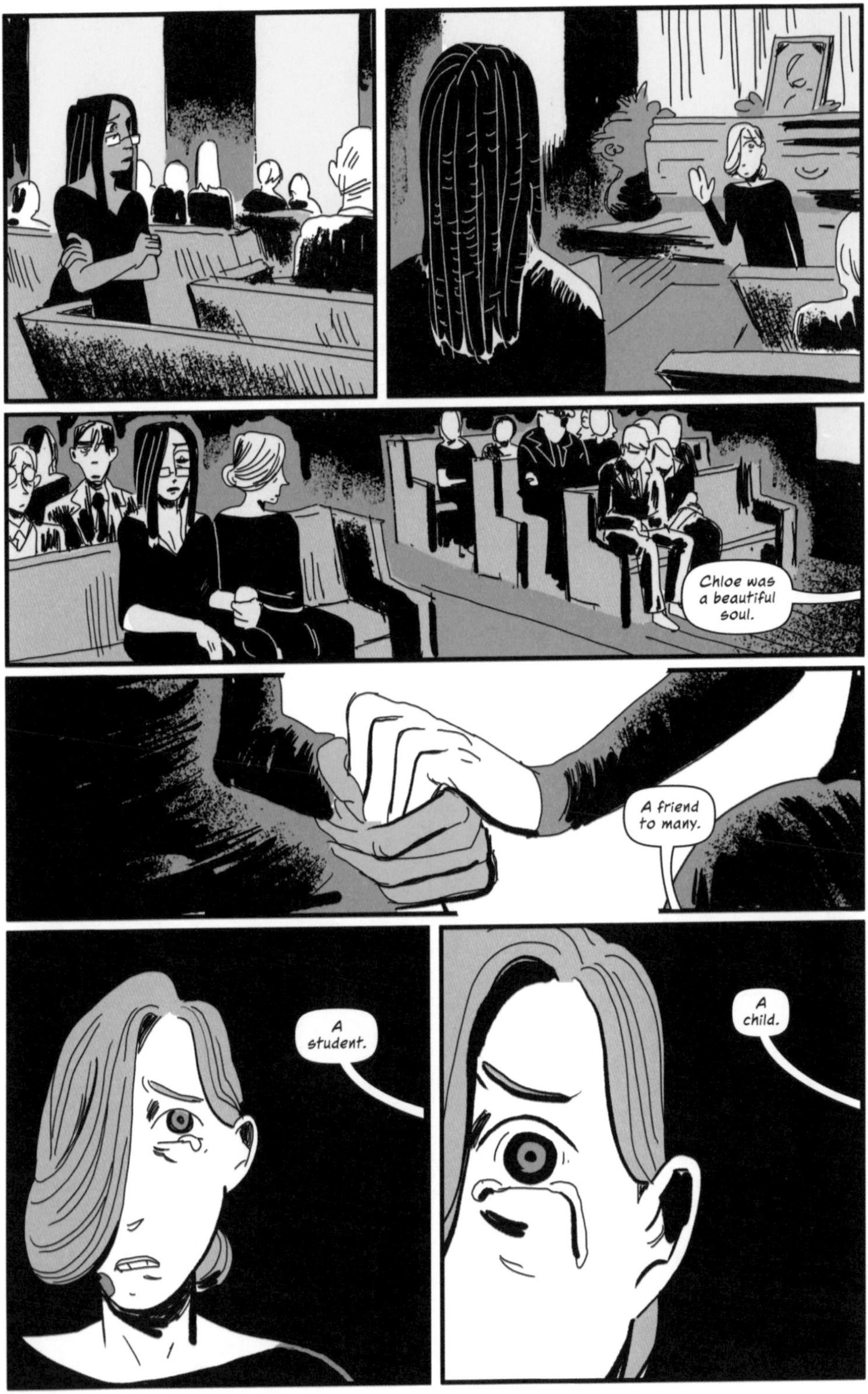
Chloe was a beautiful soul.
A friend to many.
A student.
A child.

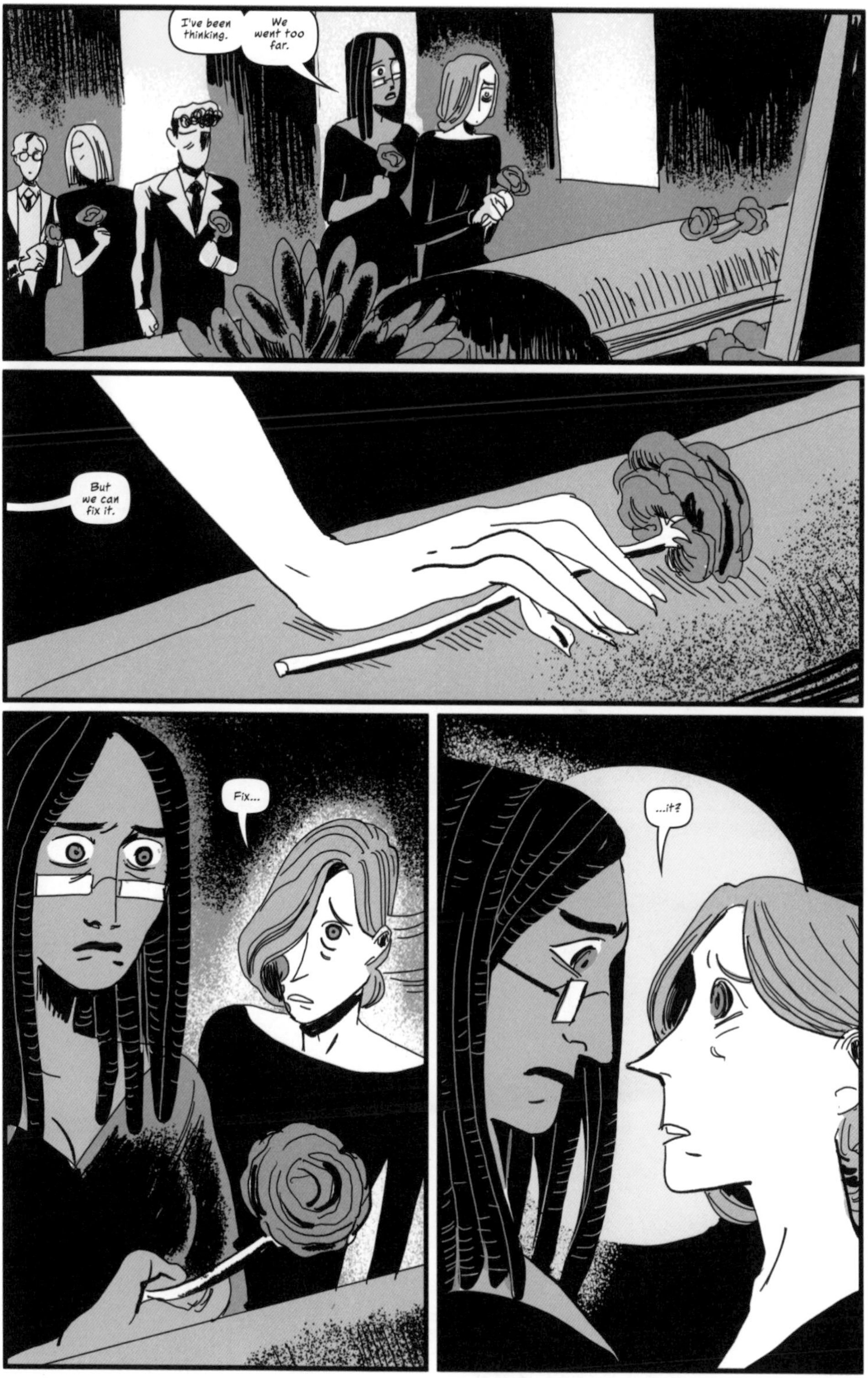
I've been thinking.
We went too far.
But we can fix it.
Fix...
...it?

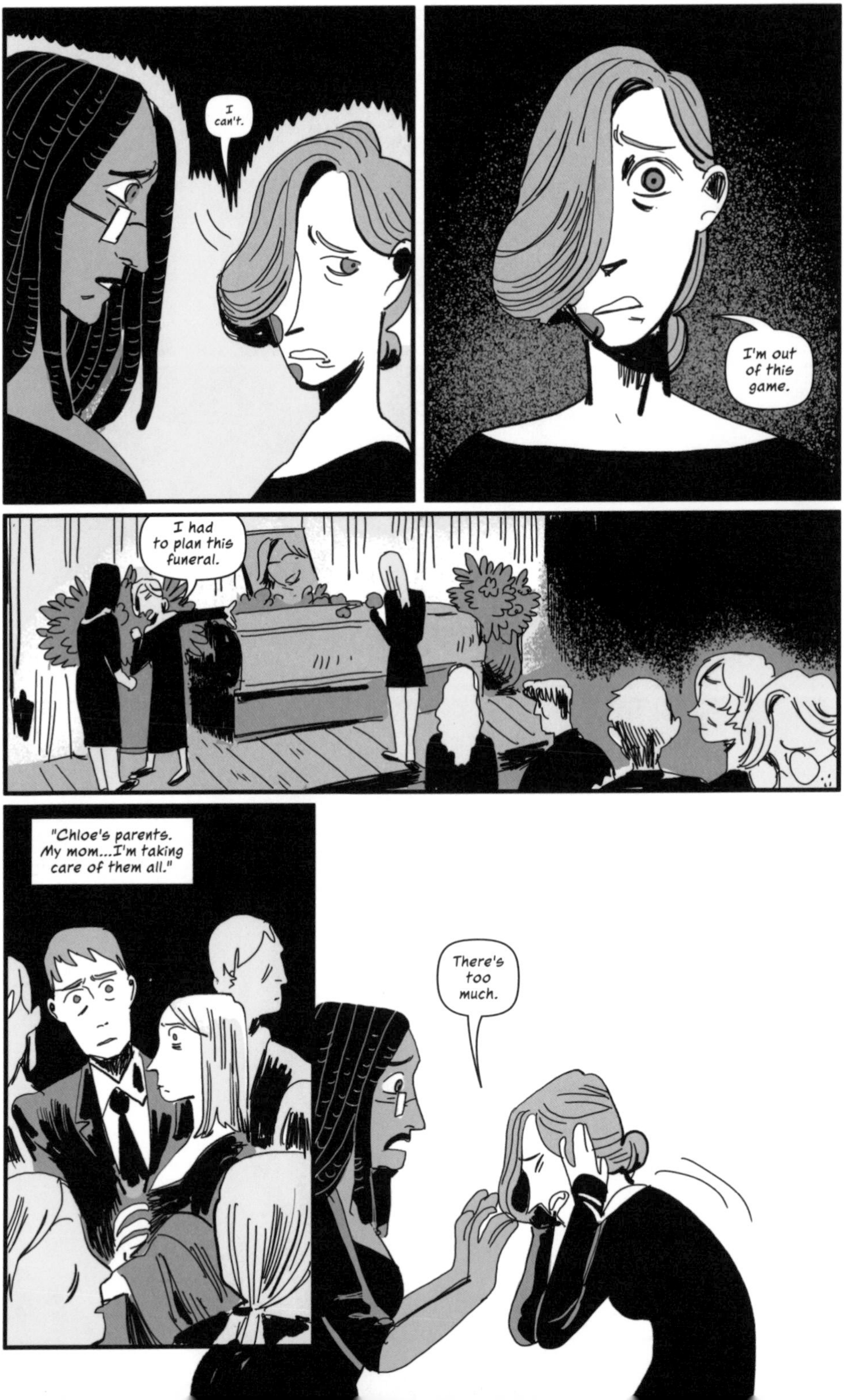
I can't.
I'm out of this game.
I had to plan this funeral.
"Chloe's parents. My mom...I'm taking care of them all."
There's too much.

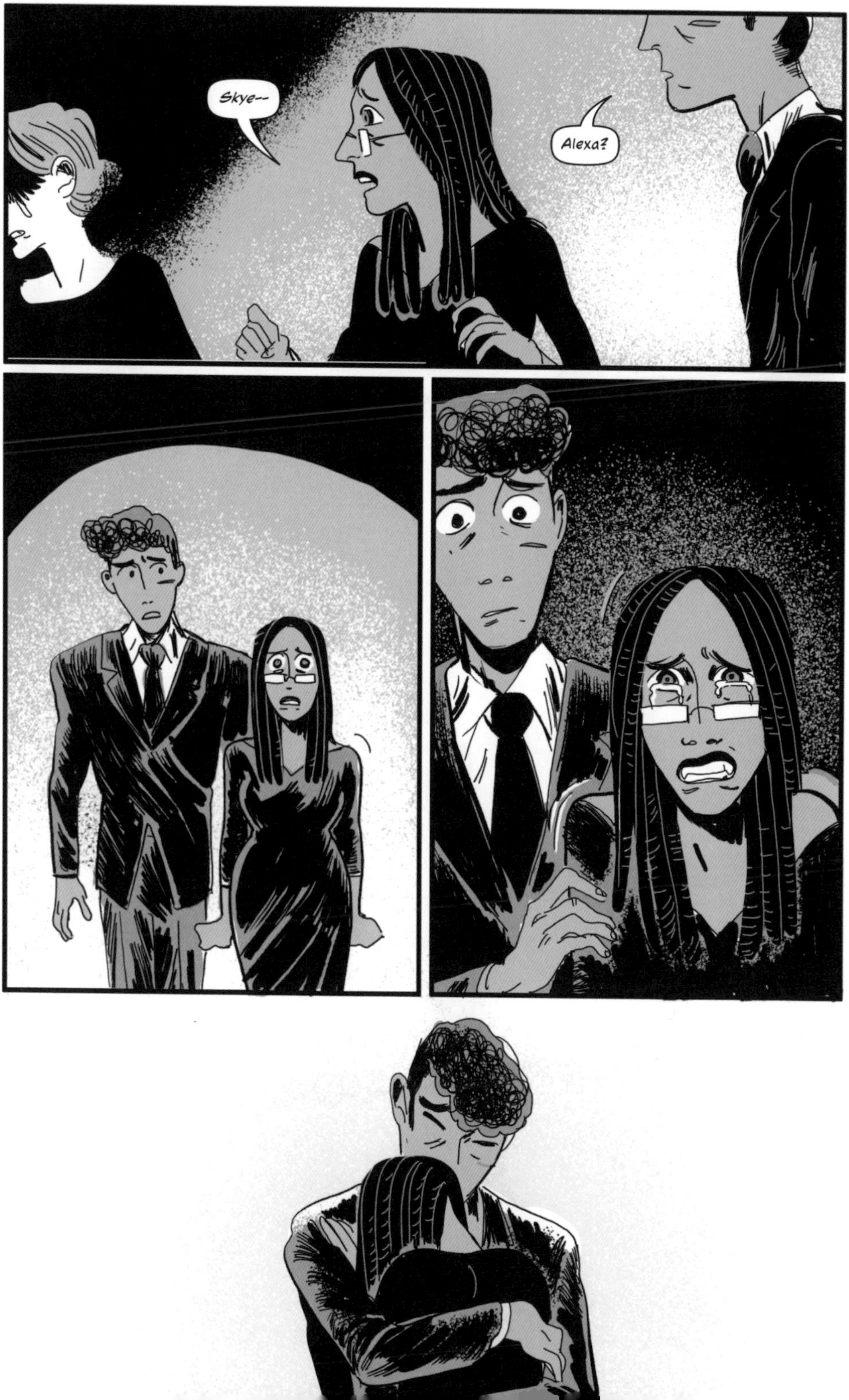
Skye--
Alexa?

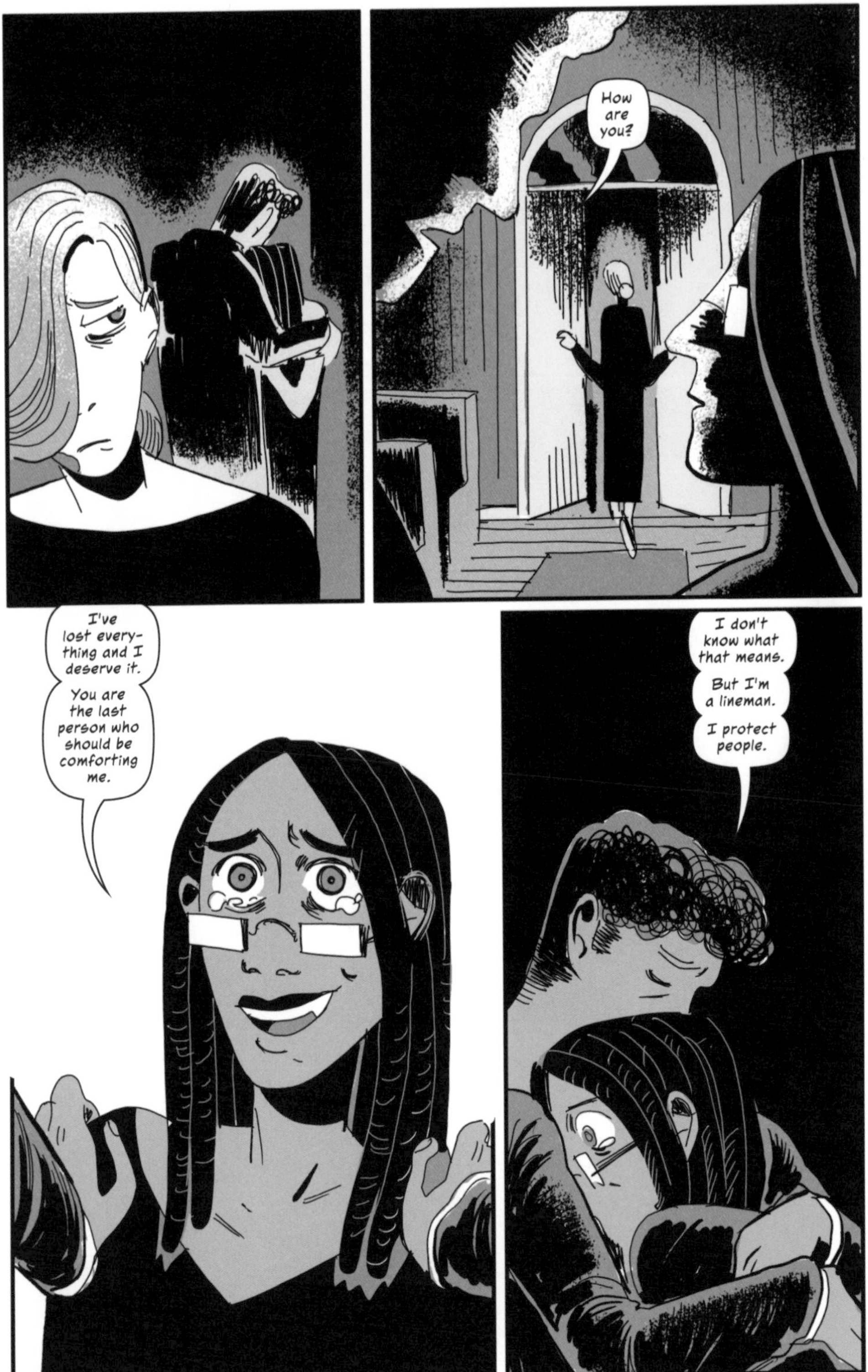
How are you?
I've lost everything and I deserve it.
You are the last person who should be comforting me.
I don't know what that means.
But I'm a lineman.
I protect people.

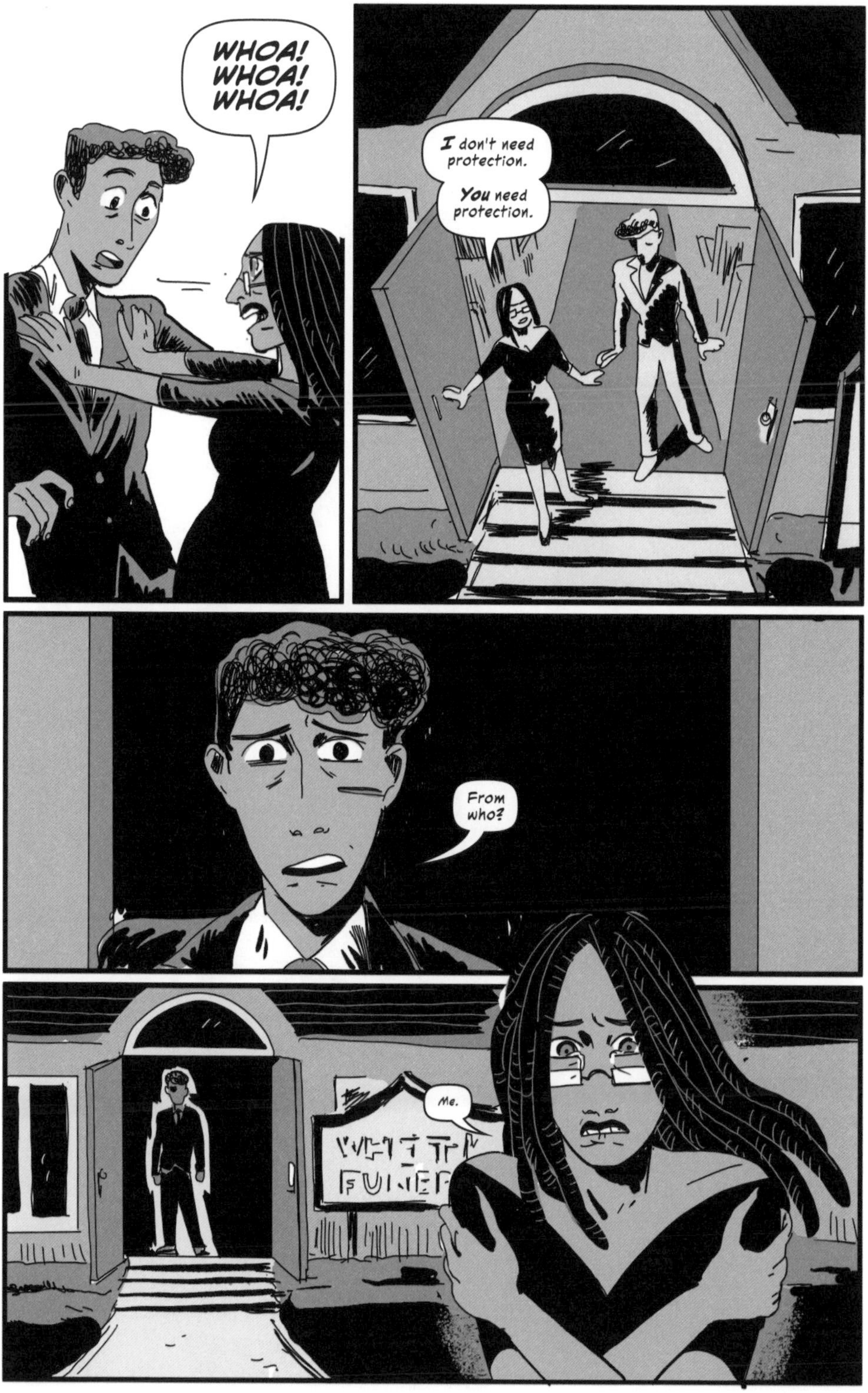
WHOA! WHOA! WHOA!
I don't need protection.
You need protection.
From who?
Me.

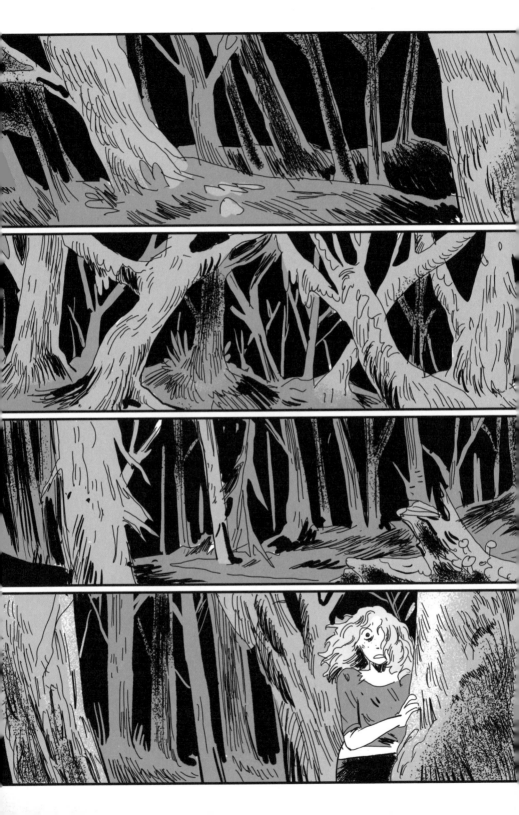

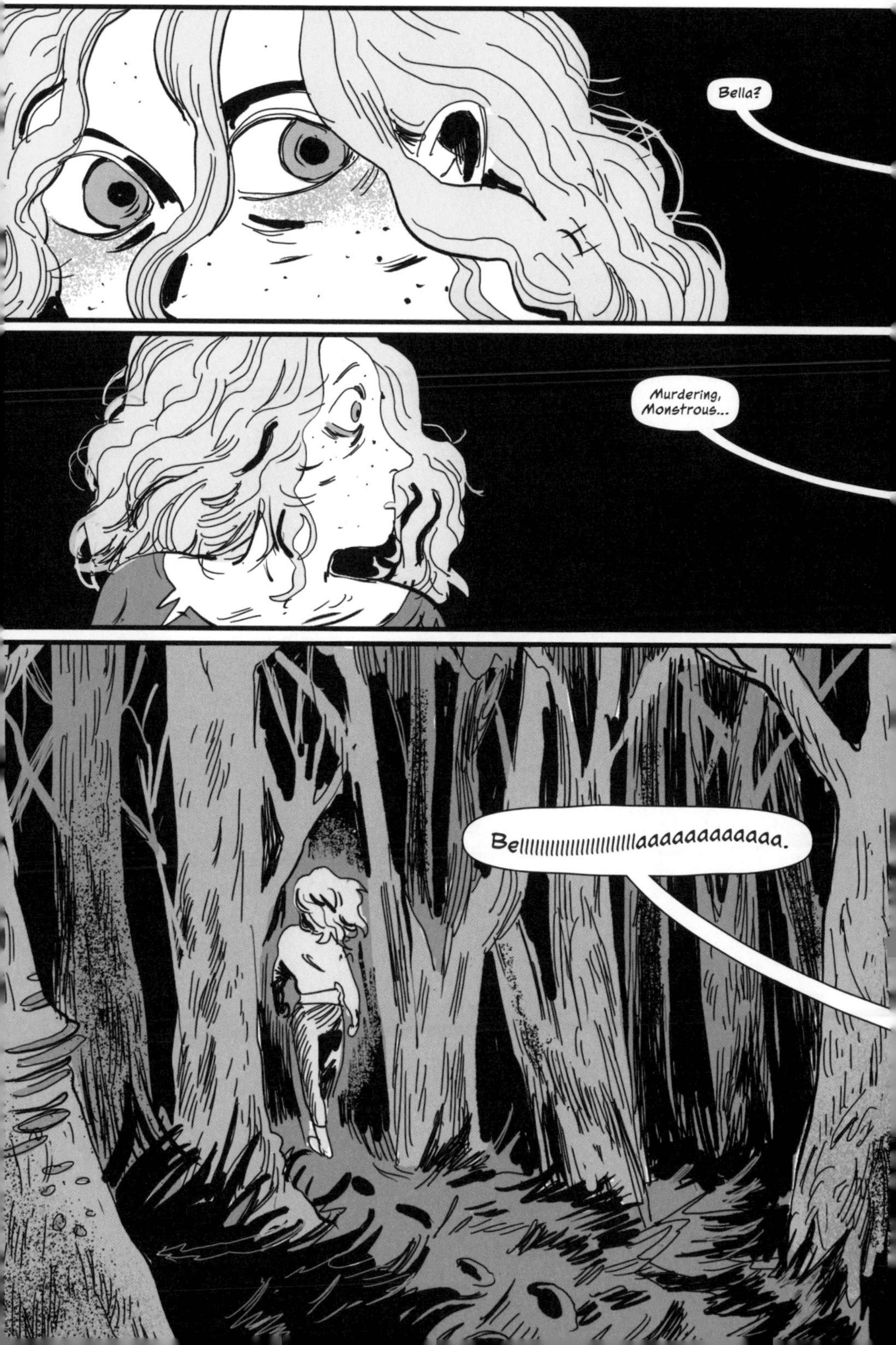
Bella?
Murdering, Monstrous...
Bellllllllllllllllllllllaaaaaaaaaaaa.

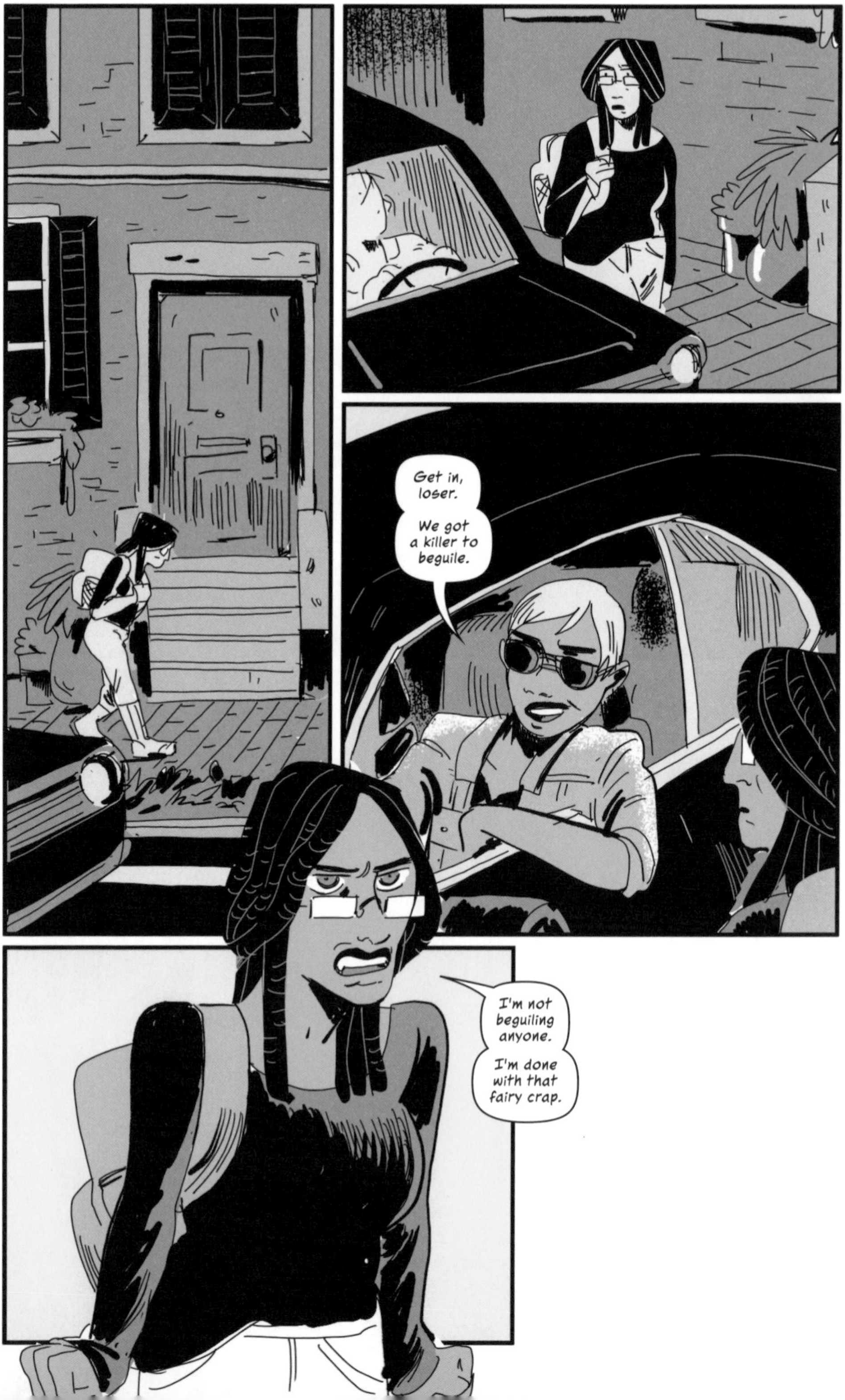
Get in, loser.
We got a killer to beguile.
I'm not beguiling anyone.
I'm done with that fairy crap.

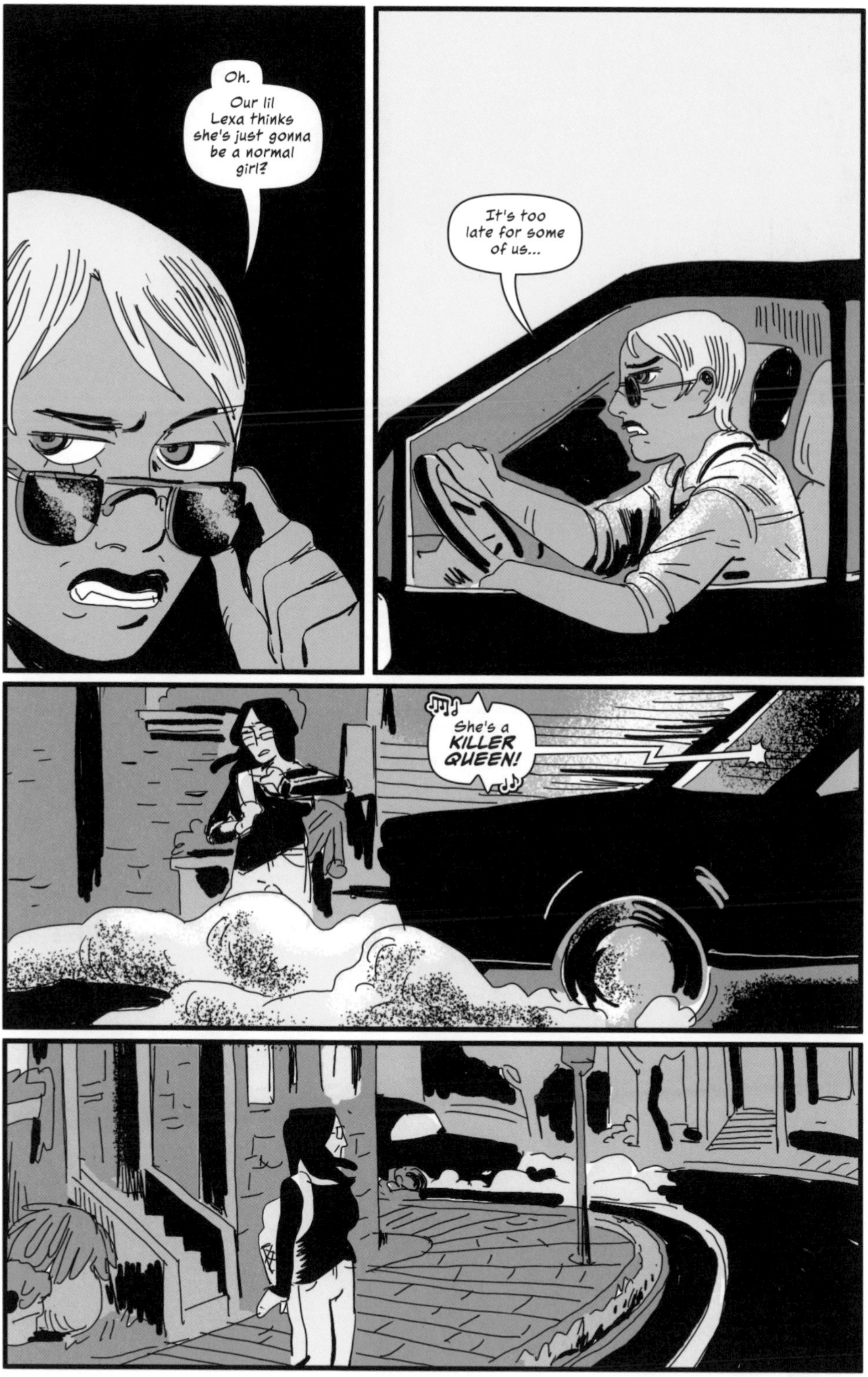
Oh.
Our lil Lexa thinks she's just gonna be a normal girl!?
It's too late for some of us...
She's a KILLER QUEEN!

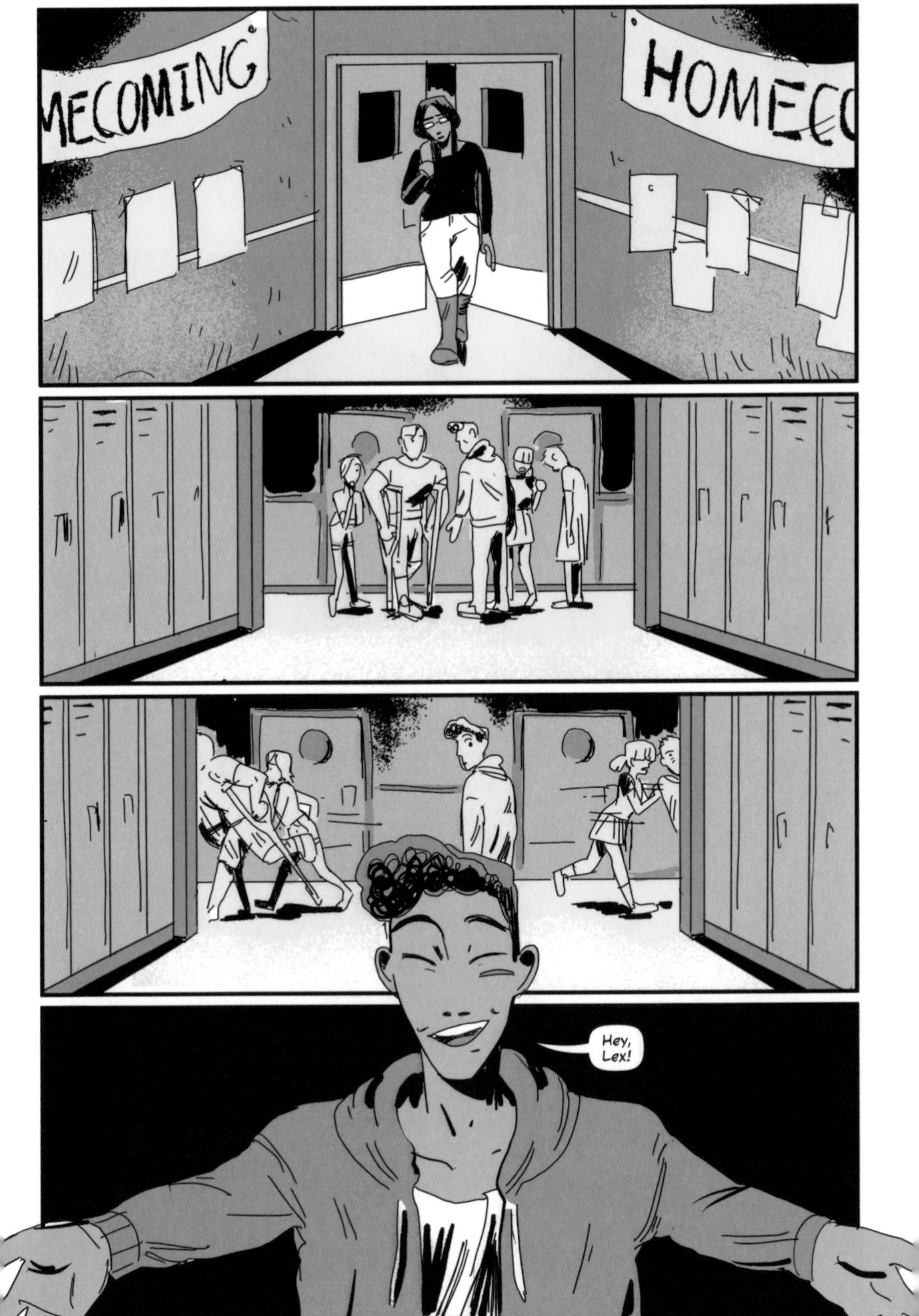
MECOMING
HOMECO
Hey, Lex!

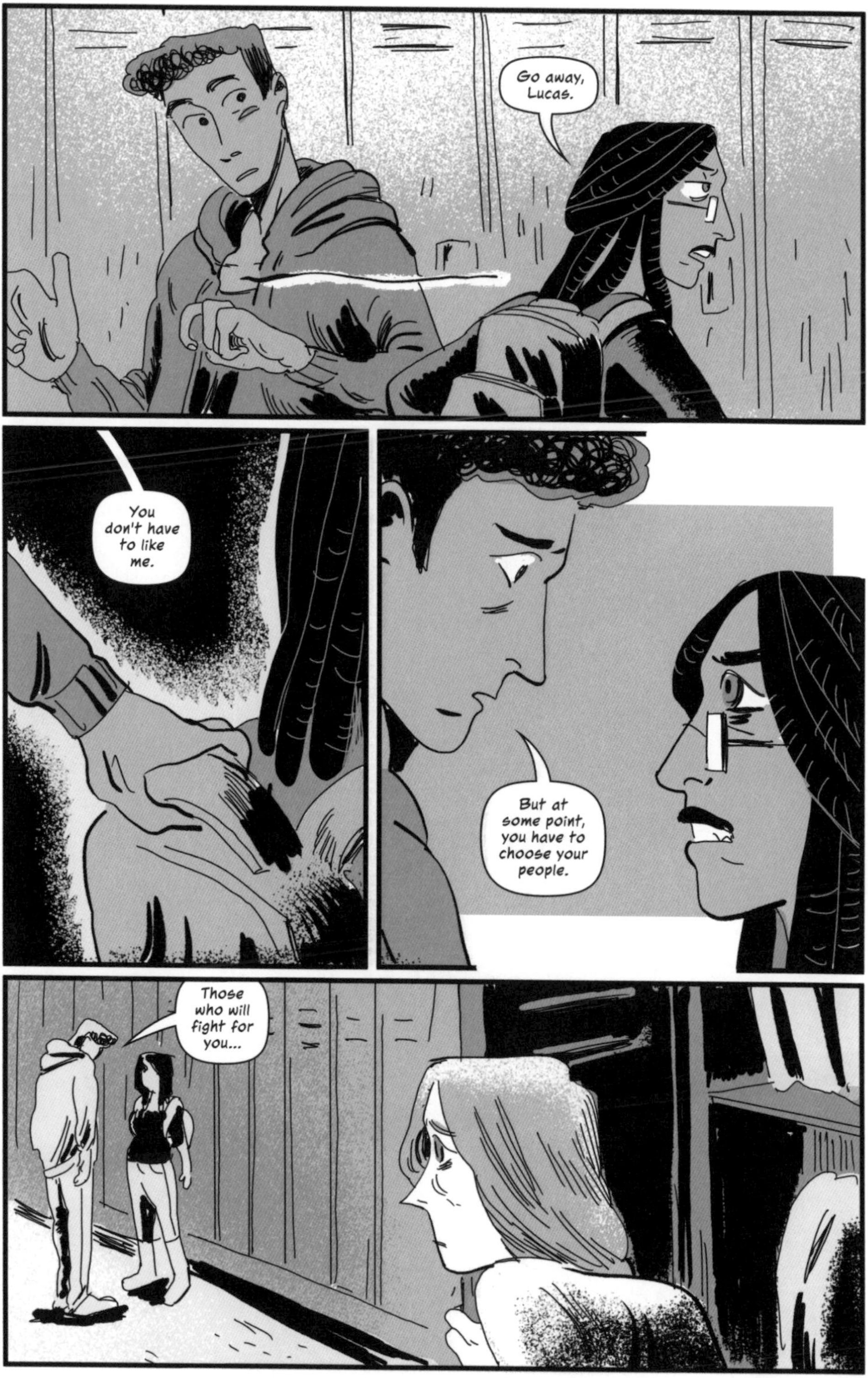
Go away, Lucas.
You don't have to like me.
But at some point, you have to choose your people.
Those who will fight for you...

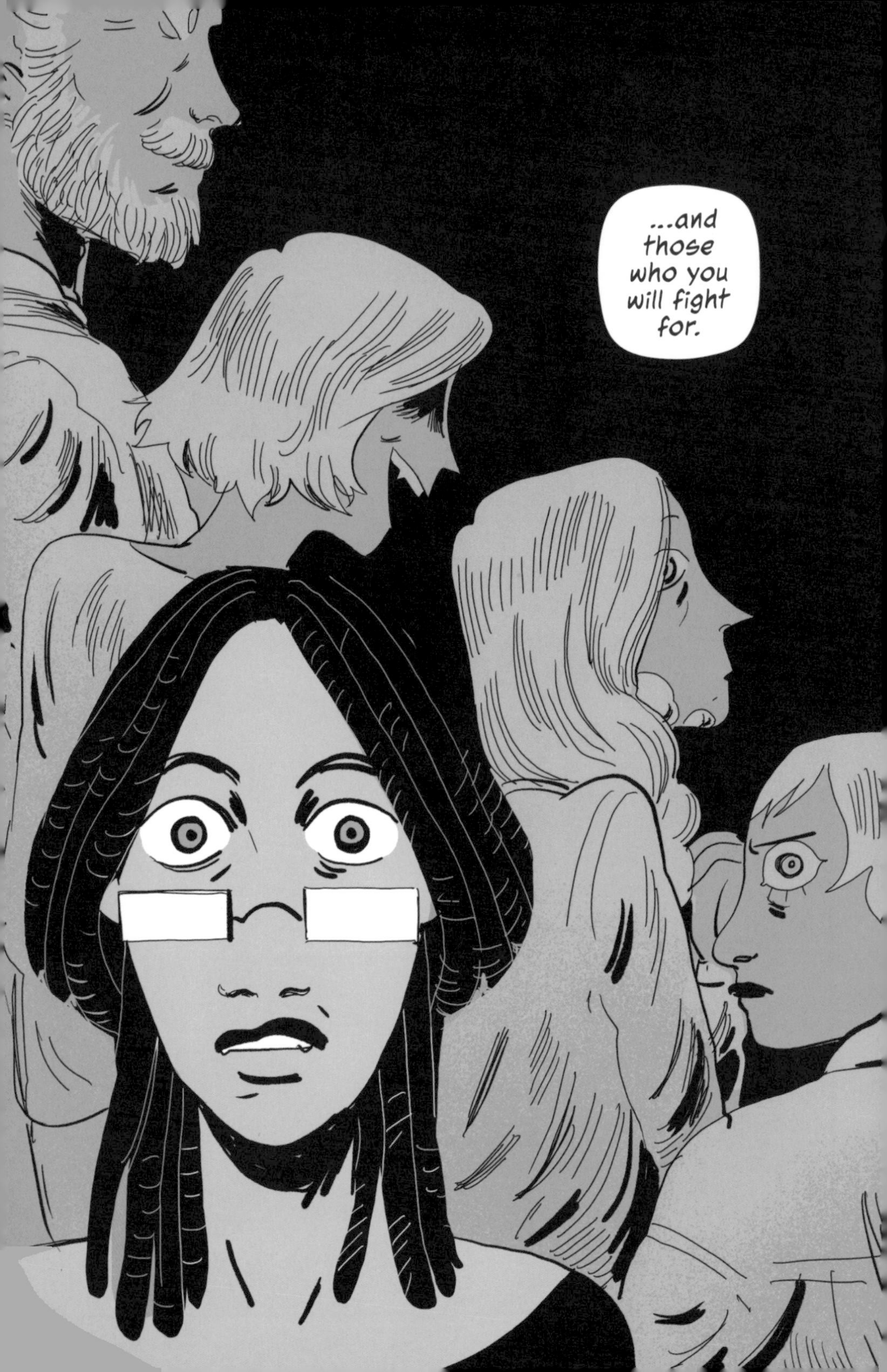
...and those who you will fight for.

The Outcast

Not much is known about this mysterious figure.
he appeared many years ago and killed every Hunter that crossed her path.
It has only been through careful negotiations
that a truce was struck.

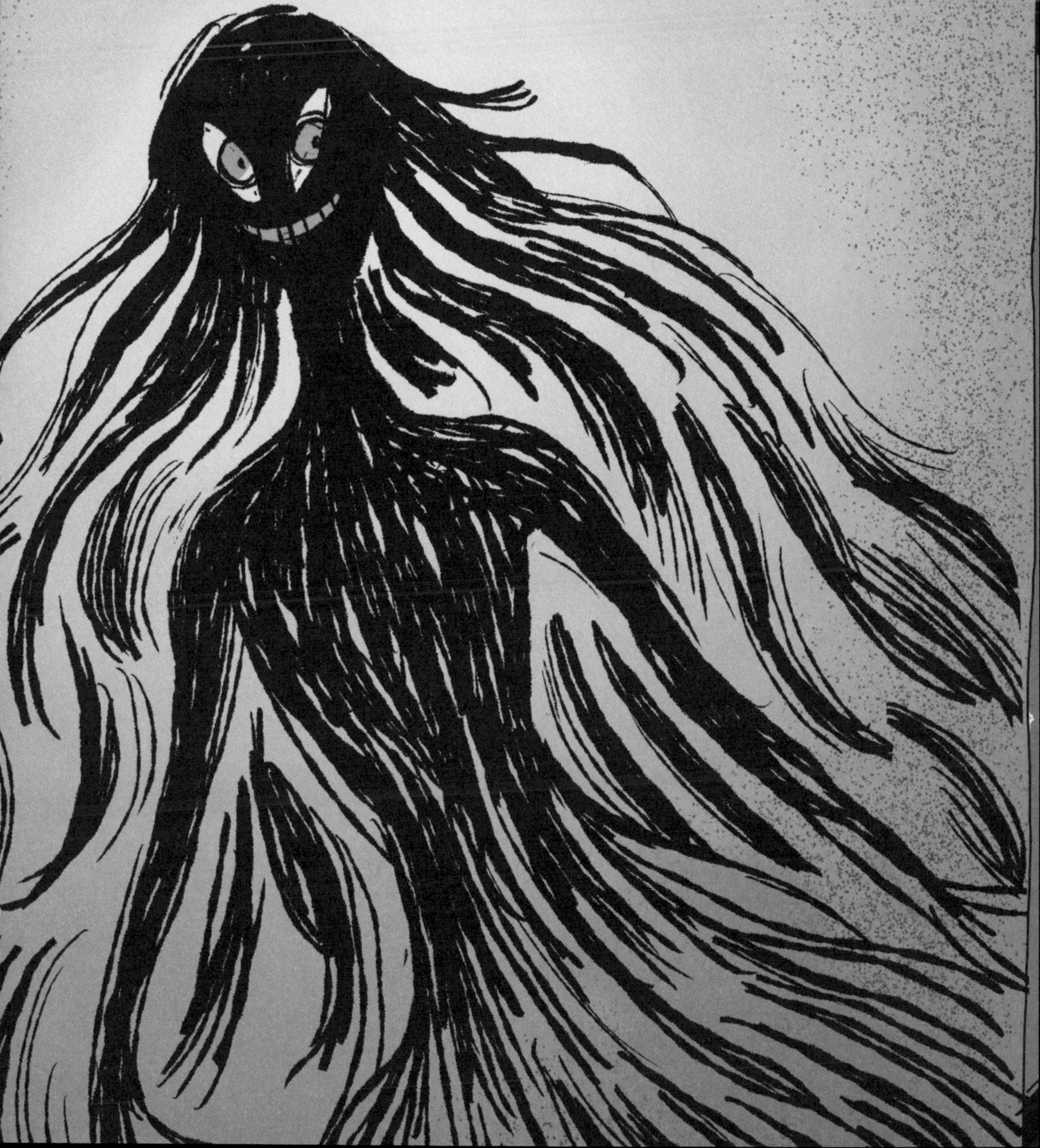

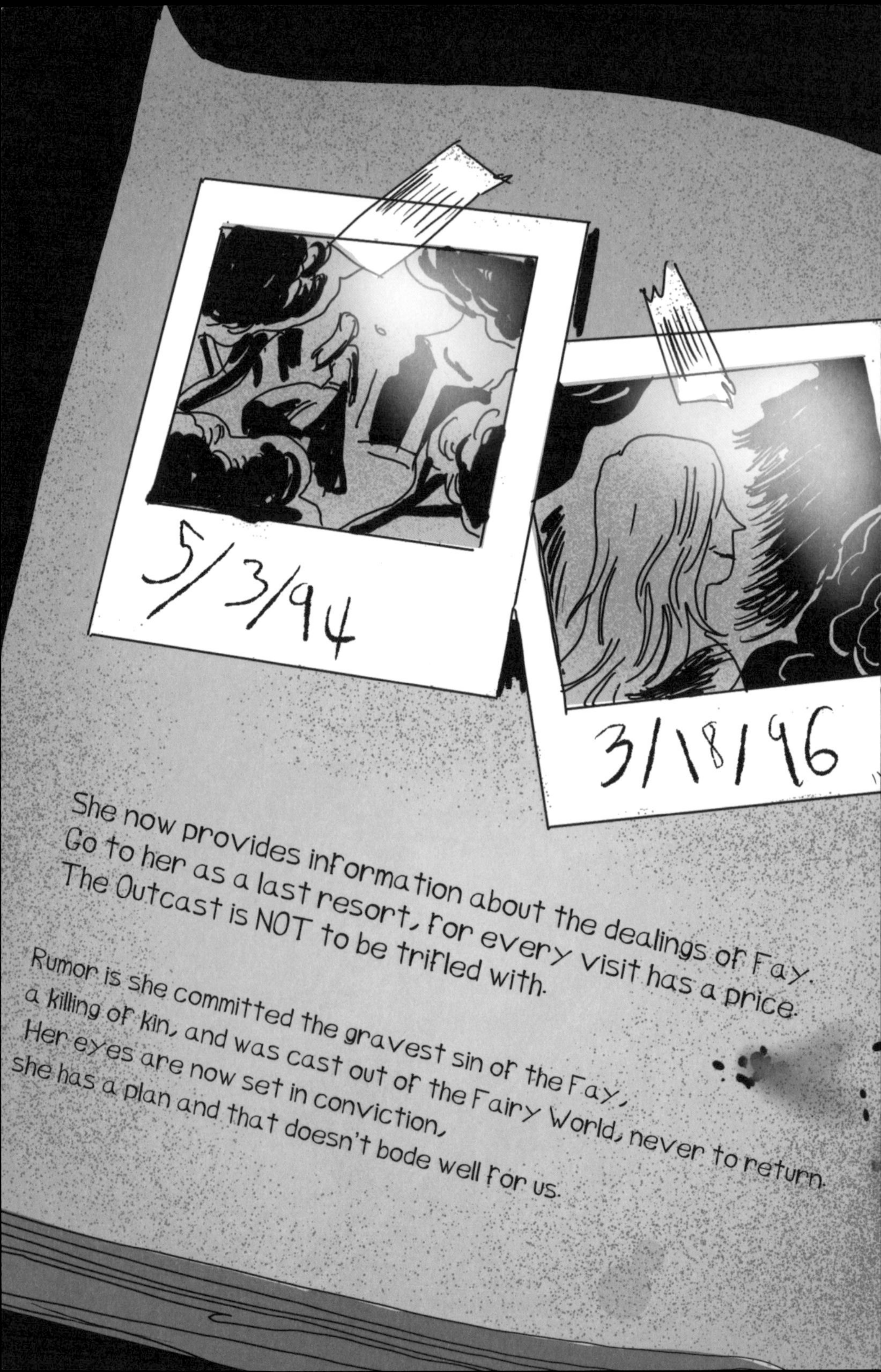
5/3/94
3/18/96
She now provides information about the dealings of Fay.
Go to her as a last resort, for every visit has a price.
The Outcast is NOT to be trifled with.
Rumor is she committed the gravest sin of the Fay,
a killing of kin, and was cast out of the Fairy World, never to return.
Her eyes are now set in conviction,
she has a plan and that doesn't bode well for us.

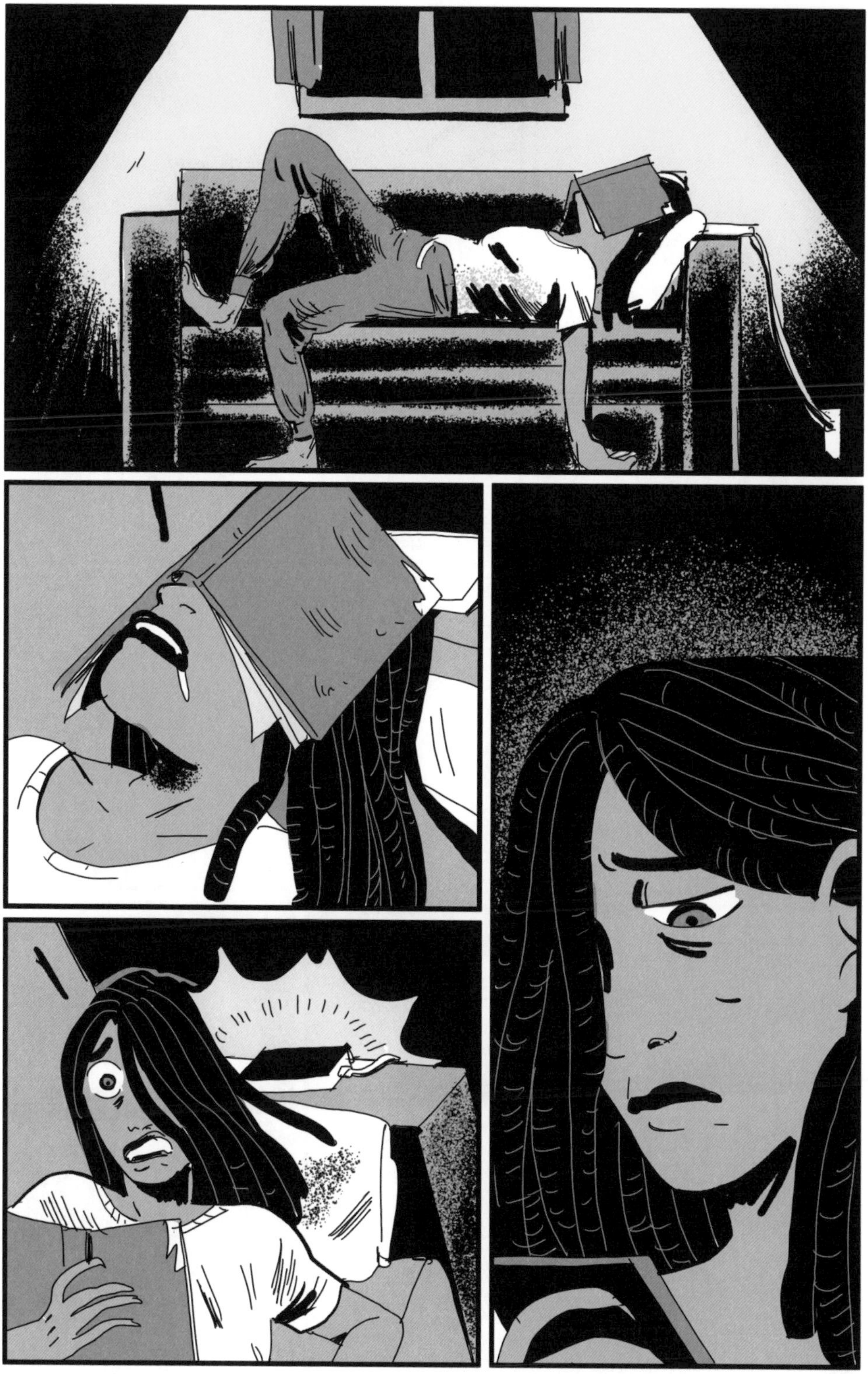

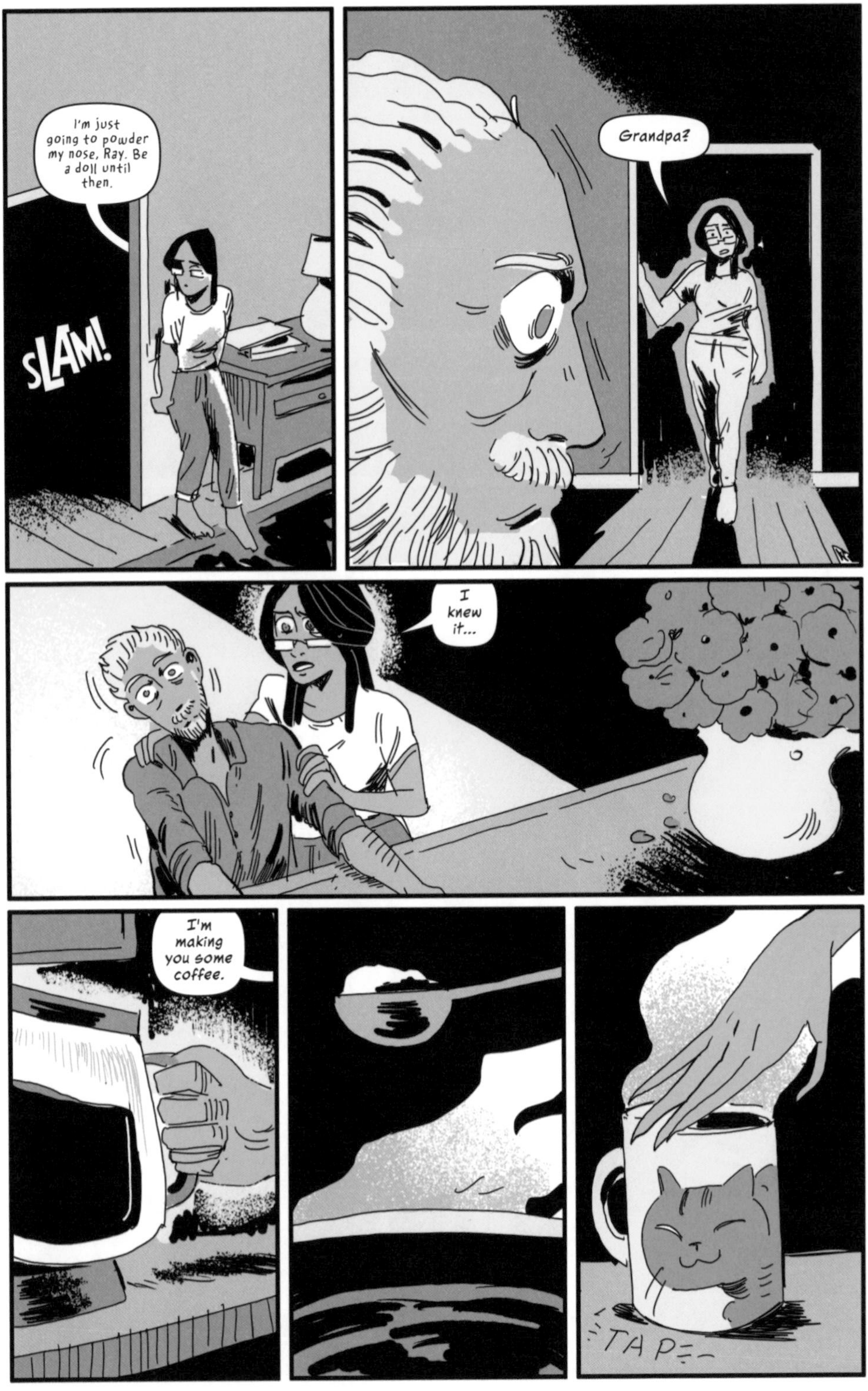
I'm just going to powder my nose, Ray. Be a doll until then.
SLAM!
Grandpa?
I knew it...
I'm making you some coffee.
TAP

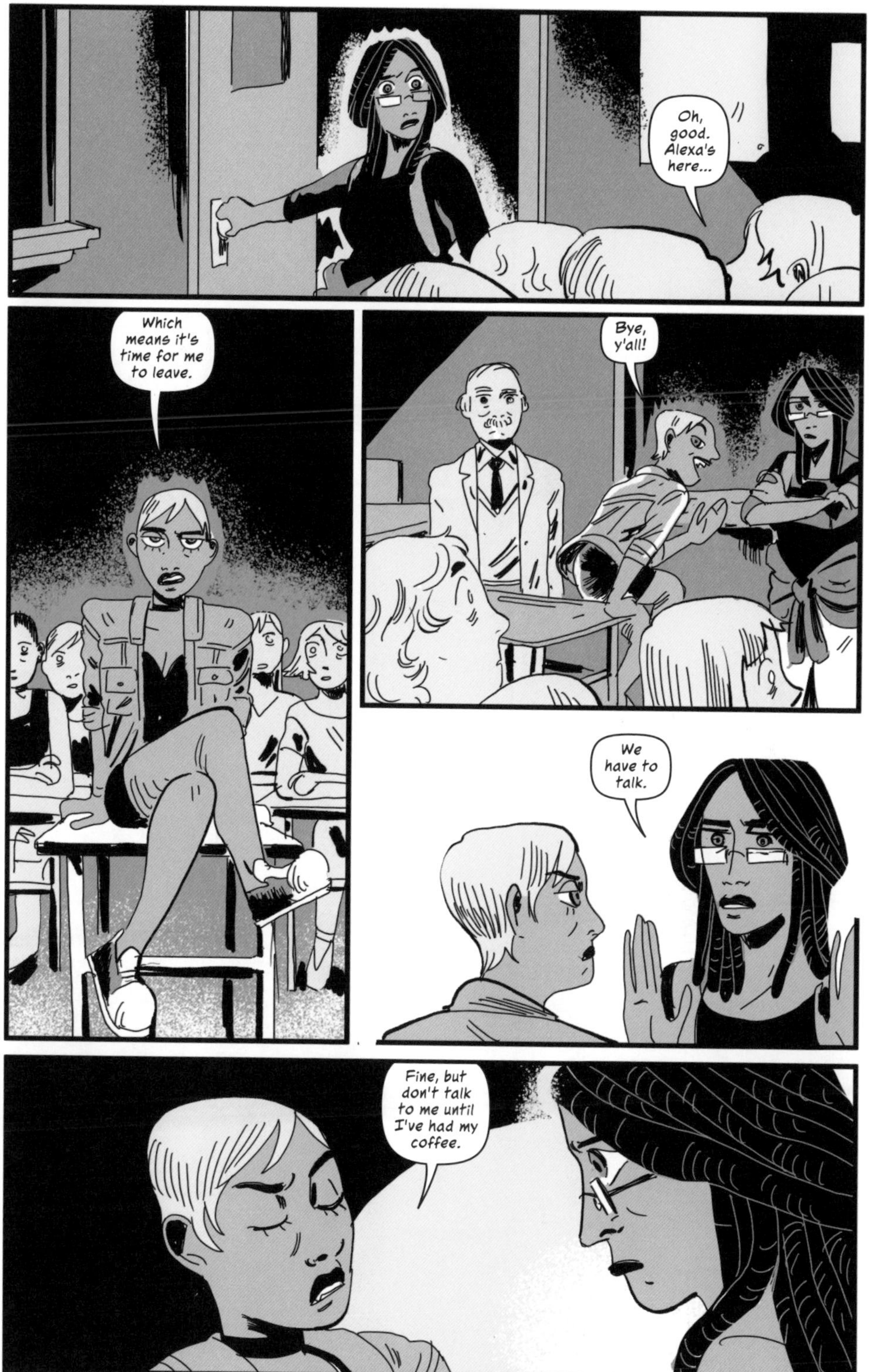
Oh, good. Alexa's here...
Which means it's time for me to leave.
Bye, y'all!
We have to talk.
Fine, but don't talk to me until I've had my coffee.

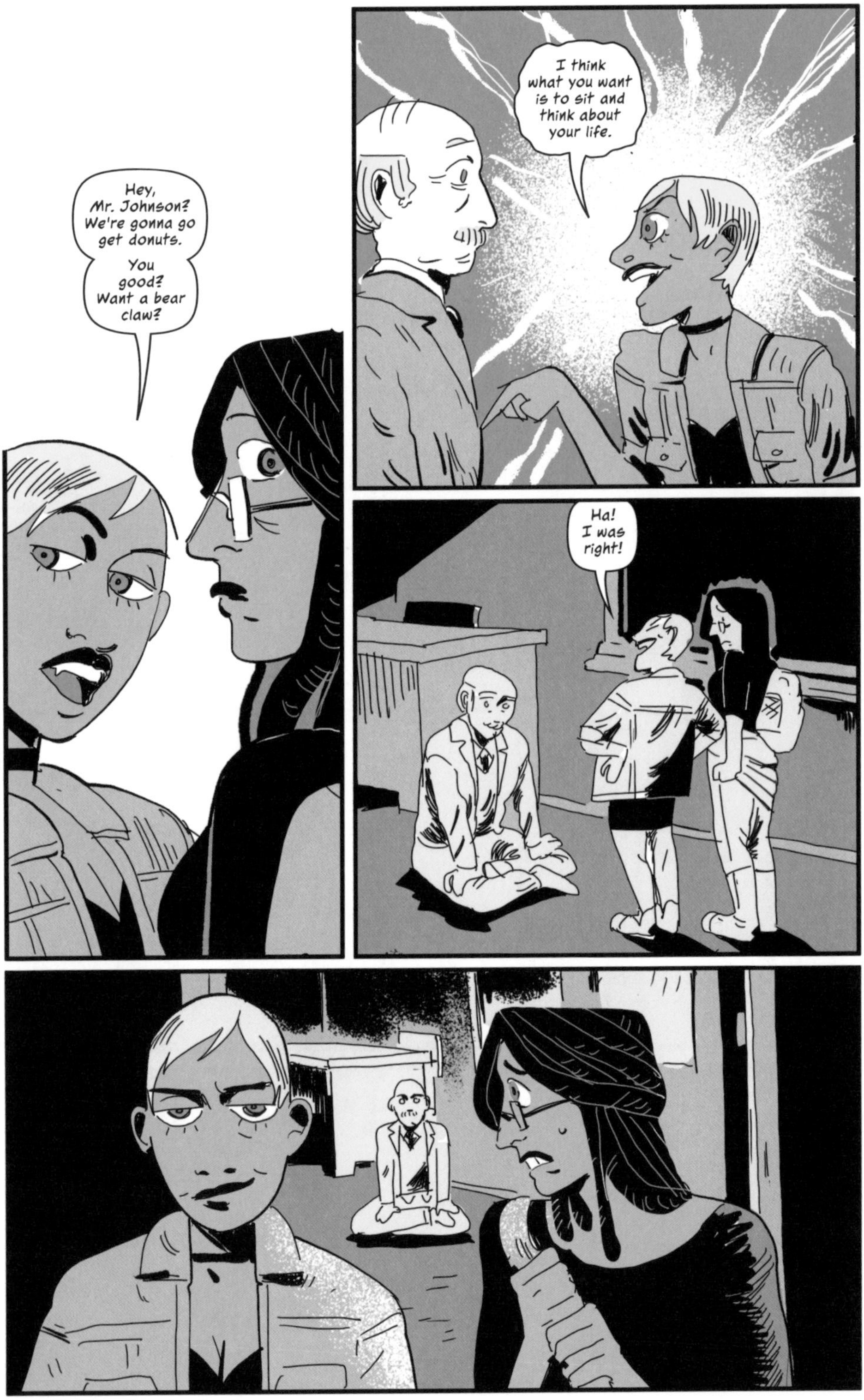
Hey, Mr. Johnson? We're gonna go get donuts.
You good? Want a bear claw?
I think what you want is to sit and think about your life.
Ha! I was right!

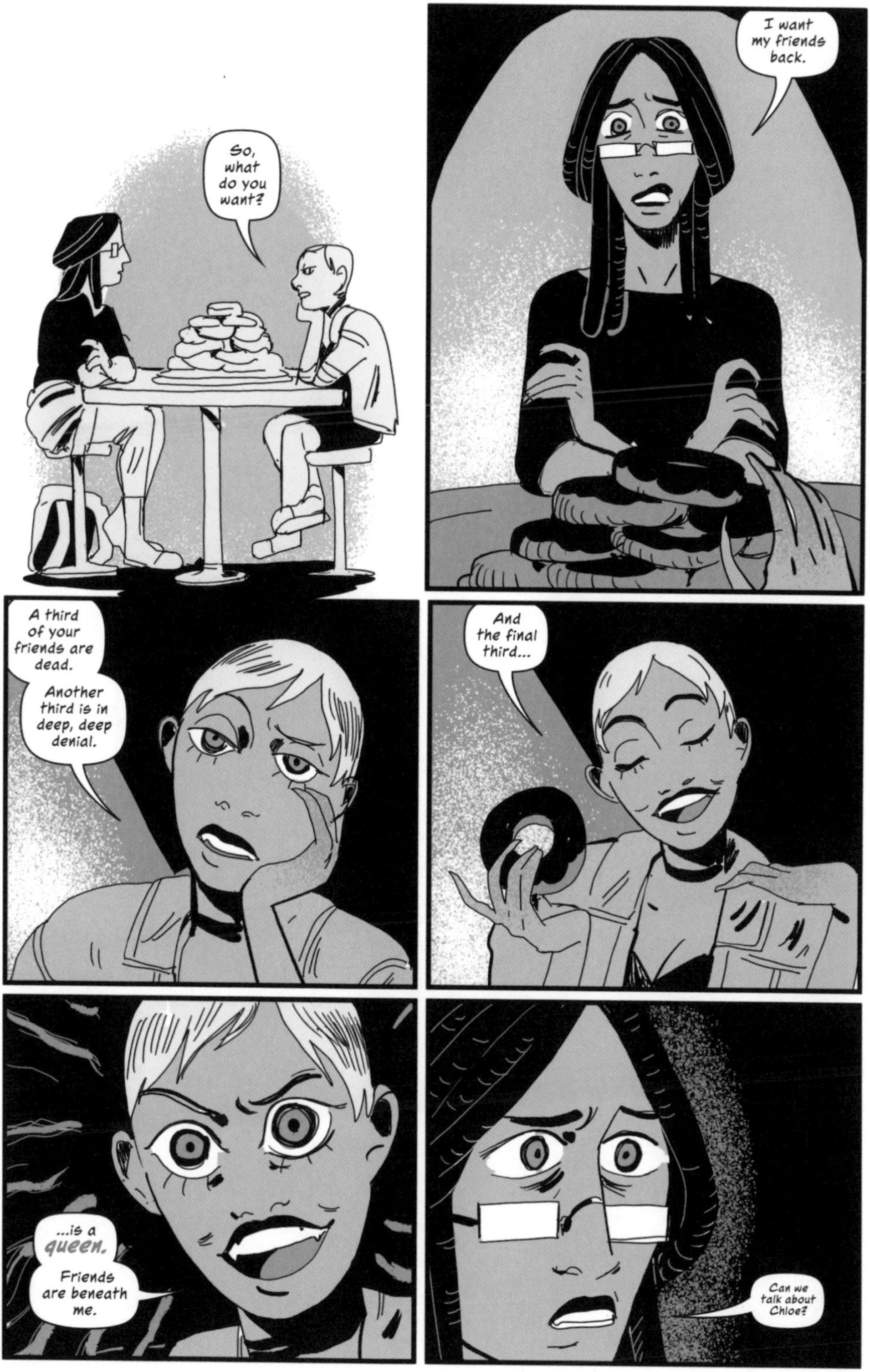
So, what do you want?
I want my friends back.
A third of your friends are dead.
Another third is in deep, deep denial.
And the final third...
...is a queen.
Friends are beneath me.
Can we talk about Chloe?

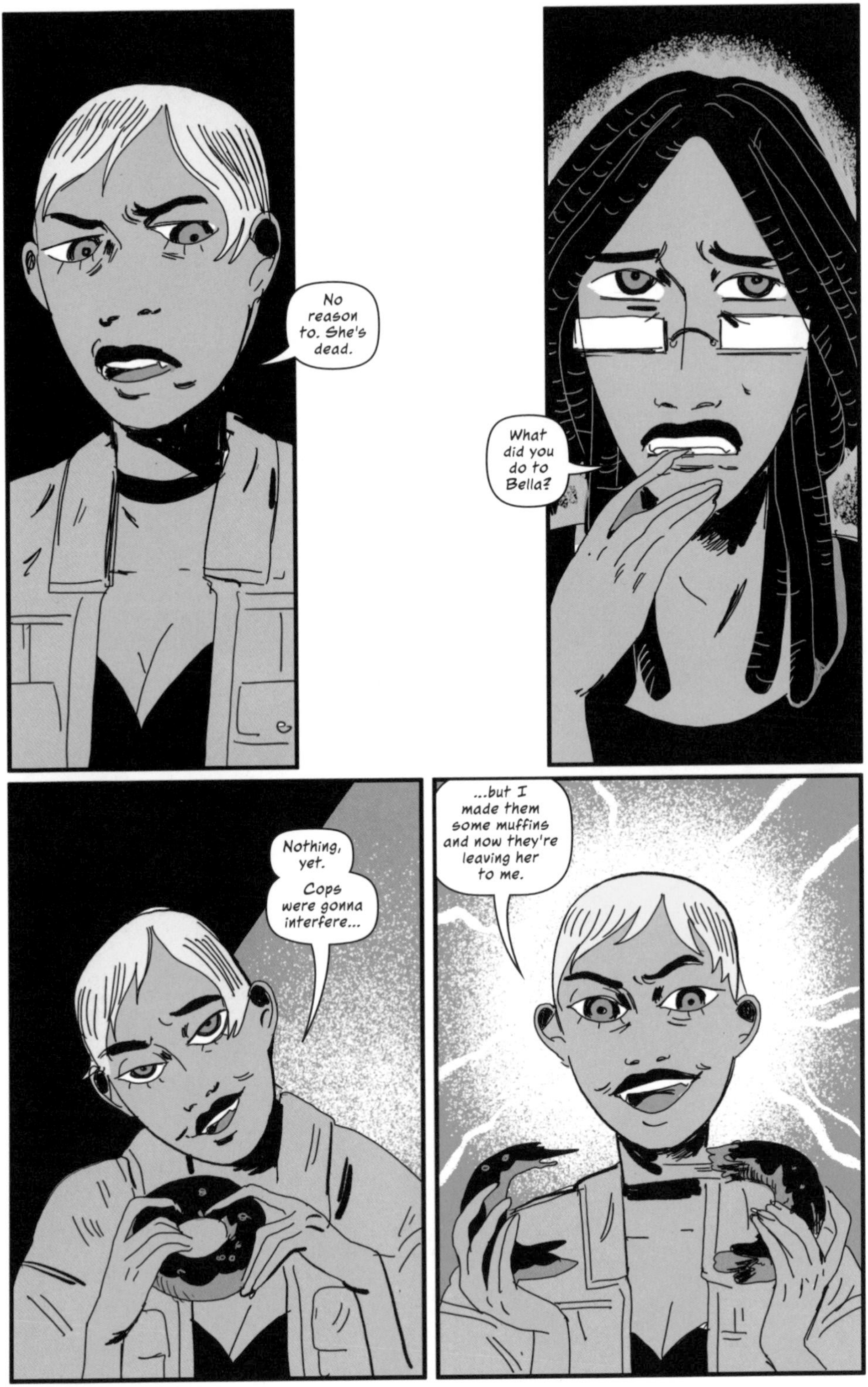

No reason to. She's dead.
What did you do to Bella?
Nothing, yet.
Cops were gonna interfere...
...but I made them some muffins and now they're leaving her to me.

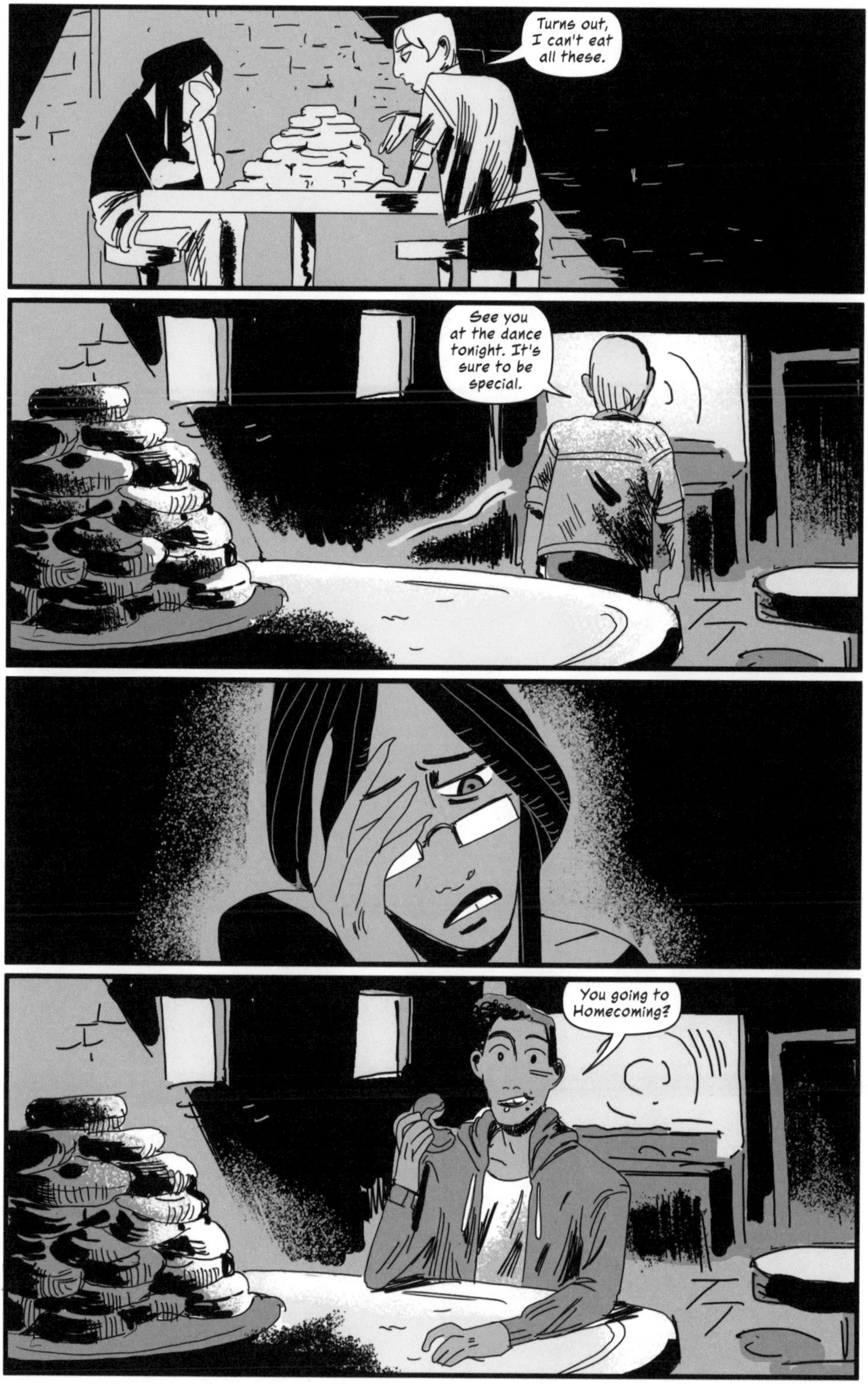
Turns out, I can't eat all these.
See you at the dance tonight. It's sure to be special.
You going to Homecoming?

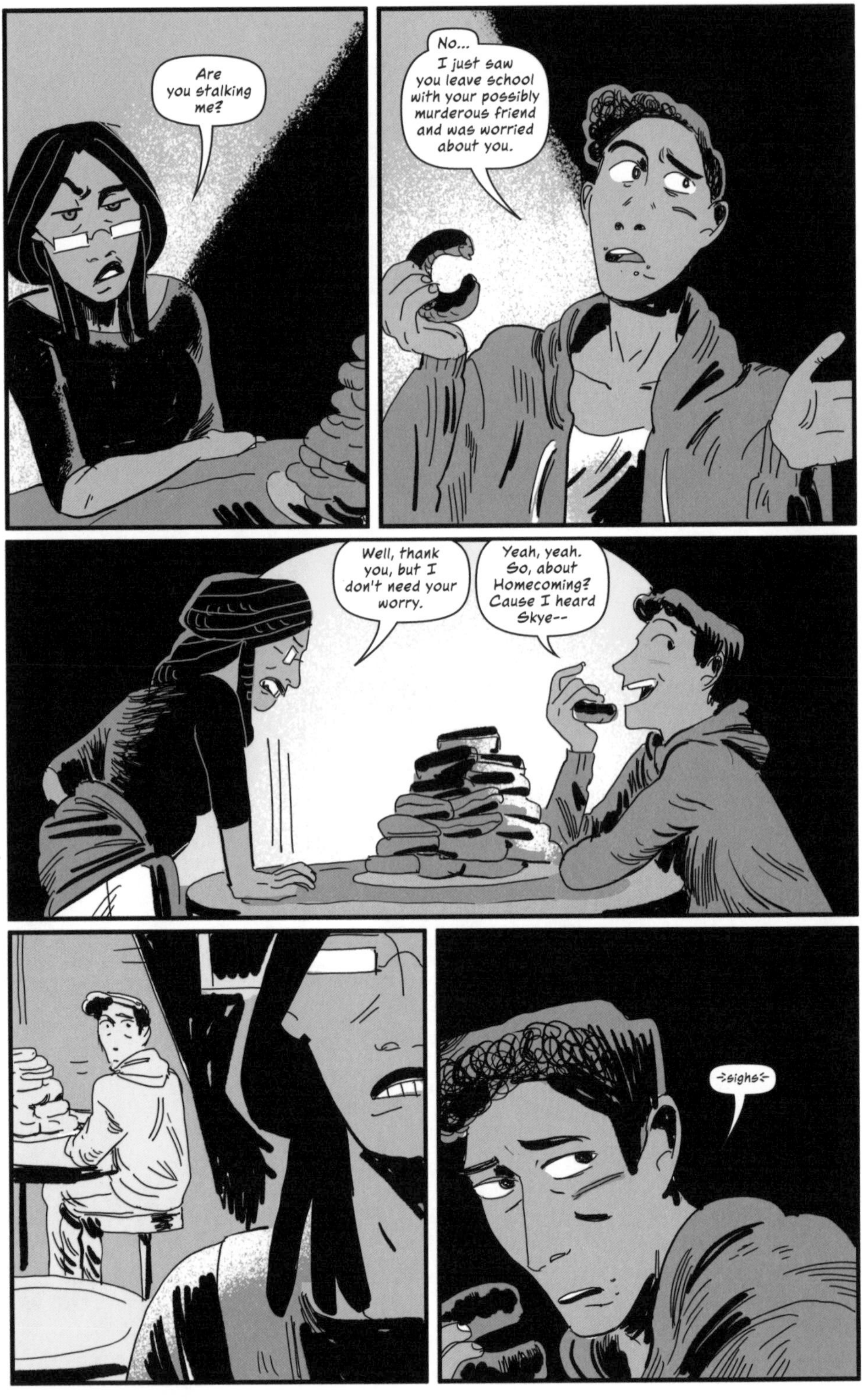

Are you stalking me?
No... I just saw you leave school with your possibly murderous friend and was worried about you.
Well, thank you, but I don't need your worry.
Yeah, yeah. So, about Homecoming? Cause I heard Skye--
sighs

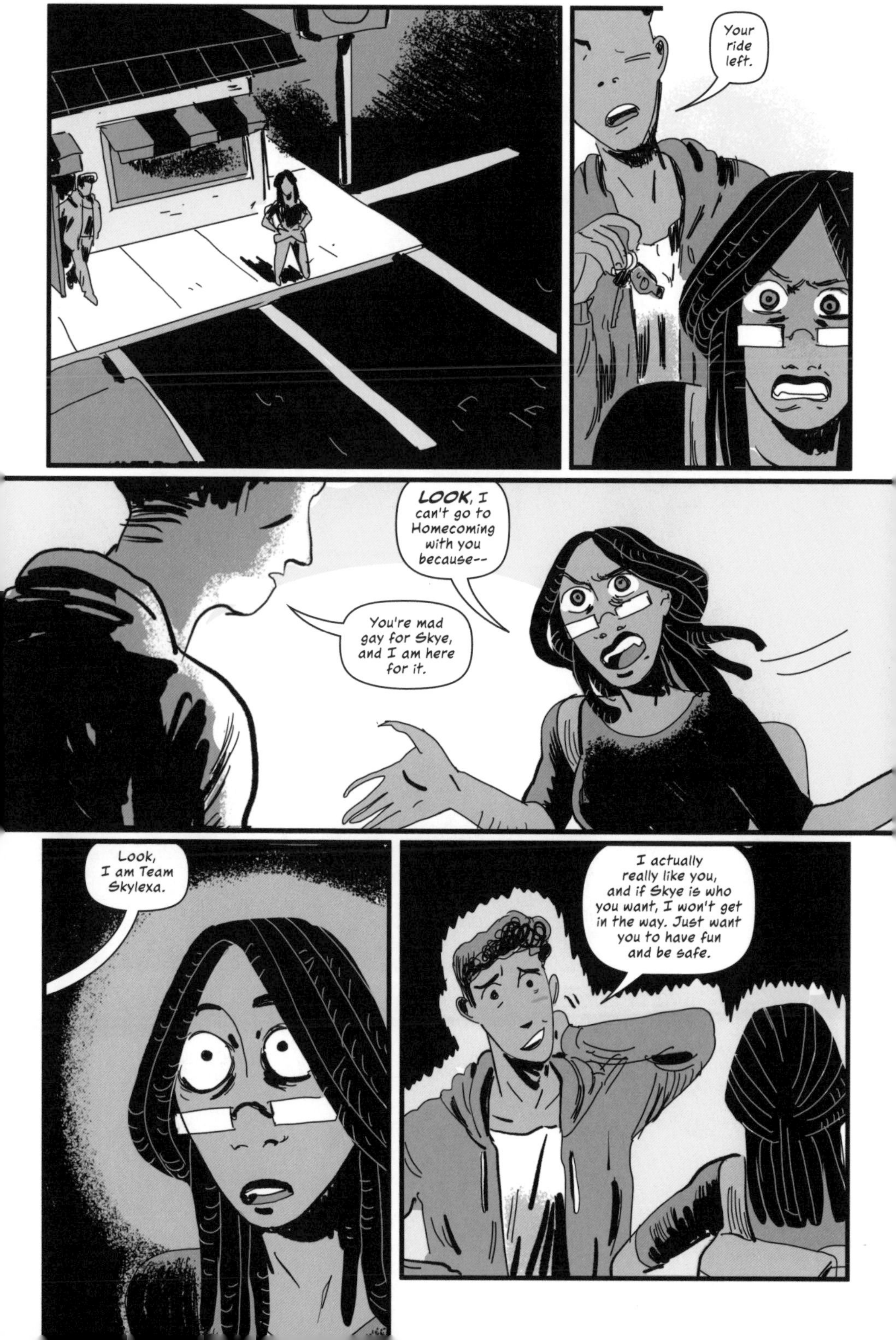
Your ride left.
LOOK, I can't go to Homecoming with you because--
You're mad gay for Skye, and I am here for it.
Look, I am Team Skylexa.
I actually really like you, and if Skye is who you want, I won't get in the way. Just want you to have fun and be safe.

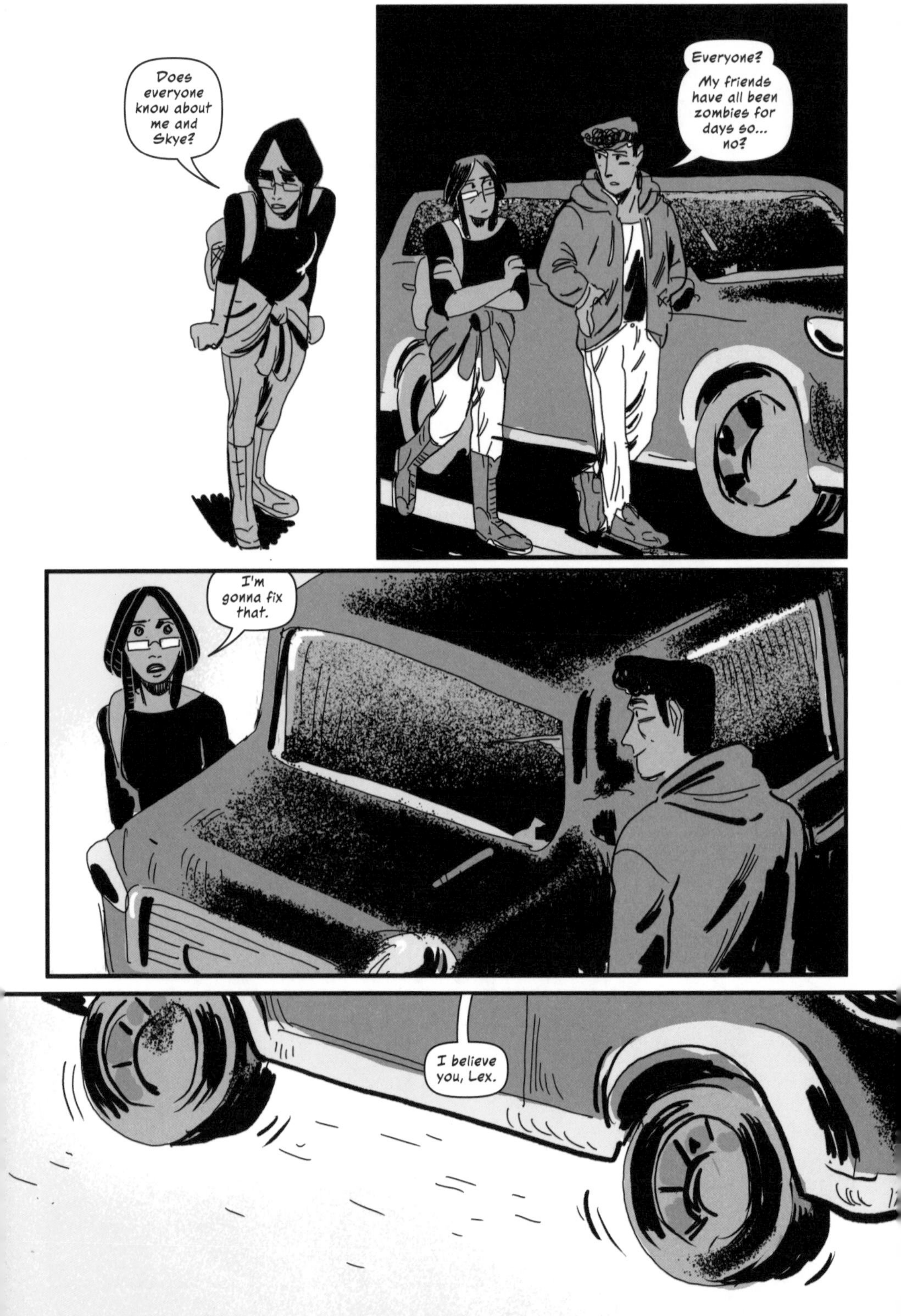
Does everyone know about me and Skye?
Everyone? My friends have all been zombies for days so... no?
I'm gonna fix that.
I believe you, Lex.

Weaknesses of Fay

Fairies are susceptible to cold-forged iron and silver.
Burning at the slightest touch.
This method is used to confirm cases of suspected fairies.

Salt weakens fay magic
and can be used to suppress them to a degree.

Dropping seeds or pebbles
at the feet of a fairy is a Hunter's preferred means of escape.
Fay must count them all before they can leave the area.

Their biggest weakness is their selfishness.
Prone to flights of fancy, a fairy, for all their tricks,
can be put in deadly situations if their ego is fed.

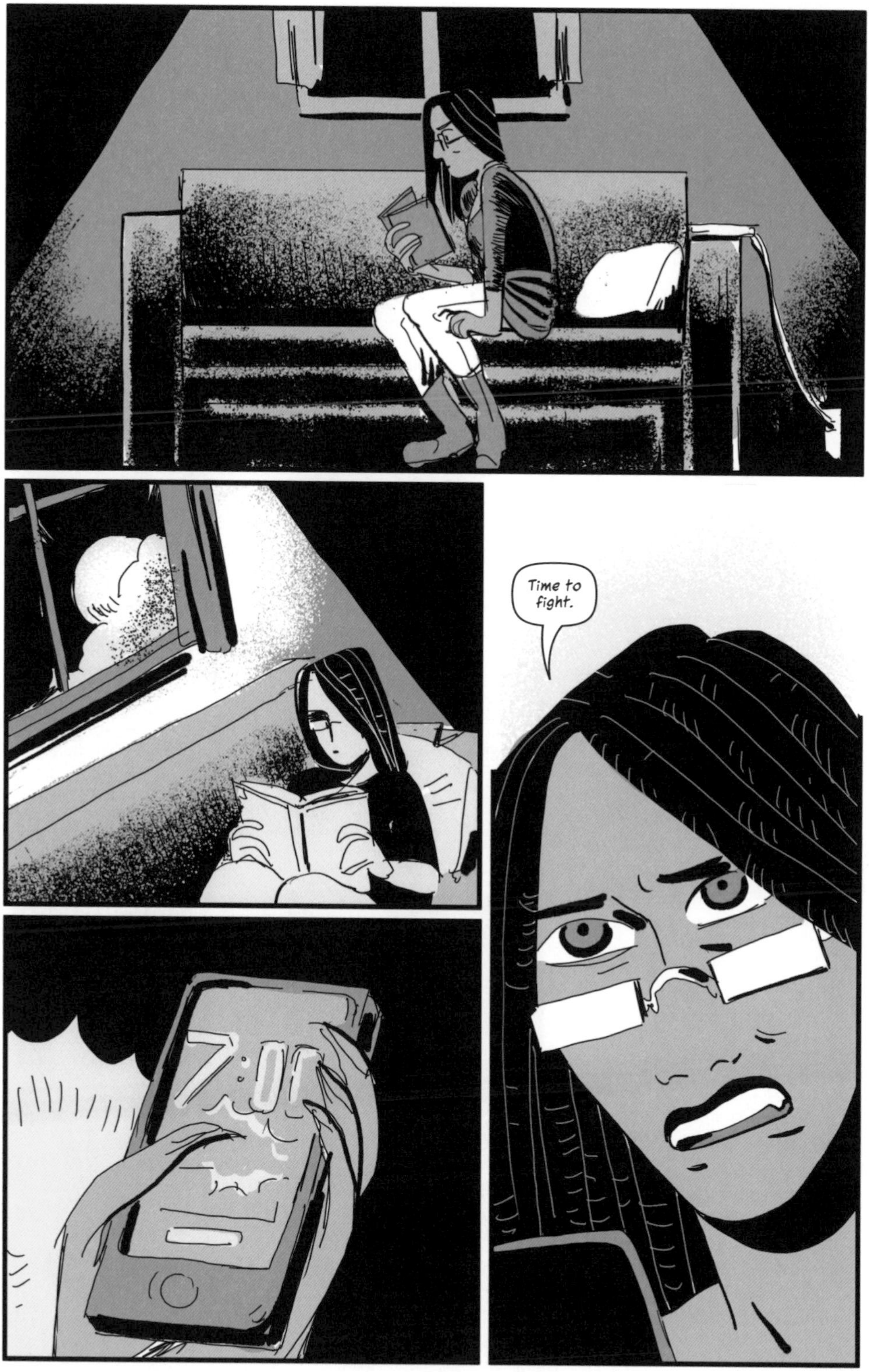
Time to fight.
7:01

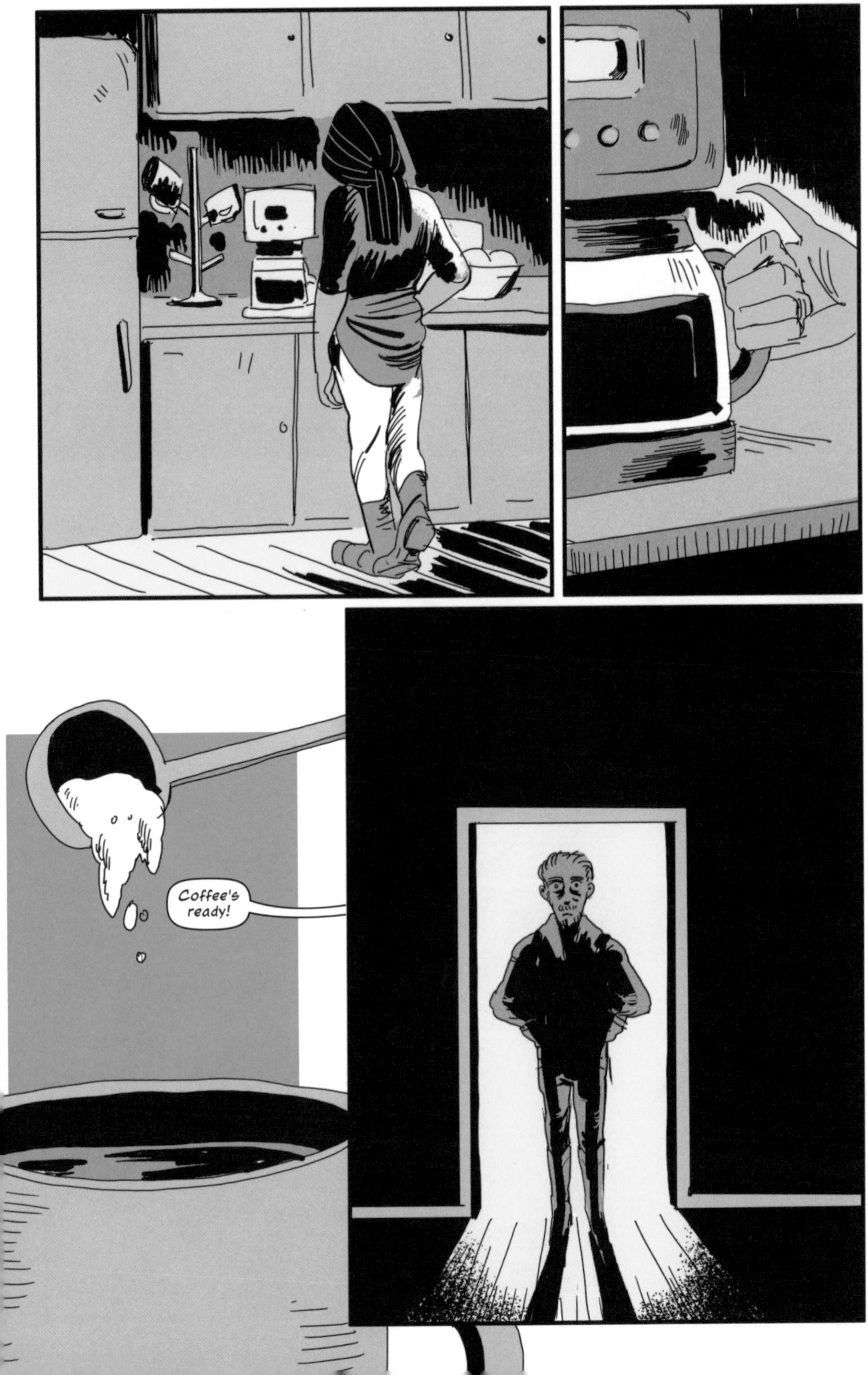
Coffee's ready!

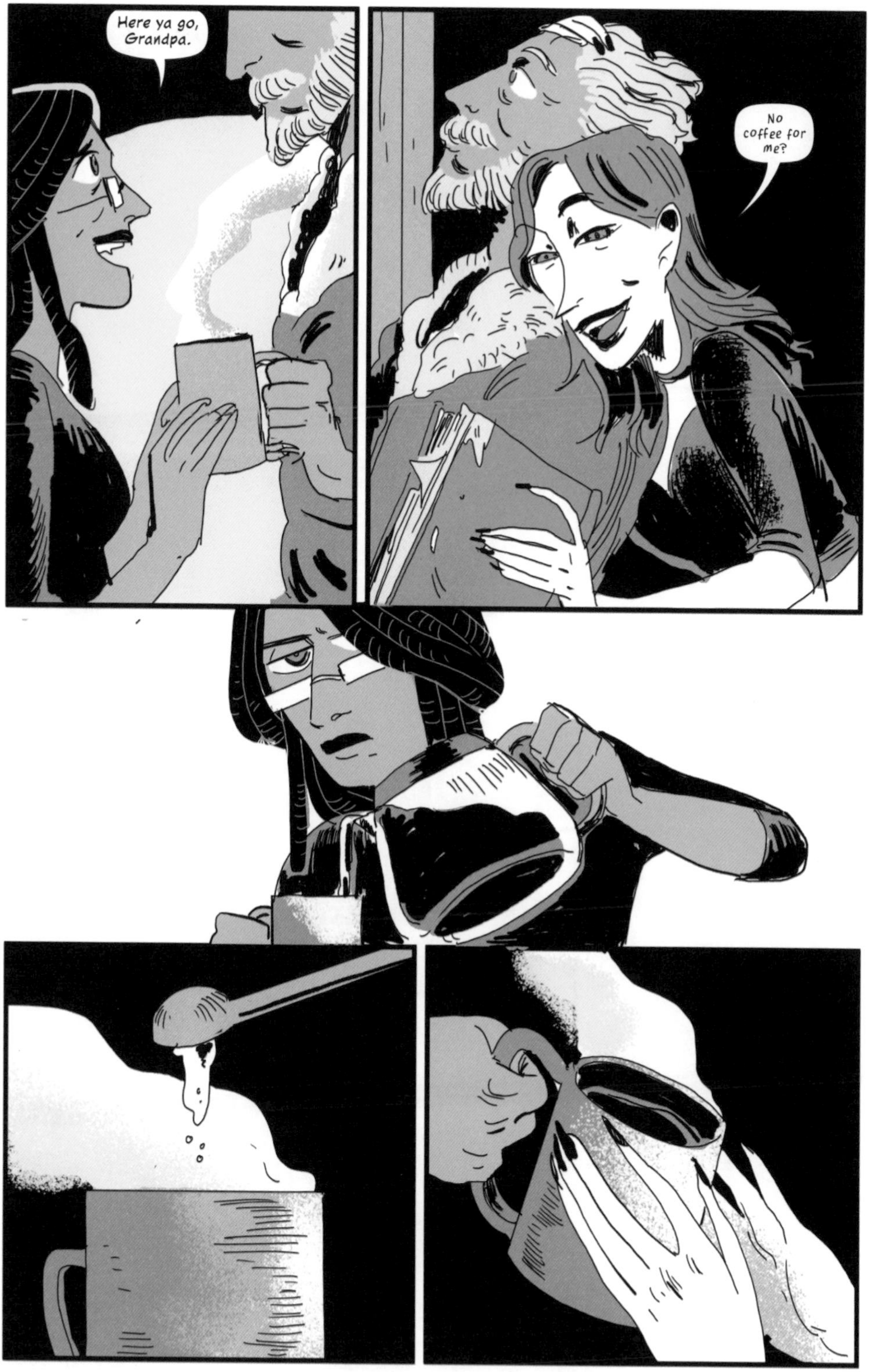
Here ya go, Grandpa.
No coffee for me?

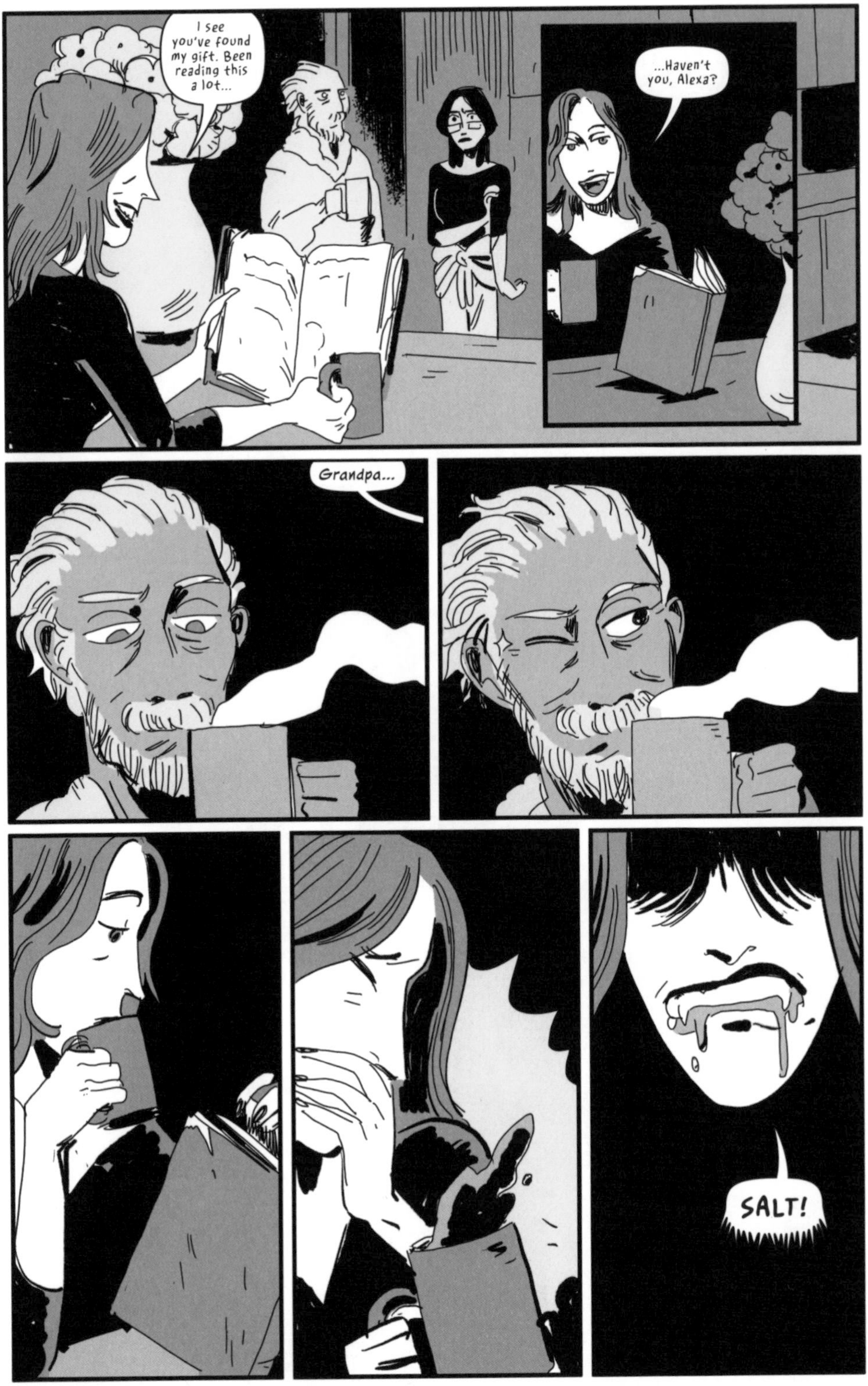
I see you've found my gift. Been reading this a lot...
...Haven't you, Alexa?
Grandpa...
SALT!

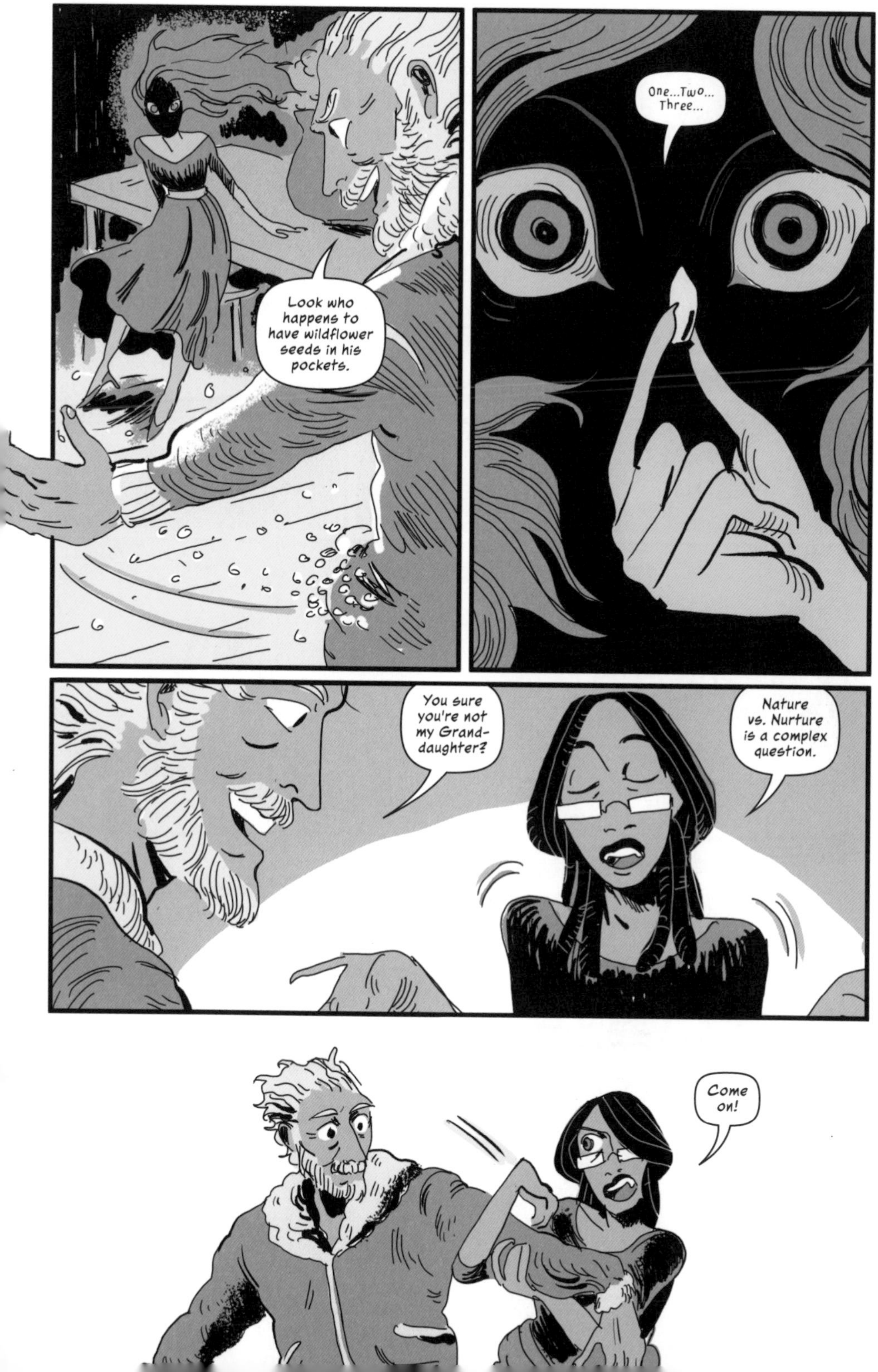
Look who happens to have wildflower seeds in his pockets.
One...Two... Three...
You sure you're not my Grand-daughter?
Nature vs. Nurture is a complex question.
Come on!

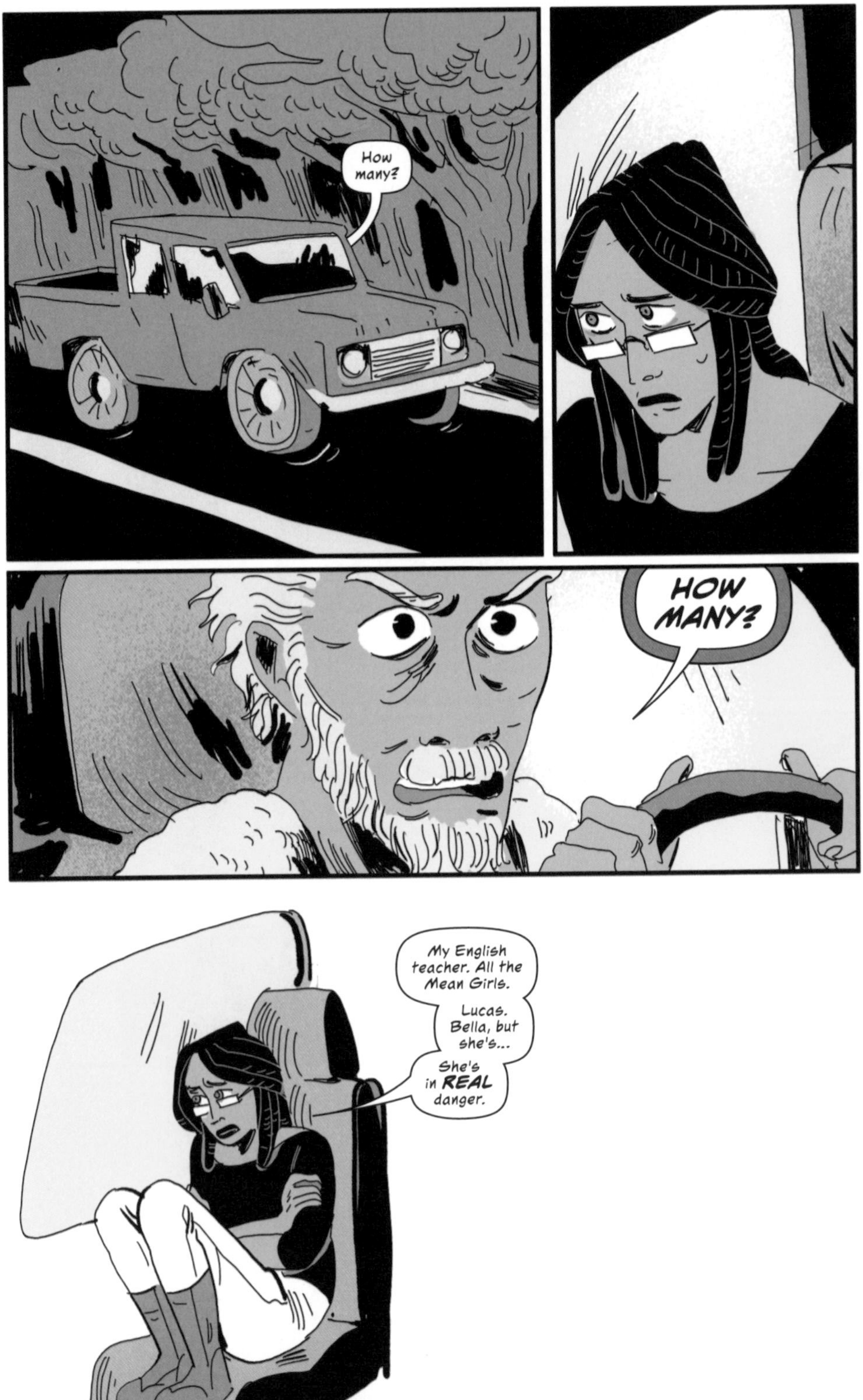
How many?
HOW MANY?
My English teacher. All the Mean Girls.
Lucas. Bella, but she's...
She's in REAL danger.

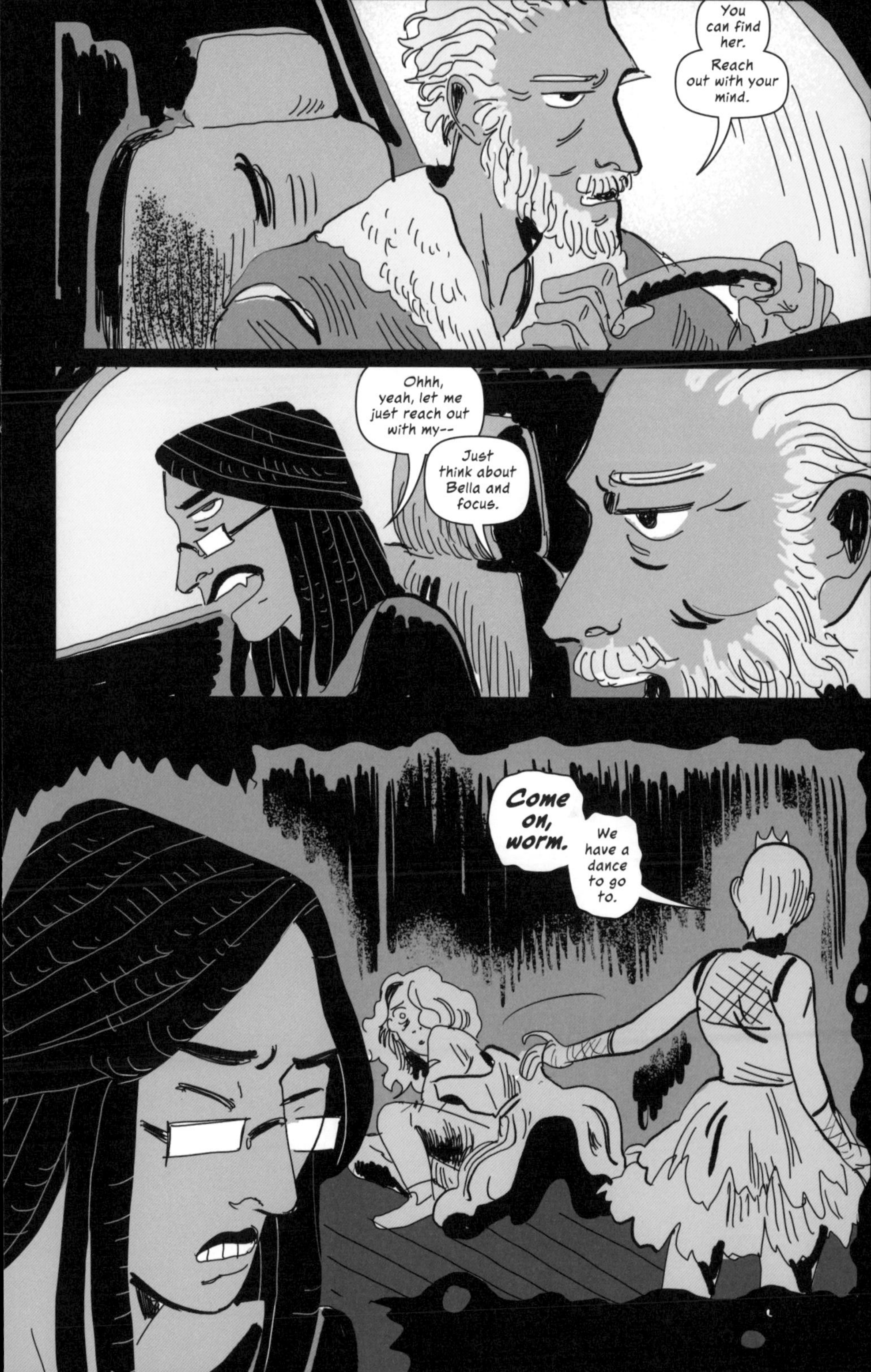
You can find her.
Reach out with your mind.
Ohhh, yeah, let me just reach out with my--
Just think about Bella and focus.
Come on, worm.
We have a dance to go to.

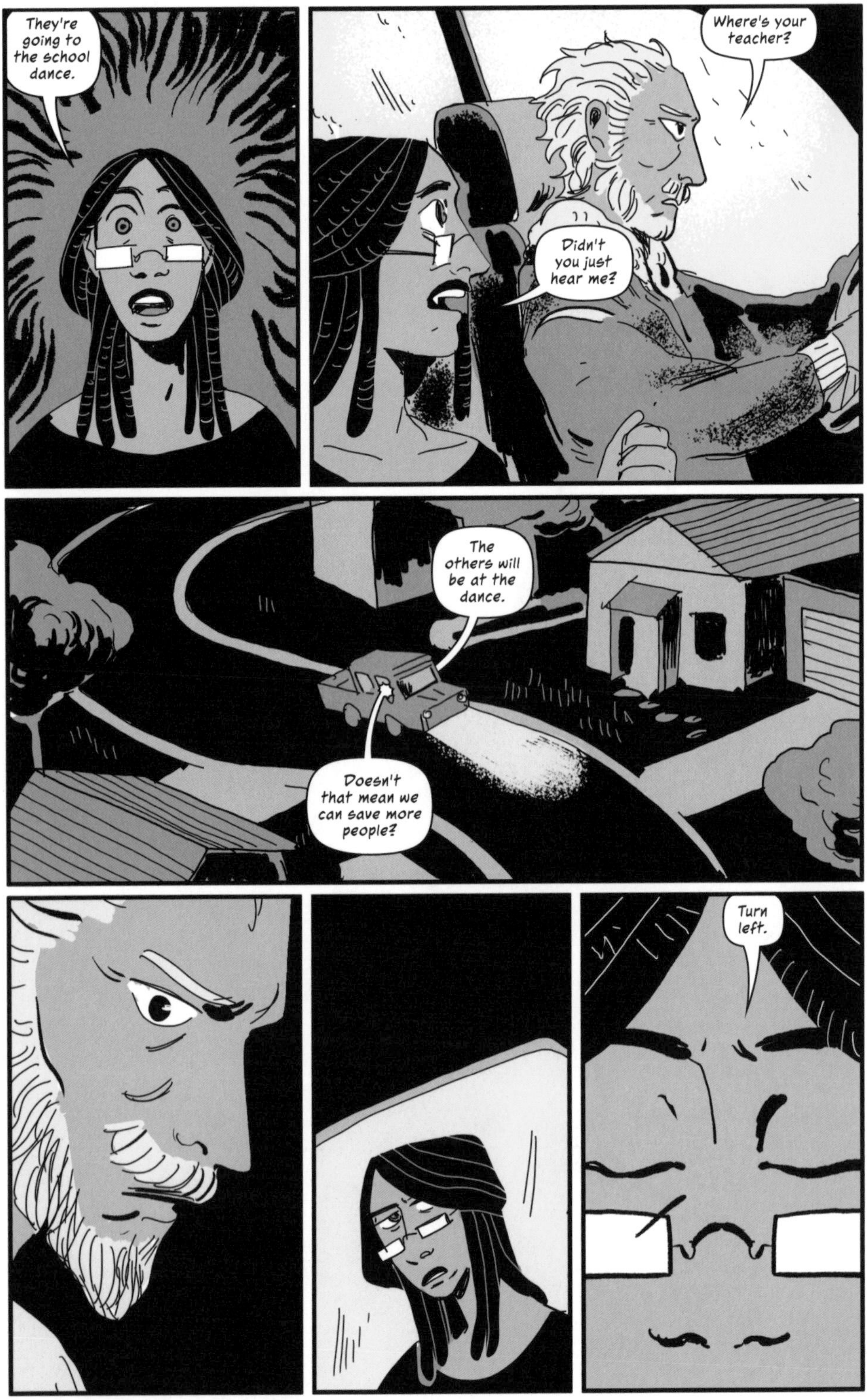

They're going to the school dance.
Where's your teacher?
Didn't you just hear me?
The others will be at the dance.
Doesn't that mean we can save more people?
Turn left.

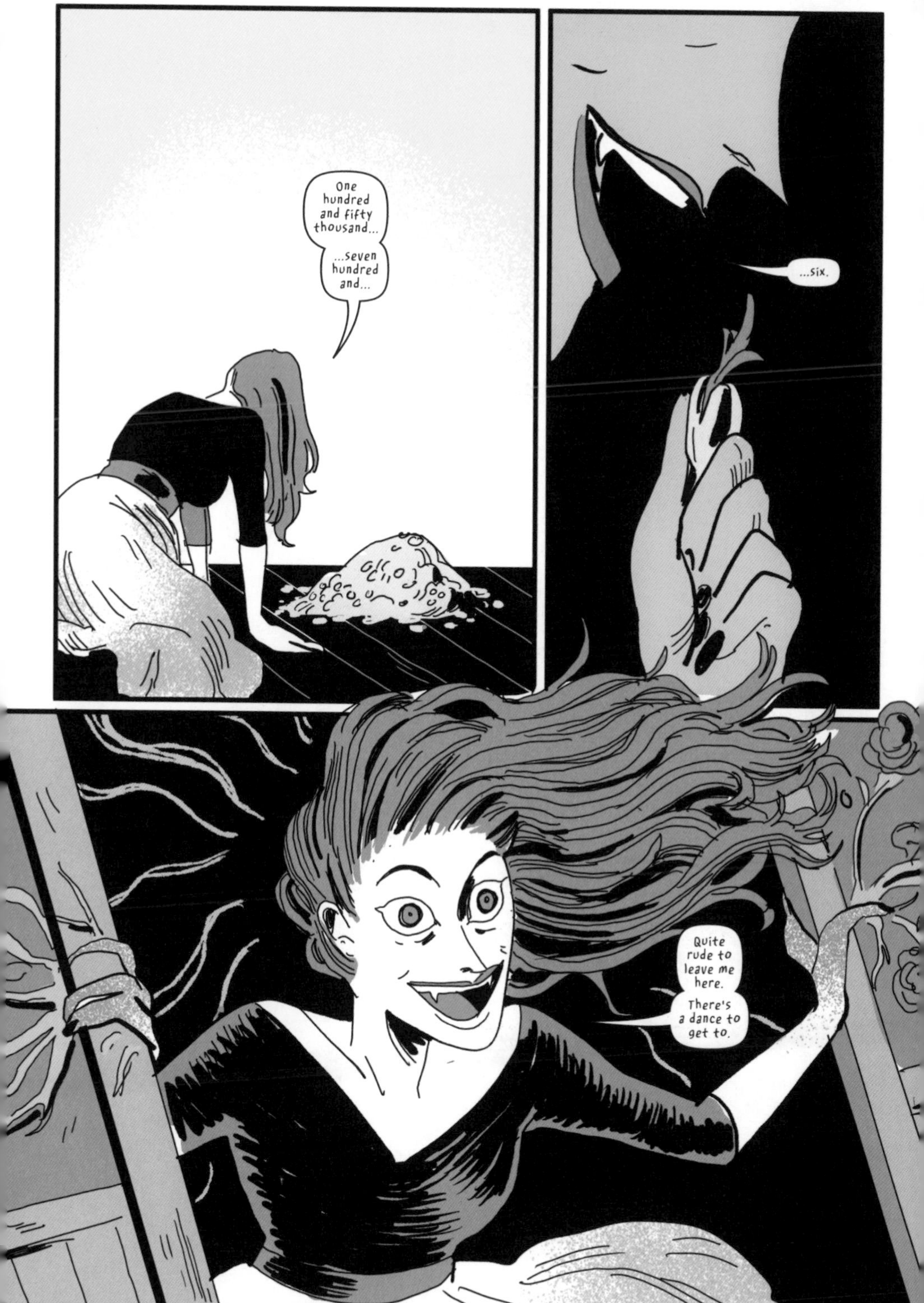
One hundred and fifty thousand...
...seven hundred and...
...six.
Quite rude to leave me here.
There's a dance to get to.

Fairy World

Described by Hunters who made
the journey on reconnaissance missions.

A wild frontier of eerie beauty, the Realm of Fay is the home of Fairies. Forests of giant mushrooms and rivers of light dance between the soil of the plane.

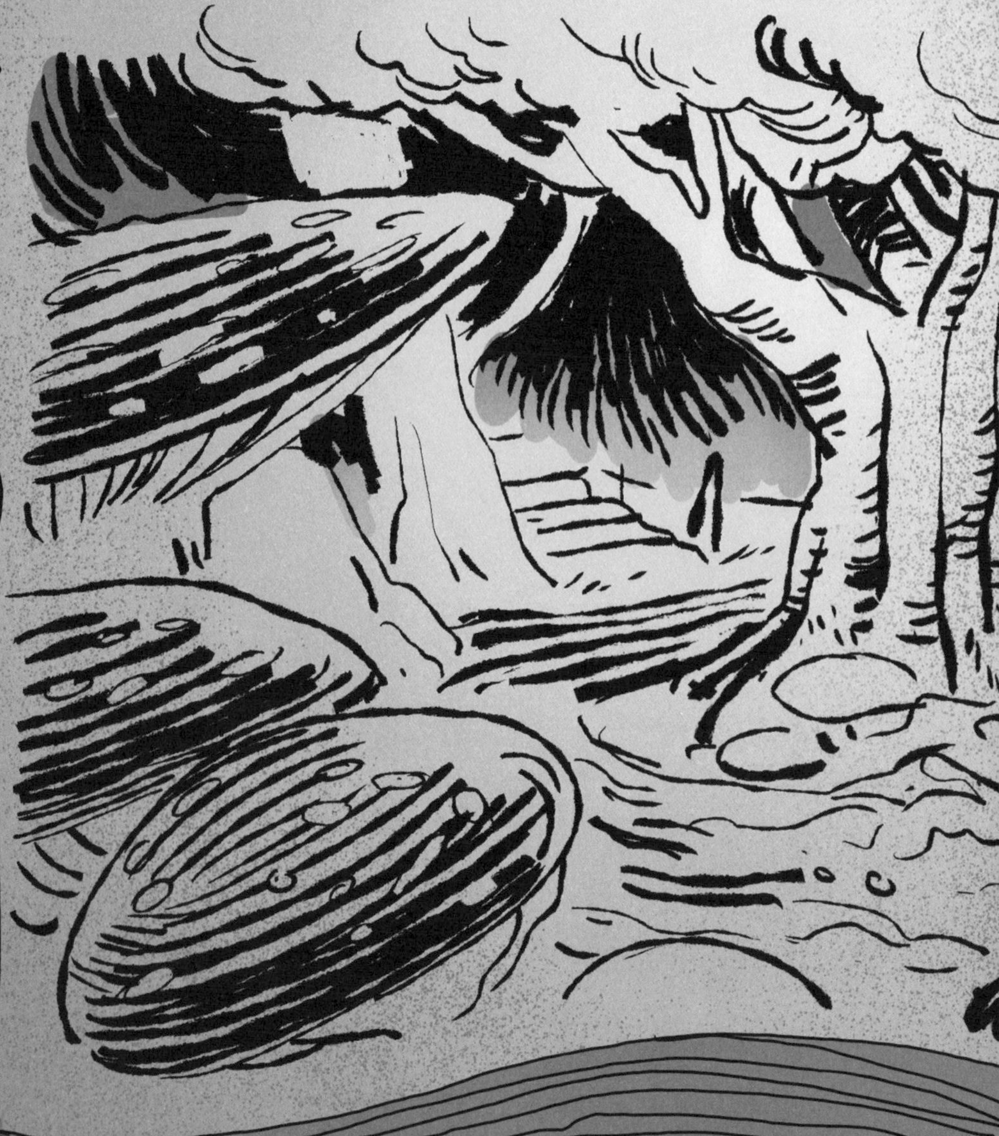

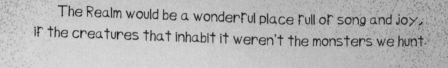

The Realm would be a wonderful place full of song and joy, if the creatures that inhabit it weren't the monsters we hunt.

The Space Between Worlds

Little is known about this plane of existence. No human has ever stepped foot in this mysterious land and it's only talked about through whispers of the eldest of Fay.

Most associated with victims of powerful beguilements. The body remains, but the spirit ends up lost in the space between our world and theirs.

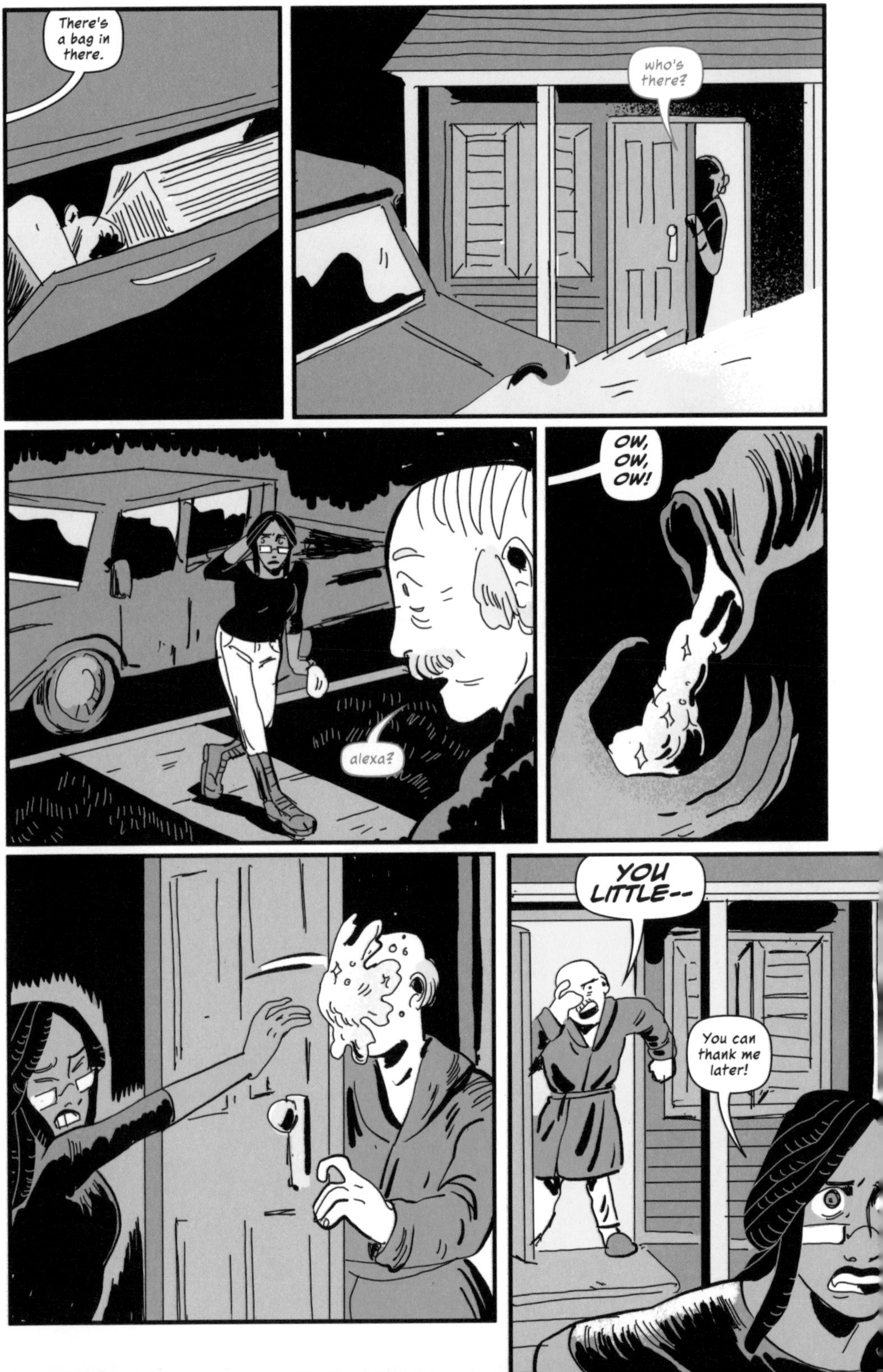
There's a bag in there.
who's there?
alexa?
OW, OW, OW!
YOU LITTLE--
You can thank me later!

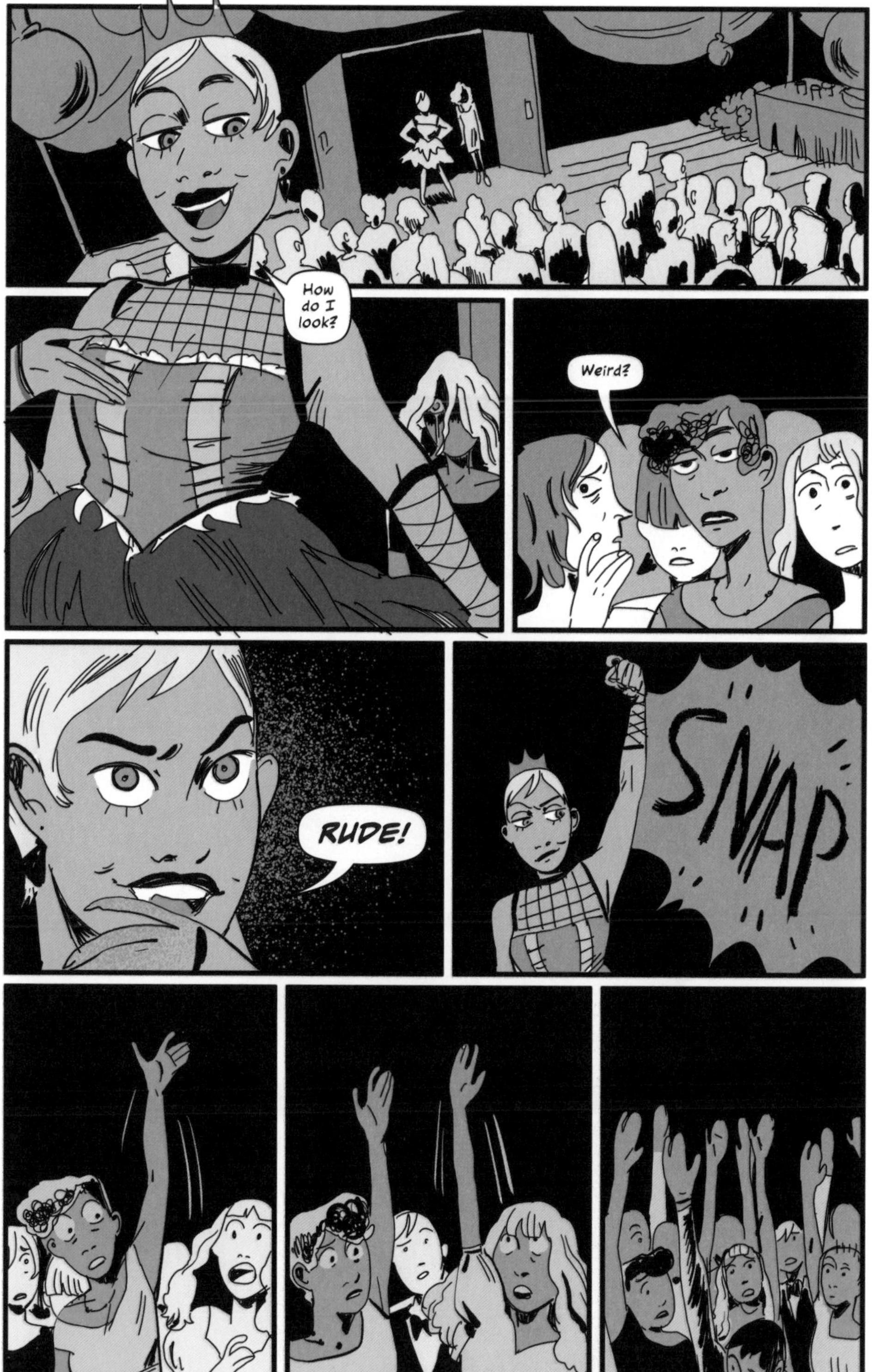
How do I look?
Weird?
RUDE!
SNAP

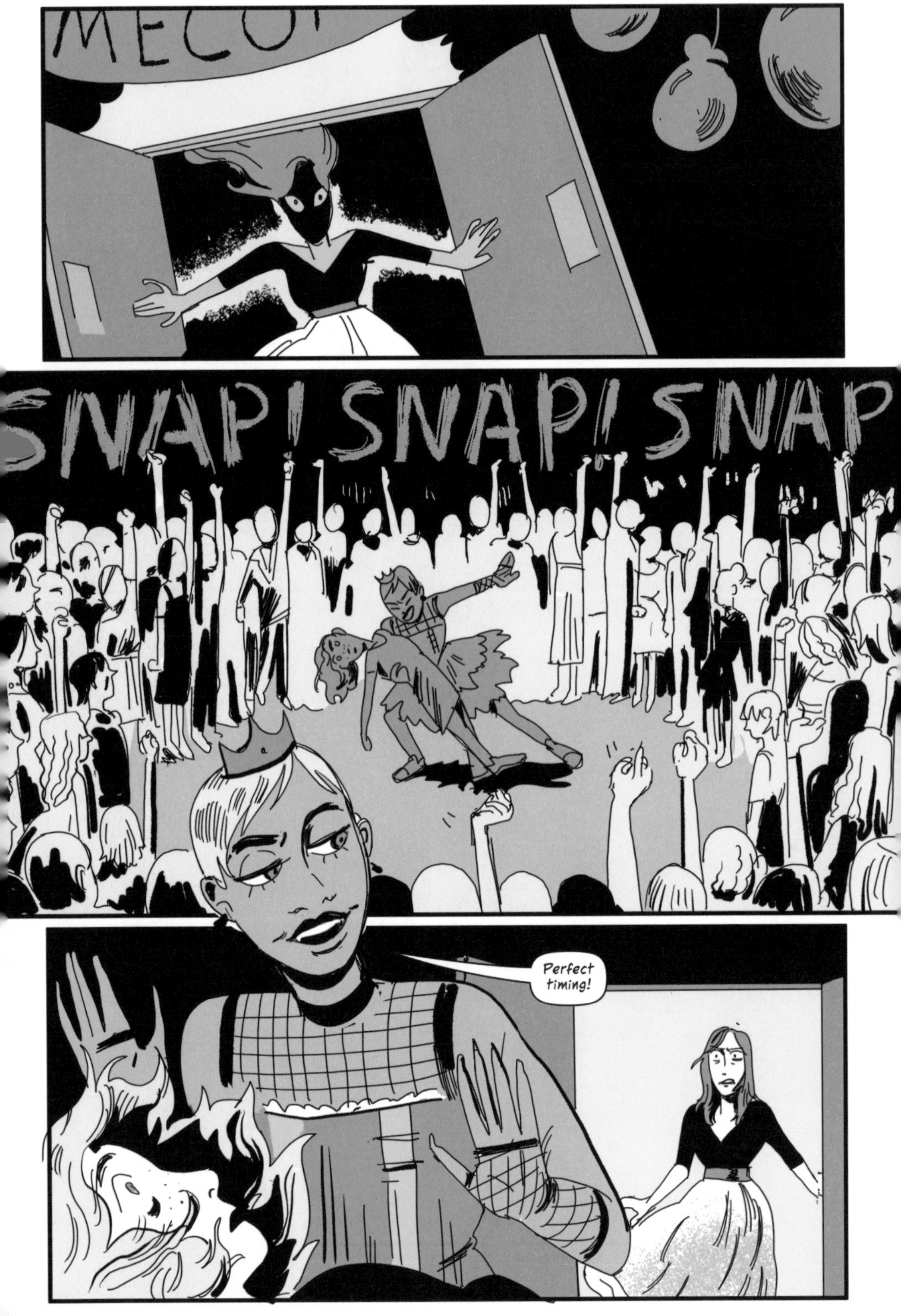
SNAP! SNAP! SNAP
Perfect timing!

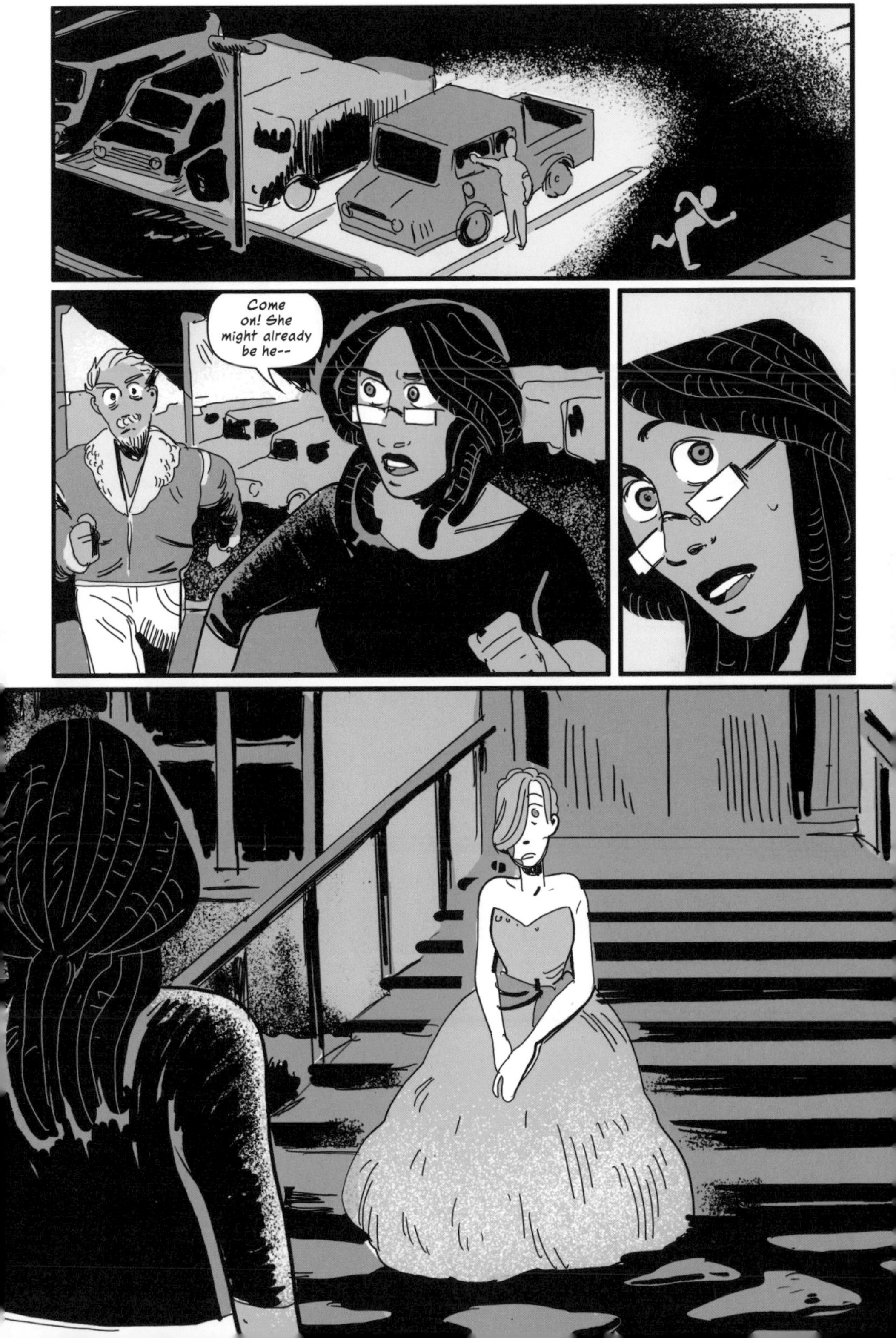
Come on! She might already be he--

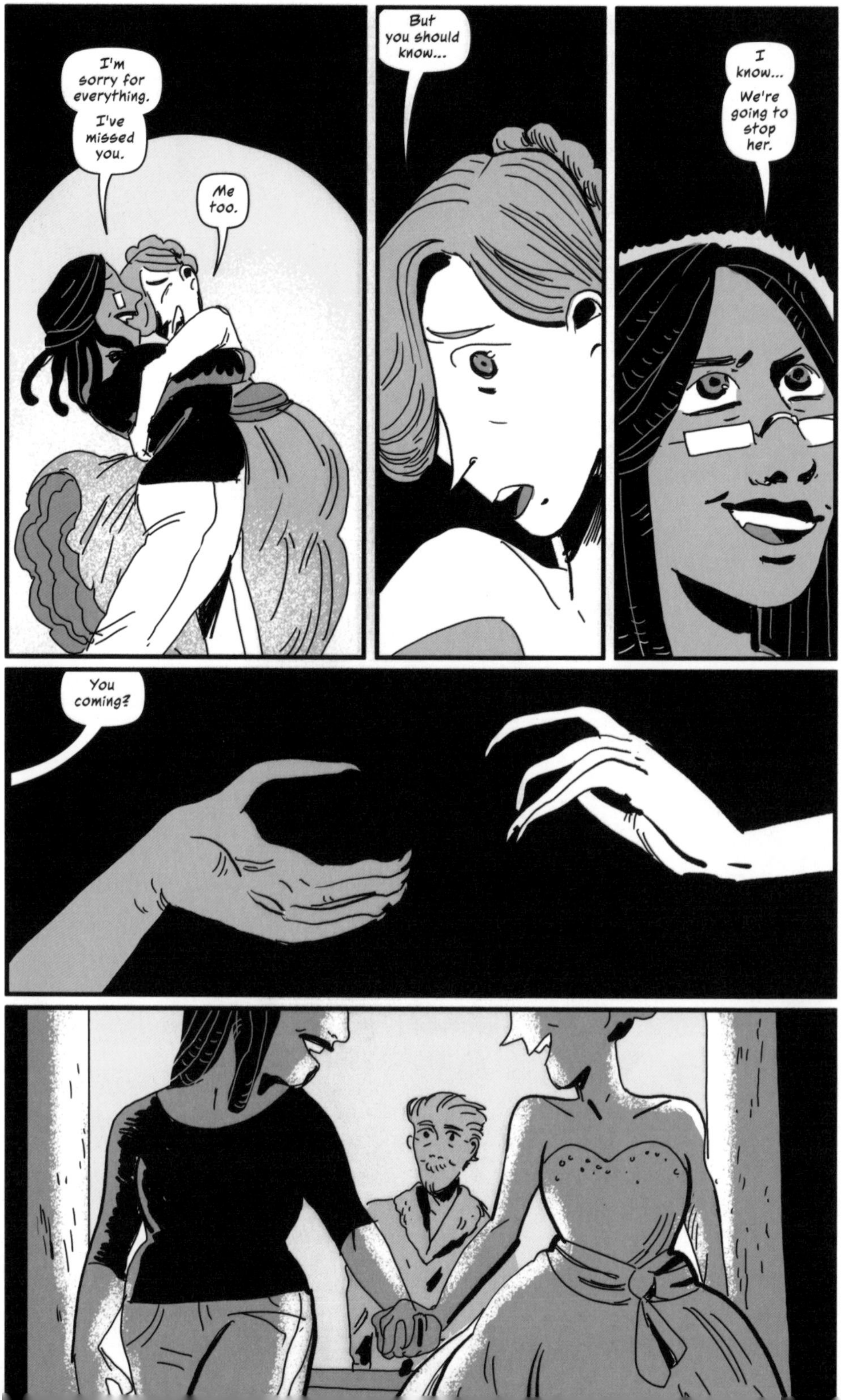
I'm sorry for everything.
I've missed you.
Me too.
But you should know...
I know...
We're going to stop her.
You coming?

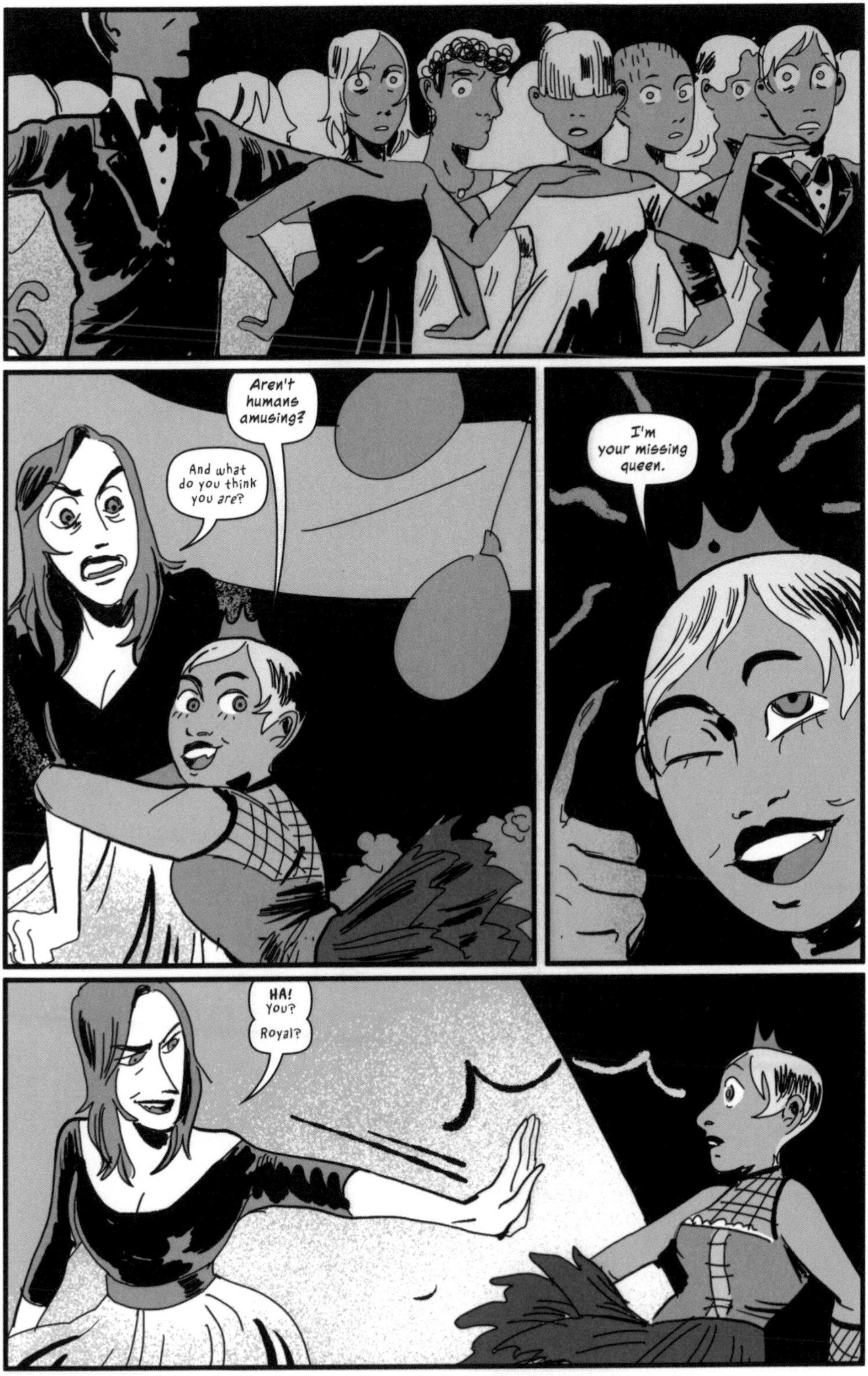
Aren't humans amusing?
And what do you think you are?
I'm your missing queen.
HA! You?
Royal?

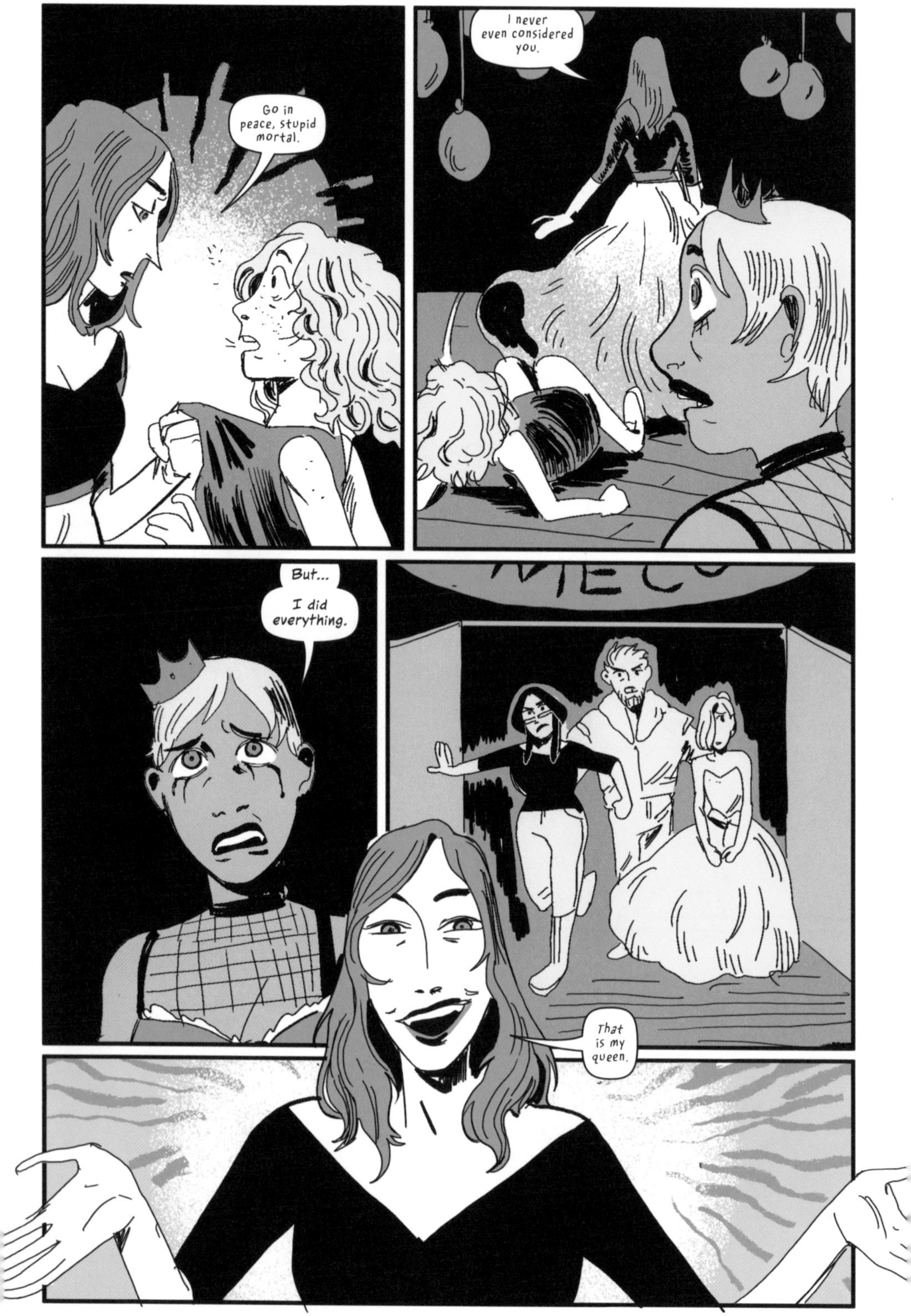
Go in peace, stupid mortal.
I never even considered you.
But...
I did everything.
MEC
That is my queen.

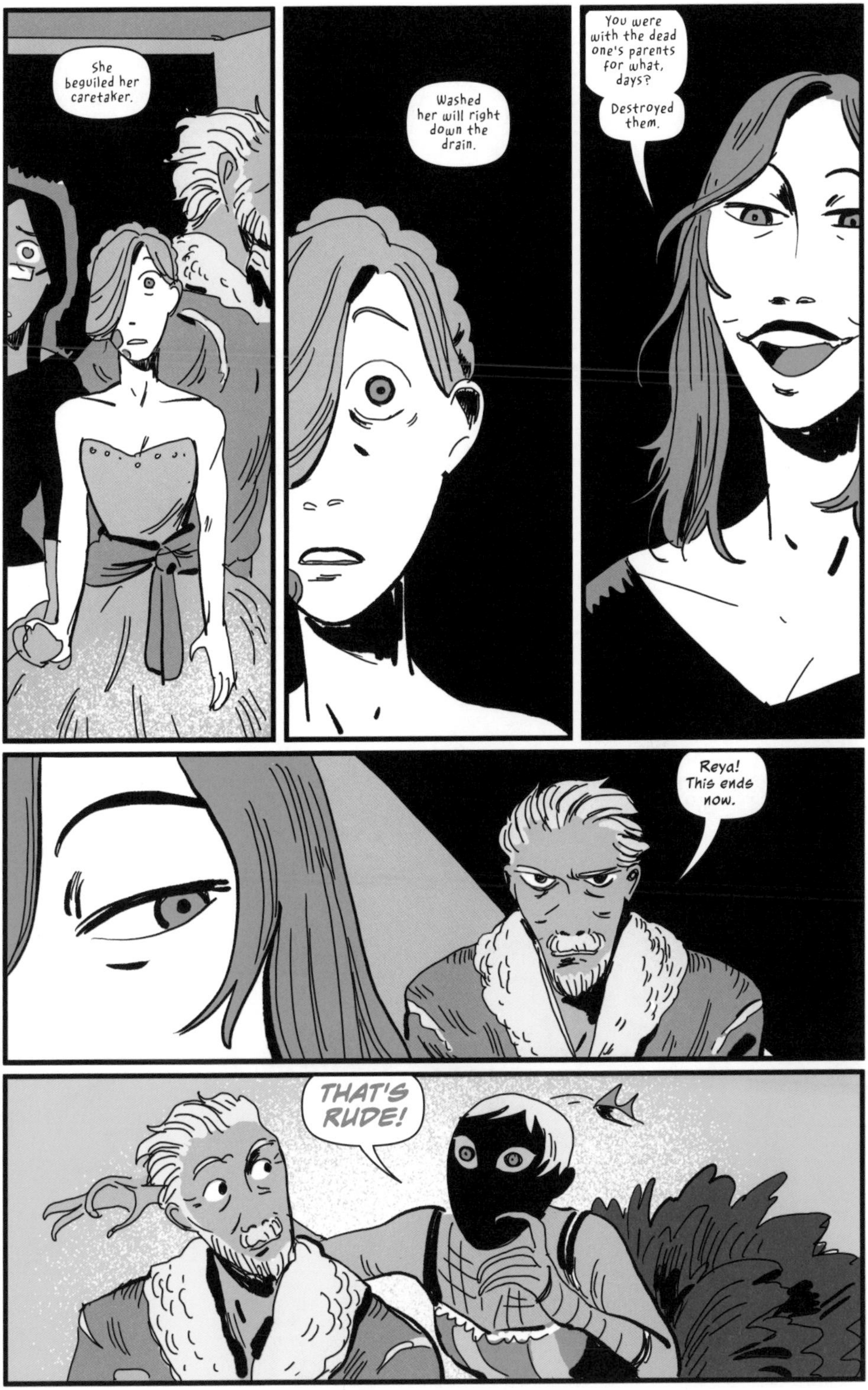
She beguiled her caretaker.
Washed her will right down the drain.
You were with the dead one's parents for what, days?
Destroyed them.
Reya! This ends now.
THAT'S RUDE!

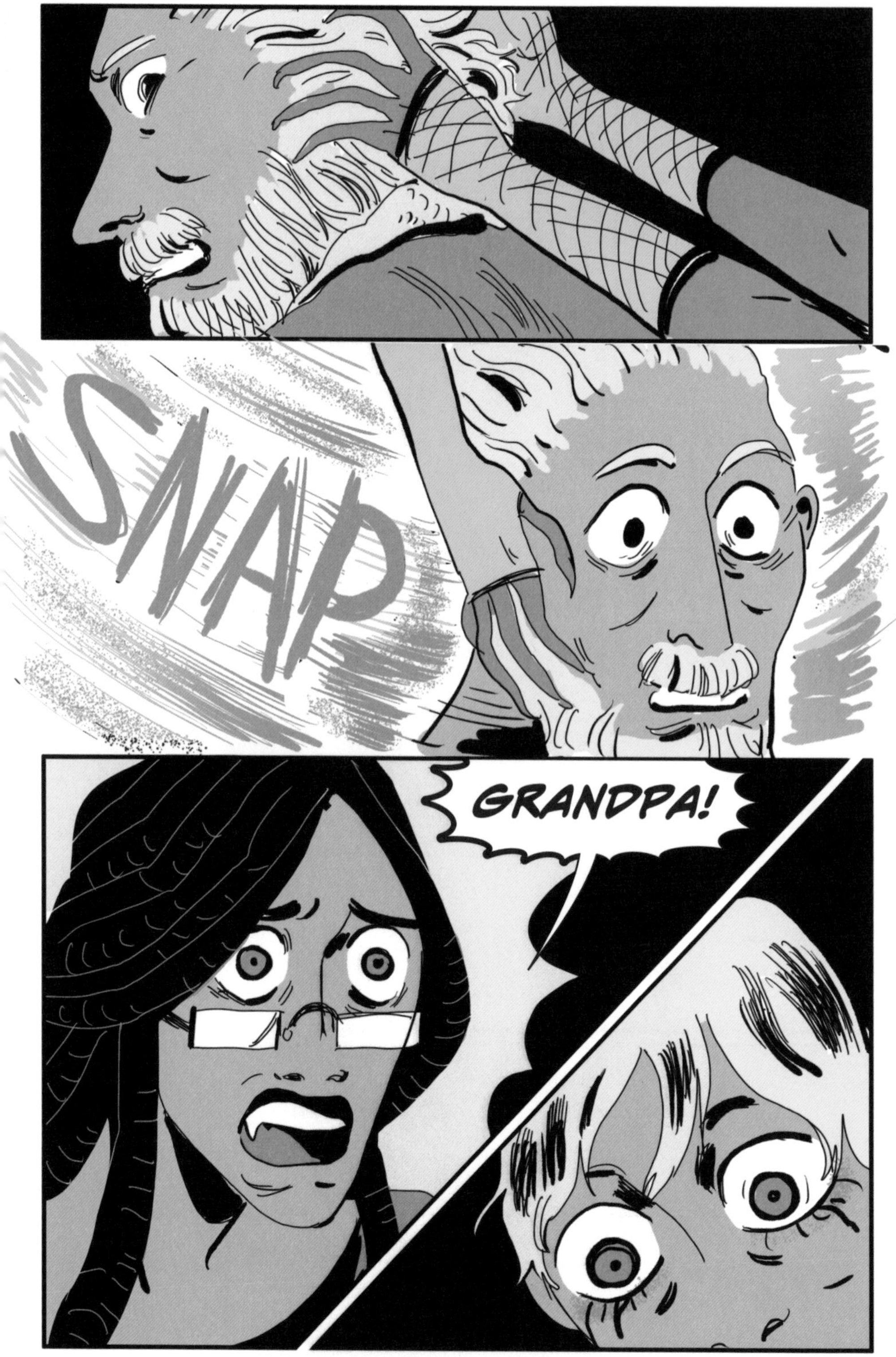
SNAP
GRANDPA!

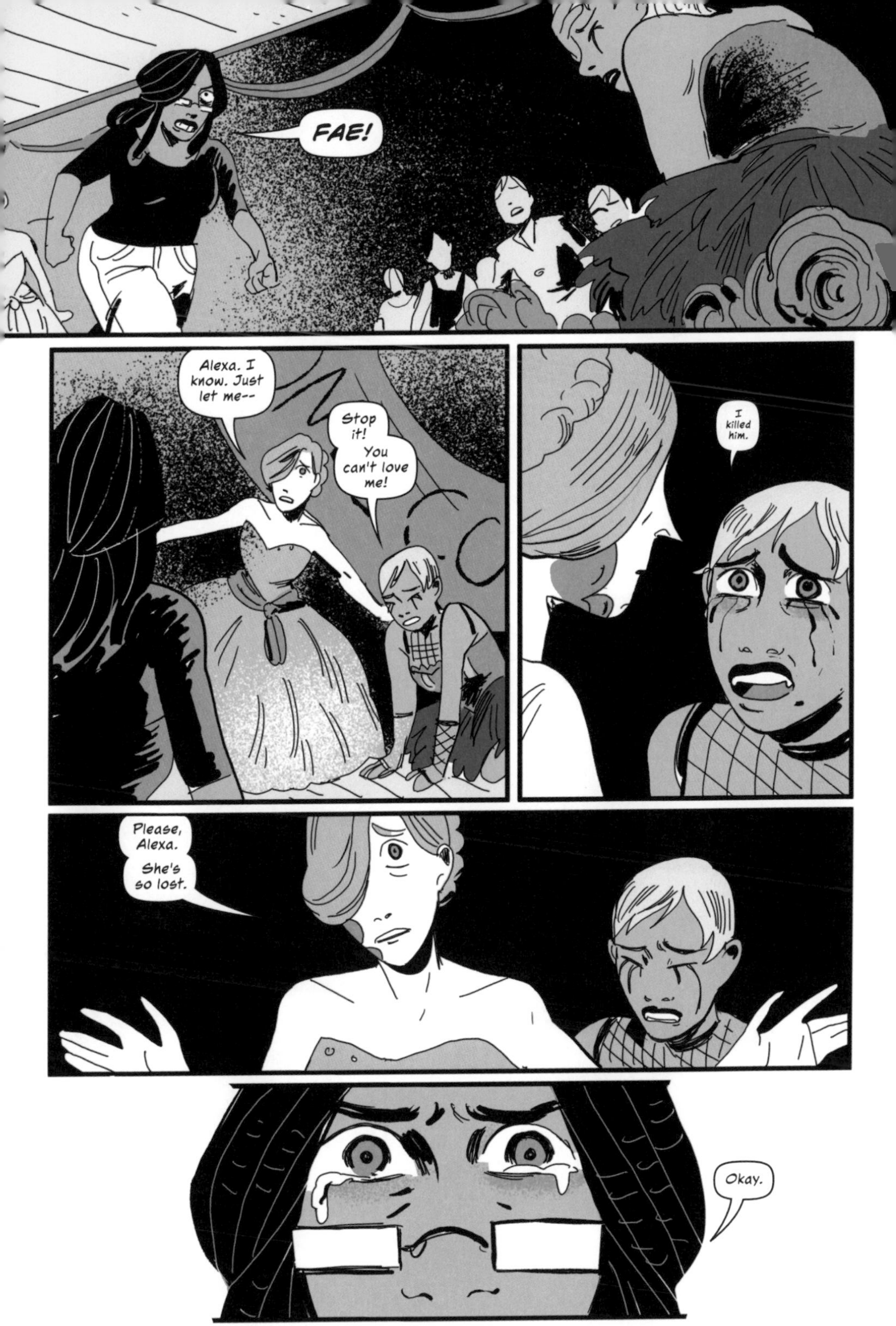
FAE!
Alexa. I know. Just let me--
Stop it! You can't love me!
I killed him.
Please, Alexa. She's so lost.
Okay.

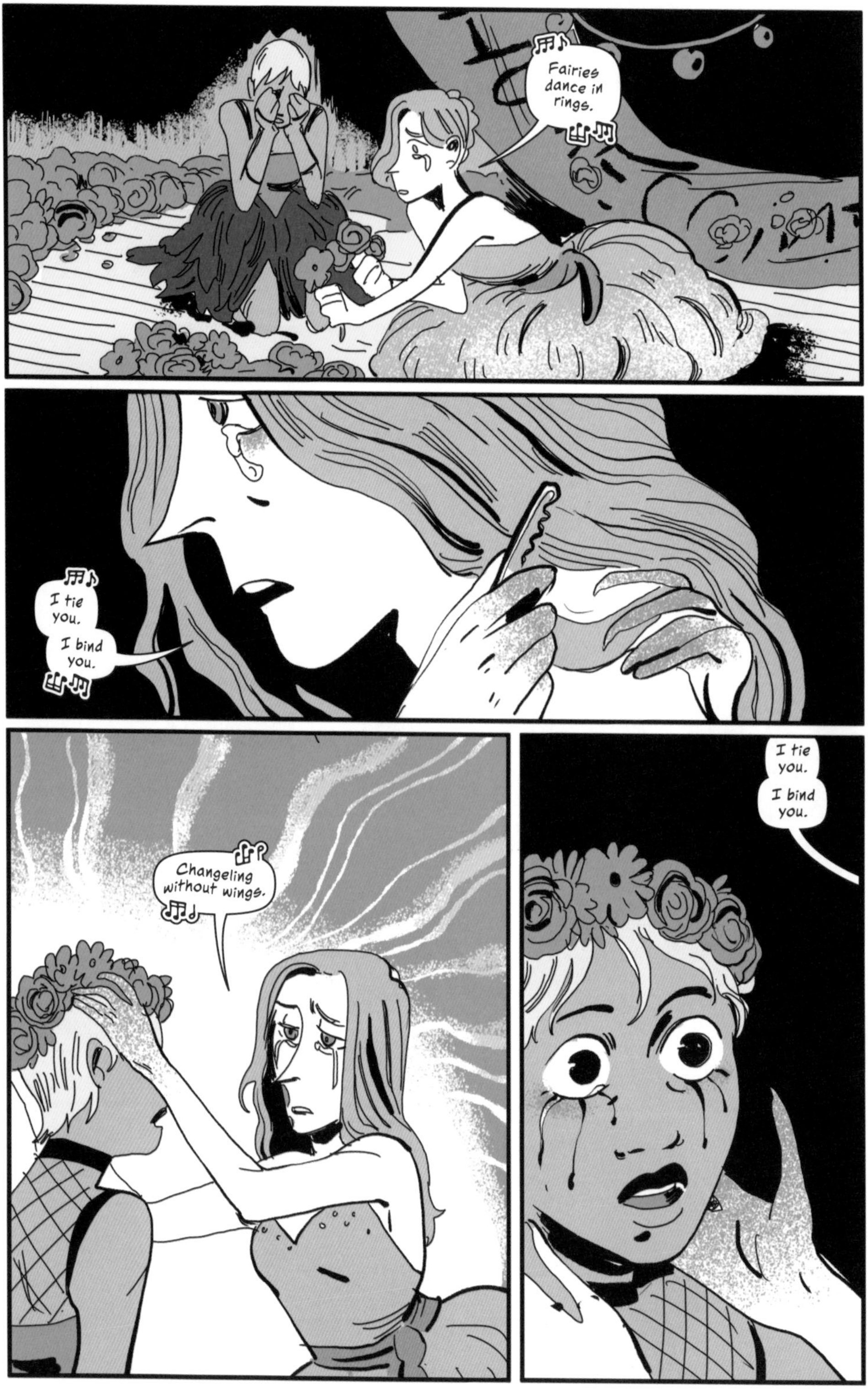
Fairies dance in rings.
I tie you.
I bind you.
Changeling without wings.
I tie you.
I bind you.

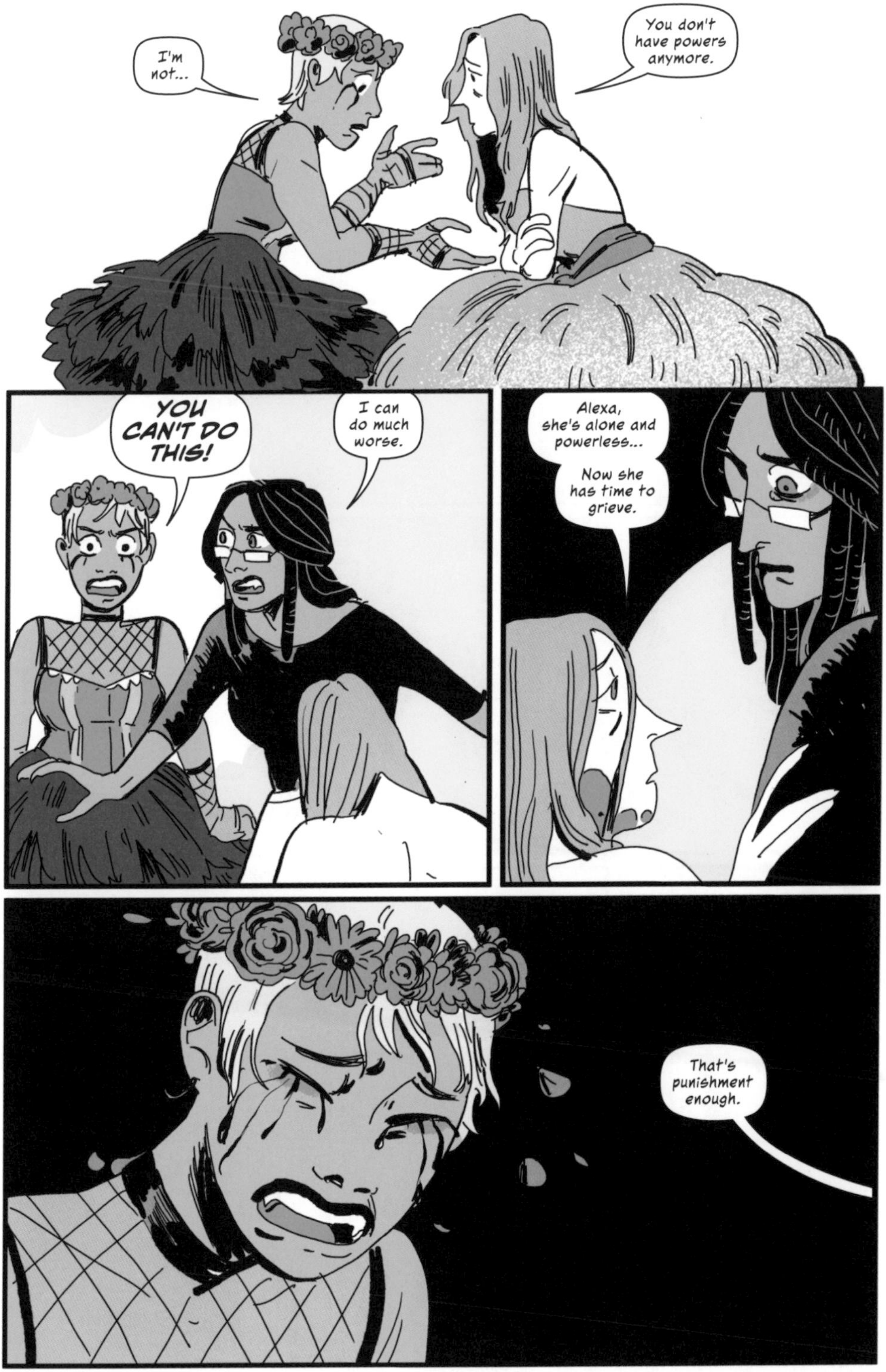
I'm not...
You don't have powers anymore.
YOU CAN'T DO THIS!
I can do much worse.
Alexa, she's alone and powerless...
Now she has time to grieve.
That's punishment enough.

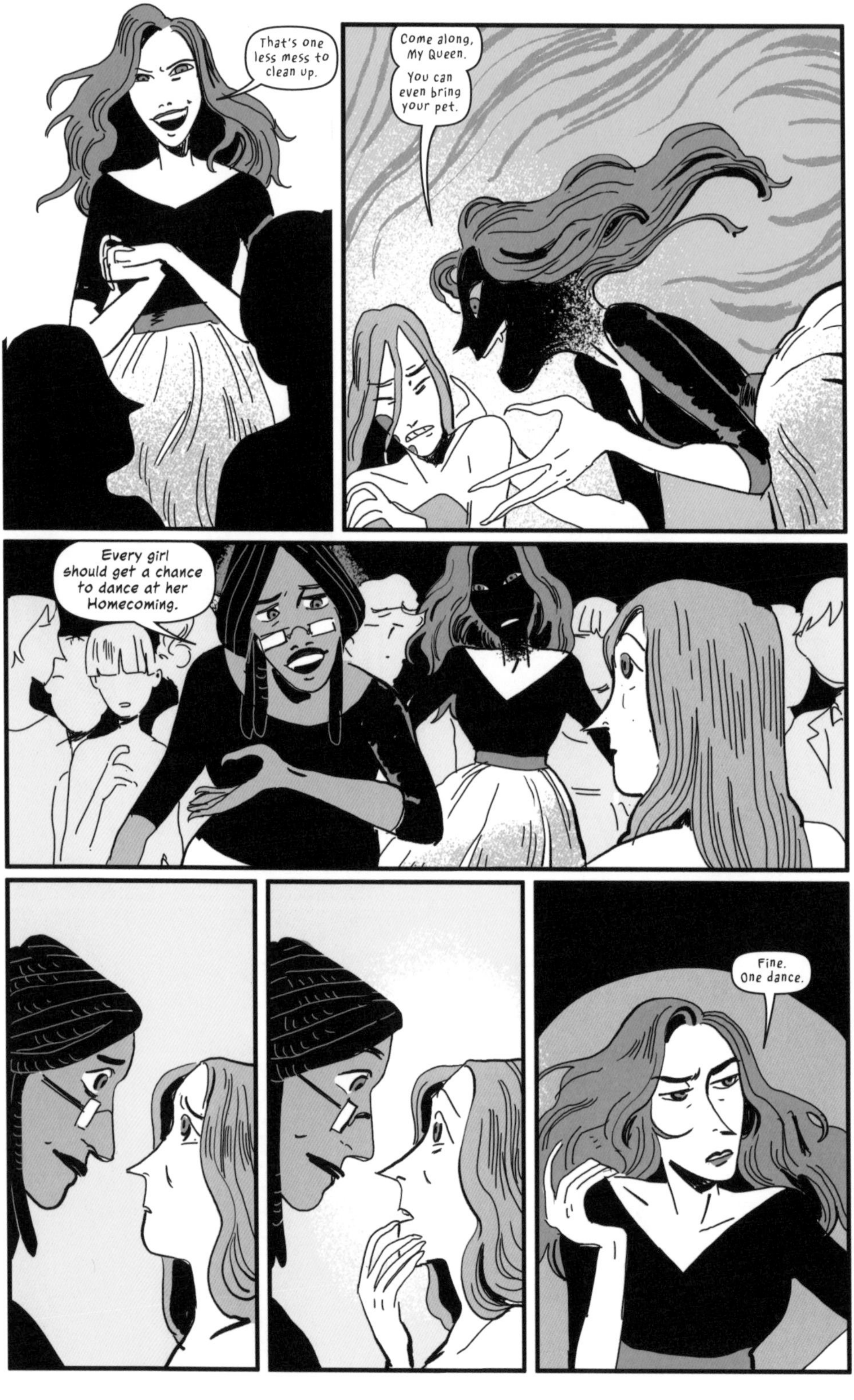
That's one less mess to clean up.
Come along, My Queen.
You can even bring your pet.
Every girl should get a chance to dance at her Homecoming.
Fine. One dance.

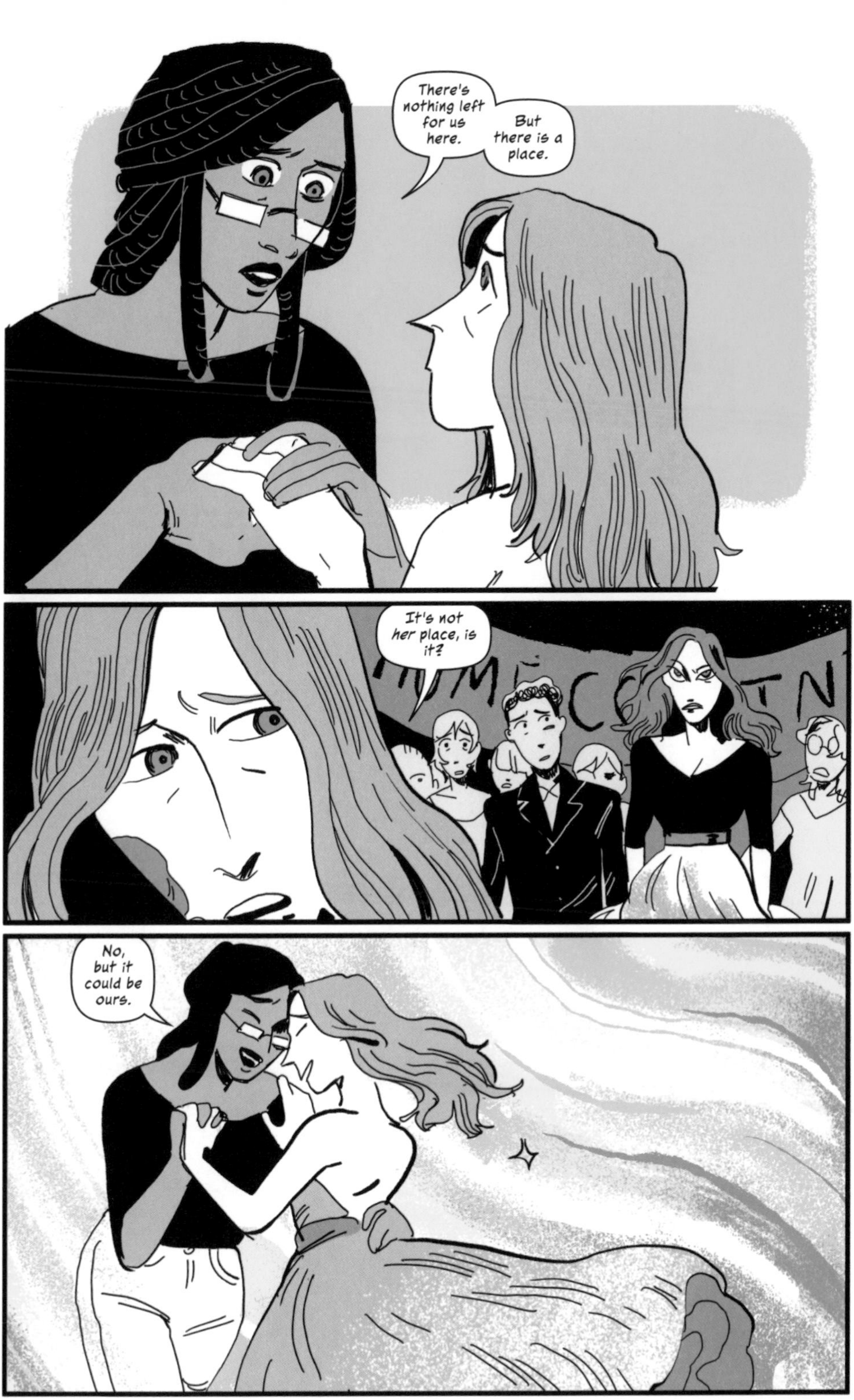
There's nothing left for us here.
But there is a place.
It's not her place, is it?
No, but it could be ours.

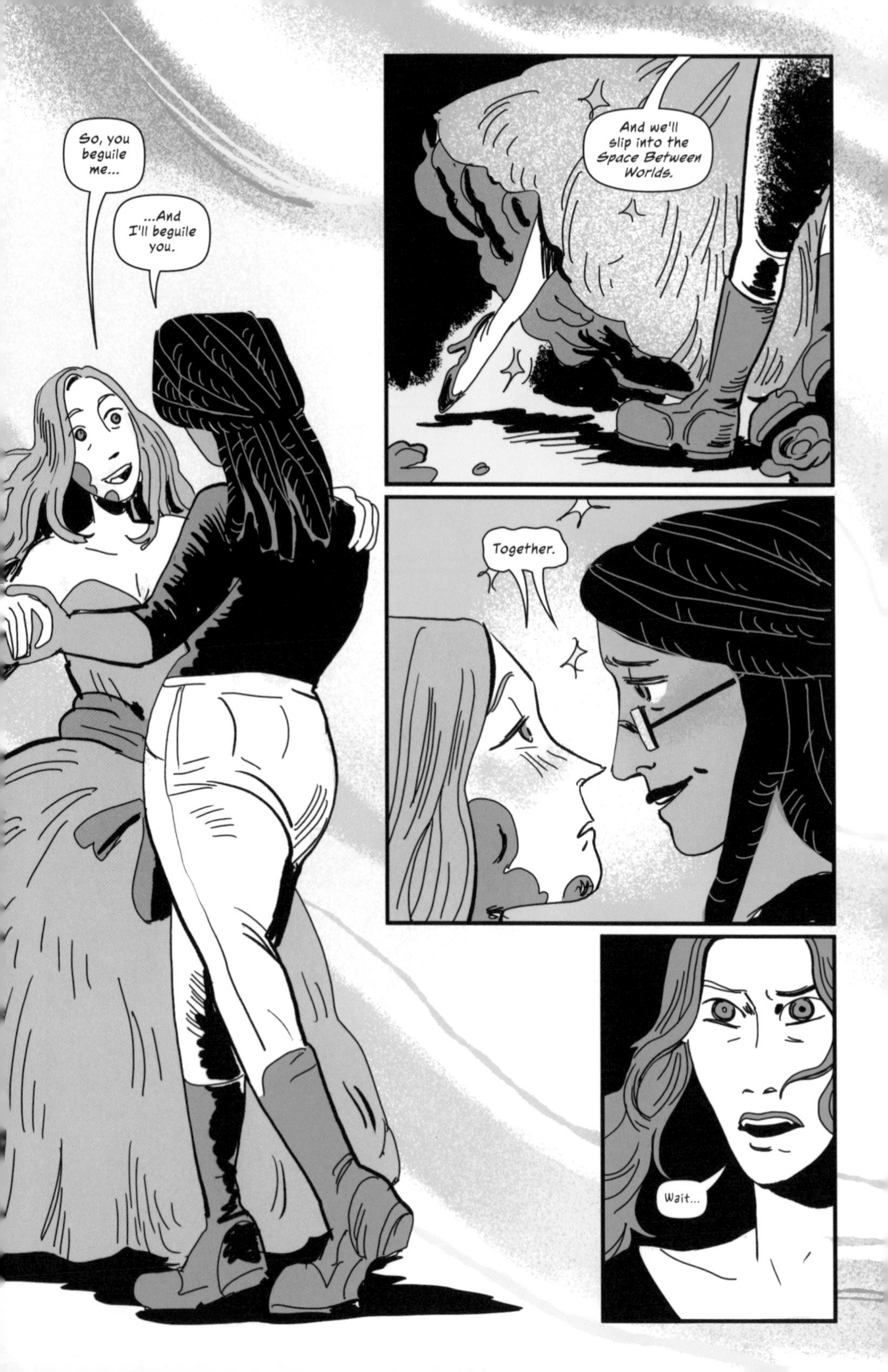
So, you beguile me...
...And I'll beguile you.
And we'll slip into the Space Between Worlds.
Together.
Wait...

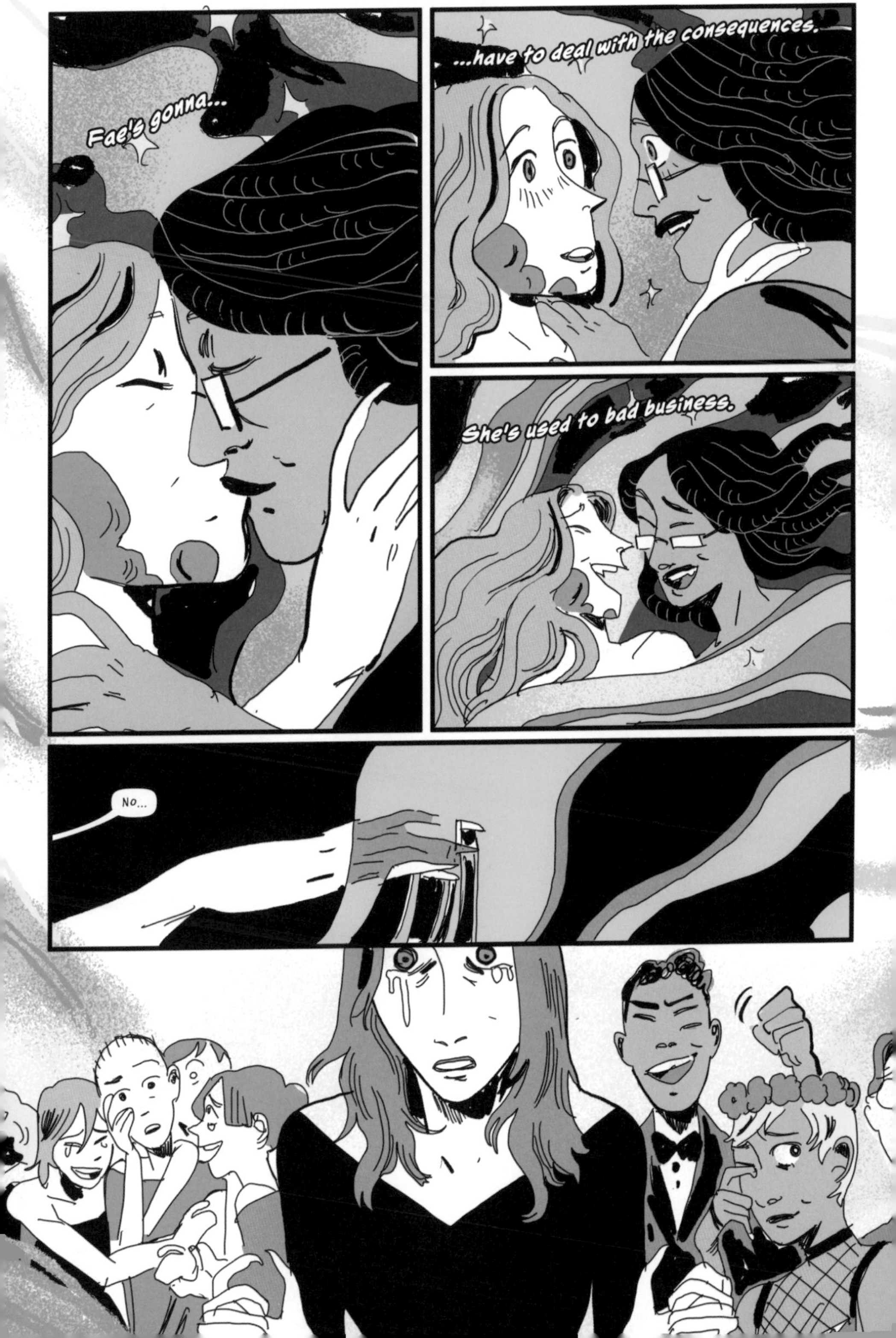
Fae's gonna...
...have to deal with the consequences.
She's used to bad business.
No...

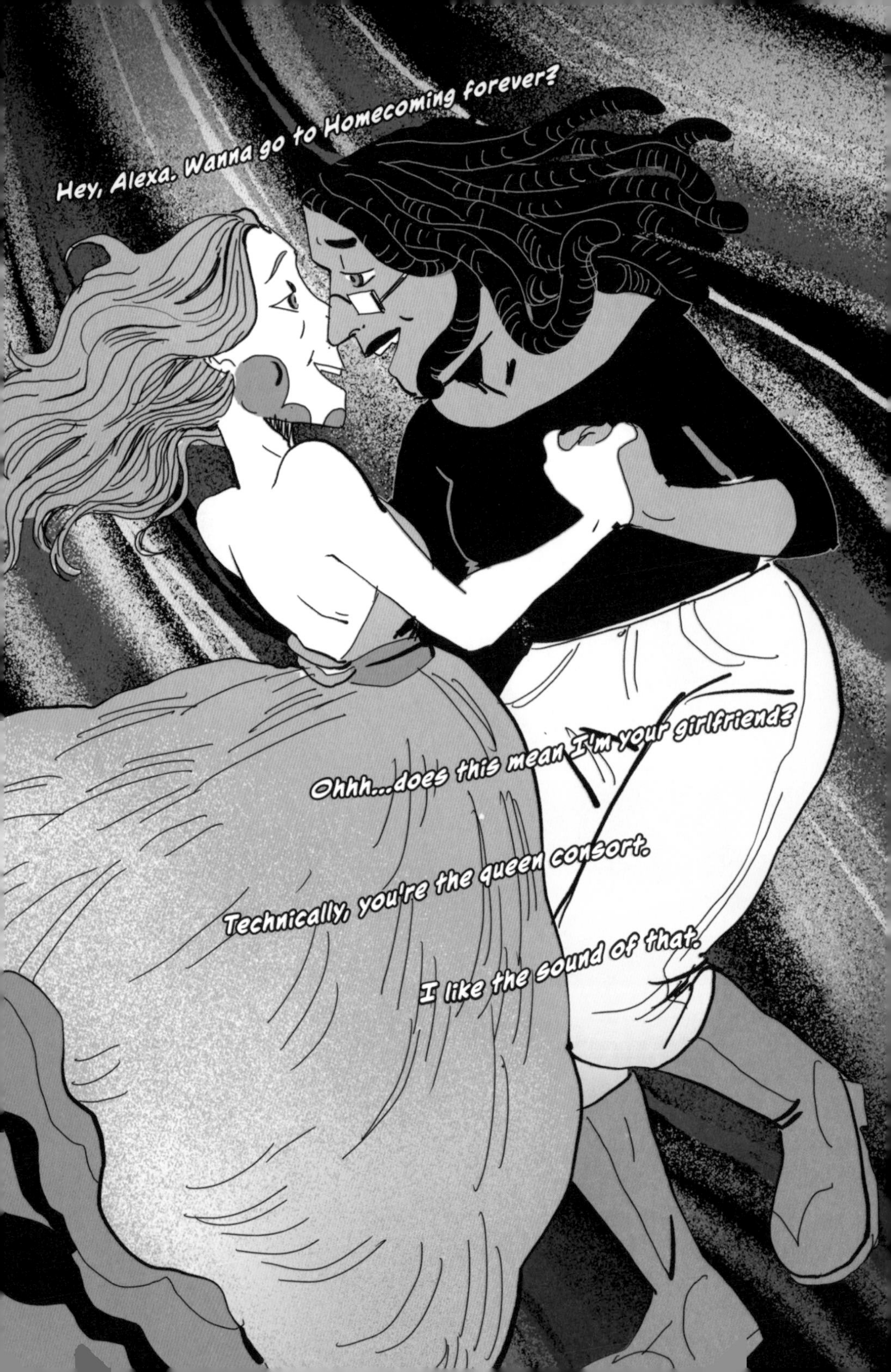
Hey, Alexa. Wanna go to Homecoming forever?
Ohhh...does this mean I'm your girlfriend?
Technically, you're the queen consort.
I like the sound of that.

CREATORS

LELA GWENN
WRITER

Has written for BOOM!, Image, Wave Blue World, and Dark Horse. She's a proud social justice warrior, and the town weirdo in her rural community. She's currently in school despite being way too old, but she loves it.

ROWAN MACCOLL
ARTIST

A comic artist who was born and raised in the New England fog. She loves her ink, her spooky folktales, and, of course, her four black cats.

MICAH MYERS
LETTERER

A comic book letterer who has worked on comics for Image, Dark Horse, IDW, Heavy Metal, Mad Cave, Devil's Due, and many more. He also occasionally writes and has his own series about D-List supervillains, The Disasters.

CONCEPT

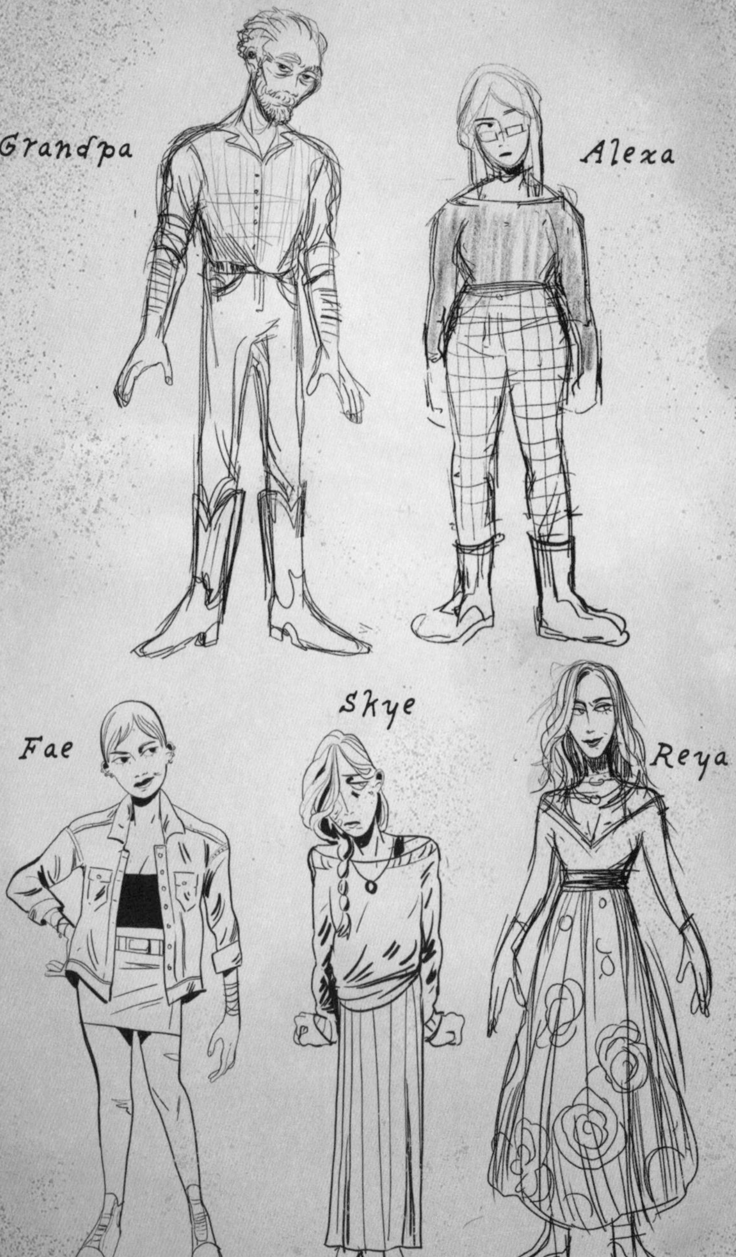
Grandpa
Alexa
Skye
Fae
Reya

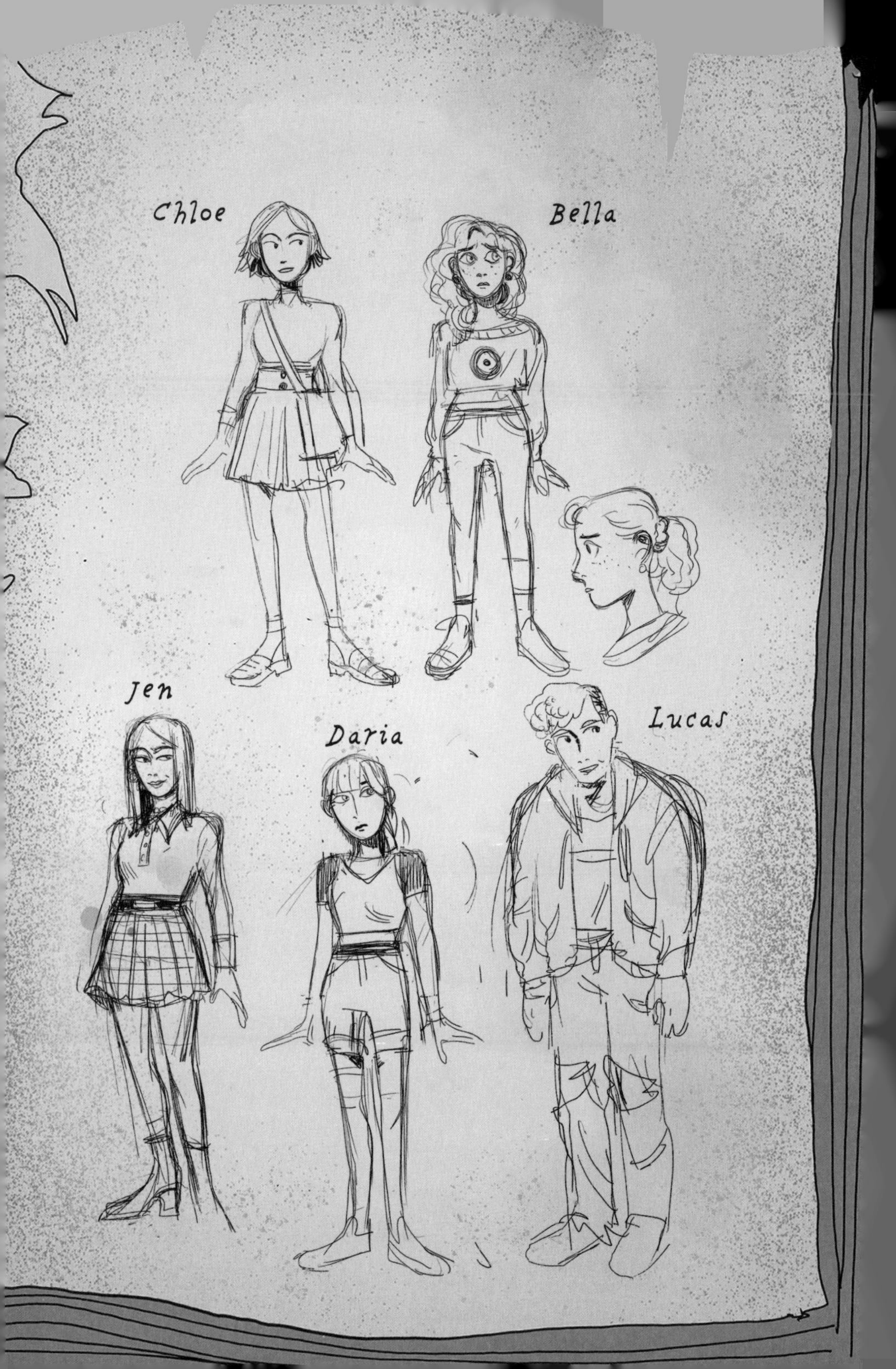
Chloe
Bella
Jen
Daria
Lucas

CONFETTI REALMS
Nadia Shammas
Writer
Karnessa
Artist
Hackto
Colorist

GOOD GAME, WELL PLAYED
Rachael Smith · @rachael_
Writer
Katherine Lobo · @Kath_Lobo
Artist - Colorist

IN THE SHADOW OF THE THRONE
Kate Sheridan
Writer
Gaia Cardinali
Artist

NEEDLE AND THREAD
David Pinckney · @HelixandMeteors
Writer
Ennun Ana Iurov · @ennunanaiurov
Artist - Colorist

NIGHTMARE IN SAVANNAH
Lela Gwenn · @LGwenn
Writer
Rowan MacColl · @Skulkingfoxes
Artist - Colorist

OF HER OWN DESIGN
Birdie Willis · @BirdieWrites
Writer
Jess Taylor · @deuxdel
Artist
Keith Chan
Layouts
Stephanie Palladino
Colorist

PAPER PLANES
Jennie Wood
Writer
Dozer
Artist - Colorist

WORLD CLASS
Jay Sandlin · @JaySandlin_WHN
Writer
Patrick Mulholland · @Pat_M_Art
Artist
Rebecca Nalty · @rebnalty
Colorist

SOCIAL MEDIA & WEB SITE

Visit madcavestudios.com/maverick to learn all about our new releases, learn more about each title, and, best of all, download.

Follow @maverick_ogn We use our outreach to shout-out the best retailers in the country!

HOW YOU CAN GET IN ON THE MADNESS

Retail/sales related inquiries or scheduling store signings? *mcastellanos@madcavestudios.com*

Want to know more about store signings or exclusives? *contact@madcavestudios.com*

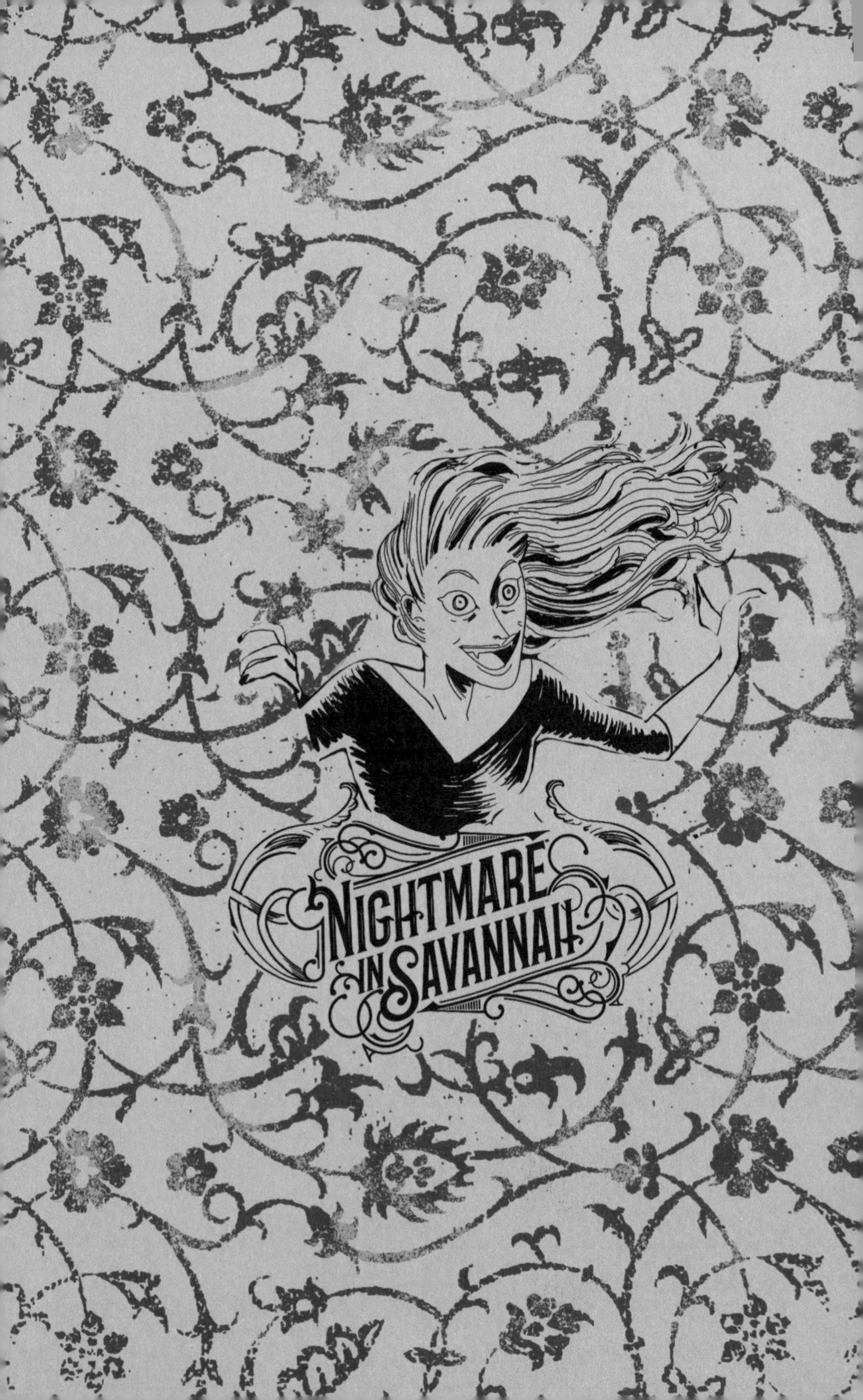
NIGHTMARE IN SAVANNAH